I0667813

Sadhana

TWO LIES – ONE TRUTH

PHIL RIBERA

This is a work of fiction. Names, characters, places and incidents are the product of the author's imagination and are used fictitiously. Any resemblance to actual persons, living or dead, events, or locales is entirely coincidental.

Sadhana. Copyright © 2015 by Phil Ribera. All rights reserved. Printed in the United States of America. No part of this book may be used or reproduced in any manner whatsoever without written permission except in the case of brief quotations embodied in critical articles or reviews.

ISBN-13: 978-0-9962103-0-0
ISBN-10: 099621030X

Published by Phil Ribera

Learn more about the author by visiting: www.philribera.com

ACKNOWLEDGEMENTS

I would like to thank my family and friends for their loving support and encouragement during the research and writing of this work. To my family of fellow writers at the Yale Writers' Conference, I sincerely appreciate the time and effort you all took to "workshop" my rough chapters. I'm also grateful for the help I received from Norma Santos, Margaret Reimche, Terry VanderHeiden, Jacob Spillner, and my brother, Tyler—couldn't have done it without you.

I am indebted to D.R. Mehta and Dr. Pooja Mukul of Bhagwan Mahaveer Viklang Sahayata Samiti—the world's largest organization for handicapped. They spent much of their valuable time taking me though the amazing BMVSS prosthetic limb facility in Jaipur. I'd also like to thank Juber Khan, my good friend and the best tuk-tuk driver in all of India.

And lastly, for my cherished memories of the gentle and gracious people I met during my journey—thank you, citizens of India, for your welcoming kindness.

Three things that cannot be long hidden:
the sun, the moon and the truth
~Buddha

One

"What is the truth?"

Many years ago, shortly after Mr. Griffiths hired me, I overheard a conversation that was not meant for my ears. It was a matter that did not concern me; a thing I wished I hadn't heard. The trouble is that once you know something, there is no way to ever un-know it.

The memory of it faded over time, yet it was always there, in the back of my mind. The day the Griffiths boy turned to me for answers, I knew that life had come to collect a debt I had always hoped I'd never have to pay.

I looked back into the boy's eyes, his black pupils wide and intense, watching me. Waiting. Thirsting for the answers I knew he deserved. And when he asked me again if I knew the truth, I lied to him. I became part of the deception.

In the lee of my guilt, I have carried out my duties with honor and loyalty, and I've served the family with integrity. I have tried to separate myself from others who would defend dishonesty on the grounds that the truth might hurt someone else, and who rationalize their deception into righteousness.

Well, I'm carrying on about opinions that are neither here nor there, because this story is not about me. And it's not about my views on morality and virtue. This story is about the man and the family that I work for. It's about an ugly past, buried for nearly 30 years—known only to a small circle of confidants, and almost forgotten by those of us who lived it.

It's about a falsehood that was told long ago. And like a stone tossed into a tranquil pond, its ripples have extended outward, affecting everyone and everything in its path.

* * *

The morning could not find Long Island under the heavy shroud of fog. An unseasonably cool air mass from Canada was keeping the staff hard at work, cleaning, sanding, painting, and readying the estate for an early fall.

The chipper mood of the house staff was stymied when there came a sudden knock at the front door. It was a harsh, authoritative rap that could only prescribe trouble. Two plainclothes detectives had come calling, and not with tickets to the policemen's ball.

Every member of the staff knew whom the detectives had come for. They had all seen the silver Hummer speed up the long driveway about an hour earlier, churning the stillness of the Sunday morning, and spitting gravel on two groundskeepers as it passed. One of the cleaning women dust-mopping the marble foyer heard the commotion and made herself scarce, even though the source of fracas remained outside the main house.

Loring Griffiths Sr., who friends and business associates referred to as "LJ," had been working upstairs in his third floor office. He too heard the Hummer arrive. A sigh escaped his lips, rippling the lace curtain of the dormer window as he watched the car slide to a cockeyed stop in the driveway. His only child, his namesake, steadied himself as he emerged from behind the wheel, then dropped his trousers and urinated into the alabaster pond beneath a bronze statue of Sir Henry Havelock. The statue had been passed down from LJ's great grandfather, who had supposedly served in India under Havelock.

So much for the new koi, thought LJ. Disgusted, he leaned back into his seat and began massaging his creased forehead.

Laughter and closing doors drew him back to the window. He watched as one young lady and then a second climbed out of the car. One of them carried a pair of heels under her arm while the other clutched a bottle of champagne and three flutes. The barefooted one paused near the pond, and for a moment LJ thought she was about to further denigrate Sir Havelock's memory. The other girl raised a glass and toasted the statue, before the threesome disappeared through the courtyard garden separating the main house from the old riding stables.

The laughter trailed off, but LJ was familiar enough with his son's complacent routine: lithe bodies frolicking in the heated pool behind the estate, more drinking, lewd behavior and rowdiness—all of which the house staff would eye in furtive glimpses through Beach Rose hedges and shuttered blinds. Later, the trio would retire to the two-story pool house where his son had resided since returning from NYU six years ago.

Failure to submit his course requests on time had resulted in the boy's unexpected return home only three months shy of graduation. It was his flagrant insolence and contempt for his father, however, that kept him from ever going back to complete his degree. It was around this time that young Griffiths announced he had legally changed his first name to Paul.

"Loring is such a pretentious name," he had told his father. "It reeks of self-important arrogance." Then he added an obligatory yet patronizing, "No offense, Dad."

But LJ felt otherwise. It *was* offensive, and he knew it was intended to be. Though it was never stated, LJ believed the boy's taking of the name Paul, was yet another slap. Paul Griffiths was the name of LJ's twin brother, with whom he was estranged and hadn't spoken of for many years.

LJ's personal attendant tapped lightly at his office door, drawing LJ away from his thoughts.

"Come in, Rupert."

The man entered the room and quietly closed the door behind him. "I apologize for the interruption, sir, but two police detectives are downstairs to see Paul."

LJ glanced out the window at the dark gray, unmarked sedan. He hadn't heard them drive up. "What did you tell them?"

"I explained that Mr. Griffiths Junior was presently indisposed, but that I would attempt to locate him."

"Did they say what they want with him?"

Rupert shook his head. "No, sir. They did, however, seem to recognize the family name."

"They should." LJ straightened the button line of his gray sweater as he stood. "I've donated enough money to their fundraising events."

Loring Griffiths had been an imposing man in his day. He was over six feet tall, but his sixty-two year old body had thinned some, as had his silver hair. Tiny creases at the corners of his eyes had softened his look, and age had brought some patience to the semiconductor mogul.

Rupert stepped aside—a matador pirouetting from the path of the charging bull—then followed his boss down the staircase to the foyer, through the double doors on the left, and into the study where the detectives waited.

LJ introduced himself and shook hands with the two men. "I understand you need to speak with my son?"

"Yes, sir." One of the detectives glanced at the other and shifted his stance. "A vehicle registered to Paul Griffiths at this address was involved in a hit and run collision last night."

Mr. Griffiths turned and said, "That will be all, Rupert."

The attendant stepped backward into the foyer, deftly sliding the doors closed as he left.

"Was anyone hurt?" LJ asked the detectives.

"No, sir. A sign was knocked down outside a restaurant over in Montauk, and a witness wrote down the tag number as the car drove away."

"Perhaps we can clear this up without fanfare." LJ stepped behind the large oak desk and took out a binder-size checkbook. "I'd be glad to make restitution to the business where the accident occurred. What was the name of the establishment?"

The detective who had been doing all the talking smoothed his hair, not completely comfortable with the proposed arrangement.

"The Sloppy Tuna," said the second detective, reading from a small notepad he had taken from his pocket. "It's a bar and grill."

LJ took a breath, bristling at the image of his own son spending his leisure time at such a place. He thought of the two young ladies his son had brought back to the house, and suddenly the name of the place seemed to fit.

"Technically, the bar wasn't the victim," said the one with the notepad. "I have here that it was a Suffolk County street sign, valued at seven hundred-fifty dollars."

The first detective fidgeted. "Yeah, okay, I'm sure a check to the county will suffice." He was clearly eager to close the case and get out of there.

LJ tore the check from the ledger and handed it to him. The detectives hustled toward the door without noticing the generous contribution LJ had added. He stepped onto the portico and watched the sedan make its way out the driveway and onto Bluff Road.

After they were gone, he strolled around the side of the Hummer and saw the gnashed remnants of its bumper. As drunk as his son must have been, thought LJ, he must have known that he hit something.

Walking back upstairs to his office, LJ did his best to ignore the inquisitive eyes of the house staff.

4

Rupert hastened from the kitchen, his wrinkled brow and steel eyes compelling the curious employees back to their work. Then he followed his boss up to his office with a cup of coffee and a poached egg on a piece of dry toast.

LJ sat down and began reading his personal correspondence. Rupert had gone through the mail, and sorted faxes and emails for him during the course of the week. He had discarded some, responded to others, and left only the most private or personal in labeled slots above the desk. One such letter was from Sheryl Beckham, Executive Director of Children's Relief Foundation International.

The foundation was created in the early 80's, thanks to substantial financial support from the Leigh Griffiths Endowment. Since his wife's death, LJ had made it a priority to maintain a close, personal, and financially supportive relationship with the non-profit. The letter from Sheryl thanked LJ for a recent donation, and included an invitation to join her and her husband, John, for dinner at their Hudson River home in Red Hook, whenever LJ had time. Enclosed in the correspondence was a colorful brochure highlighting CRF's recent initiatives in India.

Rupert set LJ's steeping mug on the desk next to the breakfast plate, as his boss lingered over the brochure on the desk in front of him.

"Is everything alright Mr. Griffiths?"

LJ's eyes narrowed, as if he was looking into the sunlight. They were focused beyond the printed words and the glossy images, into his own memory. The photographs of people suffering in India had stirred something deep inside him. His gaze shifted toward the window as he began to envision an idea—still just patches of fabric yet to be stitched together. "Sit down, Rupert."

Rupert eased into a leather chair on the opposite side of the desk. He was a slightly built man who carried himself as if born to serve royalty. Impeccably dressed in a light gray suit, Rupert's cagey eyes and wry smile often gave one the impression he knew something that you didn't. He had been Griffiths' personal assistant for more than three decades, and had proven his loyalty several times over.

"One of my greatest disappointments in life has been my son." LJ still couldn't bring himself to call his son, Paul.

Rupert nodded thoughtfully. "I know that, sir."

"He respects nothing, especially me." LJ leaned back in his chair and closed his eyes. "I've always thought that he blames me for what happened to his mother."

It was a conversation that for the past thirty years had been off limits. Rupert cleared the uneasy tightness from his throat. "If anything, I suspect his blame lies only in the fact that he doesn't really know what happened to his mother."

"How can I?" LJ had receded into a conversation with himself. "After all these years . . ." His words trailed off.

The two men sat quietly for several minutes. LJ touched the corners of his eyes with his thumb and index finger before finally speaking again. "I've tried to provide him with everything a father could give a son. I don't know where I've gone wrong. Perhaps I've given him too much. "

Rupert studied his boss and friend for a moment. "If I may, sir?"

LJ nodded.

Rupert paused to find the right words. "Sir, you created a fortune five hundred company from nothing. You, better than anyone, know that hard work towards any goal gives it meaning. To struggle and overcome adversity creates context and brings about value. Paul has never had to struggle; therefore he knows neither triumph nor failure. Life has come relatively easy to him."

"You're right, Rupert." LJ thumbed the brochure from the desk, glancing at the photos of starving children. "I think by trying to give my son the opportunities I never had, I've robbed him of important life lessons."

"You shouldn't be too hard on yourself, Mr. Griffiths." Rupert motioned to a framed picture of LJ holding young Paul—his feet dangling in the Long Island surf. "You have been his sole caretaker since . . . the terrible tragedy. You have been as loving a parent as Paul could have had, and you provided a solid foundation for him." Rupert paused to consider the boy he had known nearly since birth. "Paul is an intelligent young man, and his story is yet to be written."

LJ donned a pair of reading glasses and picked up the brochure. As he studied it, the jigsaw outline of his idea started taking shape, and then one-by-one, the pieces fell into place. The situation was perfect, and it would provide lessons that LJ was incapable of teaching Paul.

"I am going to need your help with something."

"Of course," Rupert said. "Whatever I can do."

LJ walked to the window holding his coffee mug. "With only one exception, I've never lied to my son. I promised myself that I would never mislead him again."

"You're going to lie to Paul?"

"No, not me. Anything I would say to him at this point would be immediately suspect." LJ gazed down at the driveway, and somehow the Hummer he had bought for his son served to galvanize his resolve. "I need you to lie to him, Rupert."

"Sir?"

After a full minute of silence LJ turned from the window. "Get Sheryl Beckham on the phone."

It was late afternoon, and the staff hadn't seen Paul and his two companions since they stumbled into the pool house earlier in the day.

Rupert tapped on the door a second time before easing it open. Wet towels were strewn over the furniture and empty beer bottles littered the kitchen counter. Rupert felt a crunching sound underfoot and saw buttered popcorn from a Jiffy Pop container scattered about the tile floor. He turned off the television before climbing the stairs, and then paused to knock again at the threshold of Paul's bedroom.

The room reeked of pot, and old booze secreted in the form of sweat and stale breath. Through the darkness he could discern a single figure sprawled on the bed. Rupert had already summoned the family car and ordered Terrence to return the two young women to the Sloppy Tuna.

"What the hell?" Paul's hoarse voice groaned as Rupert snapped back the window drapes. Nails of sunlight drove into Paul's squinted eyes, provoking a grin from Rupert.

"My apologies, Mr. Griffiths." Rupert made a half-hearted attempt to block the light. "I'm afraid I have some troubling news."

He handed a robe to Paul, who rolled to a sitting position and hoisted it over his shoulders. The attendant's use of the more formal title to address him made Paul pause.

"Mr. Griffiths?" he repeated as he slipped the rest of his way into the robe. Paul rubbed his eyes, trying to clear the haze inside his head. "What happened to my two friends?"

"Terrence drove them home about an hour ago."

Paul ambled into the bathroom and used a hand to brace himself against the wall as he urinated. "So what's the troubling news?"

Rupert moved to the window and gazed out at the Atlantic, glistening through the trees at the east end of the property. He turned back to face Paul as he emerged from the bathroom. "You may wish to bring your toothbrush."

"Huh?" Paul tucked himself back into his robe. "What are you talking about, Rupert?"

"Two East Hampton police detectives came to the estate today. They have a warrant for your arrest." Rupert's words were devoid of emotion. "Something about a hit and run, I believe."

Paul's eyes widened as he struggled to find some memory of the previous night. "Don't be ridiculous," he said, almost as if trying to convince himself. "What did they say I hit?"

"I wasn't privy to that information." Rupert stooped to pick up an empty bottle from the floor. "Evidently it was serious enough for them to impound your Hummer vehicle, sir."

Paul's jaw tightened. He bolted down the steps and out the door. Standing poolside, he was able to see the empty driveway as it horseshoed past the courtyard garden. "Sons of bitches," he mumbled under his breath. Then, he turned back to Rupert, who had followed him out. "Does Dad know about the cops?"

"Yes."

"Oh, he must be loving this."

"No." Rupert stepped around him. "As a matter of fact, I'm quite certain he isn't loving this."

"Get serious, Rupert. Why doesn't Loring just pull some strings and fix it?" Paul stopped talking when he heard the narcissism in his own words.

Rupert stared at him, debating for a moment the intensity of criticism he was willing to dole out to the son of his boss. He settled for a disgusted shake of the head.

"I suppose Dad wants to talk to me about this." Paul's eyes looked past Rupert toward the main house.

Rupert said nothing.

Paul snickered, "Should be a lively dinner conversation."

"You missed dinner."

"What do you mean, I missed dinner?" Paul was incredulous.

"Your father ate early today." Rupert motioned back to the pool house. "But I noticed you have an abundance of Jiffy Pop, should you find yourself weak and in need of nourishment."

Paul cursed under his breath as he watched Rupert walk up the pathway and disappear into the staff entrance. He stood there for several minutes looking up at the main house and then out over the sprawling Griffiths Manor. It was everything he loved; yet it was everything he loved to hate.

Suddenly freeing himself from his robe, Paul dove naked into the swimming pool. He swam furiously, slashing his arms into the still water in angry stokes. Pounding out lap after lap, persisting without relent. Paul's head pounded and his lungs ached, yet he beat himself until the sun disappeared and his body finally surrendered to exhaustion.

He clung to the ledge of the pool for a half-hour, his eyes closed and his head resting on his throbbing forearms. Paul might have been a world-class swimmer had it not been for his disdain of training. He certainly had the body for it: long lines and broad shoulders. Paul's build was like his father's, and he also had LJ's thick black hair. But his eyes, crystal blue and inquisitive, were just like his mother's.

His athletic physique, his good looks, and access to the finer things made Paul extremely popular with his peers—especially the women. And because of it, his social life had always taken precedence over sports and school.

With his father's plan now set in place, all of that was about to come to an end.

"Genius," Rupert said to LJ as they watched Paul drag himself out of the water and back into the pool house. "Having Terrence stash Paul's car at the garage in Brookhaven is what convinced him."

LJ offered a weak smile, but he disliked having to do this to his son. He turned away from the kitchen window with a knot in his stomach, realizing he had always taken care of business, whatever the nature, face-to-face, like a man. Trickery and deceit had long since become a foreign concept to him, yet this was the path he had decided to take with his son this time; it's what needed to be done.

LJ had involved others besides Rupert in his scheme, and once again the wheels of deception had been set in motion. There was no turning back now.

It was just after ten o'clock on Monday morning, and LJ was reading the paper and enjoying a cup of coffee in his study. He heard one of the staff greet "Mr. Paul" somewhere outside, followed by the sound of the front door opening and closing. LJ set down his mug and folded the paper neatly on the desk in preparation for what was sure to be an angry confrontation. He was pleasantly surprised when Paul sat down across from him and let out a surrendering exhale.

"Morning, Dad."

"Good morning, Paul."

Paul paused, taken aback by his dad's acknowledgement of his new name. "Rupert filled me in last night about the cops towing my car."

LJ nodded, but didn't respond.

"So . . ." Paul's fingers tapped lightly on the chair's armrests. "What happens now? When can we get it back?"

"They didn't take the car to punish you," LJ said. "It was towed as evidence of a hit and run." His father took off his reading glasses. "Do you remember anything about the accident?"

Paul swiped a hand dismissively. "It was nothing more than a fender bender. We're talking, barely any damage to the other car. I'm sure nobody was even hurt."

LJ stared at his son, astonished at his brazen lack of remorse. Paul had no idea what or whom he had hit, nor did he care. Once again, Paul was only concerned with Paul. "Well the police seemed to believe otherwise. In fact, had Rupert not covered for you, those detectives would have dragged you out of bed and tossed you in the hoosegow."

Paul rolled his eyes—mostly at the term, hoosegow. "Can't we just pay the bail or something, and be done with it? I mean, seriously Dad, you know these village cops are always making a big deal out of the smallest stuff."

LJ shook his head, even more certain now that he was doing the right thing. "I've gotten the police to back off for the time being, but there's no way I can make this one go away for you. It's going to court and the case will have to be decided upon by a judge."

"What do you mean, like, I'll be on trial?" Paul's voice was a couple of decibels louder and an octave higher. "Can't you call Nathan and have him take care of it?"

Nathan Geerts had been the family's attorney for years. He was presently vacationing with his wife in Belgium, which suited LJ just fine. LJ could claim that Geerts was representing Paul in court, and Paul would have no way of ever finding out otherwise.

"I've already spoken with Nathan," LJ lied. "He's left a couple of phone message for the judge who will hear the case."

Paul eased back in his chair.

"But I wouldn't be too optimistic," said LJ. "The district attorney is pushing for jail time. For now, you're considered under house arrest."

"This is bullshit!" Paul bellowed. "I've got tickets for the big fight Thursday night at the Garden! I can't miss that. Plus, I'm sure it would be okay for Terrence to drive me into the City, wouldn't it?"

LJ shook his head solemnly. "If the detectives happen by and find you're not at the house, you'll be looking at prison time for certain."

"Prison time," Paul swallowed hard. "What the hell did I crash into, anyway?"

"I don't know," said LJ. "But I get the feeling that your lack of accountability has a great deal to do with the direction this is going. At any rate, I'll apprise you of the details as soon as I hear back from Nathan."

The desk phone rang and LJ answered it. Paul hunched forward at the ready, but LJ shook his head, indicating that the caller was someone other than Nathan. Paul took it as his cue to leave and he skulked out of the study.

Just as LJ set the phone back in the cradle, Rupert came in and closed the double doors behind him. "Beg your pardon, Mr. Griffiths. I thought you'd want to know, Paul is querying some of the staff as to what the police said when they were here." Rupert kept his voice low. "I've already spoken to each of the employees, and they know not to say anything to him."

"Good, good" said LJ. "That was Gwyneth Eichler on the phone just now, Sheryl Beckham's deputy director of volunteer and community partnerships. She handles India outreach programs—health, water, sanitation, that sort of thing."

"So they're definitely onboard with the plan." Rupert rubbed his hands together, uncharacteristically effusive. "When do you plan on telling Paul?"

"Not just yet. Gwyneth is going to call me back in a few days with the particulars." LJ glanced at the notepad on his desk. "But it sounds as if they have a group of volunteers heading to New Delhi at the end of the month. Until I hear back from Ms. Eichler, Paul will just have to make the best of his confinement here at the house."

The return call from Eichler came on Thursday afternoon as LJ was meeting with the CFO of Griffiths Semiconductor, Inc. He and his secretary had decided the drive out to Long Island would be a nice break, and it also saved LJ the ride into the City. Unless absolutely essential, LJ's forays to the company headquarters on Madison Avenue were becoming less frequent. The three were putting the finishing touches on a PowerPoint presentation for an upcoming shareholders meeting when Rupert tapped on the door of the study.

"Please forgive the intrusion," Rupert said in a low voice. "But I have that call you've been waiting for from Ms. Eichler."

His guests excused themselves while LJ took the call. A few minutes later LJ summoned them back into the study to finish their meeting. They agreed to stay for dinner, and the group talked lightly over garden-fresh tomato soup, wedge salad, wild rice and salmon with dill sauce. Afterwards, the two men enjoyed brandy and cigars on the veranda while the secretary worked on revisions to the presentation.

Paul, who had been underfoot all week, had walked up the slight incline to the main house three times during dinner. Rupert had seen him pacing the driveway on each occasion, and then trudge back to the pool house in annoyance. Whether Paul sensed his fate was close at hand, Rupert couldn't be certain. But it was clear that not knowing had begun to wear on him.

LJ worried that the plan had to come together soon, or Paul would figure it out. The supposed house arrest had kept Paul from going out, but he still had his cell phone, his computer and access to whatever social media was the latest fad. Sooner or later someone would reveal that the hit and run had totaled only a common street sign, which had already been repaired.

Late that evening, with his dinner guests gone and the call from Eichler having finally come, LJ decided it was time.

The evening was cool, and the light breeze felt good against the heat from the two good-sized snifters of brandy he'd had with his guest. LJ strolled down the path to the pool house, trying to figure out how he would tell Paul that his life, as he knew it, was about to change forever.

The door was open and Paul was sprawled on the couch watching the fight on a pay TV channel. When he noticed his father in the doorway, Paul quickly fanned the hazy air and muted the sound on the TV.

"Sorry to interrupt," LJ said. "We can talk in the morning if you'd rather." He knew full well that anxiety had already pushed Paul to the cliff's edge.

"No, no. Now's fine." Paul flung a pile of newspapers off the couch and motioned toward the cleared space, but LJ remained standing. "Did you hear from Nathan?" Paul asked as he eyed the folder under his father's arm.

LJ's throat tightened, as if refusing to let the lie escape from it. "I did," he answered solemnly. "Nathan has been working on the judge behind the scenes, and they were finally able to reach a conditional agreement." LJ dropped his head slightly. "But Paul, what I've got to tell you is both good and bad news."

Paul sunk into the cushion and exhaled without taking a new breath. His mouth was frozen half open, and he looked as if he was about to be sick. "Tell me, Dad. Just say it."

"The good news is you can avoid having to serve any jail time whatsoever."

His father's pause seized Paul, pinning him in place as if he were paralyzed. Suddenly LJ wasn't sure he could go through with another deception.

Two

January 10, 1968

LJ tapped his trousers nervously while Paul sat back in the chair, his head cocked and his lips pinched into a smirk. They were seated in the vestibule just outside the commandant's office, waiting to be summoned.

"They know it was you," LJ said under his breath.

Paul's eyes rolled toward the office door. "Then why are you here too?"

"Because whoever saw you do it couldn't tell us apart."

Paul snickered then shrugged. "Stephens can't do jack shit to us--."

"Why is it always *us*?" LJ forced the words through clenched teeth. "I have an alibi and I'm pretty sure you don't. So maybe this time I'll just tell Commandant Stephens the truth."

"Easy there, hombre." Paul studied him. "You'd never rat out your own brother . . . Would you?"

A hissing exhale issued from LJ as he slumped back, his head resting on the top of the chair and his eyes fixed on the yellowed ceiling tiles above him. It wasn't the first time LJ had been implicated in a scheme of Paul's, but it was the first time he had ever considered letting his twin bury himself in a ditch of his own digging. LJ realized how easy it would be to simply tell the commandant to check the library records. The sign-in sheet would prove that LJ had been studying there when it happened.

Paul had climbed onto the roof of the library and pelted one of his classmates with eggs as the kid was walking to class in the outdoor hallway below. Paul and the other cadet had been at odds after the boy reported Paul absent from a mandatory JROTC meeting. But even with several witnesses having heard Paul's threats to get even, the boy was unable to positively identify his assailant. Reporting the incident to the commandant, the violated cadet could only describe the perpetrator as, "one of the Griffiths twins." In the tightly run military academy, it was cause enough to haul both of the brothers in.

"Not to mention," LJ continued, "Do you have any idea how pissed mom will be?"

The Christmas break had just ended, and only three days earlier their mother made the 1½-hour drive from Brooklyn to Cornwall on Hudson to drop the boys back at the academy.

Paul crossed a leg and palmed his hair back. "I need a cigarette."

LJ glared at him. "I don't know if you even care, but I'd like to graduate next year. And if this latest stunt of yours gets me kicked out of here too . . . Put it this way, I'm not going to sit quietly and just take it. I'm done paying the price for your screw-ups."

"Jesus, Lore." Paul lowered his voice. "It's not like I shot the little prick; it was just a couple of eggs."

Suddenly the door swung open. Both boys fell silent when they saw the school chaplain standing in the office with Commandant Stephens. That detail, not being a minor one, and the bleak expressions on the men's faces, sent a jolt of doom through the brothers. LJ knew that this time Paul had gone too far.

On past occasions, Paul had used their father's status as an alumnus and generous supporter of the academy to his advantage. But this time he wondered if even the fact that their father was serving in Vietnam might not be enough to spare him.

The commandant motioned the brothers in and the chaplain closed the door behind them.

"I'm sorry to have to tell you this boys, but I have some terrible, terrible news." Commandant Stephens came around closer to the two brothers, and then sat awkwardly on the front of the desk. "Your father has been killed in combat."

Thinking back on the dark time that followed, it wasn't his father's funeral, or the bills the family was left with, or even their abrupt departure from the military academy that stood out to the two boys. Nor was it the sudden move to the crowded home of cousins in Chicago that they would remember most. It was Mother's unrelenting insistence that their father's death wasn't fair. It was her mantra-like response to all those who tried to console her.

Lieutenant James Victor Griffiths had been killed on the first day of 1968, after the North Vietnamese Army had agreed to a 36-hour ceasefire. "Pope Paul VI had even declared January 1st a day of peace," she would say; as if the argument somehow bore influence over the hand that fate had already dealt.

It had taken more than a week for official word to trickle down from Tay Ninh Province, through U.S. Army bureaucratic channels, to their New York brownstone. Truce or not, the outcome remained unchanged: his father was dead. LJ had been transplanted into a public school in a strange city, much different than their genial neighborhood in Brooklyn.

The brothers were relegated to a converted laundry room in the basement of their aunt and uncle's Lincoln Park home. Mother had to take a job at a bakery in Cicero, and she was away at work much of the time. And even when she was not working, the once-lively woman retreated into a cocoon spun of grief, stale memories and images of what should have been. The boys would often find her sitting in her small bedroom off of the kitchen, a shoebox full of old photographs spread out on her bed. They could hear her in there weeping when came in at night.

The embracing certainty of a family had become as artificial to them as the New Year's Day ceasefire was to the NVA. Gone was the structure the boys had come to know at the academy, and with it the natural order to their lives had plummeted into chaos. As far as the twins were concerned, they might as well have moved to Iceland.

Both coped in their own ways. LJ tried to restore some sense of stability in his world with a sense of focus. He joined Mather High School's basketball team and worked afternoons and weekends at a neighborhood pet store. Paul, on the other hand, seemed to embrace the dearth of structure. He spent his after school hours hanging out under the bleachers, smoking weed with the leather-jacketed crowd.

Then one breezy Friday afternoon everything changed for both of them.

LJ left school after his last class, taking the 49 downtown bus for his afternoon shift at the pet store. It had been three months since the move to Chicago and he was finally getting the hang of the inner-city transit system. The street seemed quiet to LJ—almost eerily so. As he walked the two short blocks from the bus stop, he had no way of knowing that on that April day, a volatile brew of rage and race was boiling just beneath the surface of the West Side neighborhood.

SADHANA

The owner of the pet store had decided to go home early that afternoon, and for the first time left LJ responsible for closing the shop at the end of the day. Two other employees would be working there with him: Jules Loftgren—a retired teacher who volunteered at the store—and a seventeen-year-old clerk named Abby Townsend.

The boss had just left. LJ was changing out the puppy litter and Loftgren was working in the back. He was a fussy man who spent most of his time at the shop quietly tending to the kittens. LJ had often noticed the long sleeves he wore over his boney forearms, scratched and scabbed from the cats. Loftgren never complained about them though, and referred to the felines as his "little furries," claiming that they were the only ones who truly understood him.

The bells over the front door jingled and Abby came in.

"Son-of-a-gun!" screeched Buster, an old white cockatoo—his head bouncing up and down as he stepped sideways along his perch. "Come in! Oh boy! Son-of-a-gun!"

The blond haired, blue-eyed girl hefted her schoolbooks onto the counter—the familiar lilt gone from her step. "Did you hear what happened? Martin Luther King was shot. It's all over the news."

LJ nodded. "They announced it on the loudspeaker at school today," he said. "Pretty sad thing."

"I know. It's hard to believe anyone would do something like that."

Loftgren emerged from the storage area behind the store. "What's this about Dr. King?"

Abby told him what she had heard. The man gasped, and then as if the bones had suddenly left his body, he crumpled onto a display case of chew toys.

LJ helped him upright and steadied him as Abby handed the man a tissue. Abby walked Loftgren to the back of the store, rubbing his wilted and quivering shoulders as he dabbed at his eyes. Then LJ went to the door and looked around outside. The sun was behind the shop now, throwing a long angled shadow halfway across the street. Pages of a newspaper scrambled past the store, separating in the air—one page gripping the grill of a parked car while the others cowered against the building. The CLOSED sign was already up in the window of the dry cleaner next door and LJ saw the owner of the hardware store across West Madison, stooped against its metal security grate, trying frantically to secure the padlock. A city bus sped by, nearly bereft of passengers, leaving a sooty cloud lingering over a desolate street.

"I think we need to board up the windows and leave here," LJ announced to his two co-workers.

They both stared back with a mixture of alarm and confusion.

"Something isn't right," LJ said, not really clarifying his decision to secure the store. It wasn't even clear to him. "I just have a bad feeling."

"There are some crates and sheets of wood near the dumpster out back," Abby said. "I'll get them."

Loftgren threw a hand up to cover his mouth. "Oh, good God. Are you really sure this is all necessary?"

"No, I'm not," said LJ, "But I'd rather be prepared just in case. Can you find that transistor in the back and tune it to a news station? Abby and I will work on the windows."

With a trembling hand held tightly over his mouth, Loftgren simply nodded and went off to locate the radio. LJ and Abby brought the wooden sheets through the roll-up door in the back, closing it behind them. LJ then held the plywood pieces in place while Abby stood on a stepstool and nailed them to the window frame out front. Neither teen said much. The entire street was now cast in a blue-gray shadow, and a faint smoky smell drifted in the air. LJ glanced nervously up and down the empty sidewalk as Abby nailed the last board into place.

It was dark now and sirens cried out in the distance. With the windows covered the store took on a hauntingly confining feel.

"Come in!" squawked Buster. "Oh boy!"

"We should move all the animals to the back," said Abby.

Loftgren moved the kitten cage, while LJ and Abby slid the larger puppy cage across the concrete floor and through the door. A zesty trail of pinewood shavings and shredded newsprint trailed them into the large storage room at the back of the store.

Sensing a disruption in their routines, the animals reacted right away. The puppies yapped and panted while the kittens clung fiercely to their cages. Abby started back for Buster, but Loftgren called out.

"Come quick! The radio station," he said. "They're talking about some sort of Negro uprising."

They huddled around the small transistor as news reports were interrupted by updated reports—each worse than the one prior. It seemed that large portions of the city were under siege by black youths, hungry for retribution. Several arson fires were burning out of control in the South Side neighborhood of Woodlawn, according to the report. Broken store windows and incidences of looting were reported on the West Side, specifically in the Austin and Lawndale areas.

"That's us!" cried Loftgren.

"We should leave," Abby said, Loftgren nodding his concurrence. LJ agreed, but asked that they wait in the back while he checked outside the front of the shop. A swatch of West Madison was visible through an uncovered corner of window, and LJ saw only an empty street. He crept to the door and slowly opened it, listening for anything threatening. More distant sirens, and alarms ringing much closer.

LJ eased his head outside, glancing one way and then the other. A figure sprinted across the street about a block away, running quickly, and then two more and then the sound of glass breaking. LJ took a step further out the door and saw flames shooting from a building several blocks to his left, well beyond where the figures had crossed the street. A rapid burst of what sounded like gunshots spit into the night from a rooftop somewhere in the area, driving him backwards into the shop. He locked and bolted the door.

"I don't think it's safe to leave," LJ told Abby and Loftgren. He described the scene on the street to them, including the sound of gunshots and the building in flames he spotted.

"How close is the fire?" asked Abby.

"It's several blocks west," he said. "Nowhere near us, but it looks like it's close to the Imperial Theater."

Another news bulletin came on the air, and the three ran to the radio. It was an announcement that Mayor Richard Daley was imposing a 10 p.m. curfew for minors, and all residents were advised to remain inside.

LJ phoned home to let Paul know what was happening, that he was unable to leave the shop and planned to spend the night there. Paul asked if he should come down to help, but LJ declined his offer. "I doubt you could get though anyway," LJ said. "The news reported that the National Guard has sealed off this whole neighborhood."

At about 11 p.m. the electricity in the store suddenly went out and the neighborhood was submersed in complete darkness. Abby tried the phone and it was dead, too.

With a flashlight and a candle, the three double-checked the doors and windows and rejoined the animals at the back of the building.

Jules Loftgren had always maintained a façade of being married to a woman, whom none of the employees had ever seen. But now he was eager to get home to his own cats—admitting there was nobody there to take care of them. Anxious and afraid, he worked himself into a state of panic, adamant that he could not stay the night.

LJ implored him to remain at the pet shop where he would be safe, but Loftgren insisted he had to get home. For an hour or more Loftgren peeked through a corner of nailed plywood, watching for a lull in the barrage of smoke and tear gas grenades tossed back and forth between the opposing factions. Shortly after midnight, Loftgren made a run for his green Wolseley Hornet parked near the front of the hardware store across the street.

LJ and Abby watched in horror as a bottle struck Loftgren in the head. He crashed to the pavement like a sack of sand, and then lay writhing in the street amongst shattered glass and his own blood.

Abby clenched LJ's shirt and buried her face into his chest. LJ watched for signs of movement during sporadic flashes of light. As a helicopter spotlighted the street, they saw the National Guard troops moving away from them, down West Madison Street.

Loftgren had rolled onto his side, but was now still. The two teens sensed, more than they actually saw, the swell of rioters moving to fill the void left by the departing troops. In the distance, buildings and cars burned and the entire area was choked with acrid smoke. LJ knew it was only a matter of time before the crowd, ravenous for revenge, would reach Loftgren. Shortly following that, they would surely set the shop ablaze—killing he, Abby and all the animals.

"Try to find something to write with!" LJ told Abby. "Quickly! Paint, a felt pen . . . anything that might stand out."

Furiously, the two of them ransacked the cabinets. There was nothing.

"Got something!" Abby finally yelled from another room. She emerged from the janitor's closet with a small tube of white shoe polish.

"Good," said LJ, tucking it into his pants. "Now help me with this tarp."

They unhooked a canvas tarp used to separate the large and small dogs, and quickly bundled it into a manageable wad. LJ tucked it under his arm and went to the barricaded door at the front of the shop. "If I don't make it back in three minutes, lock the door and push the desk in front of it."

Abby's eyes were wide with terror, and she could only nod her assent.

One last peek into the murky battlefield, and LJ disappeared through the doorway. He ran as fast as he ever had, across the roadway to where Loftgren had gone down. He knelt next to him, relieved to find the man still breathing. He was bloody and moaning incoherently, but he was alive. LJ rolled Loftgren onto the canvas, afraid to look up for fear of what awaited beyond the darkness. He turned and tugged with all his might, sliding the man's dead weight an inch at a time back across the asphalt. It seemed like it was taking too long, and LJ had lost track of time. Was the angry mob moving closer? Had Abby already barricaded the door?

Abby was a year younger and attended a different high school, but the two had worked quietly, side-by-side at the store for nearly six weeks, neither of them ever imagining that a time would come when they would depend on one another for their very survival.

LJ mustered all the strength he had to tug faster, as his fingernails bent painfully outward with the force of his grip. He realized a rock or brick or bullet could strike him at any moment and he began to panic. As he considered leaving Loftgren in the street and running back to the store, an odd sensation came over him. He wondered if his father could see him.

The horrors his father had faced in Vietnam had always been an abstruse concept, but now they were vividly illustrated. LJ wondered if his father's last moments were anything like this.

When they finally reached the door, LJ paused momentarily and took the shoe polish from his pocket. He shook it viciously until the liquid filled the small spongy head. With several quick stokes against the plywood window covering, he conveyed a cryptic message to the marauding looters: SOUL BROTHER OWNED.

The door sprung open and Abby reached out to help LJ drag Loftgren through the doorway. Once safely back inside, LJ and Abby tended to Loftgren's head injury. Covering him in blankets, they moved him to the back of the shop and laid him on a foam mat atop a wooden pallet. The couple then fed all the animals and slid their cages near the roll-up door. In the event that the place was ignited, they planned to evacuate all the animals and set them loose. Many would certainly become lost in the urban landscape, but LJ and Abby agreed that it was a more palatable outcome than allowing the animals to die in the burning building.

The bark of gunfire was louder now. LJ and Abby could hear the snarling crowd approaching—the sound of trash cans thrown through store windows, and alarms blaring all around them. No smoke was visible, but a charring odor hung heavy in the air.

Something struck the outside wall right next to them, possibly a bottle. Angry yelling convulsed the roll-up door, and then the shuffle of bodies outside and the sound of trash containers being upended in the alley behind the shop. The young couple embraced each other tightly in the dark. A jarring crash shook the building—a brick perhaps, thrown against the barbershop next door.

"Oh boy!" screeched Buster from his cage near the front door. "Son-of-a-gun! Come in!"

LJ grabbed one of the blankets from Loftgren and quickly felt his way like a blind man, through the pitch-black store. He tossed the blanket over the bird's cage and then carried it into a maintenance closet. The bird continued his nervous dialogue from behind the closed closet door, but now at least it was too muffled to hear from outside the store.

The two teens watched over Loftgren and calmed the animals through the sirens and gunfire, as best they could. LJ repeatedly assured Abby that they would survive unscathed and would laugh about it someday, but in truth, he was as worried as she.

"How did you know what to do?" Abby asked.

LJ shrugged. "You mean about Mr. Loftgren?"

"About everything. Covering all the doors and windows, writing that on the boards outside, and yes, Mr. Loftgren, too. You probably saved his life."

LJ shrugged again. "Had to try something." He went to the cages to refill the water bowls. Abby followed, summarizing her life as if that night was to be its final chapter. She told LJ that she was an only child, had worn braces to straighten her legs until she was four years old, and had an uncle nobody talked about because he was mentally ill and lived on the streets. She told him that she'd always gone by a shortened version of her middle name, Abigail, and that her first name was Leigh, which she liked even less. Abby also admitted that she found LJ's eyes "captivating," because they reminded her of a Persian cat she had once adopted.

A blast nearby rattled the windows and the metal roll-up door, propelling Abby against LJ.

"It's probably farther away than it sounds." He struggled to maintain an even voice while reassuring her. "I'm sure this whole thing will all be over soon." But he could see in her eyes that she needed more of a distraction.

22

So, LJ told Abby all about himself; that his father had been killed in Vietnam, and of his worries about his mother. He told Abby of his plans to go to college, of his love of horses—though he had never actually ridden one, and he told her about his best friend: his identical twin brother.

They took turns sitting with Loftgren, and eventually they both fell asleep—Abby's head nestled comfortably against LJ's chest.

By noon the following day the smoke had cleared, the National Guard had gained control of the streets, and the young pet shop employees had developed a strong emotional bond. Along with the animals, LJ, Abby and Jules Loftgren had survived the night. And though a man named Seth Leibowitz owned the shop, LJ's makeshift signage had persuaded the rioters to bypass the building for other "white-owned" businesses.

LJ called his brother, Paul, to the shop for help getting Loftgren to Methodist Hospital. The man eventually recovered from his wounds and returned home to his cats. LJ and Abigail "Abby" Townsend began spending most of their free time together, along with Paul, who had ingratiated himself into the group. The threesome became inseparable.

Paul's demeanor seemed to mellow somewhat under the positive influences of his brother and Abby. He began working for a man named Ambrose Carter—an affable sort and a friend of Abby's father. Carter owned a small offset printing company on South Dearborn Street near Printers Row. With the earnings he saved, Paul was eventually able to buy a used Volkswagen van.

Meanwhile, LJ had applied to the University of Michigan and was admitted into the Ross School of Business. His acceptance was bittersweet, however, as by the end of summer he had completely fallen for Abby. LJ wanted Abby to come with him, but by then she was managing the pet shop and couldn't leave. She assured LJ of her requited love, and promised to wait faithfully for him.

LJ left for school on Sunday, the day before Labor Day, from Chicago's Union Station. Paul had driven him there, along with Abby, in Paul's newly painted, light blue van. Paul had been eager to show off the eight-track tape player he had just installed, and played a tape by The Rascals, all the way to the station. They all hugged goodbye, and LJ watched from the train window as his brother and his girl drove away together. During the four and a half hour trip to Ann Arbor, LJ's mind kept replaying the song, A Girl Like You.

* * *

"I'm sorry Mr. Rosenberg," Carter said into the phone. "With over a dozen artists and forty-five works of art, your order for a tri-fold leaflet has grown into a small booklet. I'm afraid you'll have to find another printer to handle a project of that scope."

Paul loitered at the file cabinet, pretending not to have heard the conversation. He watched as Mr. Carter tore the message from the pad, wadded it and tossed it into the wastebasket beneath his desk. "I'm going to lunch," Carter said as he hung up the phone and grabbed his coat from the rack.

Paul waited until he was well up the street, on his way to the Berghoff for his customary hot corned beef on rye. When the boss was out of sight, Paul picked the crumpled message out of the trash and slipped it into his pocket.

For years the company had specialized in the design and production of pamphlets, corporate brochures, restaurant menus and business cards. For the most part they were uncomplicated printing jobs that required no binding. Paul's discussions with Mr. Carter about expanding their market had always been rejected as untenable—the expertise and materials too costly. "Don't blame the boss," Mr. Carter used to say. "He's got enough problems."

Early in his employment Paul had recognized the decision not to take on larger print orders such as pamphlets and books, as both a mistake on Carter's part and a potential opportunity for Paul.

A dim light flickered through a barred window behind Carter's Print Shop. It was the middle of the night, and the alley running parallel to South Dearborn Street was empty.

Paul felt the rush of cool air on his face and chest as he propped open the back door, casting a long angled shadow across the vacant building behind the shop. He had been working there alone throughout the night, listening to music and enjoying the tranquility of the empty shop. Nobody knew he was there at that hour, which was essential for what he was doing. Paul had spent the past five hours printing material for an upcoming art exhibition at the Art Institute of Chicago. He had called Rosenberg back after Carter had rejected the job. During the phone call, which was made in secret from a phone booth down the street, Paul had agreed to handle the job himself. Only he was working on the sly, after hours, and under the name, Griffiths Printing and Binding.

SADHANA

When he had collated the copies, Paul set the eight program pages and single folded covers in 300 tiny stacks on the floor of the shop. The work had taken more time than he had planned, and he still hadn't glued the pages yet. Paul checked the clock as he donned his rubber work gloves. It was a quarter-to-three in the morning.

Paul pried the top off of a gallon container, and moving quickly from stack to stack, applied a thin bead of glue along the spine of each cover, using a one-inch paintbrush. After thirty seconds the surfaces became tacky, and the pages needed to be immediately attached. After sixty seconds the glue hardened to the point that the pages would no longer bond. It was a sloppy process that left a glut of adhesive on some pages and a shortfall on others. Excess glue dripped and spattered on the floor and around the entire printing room, inundating the shop's work surfaces with millions of tiny, golden, petrified raindrops.

"I need your help!" Paul whispered into the receiver as Abby wiped the sleep from her eyes.

"Paul? What's the matter?"

"I have to get a job done before Carter gets in to work."

"It's five in the morning," she protested. "Isn't there anybody else you can--?"

"Please Abby, I really need your help." Paul sounded unusually troubled. "I've started something down here at the print shop and it's gotten away from me. If I can't get this thing fixed tonight, I'll be out of a job."

"You're there? Tonight? Now?" Abby voice held a combination of curiosity and disappointment. "I'll be there in twenty."

"The front is locked," Paul said, "so come in through the delivery door in the alleyway."

Abby let out a disconcerted groan, and then hung up the phone. The entire drive there she wondered why she would do this for Paul; risking the shame of her father should Mr. Carter ever find out.

Convincing herself she was doing what LJ would want—helping his twin brother out of a jam—Abby showed up at the alley door. She was washed and lightly made-up, and wore a pair of bell-bottom Levis and a black tee shirt from The Doors' Midwest concert tour.

With an indicting frown she said, "I know you're not supposed to be here at this time of night." Abby tossed her purse onto a chair. "What in the world are you up to?"

Paul contemplated making up a story to garner her sympathetic cooperation, but instead he uncharacteristically opted for the truth. He explained how Mr. Carter had forsaken the job offered by Rosenberg of the Art Institute, and how Paul had agreed to do it under a ruse company. He tried to justify to Abby that he had only done it out of a long-standing love for the arts. Abby had been around Paul long enough to know his deceptive ways, however she was already there and agreed to help him anyway.

With feverish precision the two teenagers glued the remaining programs and stacked them in boxes by the back door. They then went to work scouring the excessive overspill from the countertops and floor. It was difficult work and the stubborn adhesives clung to the surfaces like crustaceans in a tide pool.

With Carter's reputation as an early riser, the clock was ticking for Paul and Abby. Just prior to sunup they decided to cut their losses and take the boxed programs out through the rear door, even though the cleanup was only fractionally completed.

The sky blue Volkswagen van sat idling in the Art Institute parking lot. With the heater turned high, the two drank coffee from Styrofoam cups and listened to Sunshine of your Love, while they waited to deliver Rosenberg's programs.

"I was just thinking," Paul said as he gazed through the frosty car window. "If we got a few more jobs like this one, we could make beaucoup bucks."

"We?" Abby tucked a bent leg under herself as she turned to face him. "I only helped you because you were in a fix. I'm convinced this whole thing is going to backfire, and you're still going to lose your job."

Paul smiled smugly.

"And since Mr. Carter is one of my dad's best friends, I don't want to be anywhere around when that happens."

"You're forgetting that Carter turned down this job," Paul said. "All I did was help a paying customer get what he wanted."

"Yeah, and you used all of Mr. Carter's equipment and materials to make yourself a tidy profit."

Paul laughed and Abby rolled her eyes in mock annoyance.

They waited together in the van and delivered the boxes to Rosenberg when he arrived at the Institute later that morning. Immediately, Paul went to work searching out more binding jobs for his clandestine new company.

SADHANA

But a week later, as Paul was trying to find more printing jobs, Rosenberg was trying to find Paul. The materials he had prepared for the Art Institute had been a disaster; many of the pages were out of alignment, some had stuck together and others had come loose from their bindings. In addition, Paul's boss, Mr. Carter, had begun questioning all the employees about the beads of hardened epoxy that were spattered on all the printing equipment.

Paul couldn't help but think of Abby's prediction: that his plan would backfire and he would lose his job. But Paul also felt he had covered his tracks well, and he was determined to play dumb about the gluey mess, regardless of whatever Carter may suspect.

Two weeks had now passed and Carter had just left on his lunchtime walk to the Berghoff. Paul and two other employees were working in the back when the bell above the door sounded, alerting them that a customer was at the counter.

Paul peeked through the curtain that separated the office from the workshop. It took a second to register the irate face glaring at him from the other side of the counter. The man stood there holding several detached pages of a printed program.

Paul tried to swallow the lump in his throat as he stepped into the office wiping his hands on his apron. "Mr. Rosenberg--"

Three

Paul was infamous among the estate staff. Most of us could never have afforded even the most trivial possessions that he took for granted. The damage to Paul's Hummer would be repaired or the entire car replaced; there was little doubt of that. But when talk of a jail sentence began circulating, a cathartic stir of excitement swept through the house.

We had all endured Paul's grouchiness, his careless remarks, drunken antics and sloppy quarters. It was not unusual for someone on staff to greet him in the morning, only to be ignored. Worse, there were occasions when he was downright rude.

And how could any of us expect otherwise? The boy's childhood had been purchased for him. He had experienced teenage angst from the backseat of the family car, with a beeper and a pocket full of cash. Paul's entire life had been lived on the glass shelves of a curio cabinet.

Add to that, he never even knew his own mother.

* * *

"India?" Paul could barely catch his breath. "That's the stupidest fucking idea I've ever heard . . . India! What ignorant dumbass came up with that one?"

LJ clenched his jaw to keep from firing back something he'd surely end up regretting. More than anything, LJ was angered by Paul's profane language. It wasn't that he was unaccustomed to it, but LJ didn't allow it in his home. Paul's mother never cursed, as far as LJ knew, and he had always been emphatic about raising his son to speak the same way: with respect—mostly out of deference to her memory.

But his son was no longer a boy. He was a grown man. They were two men, who were nothing alike and seemingly had little respect for one another. LJ realized that like it or not, they had to live nearly under the same roof. Besides, Paul was the sole heir to the Griffiths fortune. He was the last of the family. This was uncharted terrain for him, and the rules that LJ once insisted upon were no longer applicable.

"You ought to fire Nathan Geerts, better yet sue the son-of-a-bitch for incompetence." Paul slammed his balled fish into the pile of old newspapers on the couch next to him. "This so-called *deal* he negotiated with the judge is total shit. I'd rather go to prison than spend a single night in India."

LJ smiled to himself as if a lion's head mask had slipped off Paul and his roar had withered to nothing. It suddenly occurred to him that Paul was not only naïve, but he was also scared. The furthest he had ever been from home was a private penthouse dorm room at Palladium Hall, not more than a couple of hours away. LJ suddenly felt the gravity of his own mentorship role—one that he saw as a failure to this point. He knew there would be no second chance to redeem their relationship, and likewise, there would never be a better opportunity to intervene—to right Paul's badly canted character with a ballast of value and morality. Rupert was right; life had come relatively easy to Paul.

"Six months, Paul. How hard could that be? A lot of college kids participate in foreign exchange programs, do volunteer work, or get internships with non-profits, and most find the experiences quite rewarding."

"I may not survive six months in that armpit," Paul shot back. "I'll probably get killed by a roadside bomb or something. You never know what those damn terrorists carry under their turbans!"

LJ tilted his head back, looking for patience. "Paul, I think you're confused. Dozens of cultures wear turbans and other headdresses. Hindus make up over eighty percent of India, and terrorist incidents are rare in that country."

Paul eyed his father, doubtful that he knew what he was talking about. "In any case, what's the bottom line here, Dad? Can't Nathan work a better deal than me being exiled to India? I mean, I wouldn't even mind sweeping up garbage along the turnpike, or handing out sandwiches to the homeless, or walking old folks around the park, whatever."

LJ shook his head. "I'm sorry Paul, but it's the best we could do given the circumstances." He held up the folder he'd carried in. "Here is all the contact information. Evidently you'll be part of a group of about two-dozen volunteers leaving out of JFK on the 30th."

"Of September?" Paul dropped his shoulders, suddenly struck by another blow. "That's only ten days from now. Totally impossible! No way I could even get a travel visa by then."

LJ tapped a finger on the folder. "I had my secretary send your paperwork to the Indian consulate with a rush request. The printout and tracking information are also in the folder. Your passport and travel visa will be here within the week."

Paul's eyes narrowed as he assessed his father's brazen bearing and indomitable demeanor. This was obviously a done deal—a preordained course of action. Paul saw that his father had won another fight; somehow able to once again tip the scales of life in his favor.

"What if I don't go?" asked Paul. "What if I say no, and just don't do this *volunteer* thing?"

"According to the judge, you either do this or you go to prison." LJ set the folder on the coffee table. "Think of it this way, the sooner you leave, the sooner you'll be done with it. Six months puts you back home in time for Easter."

"Wow, really? Easter? Nice conciliation." Paul reached past the folder to pick up the TV remote, then turned back toward the set. LJ walked out of the pool house with the sound of the boxing match blaring behind him.

For several days Paul kept to himself, out in the pool house mostly, but he was seen by a few staff-members making early morning forays into the library at the main house. These "sightings" were reported to Rupert, who promptly informed LJ. The two men speculated about what Paul was up to, but it wasn't until he unexpectedly showed up at the main house for dinner one night that it became clear.

"Did you know that I'll be arriving in New Delhi during their monsoon season?" Paul said as the white bean and chopped zucchini salad was being served. "How do you like that? Monsoon season."

LJ raised his eyebrows, unsure how to answer. Instead, he took up a forkful of salad and chewed it in thoughtful silence. LJ was aware that India's monsoons generally ran from May through October, depending on the area of the country. In any case, Paul's arrival was at the tail end of the season, and it was unlikely the rains would affect his stay.

"They're putting us up for the first few days in some corporate housing in a place called Jaipur," Paul said. "Probably some kind of slum."

"Or maybe not," said LJ, patting his mouth with a linen napkin.

"Dad, are you kidding? I can already feel the head lice and bedbugs crawling on me."

LJ took another mouthful.

"It's like, we'll be put up at their training site or something. I'll bet they shuffle thousands of those people through a place like that every month." Paul flicked a bean with his fork, but still hadn't eaten anything. "And check this out, we gotta sleep three to a room. Three people in one room! What the hell is that, Band Camp?"

LJ nodded. He thought of making a crack, almost too tempting to resist. Paul certainly hadn't minded bunking three to a room when his girlfriends from the Sloppy Tuna visited.

But LJ decided it was better to let it go. He just kept nodding, realizing that this trip was exactly the thing Paul needed.

"Did you know that India has the second highest population of any country in the world? In fact they're on course to pass up China in another ten years." Paul let out a snarly snicker. "Seriously? Like, over a billion people all in one place? So yeah, I'm betting they'll probably try to cram a few more into my room."

So that's what he's been doing in the library. LJ smiled as his salad plate was cleared. "Do you spend the whole six months there in Jaipur?"

Paul shook his head, finally shoveling a helping into his mouth. "We take the bus there from Delhi Airport, and we get trained for a few days. Then they split us up into smaller groups. Don't know where I'll be sent yet, but I'm sure it'll be some septic tank of a village, where I'll contract hepatitis or amoebic dysentery, or maybe if I'm lucky only an acute case of jock itch."

A troubling thought nagged at LJ, though it had nothing to do with Paul's melodramatic predictions. He was so bothered that he just remained there in the dining room after Paul finished his meal and left for the pool house.

Rupert stepped into the room, finding LJ alone at the table. "Will there be anything else before I retire for the evening, sir?"

LJ dribbled some cream into his mug and stirred the coffee to an almond-brown. "Paul will be traveling outside of New Delhi," he said to Rupert. "He told me that the group will attend training in Jaipur for a few days, then they'll assign him wherever he's needed. Who knows where he'll end up or what he might come across?" LJ started to bring the mug to his lips, and then abruptly set it down before taking a sip. "What do you think the chances are--?"

"It's been over thirty years since all that," Rupert said, "and India is a big place. Besides, I don't see this as anything but an opportunity for Paul to grow. Are you having second thoughts?"

"I don't know." LJ slid the mug away, then crossed a leg and leaned back in his chair. "Once he's over there, it's all out of my hands. I'll have no control over where he goes or what he does."

Rupert stood there—a pressed suit, starched and straight, as if he were hung on a hanger. "Whatever happens over there, sir, whatever course things take on their own, or however events unfold, I'm sure everything will turn out for the best."

LJ eyed his friend, still unconvinced.

On the Monday before Paul's departure, a tan Lexus swung into the drive and stopped just past the house. A staff member went out to greet the solo driver, spoke briefly with him and then returned to the main house. The man took a silver briefcase from the trunk of his car then walked down the path to the pool house where he disappeared inside.

Moments later Rupert tapped on the study door, having been apprised by the staff member and then having conducted a brief background check via the Internet.

"Paul has just received a visitor at the pool house," Rupert said as LJ leaned back and removed his reading glasses. "A medical doctor, evidently, by the name of Koenigs."

"Is Paul okay?" LJ asked. "We should call Moretti, he's been our family's physician since Paul was born."

"I think it's something to do with his trip," said Rupert. "The only Dr. Koenigs I was able to find on Long Island is from a travel clinic in Brookhaven. He specializes in preventative medicine and inoculations for international travelers: anti-malaria, tuberculosis, hepatitis, those kinds of things."

"Hmm." LJ caressed his chin. "And Paul did this on his own?"

The doctor left the pool house about twenty minutes later, and LJ watched from the window as the Lexus drove away. He stared out at the grove of pink-flowering cherry trees, which blended with stately elms to comprise the center of the horseshoe driveway.

"Rupert," LJ paused in thought. "Do you still think I'm doing the right thing?"

"Sir?" Rupert studied LJ carefully. "I believe this experience will do one of two things for Paul; it will either make him or break him. Regardless, it is a challenge that your son needs to face."

LJ let out a long, heavily weighted breath. "I know you're right. But doing this in the way that I've done it . . . well, it feels wrong somehow. It reminds me too much of the old me."

A long silence followed as the two men stood in deep thought. Finally LJ spoke again. "I wonder what my brother would do."

Rupert kept his eyes down; it was a comment to which there was no adequate response.

The drive to JFK was uncomfortable for Paul, partly because of the ungodly hour. He was more accustomed to coming in at 4:45 a.m., than going out. Paul sat on one side of the limousine and his dad and Rupert sat across from him. It felt like opposing teams facing off, and for the first time he wondered if the two had somehow conspired to make these events unfold the way they had.

"Did you need anything for the trip?" LJ asked. "I can have Terrence stop at a Duane Reade along the way."

Paul shook his head. LJ saw that his son was nervous, and he understood why. Paul's self-confidence had been crippled by his surroundings—his growth stunted since birth by pampering and overindulgence. He was a boy who could not walk, and now he was being pushed out into the world. Paul would either learn to stand on his own, or he would come crawling back home. In either case, LJ realized it was something that needed to happen.

Terrence eased the limo against the curb behind a mini-van surrounded by suitcases and Japanese businessmen. Even at this hour the international departure terminal at JFK was in full swing. Terrence pressed the trunk release and then hustled around to open the curbside doors for his passengers.

Rupert handed Paul a small, unsealed envelope, which appeared to be some kind of card. "I'll go help Terrence with the bags," Rupert said, as LJ took Paul aside for a private word.

He held out a folded bundle of cash, but Paul pulled away. "Take it, Paul. You may need it for some unforeseen--"

"No. I don't want your damn money."

Terrence and Rupert turned their heads away, pretending not to notice the interaction. LJ immediately regretted what he had done. He realized his offer of money was more to assuage his own guilt than to help Paul. Besides, a portion of Leigh's life insurance premium had been put into a trust for Paul when she died, and it had been available for him whenever he needed to access it.

"If you really wanted to help me, you should have gotten this shit taken care of before I was sent to India." Paul grabbed a small tote in one hand and hoisted a larger duffel bag over the other shoulder. "See you in six months." Paul turned away and was swallowed by the throng of international travelers.

"It is 9:50 p.m. local time," the pilot announced as they touched down in Helsinki, Finland.

Paul peeled off his eyeshades and tossed the headphones onto the empty spot next to him. He had slept well after downing two glasses of champagne and stretching out on the fully reclining, first-class seat. According to his tickets, the layover gave Paul just enough time to use the restroom and find his gate before departing on the final leg of his trip.

He located the departure gate in Terminal 2, and had to shoulder his way through the mass of people crowding around the counter. Through bits and pieces overheard along the way, it seemed there was a problem with his flight. An angry exchange between a traveler and an attendant confirmed it.

"Heavy rains in the northern parts of India are delaying traffic in and out of Delhi," she said. "Flight twenty-one has been cancelled."

At once, Paul pulled out his cell phone and started dialing his father's number—his mind already rehearsing a list of criticisms, protests and complaints. He stared at the phone for a second. It was his lifeline—everything from social media to online betting, a ready file folder of old girlfriends and his easy access to quick money. Paul realized the phone number he was about to call was also his crutch, one he both detested and took full advantage of. He suddenly shut the phone off.

"Are there other flights?" Paul asked the woman behind the counter.

She told him that their next flight wasn't until the same time the following day, but another airline had a scheduled flight to New Delhi at ten o'clock the next morning. The woman gave Paul a flight voucher and directed him to the Aeroflot ticket counter.

Aeroflot turned out to be a Russian airline with a stop in Moscow, and it was filling up quickly. As it was, they could only offer Paul a standby seat. He figured if the twelve-hour wait didn't kill him, the Russian aircraft probably would.

"Please, try to get me on that flight, if you can." Paul surprised himself at the fervor of his appeal, wondering when it had become important to him. He quickly chalked it up to not wanting to waste any more time sitting around a foreign airport.

Paul passed the time listening to music and wandering around the cavernous airport. He found the Finnish women attractive, with their light skin, eyes and hair, and their modish, seductive style of dress. But most of them seemed to travel in pairs, which made a casual approach difficult. And their language, with its clipped, rapid-fire words, sounded brusque and unfriendly.

After a time of checking out the women, Paul began to feel like a stalker and decided to give up his search. Paul spotted a sign across from the shopping arcade that read *Café Tori,* and realized he hadn't eaten since he first boarded the plane that morning. Most of the foods offered on their menu were unfamiliar to Paul. Feeling rushed and unnerved by the cashier, he quickly decided on a small coffee and an oval-shaped pastry. He winced as he inspected the peculiar, sawdust-like filling.

When Paul turned to find a seat, his eyes immediately settled on the pale waistline of a young woman bent over to get something out of a pink carryon bag. The small of her back bore a colorful tattoo, which gently arched above the string of her panties and then disappeared like the point of an arrow beneath them. She pulled out a paperback book and took a seat facing the broad wall of windows. The girl's powder blue eyes were nicely framed by blond hair tucked tightly into a bright pink headband.

"Terve," Paul said as he approached her table. It was the only Finnish word he knew, having been greeted with it several times throughout the day. "Paul." He patted on his chest, exaggerating the movements as if speaking to a deaf person. "Me . . . Paul. You?" He motioned toward her, his finger inadvertently pointing at her compact but shapely breasts. He tried again; "Me, Paul . . . You?"

"Me . . ." The woman paused as if she was starting to understand. "Me, sick to my stomach. You . . . total idiot."

Paul stood there speechless as the girl raised the book in front of her face and began reading.

"Oh," he said. "You're American." Paul set his pastry on the table and his two bags on the floor next to him. "Mind if I . . ."

She peered over the top of her book. "Do I have a choice?"

He smiled as if unfazed. "Hi, I'm Paul."

"Yeah, I heard."

Paul forced a laugh. "So, I got this weird pastry thing and would be happy to share it if you're hungry."

The girl eyed his plate and then lifted the book in front of her again.

He poked the pastry with his fork before pushing it away in disgust. "Anyways, here I am stuck in the airport for, like, five more hours, and saw you sitting here all by yourself. I just thought . . . "

"I think I have a pretty good idea what you thought." The woman stood and gathered her things. She stuffed the paperback into her bag and turned back to Paul. "Karelian pie."

"What?" His eyes widened.

"Your pastry, it's called *karelian pie*. It's made of rye bread, with rice and a boiled egg. They're actually not too bad." She slung her bag over her shoulder. "And thanks for the friendly chat, but I'm really not interested. Enjoy your trip, wherever you're headed."

It wasn't the first time in his life Paul had been shut down by a beautiful woman. He realized his opening line had been a lame one, but suspected it would have gone over better back home. At least there people knew him, or recognized the Griffiths name, or at minimum could detect his affluence. Paul was suddenly awash with an unfamiliar sensation that fell somewhere between loneliness and embarrassment. He felt naked without the trappings that had become synonymous with his identity.

When he checked back at the Aeroflot gate Paul found that his name was on the flight manifest for the 10 a.m. flight, and it was scheduled to take off on time. For that he was thankful, although he would be traveling in a coach seat for the first time in his life.

The plane was full, and Paul suspected it was the result of the previously cancelled flight. As he wedged his way down the aisle, past the first class and business class sections, the cabin seemed to close in on him. He glanced at the overhead bins and noticed they seemed to be filling faster than the seats. When he found his row, the bins above were full. Paul waved an attendant over.

"Someone's taken my bin space." He pointed to an oddly familiar pink bag.

"The bin spaces are first come—first served," said the attendant. She took his duffel bag from him and stuffed it roughly into the overhead compartment. Then, motioning to Paul's small tote bag she said, "You can stow that one under the seat."

Paul glanced across the aisle to see the young woman who had so soundly scorched him earlier in the café. She glanced up at her pink bag, then back at him in disgust and then back to her book.

"Ahem!" An impatient man nudged Paul with a camera case. The guy was bald and wore wire glasses that seemed to perspire on their own. His miniscule chin, hidden behind a grayish beard, barely moved when he spoke. "Can we please get by, son?"

Paul quickly stuffed his bag under the seat in front of his and slid into his assigned row. Though thankful that the young woman was across the aisle and not right next to him, Paul was hopeful she was not part of his CRF, International group.

He settled back into his narrow seat and did his best to imagine himself up front in first class.

Four

Paul did his best to excuse the poorly bound programs, blaming them on one of *his* incompetent employees. He assured Rosenberg that the employee responsible for the shoddy work had already been fired, and that any future printing and binding needs of the institute would be done by Griffiths Printing and Binding at a discounted rate.

"I don't need your lousy discount," demanded Rosenberg. "I just want my money back."

Paul cringed at the idea of returning the earnings from his first solo business deal; in fact he had already spent Rosenberg's money.

"And what's with this 'Griffiths Printing and Binding' bullshit?" Rosenberg craned his head, exaggerating a search for a business sign. "This place is called Carter's Print Shop, and I doubt you even have a legitimate company of your own. I'd like to see your business license."

Someone in the backroom called for Paul to fetch a container of blue ink from the stockroom, and both lines of the phone began ringing at once. Paul glanced up at the clock and knew that his boss would be back from lunch any minute, and the old man would quickly figure out that Paul had gone behind his back in accepting Rosenberg's printing job. Once Mr. Carter learned that Paul had done the job there at the shop, using all Carter's materials, he would be furious. Paul had to get Rosenberg out of there in a hurry.

Paul's wallet held only fourteen dollars. He glanced back at the clock, then past Rosenberg's angry scowl to the street behind him. Still no sign of old man Carter, but Paul knew he was coming. Bending beneath the counter, Paul flipped open the cash box and removed a zippered bag containing the week's receipts. He had been paid $300 to do the art Institute's programs, but found only $265 and some change in the cash bag.

"Here," Paul said, handing the contents to Rosenberg. "Ill come by with the rest tomorrow."

Rosenberg smirked at the cash, but took it just the same. His expression softened a bit as he counted the money, and Paul knew that for the moment at least, part of his problem had been solved.

As he quickly ushered Rosenberg out of the shop, Paul's arrogant curiosity couldn't help but get the best of him. "By the way," he asked, "how did you find me here?"

"Not all that difficult," said Rosenberg. "The programs you brought me were in boxes that had *Carter Print Shop* stamped on them."

Paul felt like kicking himself for the stupid oversight. But more urgent than that was the need to replace the money he had just taken from Carter's cash box. As he glanced up the street he saw Mr. Carter making his way through the lunchtime flock, back toward the shop. Rosenberg and Carter nearly bumped into one another as they passed, but thankfully neither seemed to pay notice to the other.

Paul ducked back inside before Carter arrived, and then went straight to the phone in the backroom. He dialed the pet store and hunched himself against the wall. "Abby," he said in a hushed voice. "I need your help."

"This is beginning to be a habit," she said. "What is it this time? Did you get the contract to print all of Cook County's phone books?"

"I need to borrow four hundred dollars right away."

Abby was silent on the other end.

"Please, Abby. Can you do this one favor for me? I'll never ask you for another thing."

An hour later Abby was standing at the back alley door where Paul had instructed her to meet him. She had gone to the bank and withdrawn much of what she had saved from her meager paycheck. Again, she was conflicted about her role in whatever Paul was doing. But she was equally enticed by the eccentric naughtiness of her boyfriend's brother. In the end, she justified her help by telling herself it is what LJ would want her to do.

Abby held an envelope in one hand and the other was firmly planted on her hip. "Are you going to tell me what this is all about?"

Paul's eyes told her that whatever he was about to say would bring her no closer to the truth.

"Paul!" a voice cried out from the shop. Suddenly the back door swung open and Ambrose Carter dashed into the alley. "We've been robbed!"

Paul's eyes darted from his boss to Abby, and immediately Abby knew that the *"robbery"* had something to do with Paul's urgent request for cash. Carter followed Paul's gaze, first to Abby and then to the envelope in her hand. He immediately suspected that this, too, was somehow connected to the missing money.

Carter folded his arms slowly across the top of his portly abdomen and cocked his head. "Abigail? Paul? What's going on here?"

"It's all very simple to explain," Paul said as he snatched the envelope from Abby's hand. "You see, Mr. Carter, Abby needed to pay a veterinarian over at the pet store in order to save a little cocker spaniel from being put down."

Carter squinted through one skeptical, frowning eye, and then glanced toward Abby. Her face held a similar expression as she listened to Paul's story.

"Poor thing had a gimpy little paw," Paul continued. "And, well, I don't want to bore you with the details. At any rate, I know Abby's father is a dear friend of yours, and I just thought that you would want to loan her the money for just a little while, until she was able to get to the bank." Paul hurried through the narrative leaving no space for old man Carter to interject his questions. "And of course, Abigail, being such a conscientious young lady, rushed right over to the bank as soon as the puppy's little paw was straightened out. And here is the money we loaned her, all accounted for. So, no harm – no foul."

Paul plucked $250 from the envelope and realized that there were no small bills with which to make up the rest. He then fumbled through his own wallet, contributing the fourteen-dollar sum of its contents. He was still a dollar shy, but didn't think Carter would notice.

"That was quite a story, Paul." Carter turned his gaze to Abby. "Abigail, is this true?"

Her eyes narrowed at Paul, waiting in silence just long enough to strike fear into him. Afraid to open her mouth for fear she might unleash a scathing rebuke, Abby merely nodded.

Carter took the money and walked back inside, leaving Abby and Paul standing silently in the alley, their eyes locked on one another. Once the door closed behind his boss, Paul quickly held up his hands in surrender.

"Do you realize how bad you made me look?" Abby demanded. "Mr. Carter is a family friend."

"What do you mean?" Paul's tone and body language feigned ignorance. "You don't look bad. He sees you as a kind-hearted animal lover. That's a nice thing."

"Gimpy paw," she said, shaking her head. "Why did you take that money from him in the first place?"

Paul didn't want to tell Abby about the poorly bound programs he'd done for the Art Institute, nor did he want her to know he had been careless enough to leave a trail for Rosenberg. So instead, Paul told her he needed the money to get his Volkswagen registered.

"So you stole from your boss?" Abby looked disappointed, but not really angry. "And what about the rest of the money? I saw how much you took from the envelope, and there's still a hundred and fifty dollars left. What else are you up to?"

"I got a lead on another binding job," he said. This time he was telling the truth. Paul explained that St. Alphonsus Church was putting together a new hymnal for the choir, and he had spoken to the monsignor about doing the job. He had promised the monsignor he could print and bind the hymn booklets for a good price.

Abby was suspicious. "It still doesn't explain why you need the extra money."

"I'm not going to use any of Carter's materials this time," he said. "Also, I might have screwed up the glue on those programs we did for the artist thing, and if I get the church job, I'll need some money to do it right this time." It was only half true. Paul still planned on printing the songbooks at night, using Carter's equipment, but he was also determined to figure out where he went so wrong with the bindings.

Abby studied his face, looking for a telltale clue as to what part, if any, of what he was telling her was the truth.

"I'll pay you back as soon as the church cuts me a check," he said.

"I'm not worried about that." She brushed aside his assurance. "Go back to the thing you said before that. What do you mean, you *might* have screwed up the glue?"

Paul was silent.

"You did screw up those programs, didn't you? And that's why you needed money in such a hurry. What happened? Did that guy from the Art Institute threaten to sue you? Was he going to blow the whistle on you? Tell Mr. Carter?"

Paul's face softened to an angelic smile. Abby tried to be angry, but couldn't help laughing. She playfully swatted at him, slapping Paul on the shoulder. She raised the other hand and Paul took her by the wrist.

They froze there for a heartbeat; breast-to-breast in mid-step of a sultry dance that neither of them had prepared themselves for. Paul's eyes questioned hers as the steamy silence descended around them. A second later they had released one another and the moment was over. Abby stepped back, embarrassed and confused. Paul held the spot, his unyielding eyes boring into hers.

That afternoon Paul left work and drove straight to the Central Library on Michigan Avenue. Surprised to find an abundance of materials on the subject, Paul checked out as many of them as the library would allow: Severin's History of Bookbinding; From Cover to Hardcover, by J. Graves; Binding Glues and Adhesives; and Kenny Talton's Step-by-Step Guide to Perfect Binding.

The nights that followed were spent at Carter's Print Shop, though this time he wasn't alone. After dinner Paul would swing by to pick up Abby, and with the radio playing softly in the background, the two would sit across from one another, working beneath a hanging fluorescent lamp in the backroom. Together they would pour over the library books, learning everything they could about bookbinding.

"It's no wonder those programs fell apart," Abby said, sliding the manual around to face Paul. "Look at this. It says that the glue needs to be flexible, and the paper should be rough cut in order to absorb the heated adhesive."

"Hmm," Paul followed along the page with his finger.

"That stuff we used dried as hard as a rock," she said. "And it was never even heated. What kind of glue was it?"

"Just some adhesive I bought at the supply house where Carter gets his ink. It's a big warehouse out on Howard Avenue." Paul frowned as he read further down the page. "I think this is going to cost more than I thought. We're going to need something to score the paper with. And it says we need a special machine, something like a hot griddle, in order to set the glue."

It turned out Paul was right about the cost of equipment. He found that the price of even a small thermal press was over a thousand dollars. And high temperature bonding agents, usually marketed to large publishing houses, were only sold in bulk quantities. He didn't need a fifty-gallon drum of the stuff, nor did he need a brand new pressing machine. But those seemed to be his only choices. Paul's frustration turned to desperation as he searched the want ads and auction houses for a cheaper option.

SADHANA

One night after working late on their binding research, Paul dropped Abby off at her house. She had sensed his aggravation and assured him that it would all work out okay.

Paul arrived home just after midnight and noticed a light on in the kitchen. His mother had returned from her job, and he found her sitting alone at the table, embracing a cup of coffee and crying. She told Paul that her boss had decided to close the Cicero bakery and move to Florida. The man had given layoff notices to all of his five employees at the end of their evening shifts. Paul made a meager effort to comfort his mother, but was consumed with his own troubles. He squeezed her shoulder awkwardly. "It'll all work out okay," he said, stealing the line Abby had used on him. His mother smiled weakly and then went up to bed.

Paul poured the remainder of the coffee into a mug and added a healthy shot of brandy from his uncle's liquor cabinet. As he sat there sipping it, Paul spotted a message on the notepad next to the phone. Monsignor Ryan had called to give Paul the church's printing and binding contract. It was good news in one respect, but it also made things more complicated. When added to the loss of income from his mother's layoff, the hymnal booklet job created a tremendous sense of urgency for Paul. He had to find a solution to the binding situation, or it would be a disaster worse than the Art Institute booklets.

Paul poured another shot into what was left of his coffee, gulped it down and then headed back out to his van. He had decided to break into the printers' supply house on Howard Avenue.

The wind rocked the van as Paul turned out the headlights and coasted to a quiet stop. He had parked near the loading dock at the rear of the warehouse, where it was dark and out of view from the street. Against the gray rollup doors, the van showed up as little more than a faint silhouette. Paul hoped a passing security guard or cop would not spot it. The warehouse was also in the takeoff path of the airport, which Paul was fairly certain would drown out any sounds he might make.

He took a mallet and a crowbar from under the seat, and then removed a small flashlight from the glove box. Paul cursed when he turned the switch and found that the batteries were dead.

The rear of the warehouse was dark, and it took Paul several seconds for his eyes to acclimate enough to even make out the contour of the building. What he saw was the outline of some kind of steel

43

security door at the back entrance. Paul ran his hand along the frame and felt a metal plate covering the latch. He guessed it would take several hours to pry it open, and even then he wasn't sure that his lack of lighting and his paltry collection of tools could accomplish it.

Paul then turned his attention to the rollup door, which seemed a bit flimsier and was closer to where he had parked. But it had a latch that was secured with a heavy padlock. He gave it several whacks with the mallet, and then tried to pry it. After a few noisy minutes with no discernible results, Paul jammed the crowbar into the narrow space between the building's frame and the door slats. It was quieter work, and after a few minutes it seemed to pay off. The aluminum had bent slightly away from the track.

Flattening his face against the building, Paul tried to peek through the two-inch gap. He muttered into the dark warehouse, again cursing his stupidity for not checking the flashlight batteries earlier. An idea suddenly came to Paul and he dashed back to the van. Digging in the darkness beneath the rear seat, he found a twenty-foot length of rope he had once used to tow a friend's car. Paul tied it firmly around the middle of the crowbar and then fed the curved end of the bar through the gap he had pried, until it hung along the track just inside the door. Keeping the rope taught, he tied the other end to the bumper of his Volkswagen and started the engine.

Paul held his breath, shifted into first gear and let out the clutch.
He felt the Volkswagen catch, as if he had forgotten to release the emergency brake. He gave it more gas and it groaned a foot or two forward before abruptly giving way in a deafening crash. In the rearview mirror Paul saw that the entire rollup door had sprung off the track and was clattering in a jumbled heap behind him.

With the thunderous sound still reverberating in the night air, Paul considered for a second, driving away from the building as fast as he could—pieces of the door snaking behind him and all. But he steadied himself and stopped the van. Untying the rope from his bumper, Paul quickly backed the van over the crumpled remains of the door. He left the van running, it's backend just inside the building. With its lights now on, Paul realized he would be more visible. But he also knew that without his taillights to illuminate the dark interior, all his efforts would be worthless.

Near the center of the cavernous room, Paul found what he thought were several thermal press machines on large racks. They were all too large for him to move. A smaller press sat on a pallet closer to the van. It wasn't as heavy as the others, but Paul still couldn't carry it by himself. He grabbed a blanket from the van and used it to slide the press the rest of the way across the floor. Fed by a healthy dose of adrenalin, Paul hurriedly hefted the machine onto the bumper and slid it inside. He then scampered back through the building, trying to remember the section where they stored the binding compounds.

As he made his way through the maze of racks and stacked boxes, Paul noticed a blinking red light coming from a metal box on the wall. A hot searing panic shot through him as he realized he had probably set off a silent alarm. Paul spun in a half-circle, eyes searching wildly, and then lurched toward a towering stack of plastic bottles and gallon-size tins. He scooped as many as he could in his arms and heaved them into his van, then ran back for more. Grabbing another clumsy armful, Paul shoved them carelessly into the rear of the van with the others. He wanted to go back for more, but couldn't bring himself to do it. Instead, Paul jumped back into the driver's seat and sped out of the building.

After a few long blocks he cut down a side street, flew past a high school, then slowed to the posted speed limit as he emerged onto Lee Street. As he made the turn, Paul saw two Chicago PD patrol cars approaching from the opposite direction. Speeding toward him with emergency lights flashing, they were undoubtedly heading to the silent burglary alarm at the warehouse.

The first car whizzed past, making the turn and continuing toward the alarm. The second slowed slightly, the cop inside eye-to-eye with Paul as he passed. It took only a second, but the cop's piercing glare held both suspicion and intense scrutiny. Paul knew that the cop got a good look at his van, and worse still, at him. But the squad car sped up again, its flashing red lights fading in Paul's mirror.

Paul scanned the street, continuing on at a normal speed. It would only take a minute or so for the cops to find the busted rollup door, he thought. And they'd either broadcast a description of his van to the rest of the force, or turn around and come after him themselves.

The street behind him was still vacant however, and there remained no signs of any other police cars. Within another minute or so he had driven well out of the industrial district. Traffic now joined him on the road, and Paul began to feel the confidence that came with blending in. He was convinced that the passing was too quick for the cop to have seen his license plate. But just in case he did, Paul decided to unload the stolen property before going home.

Abby's house was across town in Wicker Park, and it took him twenty tense minutes to get there. The homes were nice—large and neatly landscaped. The cars parked on the street were nicer still, and Paul knew his van did not fit in. Abby's house was dark when he drove past, so Paul called her from a phone booth a few blocks away.

"Hello?" Abby's voice was raspy and her consciousness blurred.

"It's Paul, I need to ask a small favor."

Abby wanted to ask if he had any idea what time it was. She wanted to remind him that he already promised he would never ask another favor of her. She wanted to hang up the phone and go back to sleep. But she didn't. "Alright," she heard herself say.

A light was on in Abby's second-floor window when Paul drove up the second time. She came to the front door in a pale green bathrobe and thick striped socks. Paul studied her for a moment under the porch light. With her hair tucked back under a stretchy band and without any makeup, Abby had a different look. It wasn't a bad look, he thought. In fact, she looked even softer and maybe a little younger. But he liked what he was seeing.

"Paul!" she croaked. "What? What's the favor?"

He told her that he needed to store a few things in her garage for a couple of days.

Abby's head and eyes rolled back in tandem. Before she could even form another question, Paul interjected. "It's nothing bad," he said. "My mom lost her job and my uncle is probably going to kick us out. I just don't want to piss him off by keeping all this stuff at his place."

"All what stuff?"

"Just open the garage and I'll explain everything to you in the morning."

"It is morning!"

Paul crossed the lawn toward his van.

Abby stood on the porch for a second weighing whether or not she should help him. "You've probably managed to wake my parents by now. They'll want an explanation."

"Just tell them that there have been some car break-ins in my neighborhood and I was afraid my stuff might get stolen."

"Exactly what stuff are you talking about?" she called to him, but he had already reached the van and started the engine. Abby let out a deep sigh, and then went around to the back of the house to open the door for him.

SADHANA

It was a good-sized space that opened to an alley running behind the house. Even with her parents' El Dorado parked inside, Paul had enough room to stack *his* newly acquired equipment. He quickly unloaded the press and the hodgepodge of canisters onto the floor of the garage and covered it all with a tarp. Abby watched from the steps, shivering in her nightclothes and wondering what he was up to and how she would account to her parents for the late night intrusion.

When Paul was finished he closed the garage door, got back into his van and drove off. Abby went back upstairs to her room and had just turned out the lights when she heard a car approaching. Expecting to see Paul's van returning for yet another one of his favors, Abby pulled back the curtain and peeked out the window. A Chicago police car sped past, in the same direction Paul had just gone. A second later another patrol car came, driving much slower and shinning a spotlight into bushes, cars and between houses on both sides of the street.

Abby had a pretty good idea that whatever the cops were searching for was sitting under a tarp in her garage. She closed her eyes and buried her face in her hands. Whatever Paul had just gotten himself into, he had now managed to involve Abby and her family.

Five

In light of the fact that there was no news of a plane crash or other disaster, we all assumed Paul had made it to India in one piece. And though one might have expected that the boy would call his father to let him know he had arrived safely, not Paul. There was no word—no call, no email, nothing.

I can't say that any of us were too surprised by it. We all automatically assumed that, remaining true to his *spoiled kid* reputation, Paul was still in a stew over being sent to India in the first place. And nobody on the staff believed for a minute that he had truly gone there of his own accord.

As for the estate, it hadn't been this quiet since Paul had taken a sloppy jab at college. The unproductive and pointless stint at NYU had not only wasted five years of tuition, but it had been widely rumored that Mr. Griffiths pulled strings on more than one occasion, just to keep Paul enrolled.

Back in those days however, before he changed his name, most of the staff malevolently referred to Paul as *"Junior"*.

And after the dented Hummer showed up, shortly followed by a visit from police detectives, talk amongst the staff was that *Junior* had again managed to dig up some drama—another, *"dog's breakfast,"* as one of the gardeners put it. Yet one more pile of garbage that Mr. Griffiths had pulled strings to help the boy out from under.

My hope was that this time Paul would somehow find the resources within, to work *himself* free of the mess.

* * *

SADHANA

Paul-

Each journey to a new land is also a discovery of the landscape within the traveler. Beyond simply seeing an unfamiliar world, a man will see the world through unfamiliar eyes.

May life's journey help you to see your world more clearly and bring you the richness of life you deserve.

Safe travels.

> *Fondly,*
> *Rupert*

The note was handwritten on a simple card inside the envelope Rupert had given him in the car. Aside from the card, the envelope was empty. It was like opening a box of Cracker Jack; Paul found the witty little message as useful as a plastic decoder ring. The meaning of Rupert's words had completely escaped him.

"Life's journey," Paul muttered as he stuffed the note back into his pocket. "More like indentured servitude." If anyone needs to see life more clearly, it's Rupert—my father's lifelong, professional errand boy. The only difference is Rupert does it of his own free will; he deserves his lot in life. I've got no choice in the matter. If not for those donut-eating cops, my dad's useless attorney and that prick of a judge, I'd be out partying with my friends tonight. Instead, I'm inhaling the recycled curry breath of everybody else in this cattle car.

Paul stood again and groped for his duffel in the compartment above him. He had brought with him a travel book and a couple of magazines, which he now plucked out before zipping his bag closed. He sat back down and stared at a book that he did not recognize. Paul had no idea how it had gotten into his duffel bag.

Sadhana didn't look anything like a travel book. Paul fanned the dusty-smelling pages and saw it was a collection of short stories. It reminded Paul of a literature course he once failed at NYU. The book, apparently translated from Sanskrit the year Paul was born, seemed like a worthless relic that was unlikely to contain any current or useful information. Paul thumbed through a few pages before slapping it shut and tossing it on his tray.

Flipping over another publication, he was relieved to find the LONELY PLANET'S TRAVEL GUIDE he had purchased during his extended layover in Helsinki. He read through the first few pages of the *culture* section, learning that it is impolite to go to dinner at someone's home without bringing a gift, and to address the eldest male in the home when speaking. Not that he expected to be invited to a family dinner in India, anyway. The guide also warned against taking photos inside a temple, which didn't matter to Paul since he had neither a camera nor any interest in visiting a temple.

He stood to put the assortment of reading materials back in his suitcase, when the pilot announced that the aircraft was beginning its descent into Indira Gandhi International Airport.

A pocket of turbulent air caused the plane to bounce suddenly. A book from Paul's reading collection slipped from his grasp, toppling into the aisle. As he made an ineffectual swipe to catch it, Paul's hand caught the top of a man's headdress and knocked it cockeyed on the man's head. A grumble surged from the surrounding seats as the man readjusted his *Pagri*.

Paul had to get onto his knees to see the book, which had landed beneath a seat across the aisle. His nose was an inch from the thigh of the middle-aged Indian woman seated there, as he stretched to reach the book. Paul gazed up from under the cocoon-like dress the woman was wound into. "Sorry," he said.

Her single eyebrow drew into the crease of her forehead as she glared at him in confusion.

"Sir, you'll have to take your seat now," a flight attendant's voice ordered from behind Paul.

He quickly stood, holding the book outstretched as evidence to the other passengers—all but one of whom looked away. The Caucasian eyes staring back at him in disgust were not new to Paul. In fact, at the beginning of the flight he had seen the same blue eyes glaring from beneath the short blond hair and pink headband.

Paul turned back toward his seat, deciding to forego the overhead compartment and keep the book with him.

"Is this yours, sir?" The flight attendant held a folded sheet of paper in her hand. "I think it dropped from your book."

Having no idea what it was, or even if it belonged to him, Paul took the paper and squeezed back into this row.

"Seat and tray table in full upright position!" the flight attendant barked. "And seatbelt securely fastened!"

SADHANA

The sudden and chaotic rush toward the front of the plane, even before it came to a complete stop, barely gave Paul time to get out of his seat. No orderly queue, no consideration of row number or seat location, and no apparent concept of personal space. Paul was shoved and jostled as he stood to grab his bag, the entire time bathed in the steeping breath of a man hunched against his back.

"Do you mind?" Paul bristled.

The man's head bobbled slightly as he gave Paul an odd smile. The older woman across the aisle reached up for her bags, surrendering a gust of fetid body odor, and then pushed past both of them with an armload of what Paul estimated to be six pieces of carry-on luggage.

The jetway was a steamy vault—part spice pantry and part locker room. Paul was nudged and bumped, and then squeezed as if from an accordion, toward the top of the ramp. Worried that he would be pick-pocketed, Paul quickly took his wallet out of his pocket and slipped it into his large duffel bag.

The crowd of passengers separated into two lines as he approached Immigration and Customs; one said *INDIANS* and the other said *VISITORS*. Though Paul's line was much shorter, it seemed to move slower. Once at the window, he was told with some impatience that he was supposed to have received a form on the plane. Paul had to step out of line, fill in the answers to a series of health and travel questions on a form, and then edge back into the line.

It was after 8 p.m. when Paul was finally cleared. He emerged into the cavernous concourse looking frantically for a bathroom, but the only signs he found pointed to a prayer room. After a short hunt, he managed to locate a restroom, relieve himself, brush his teeth and wash up. Paul cursed at the empty paper towel dispenser and then dried his hands and face on his shirt.

A beggar with no legs sat on the grimy floor with a display of wilting candles, just outside the restroom. Paul tossed a 5-rupee coin into his cup. "Keep it," Paul said as the man extended a candle to him, "I don't need it."

The whites of the beggar's eyes were intensified against his black skin. He stared back at Paul, hand still outstretched with a candle—a silent refusal to accept something for nothing. His stolid expression said: *I am a businessman, not a beggar.*

Paul hastily grabbed the candle from him, stuffing it into his small tote bag. Only then did the legless man give Paul a knowing smile, then clasped his hands together in prayer and bowed his head.

Stepping out into the New Delhi night was nothing less than stupefying. A yellow nylon cord attached to wooden stanchions held back hundreds of men waving handwritten signs. Paul scanned the pandemonium, looking for his name and hoping that the CRF International group had sent a driver to pick him up. After checking several dozen of the placards, it occurred to Paul that his original flight had been cancelled and his arrival here had been delayed twelve hours. Paul assured himself that CRF would surely have gotten the word. After all, according to his father, others from the group were traveling on the same flight.

After another half-hour of elbowing his way through the hordes of arriving passengers, a thought came to Paul that made him feel stupid: *The packet of papers that CRF had sent might have listed a contact phone number.* He turned on his cell phone and began searching through his duffel bag for the paperwork.

Somewhere in the mass of hysteria surrounding him, Paul thought he heard someone speaking English. He instantly stood up, his eyes sweeping through the crowd. Over the heads of the surging chauffeurs and beyond the rickshaw drivers, Paul spotted a pink headband bobbing away toward the parking lot. He stood on his toes and saw that the blond girl from the plane was now in the company of two people, another young woman and a man. They were headed for a rickety white bus, idling just across from the pick-up lane in front of the terminal.

Paul thought that the threesome seemed to know their way around the airport, at least well enough to find a bus. Regardless of where it was headed, Paul figured he was better off joining up with someone he could at least communicate with.

Then just as the decision jelled in his mind, the bus grinded into gear and lurched away from the curb. A shudder of panic coursed through him as he saw the American girl and her two companions through the bus window.

Paul dropped his duffel bag and pushed his way toward the road. He tripped over a family that had apparently decided to spread a blanket in the middle of the sidewalk and eat their meal, then caught his balance and raced along the curb. As the bus rumbled past him, Paul saw the CRF International logo painted in black on the side panel. Paul's lungs tightened as he sprinted into the street, waving his arms and yelling for the driver to stop.

Between the din of the terminal and the clamoring car motors, nobody on the bus even noticed him. Several horns sounded as drivers swerved to avoid Paul, but he continued after the bus, dodging and weaving through traffic.

The bus slowed enough that Paul was able to close the distance, though the pall of smoky exhaust combined with the sweltering heat made it difficult to breathe. As the bus accelerated again, Paul made a last ditch dive to get the driver's attention by pounding on the back of the vehicle with his fist. A muffled *whump* resonated like a wheel rumbling over the shank of a pothole, yet it failed to attract anyone's attention.

Immediately, there was the fractured clatter of his cell phone somersaulting across the traffic lane. The battery went flying in one direction and the phone went another. A taxi whizzed past Paul, barely avoiding him, but further punishing his phone. The noise behind Paul sounded like eggshells in a garbage disposal, though he hadn't time to look back.

Managing to dive off the road to safety, Paul tore the thigh of his pants on a piece of rebar jutting out of the ground. By the time traffic had cleared enough to foray back into the street, the bus was gone from sight, the battery was nowhere to be found and what remained of his phone looked like a handful of garden beetles that had been trampled by school children.

When Paul got back to the Arrivals annex he couldn't find his duffel bag. He didn't recognize any landmarks along the curb or along the front of the terminal, and wasn't even sure he was in the same spot. Looking frantically back and forth over the sea of bodies, he was still unable to orient himself—nothing looked familiar, yet everybody looked the same.

Scouring the sidewalk, searching through the teeming mass of pajama-clad bodies, Paul finally spotted the picnickers he'd passed on their blanket. He retraced his steps to the area near the waiting drivers where he had set down his bag. It was gone.

Travelers and drivers moved past him in all directions, oblivious to his troubles. As Paul's angry blue eyes scanned for someone making off with his duffel bag, it seemed like the entirety of India's 1.2 billion residents were there in front of the Arrivals gate.

Paul lowered himself to the pavement and slumped against a metal signpost. All my paperwork, he thought. All my clothes.

He unclasped and opened the small tote bag he had slung across his chest. Just then, frozen and unable to take in another breath, Paul realized the depth of the nightmare he had fallen into. He had put his wallet into the duffel bag as he exited the plane, and now, it too was gone. The tote bag he had managed to keep with him contained only his passport and the useless book he didn't even intend to bring—a ridiculous Indian storybook about, who knows what?

Paul had no credit cards, no money and no phone—no means to get in touch with his CRF group or contact anyone back home.

Six

The rap on her door startled Abby awake. She had been dreaming about Loring; that he had taken the train home to surprise her. In the dream, she could hear him talking to her parents downstairs—the men's voices resonant and warm. She had dashed down the stairs wearing only her silky chemise, coming up behind Loring with outstretched hands. Abby had playfully reached around to cover his eyes, but as he turned to face her she saw that it was Paul. Her heart had quickened as she was gripped by a peculiar feeling. Though she couldn't identify it, the feeling both scared and excited her at the same time.

"Abigail!" her father's voice boomed from the hallway.

She shook off the dream and slipped on her robe. Her father's austere face glared at her when she opened the door, as if he had somehow seen into her dream.

"The police are here to speak with you," he said. "It has something to do with Loring's brother, Paul."

Abby followed her father down the stairs where she found two large uniformed officers, and Paul hunched contritely between them. He was not in handcuffs, but there was a definite sense that he was *not* free to go.

"Do you know this guy?" asked one of the policemen.

Abby nodded. "He's my boyfriend's brother."

The cop grimaced and the other rolled his eyes. Abby's father caught the exchange.

"What's this all about, officers?" he asked.

"Someone broke into a warehouse earlier this evening, out by the airport," he said. "This young man was seen driving out of the area, not too far from where it occurred."

Paul glanced at the officers and then at Abby and her parents. Mr. Townsend's scowl was only eclipsed by Abby's burning stare. Her mother's benign expression seemed the most sympathetic, so Paul turned to address her. He was about to speak when the other officer gripped his arm.

"We stopped the kid a few blocks from here." The officer sneered down at Paul. His eyes had the same condemning look as the cop who had passed him. Paul was certain it was the same guy.

"He probably dumped off the stolen property before we pulled him over," the cop snarled.

Abby's mother raised her hand in the air, as if in grammar school. "Are you sure it was Paul?"

"Couldn't miss the periwinkle blue Volkswagen," said the other officer.

"It's called *azure* blue," Paul mumbled under his breath.

Abby glanced at her father's face, without making it obvious. His expression hadn't changed at the mention of Paul "dumping" the stolen property. She realized it hadn't registered with him, which meant that her parents were still unaware of the things Paul had stacked in their garage, and that they were oblivious to the fact he had even come by the house an hour earlier. She wondered how they could have slept through that racket.

"I don't know anything about a robbery, Mr. Townsend." Paul turned toward Abby's father, speaking to him for the first time.

The officer tightened his grip on Paul's arm. "I saw you with my own eyes."

Paul grimaced. "Yeah okay, I admit I was driving near the airport last night, but I didn't break into any warehouse."

"What were you doing there then, all alone in the industrial area?" The officer smirked at what he thought was a dead end for Paul.

"I wasn't *all alone*," Paul said. The landing at the bottom of the stairs fell silent as the group waited to hear the rest of Paul's alibi. He let the tension build just long enough to lock his gaze on Abby.

She closed her eyes, knowing what would come next.

"She was with me," Paul said.

Five sets of eyes shifted to a mortified Abby. She took in an unsteady breath, knowing that Paul's fate rested on her response.

Quickly running through the list of reasons to refute him, Abby realized he had used her money, exploited her trust, jeopardized her family and now implicated her in who-knows-what.

"Abigail?" both of her parents said at the same time.

She slowly lifted her eyelids and rolled her gaze upwards to meet theirs. "Yes," she said. "I was with him." Abby strained to swallow the bitter taste of her own lie.

"He was alone in the van." The angry cop angled forward. "I saw it as clear as day as he passed me."

"She was lying down in the back," Paul shot back.

Abby found her hand clasped over her mouth.

"Why?" asked Mrs. Townsend. "What in the world were you doing out there?"

Abby shook her head, unable to come up with a tenable answer.

"What do you think we were doing?" Paul asked, emboldened now that Abby had buttressed his defense.

Mr. Townsend shook his head, not wanting to hear any more. The policemen looked at one another over the top of Paul's head. One rolled his eyes and the other eased his grip on Paul's arm.

"We did find a blanket in the back of his van," the other officer said.

His partner released his grip altogether, then looked at Paul with disgust. "With your brother's girlfriend?"

"My twin brother," Paul said, as if it brought some clarity to the affair. "We're identical."

The group stared at him, baffled by the absurdity of his comment and dumbfounded by his gall. Abby wanted to dive from between her parents and slap Paul. She clenched her jaw, aware now that in the eyes of everyone in the room she was some kind of slut. All except Paul, who knew the truth but held it like a prize, locked behind his sardonic grin.

The police took Paul back to his van, where another squad car was still parked. A different set of cops had tossed just about everything that had been in the van, out onto the sidewalk. Finding nothing that could connect Paul to the burglary, they took down all his identifying information for their report and then let him go.

Paul hurried to load his things back into the van, flinging seat cushions, blankets, papers and eight-track tapes in a heap onto the passenger seat. He then drove to the phone booth at the end of Abby's block and dialed her number. He knew he had to find a way to get the stolen equipment out of Abby's garage before her parents spotted it.

They would surely call the police back to the house, he thought. And as livid as Abby must be at him, it seemed unlikely that she would continue the charade to protect him.

"Hello, Mr. Townsend," Paul forced a confident tone. "Turns out it was all a big mistake. The officers realized they had the wrong man and apologized sincerely for their blunder --"

"I'd like you to stay away from Abigail," Townsend interrupted. "Of course, she's nineteen now and I can't dictate who she chooses to spend time with. For the life of me I don't know why she would see you in the first place; you're nothing like your brother."

"Yeah, I get that a lot." Paul silently pumped a closed fist up and down over his crotch as he rolled his eyes skyward. "Can you just put Abby on the phone?"

"I'll let her speak to you this one time, but you've caused enough problems for us and our daughter. What you do is your business, but I don't want you to call or come by our home in the future."

Paul heard muffled words through a covered receiver, then the exchange of the phone. Abby was silent on the other end, but Paul knew she was there.

"Abby, I'll explain everything to you later." He whispered into the phone as if all this was their little secret. "I just need you to unlock the garage door."

A brittle silence stretched across the phone line until Abby finally spoke. "You've gone too far this time, Paul. I'll unlock the garage door, but I want all your stuff out of there this morning." Abby sounded resolute, and Paul could tell she could not be kidded out of it.

"Let me apologize," he said. "I really didn't mean to involve you in anything."

"Well you did," she said. "Now my parents think I've been tramping around with *you*, under a blanket in the back of your van."

She said it with such revulsion that Paul felt a twinge of pain inside. He wondered if that would really be so bad, yet he said nothing in response.

"My parents are upstairs getting ready for church," she continued. "You have less than an hour to get all that crap out of our garage. Because if it's still there when my dad goes to get the car out, he'll see it and call the police. And I'm not covering for you anymore. I'll tell them that everything you said this morning was a total lie. Especially the part about--"

"I know, I know," he said. "Especially the part about you and me." The backbone was gone from Paul's tone. "I get it; angel – devil, Boy Scout – trouble-maker, good brother – bad brother . . . trust me, I've heard it all before."

Abby instantly felt remorse for treating him so harshly. She had blistered Paul entirely out of frustration. Not that he was blameless, but Abby realized she had overstated her aversion to the idea of being with him. She was annoyed that she had allowed herself to be manipulated, and the scene that had just taken place in front of the police officers and her parents embarrassed her.

But Abby realized she was also disappointed in herself. She had developed feelings about Paul that she didn't like and didn't fully understand. Paul Griffiths was an enigma—unlike anything in her conventional world. He was wild and spontaneous. And he had a bad side that she found curiously exciting. Abby loved her boyfriend, Loring, but his twin brother intrigued her.

"Just come get your stuff," she said. "And please make it quick."

It was noon on Sunday and Paul knew the shop would be empty. He parked in the rear alleyway and carried in the canisters and bottles he had swooped up from the warehouse. A small crawlspace above the office bathroom, which Paul had found once by accident, provided enough room and concealment for his stolen goods. He had occasionally used it to conceal marijuana or alcohol from his co-workers and from Mr. Carter. A sheet of plywood laid across the ceiling joists rendered it sturdy enough to support the heavy tins of liquid, but before stashing them there Paul wanted to figure out exactly what he had taken.

He hoped at least one of the labels would read, *book binding glue*, or some version thereof. But none of them did. One metal canister contained silk-screening ink, and another gallon-sized plastic jug was a common solvent. Paul lifted a glass bottle with a red warning sticker, and held it under the light. Though it was labeled *Epoxy Resin*, the warning sticker indicated it contained some type of methyl ether.

Until then Paul hadn't even realized that one of the containers was made of glass, and after reading the label he was grateful it hadn't broken during his wild exit out of the warehouse. The two remaining containers, both plastic, were basic printer's ink—the same type that Carter used in the shop. With the exception of the last two, which Paul left in the ink closet, the rest were stashed in the crawl space.

The heating and binding press he had stolen, though the smallest one he had been able to find in the warehouse, was still too large to hide in the shop. That, he was forced to leave covered with a blanket in the back of his van.

* * *

Loring Griffiths' first year at Michigan was an adjustment; other than boarding school, he had never been away from family. And even then, he still had his brother, Paul.

LJ rushed a number of fraternities at Ann Arbor, and ultimately pledged Phi Kappa Psi. By the time his junior year rolled around, LJ was a Dean's List student and a popular fraternity member in his house. He worked a part-time job as a clerk in a real estate law firm near campus, and had paid his own way through his first two years of Michigan's Ross School of Business.

Tommy McDowell had become almost a surrogate brother to LJ. The two had pledged together as freshmen and had been roommates since joining the house. Tommy's girlfriend, Lisa, had tried several times to fix LJ up with her friends, but Loring always resisted. "I'm already taken," he'd say. "I have a steady girl back in Chicago and we're going to get married as soon as I graduate."

LJ would make the 4-½ hour train trip to see Abby whenever he could—mostly on holidays or long weekends. He would usually take the 355 Wolverine after classes on Friday, getting him into Chicago around eleven at night. But as his courses grew more difficult and his fraternity obligations more demanding, LJ stayed on campus more often than not and his visits home to see Abby were grudgingly replaced with late night phone conversations. Even those became infrequent after a while.

"Are you still in love with me?" LJ asked Abby, as they wrapped up a call one evening.

"Of course," she said. "Why?"

"I don't know. Sometimes lately, I hear something in your voice that makes me not so sure." Loring paused as he listened to silence on the other end of the phone. Tommy's heavy footsteps coming down the hall forced a quick ending to the conversation, leaving LJ feeling empty and Abby somewhat relieved.

He couldn't shake the unsettled premonition he felt after hanging up with Abby. LJ sat on his bed staring at the phone, then to the large brown *Principles of Microeconomics* study guide lying dog-eared between his legs. He was about to pick it up when Tommy walked in. He had just returned from a night out with Lisa. "LJ," he said. "We need to talk."

His roommate was a welcome distraction to the funk that LJ found himself in after the call. He put down his book and propped the pillow behind him. "I'm all ears, brother."

"It's not working out with Lisa," Tommy said. "She's a great chick, but I can't deal with all her expectations and plans."

LJ frowned. Until now he had thought they were a perfect fit. Lisa was a vibrant woman who seemed to have it all together. She was a scholarship music student, the president of her sorority, and she had stunning looks to boot. "What happened?" he asked.

Tommy sat down at the bottom of LJ's bed, his head dropping to his chest. "Lisa has been talking about getting married after graduation. She has her life all figured out, like a graph or a timeline on the chalkboard: graduate early, get married, teach music to inner-city youth, have 2.1 kids, blah-blah-blah."

LJ raised his eyebrows. "She knows what she wants out of life and she's tenacious enough to go after it. You could do a lot worse than Lisa, Tommy."

"Yeah, but I'm not ready for all that. She's smothering me." Tommy turned to watch the snow collecting on the sill outside the window. "It might be a mistake, but I just can't get tied down at this stage of my life. I'm too young for a wife and family."

LJ thought of how much Tommy reminded him of his brother, Paul. "Yeah, and while you're off playing the field, she'll get snatched up by another guy." He paused for a second, picturing Lisa's seductive green eyes and wavy brown hair. "Lisa is a beautiful girl, you know?"

Tommy looked up at LJ with surprise. "Ya think so? Maybe you could help me break this thing off."

"No," LJ said. "Whatever you're talking about, the answer is no!"

"Just hear me out," Tommy said. "The three of us make a date to meet at D'Amato's for dinner." He swung his body around to face LJ. "But then I get hung up and don't make it to the restaurant."

LJ closed his eyes and caressed his forehead.

"Then you and Lisa go ahead and have a nice meal without me. Later on you get to rap'n, and so-forth and so-on, and before you know it, voilà: you two are get'n it on. And it's like, Tommy? Tommy who?"

"No way, Tommy. Lisa and me are not going to be 'get'n it on,' whether or not you break it off with her. No way."

Tom held up a hand. "You know what I mean. But seriously, a casual night out with someone else, *you*, will help get her adjusted to the idea. It'll ease the blow. Think of it as doing her a favor, and me!"

"I couldn't deceive someone like that," LJ said. "Especially not someone who I . . ."

Tommy stared at LJ with a sly smile and an eyebrow cocked upward. "Especially not someone who you care about?"

LJ didn't answer, but that in itself was all the answer Tommy needed. "I knew it! You got the big banooch for Lisa!"

"No I don't," LJ cried out, a little too loud to appear indifferent. "I mean, sure I like her as a friend. But me and--"

"I know," said Tommy. "You and Abby are going to get married, and you won't cheat on her. But I'm not asking you to cheat on Abby. Just go along with this for a few days until I can figure a way to break it off with Lisa. C'mon . . . as a brother Kappa?"

It took Tommy another day of persuading, but LJ reluctantly agreed to participate in his fraternity brother's plan. The three of them had gone out together many times, so a Saturday night trio at Tommy's favorite restaurant wasn't out of the ordinary.

LJ tucked his hands into his coat pocket as he crossed South Main Street. He was thinking about Abby, and what she would think of him if she knew what he was doing. LJ had covered the ten blocks to D'Amato's before he knew it. Lisa was sitting by the window in a rust colored turtleneck sweater and bellbottom jeans. She rubbed her hands together over the table candle, and smiled up at LJ as he carefully hung his puffy down jacket over his chair.

"Where's Tommy?" she said, looking past him. "I thought you two were coming together."

LJ immediately felt a pang of guilt. "Uh, no, I had to walk over alone." LJ eased into his seat. "Tommy got hung up at the house, I think. Hopefully he'll be able to meet us. Later."

Lisa regarded him warily, and LJ wondered if she could tell he was lying.

"Should we wait?" She glanced out the frosty window.

LJ shrugged. He knew his answer didn't sound quite right, but couldn't think of anything to say that would. Instead, he waved over the server and ordered a pitcher of draft beer. "We can get started and he'll catch up."

After a few hearty swigs, LJ relaxed a bit and the conversation between the two flowed comfortably. However, the content was a different story; Lisa continually brought up Tommy and kept asking about LJ's girl back in Chicago. Both topics made him feel guilty and regretful about what he was doing with Lisa. LJ finally changed the subject to Michigan's football team, which had just beaten Iowa 31-0 and were on their way to what they hoped would be an undefeated season.

They ordered another round, which further helped to ease LJ's feelings of remorse. He watched Lisa as she talked and laughed, thinking all the while that Tommy was making a huge mistake. She flung her hair as she turned her head and LJ caught her sweet perfumed scent. She was fun and lively. He couldn't help wondering what might happen between them if she didn't have Tommy and if he didn't have Abby. LJ tried to shake the thought from his mind as they laughed their way through dinner.

As LJ and Lisa stepped out of the restaurant, the wind pushed and pulled at them, catching their coats like boat sails and pitching their bodies into one another. With D'Amato's disappearing into the gray squall behind them, the couple huddled close as they headed back toward campus. Small powdery drifts had begun to form at the curbs, and as they stepped over one of them a sudden gust brought a shower of snow down from a limb above. Lisa laughed until tears filled her eyes, and he laughed too—hardy and carefree. It felt really good to be with her, LJ thought.

At one point, close to her sorority house, Lisa crossed behind LJ and snuggled playfully against his back. She tucked her hands inside his coat pockets, just as Abby had done many times in Chicago. The weightless warmth of the alcohol had loosened LJ, and he knew it had done the same to Lisa. He told himself that her amorous overtures meant nothing, but when they arrived at the front of her house she drew herself close, face-to-face.

"You and Tommy are best friends, right?" Lisa's soft lips slowly forming each word.

"He's like a brother," LJ said.

Lisa feigned an exasperated pout as she let go a steamy sigh. She hung a slack arm over his shoulder and leaned a bit closer, so that their noses where now touching. "Does that mean that you tell each other *everything*?"

LJ felt her warm breath against his neck. He swallowed hard, wondering what she was leading up to. A picture floated through his mind of the two of them unclothed in her room. It was a dizzying image that stirred senses throughout him. He took a half-step back, the whole time gazing into her inviting eyes and wondering if he would actually be able to resist her. "I think I know where you're going with this," he said.

"You do?" Lisa flashed a mischievous smile. "And here I thought I was being so subtle."

LJ smiled uncomfortably. "I'd be lying if I said I hadn't thought about going to bed with you too, I have. And if things were different between me and--"

"What?" Lisa stepped backwards abruptly. "What the hell are you talking about? I was about to ask you if Tommy has ever told you that he wants to marry me!"

"I'm sorry." LJ stammered the words. "Seriously, Lisa. I'm so, so sorry. I thought . . . I don't know what I was thinking."

"I know exactly what you were thinking." Lisa rolled her eyes and pushed past him onto the covered porch. "LJ, you're, you're . . . I don't even know what to say. We *were* all friends, for Christ's sake!"

LJ paused, trying to find words that could fix it. Tommy wanted to break it off with Lisa, but LJ didn't want Tommy to know how badly he had muffed the job. "Can we just not say anything about this?"

"Don't worry," Lisa stopped in the doorway. "I won't tell your supposed '*best friend*' what you just said to me. He'd be too hurt. Just have him give me a call when you see him."

LJ walked the rest of the way home, humiliated by the exchange and angry with Tommy for having him go out with Lisa in the first place. And then he imagined Abby, at home waiting for his call, and all the while he was out with Lisa. His bedroom was empty when he got back to the house, and he wanted so much to call Abby, whether out of guilt, loneliness or drunkenness, LJ wasn't sure. He just wanted to hear her voice.

The line rang for the fifteenth time before he finally flung the phone back into its cradle. LJ slipped off his shoes, socks and pants and flopped back onto his bed—woozy from all the beer. But he was alert enough to realize it was after 1 a.m., which meant that Abby was still out. LJ wondered where she could be at that hour, and he blamed Tommy for that, too.

SADHANA

He cursed at the empty bed next to him. If Tommy hadn't strong-armed him into going out with Lisa, LJ would have called Abby much earlier and probably would have connected with her. He would never have made such a jerk of himself with Lisa, and wouldn't have . . . LJ stopped himself in mid-thought, reached over to the nightstand and shut off the lamp—too ashamed to see the light of truth.

Somewhere deep beneath his polished exterior, temptation and weakness and desire were part of his makeup. It was one more thing he was angry with Tommy for.

LJ awoke later than usual, to the sound of his frat brothers playing Frisbee in the hallway outside his room. He looked through the haze of his booming headache to see Tommy's bed, empty and still made up. He fumbled into his clothes and went downstairs, directly to the coffee pot. Frank, the chapter president, was on the wall phone in the kitchen when LJ walked in. Something in his somber tone caught LJ's attention. The color drained from Frank's face as he responded in monosyllables. Two other housemates made their way into the kitchen to listen as well.

Frank hung the receiver in the cradle and stood facing the wall for several seconds. Finally he turned around and LJ saw the shocked expression and teary eyes. "It's Tommy," Frank said. "He was in an accident last night."

"Where is he?" LJ asked, his heart launching into a hammering cadence. "Is he alright?"

Frank shook his head. "Tommy's dead."

Şèvèɳ

Mr. Griffiths spent most of the day upstairs in his office. He had been invited to an artist's reception at the Guggenheim Museum in the City, but decided at the last minute not to go. I suppose he wanted instead, to stay close to the phone in the unlikely event that Paul called.

In this way, I have always felt sorry for my boss—he seemed to suffer the ugliness of the painting that he himself had created. For Mr. Griffiths, Paul's selfishness must at times have been like looking at his own reflection in the mirror. Not that he wasn't a good father to Paul, he was; he provided Paul with many things. But "things" were easy for my boss to give his son. It was more difficult to give himself. In the early years especially, Mr. Griffiths spent his time focused elsewhere. He worked hard and long to rebuild his fortune, but now he was paying a price for those days—a price that could never be measured in dollars.

* * *

Paul fished around his pockets, finding $63.29. He had withdrawn several hundred dollars from an ATM during his layover in Helsinki, but all of it was in his *missing* wallet, which was in his *missing* duffel bag. The money in his pocket was all that remained.

He ran back into the terminal and found a Bank of India currency exchange kiosk. They would not accept the coins, but for his bills Paul received 3,580 Indian rupees. It seemed like a lot more that it should have been, but Paul wasn't going to argue with their accounting error.

He thought about trying to find the American Embassy, maybe sending word back home. His dad could wire him the money, arrange transportation with CRF and take care of getting Paul some new credit cards. The more he thought about it, the more Paul saw himself as a complete failure. He exited the building, hoping to somehow blink away the scene outside, but the bad dream was still there.

"You need ride, Boss?" a slightly built man asked.

Paul waved him off as one would a mosquito. Paul continued walking, but the man tugged on Paul's sleeve. "Boss, I give you good deal ride in very clean and gorgeous tuk-tuk. India Gate, Red Fort? Many lovely and beautiful place to see in New Delhi. Where you want to go first?"

It was a good question. The floundering American had no idea where he wanted to go. Paul slowed to survey the pandemonium outside and a half-dozen men ran up to him. As if on cue, they all began asking, using various levels of hacked English, to come with them for a ride. Overwhelmed and under siege, Paul motioned toward the first driver, who was still trailing and tugging on his arm. "Already have a ride."

"Good, Boss. Which you want to see first?"

"Nothing," Paul said, as the man guided him through the crowd. "Just a place to sleep. Do you have a Ritz-Carlton, Fairmont, Hilton, something like that around here?

The driver's eyes widened and his step quickened. Paul assumed the guy saw big bucks coming his way from the wealthy American.

If he only knew.

The driver marched across the parking lot, shooing away all the other drivers, hawkers and beggars that approached. A dark woman with a face like shoe leather walked up to Paul, her gnarled hands cupped together and her tattered saree hanging on her cadaverous frame. "Baksheesh, baby, hospital? Baksheesh, baby, hospital?"

Paul tried to ignore her, but she grabbed the rolled-up sleeve of his dress shirt. "Baksheesh? Baksheesh?"

Surprisingly, the driver didn't shoo the woman away. He only looked at her with sadness as he continued walking. "Much great hardships here in India," he said to Paul. "This old woman, she is behind some rocks and a very hard place."

Pulling away from the woman again, Paul hurried to catch up to the driver. He stopped abruptly in front of a tiny, yellow and green 3-wheel scooter.

"What the hell is this?" Paul asked, sticking his head into the covered back seat. "You steal this from the golf course?"

"Steel, yes. Very strong tuk-tuk." The driver gripped the window frame to show Paul. "You wanting golfing course? I take you."

"No, no, never mind. Just the hotel." Paul got in and was immediately tossed sideways as the motorized rickshaw jerked onto the roadway. The driver never looked to see if anyone was coming, and Paul noticed that both of the vehicle's side mirrors had been pulled inward and were facing the floor.

As insane as the chaos at the airport was, the roads outside it were worse. There were few signal lights—mostly roundabouts—and nobody seemed to slow down for anyone or anything.

Paul gripped the bottom of his seat as the driver split the lane between a double-decker bus and an oxcart loaded with scrap metal. A man and woman with no shoes emerged from the bushes and dashed across the road, while drivers whizzed by within inches without ever slowing. And all the while, the chorus of blaring horns never ceased. The tuk-tuk came abreast of a motorcycle with a family of four on it, including a toddler sandwiched between the parents, and a younger infant lying precariously on the gas tank.

"Look there, Boss." The driver pointed toward a lighted archway. "Ajmeri Gate. Is a very gorgeous and lovely place. A lots of tourist take beautiful picture of this place. Lots of Japan people, too."

"Good for them," Paul groused. "And I already told you I'm not sightseeing. Just take me to the hotel, buddy."

"You no want to see sightseeing in Delhi?" The guy kept turning around, waiting for an answer. So much so that Paul thought he was going to run the cart off the road.

"Look, friend. I got my bag stolen at the airport." Paul's voice became louder, as if blaming the driver for the actions of one of his countrymen. "My suitcase—*stolen!* And all my money—*stolen!*"

The driver suddenly looked sad. He continued driving for another few minutes before pulling under a covered circular driveway. "JW Marriott Hotel, Boss."

"You don't even have a meter in this rig," said Paul. "So how much are you going to tell me I owe you?"

The driver scratched his head. "You go first inside."

"I can pay now," said Paul. "Just tell me how much for Mr. Toad's Wild Thrill Ride."

The driver's head bobbled side to side. "One hundred rupee?"

Paul squinted as he did the math. "What's that, like, not even two bucks?" He peeled off two, hundred rupee notes and stuffed them into the driver's hand.

SADHANA

Inside the lobby, Paul found the décor much more familiar and accommodating. White stone pillars reached three stories high, with huge sculptured mobiles reflecting light from overhead. And long, white leather couches, spotlessly clean.

"May I help you, sir?" A young woman asked from behind the registration counter.

"I'd like a room for the night," he said. "And I'll want some food sent up as soon as you can get me checked in, and oh yeah, I'll need to have some money wired to me from the U.S., can we do that?"

"Certainly, sir." The woman smiled warmly. "We'll just need a credit card for a one night deposit and incidentals."

Paul arched his neck, uncomfortable with a situation he'd never found himself in before. Negotiating, when it came to something he wanted, was as unfamiliar to Paul as everything else in this country. "You see, Honey, my duffel bag was stolen at the airport . . ."

Her face transitioned from curious to guarded skepticism.

"And my wallet was inside it, and it had all my money and credit cards . . ." Paul paused to assess his progress, and then seeing her face had become set like a librarian, devoid of expression, he pulled the wad of Indian notes from his pocket. "Here, I have a few thousand rupees on me. Can't you just take them as a down payment, and I'll have plenty more wired tonight? I'm definitely good for it."

The woman was Indian, but with a decidedly European style and an eloquent British accent. She had the bearing of someone used to being around wealthy people. Paul was about to ask her to look up his name on the Internet, or that of his father, when he saw the woman eyeing his torn pants over the tops of her trendy eyeglasses. A moment later she pushed his rupees back across the counter.

"I'm very sorry, sir." She had obviously made her decision. "Our most affordable room goes for 10,750 rupee per night. Even the Courtyard Marriott across town has a rack rate of 7,000. You have less than 4,000 there. Without a credit card, you're going to have to settle for a budget class motel or perhaps a guesthouse."

Paul stood there, as insignificant as a dog turd. He thrust his hands into empty pockets. Then he wandered out of the lobby, dreading going back onto the Delhi streets. He looked at his wristwatch. It was nearly 11 p.m., and still as sweltering hot as when he'd arrived. He checked his watch again, suddenly realizing its value. The Patek Philippe, stainless steel Aquanaut had been a gift from his father. It had to be worth several thousand American dollars, Paul thought.

He turned back toward the reservation desk and then stopped. Asking the woman if she would hold his watch until he could get his father to send money suddenly felt humiliating. Paul's head hung heavy as he stood there. Never before had he seen himself through this lens. He sensed a fear of looking into himself any deeper than he had, but the core had already been exposed. Paul saw that his own identity had always been enmeshed with his father's money. And without it, Paul realized he was nothing.

Paul stood there looking at his watch, and then across the lobby at the woman behind the registration desk. *I can't do this.*

Stepping back outside to hail a cab, Paul noticed his driver leaning against the yellow and green tuk-tuk at the far end of the portico.

"I wait for you, Boss." The man stubbed out his cigarette. "You not liking this place, I take you to better hotel."

Paul suspected the driver knew better. He had realized Paul didn't have the money to stay there. But instead of saying anything that would embarrass Paul, the guy had allowed him to save face. Paul climbed into the back seat, then reached up to pat the driver's shoulder. "Thank you, buddy."

They traveled back across the city, past the airport, into an area with fewer streetlights but even more traffic. The tuk-tuk shook violently as the driver turned off the paved street into Chandni Chowk—also known as Old Delhi. The heavily rutted dirt roads, barely wide enough for two bicycles to pass one another, seemed to get narrower with each turn. Open air bazaars selling anything colorful and flavorful, stretched from one block to the next under a tangled mesh of electric wires. The area gave Paul the creeps and he hoped this was only a shortcut that the driver had decided to take.

The vehicle veered suddenly, barely avoiding a younger man who was carrying a basket containing a live chicken. The tuk-tuk's horn sounded more like a doorbell buzzer, but it seemed to capture the pedestrian's attention. The two exchanged words, the nature of which Paul could only guess by way of their body language, and the fact that one had nearly run over the other. More words were exchanged, and when the man set down his basket and leaned into the tuk-tuk, Paul was certain a punch was about to be thrown. He had seen it on the streets of Manhattan a dozen times.

Amazingly, no assault took place. The driver slid over as far as he could, allowing the man with the chicken enough room to squeeze in next to him. The men were seated so close that the guest had to rest one arm around the shoulder of the driver, while he clung tightly to the basket with the other. After two bone-jarring blocks, the other passenger pointed down a side road, then jumped off with his chicken-in-a-basket.

"Do you know that guy?" Paul asked.

The driver shook his head, seemingly confused by the question.

"I thought you two were going to fight," Paul said. "What did you say to him?"

"I ask, does he know Punjab Palace."

"That's it?"

The driver looked even more confused. "He say, he help me find Punjab Palace, and I give him ride in tuk-tuk."

Odd, Paul thought. A guy with a chicken nearly gets run down, then takes a ride from the guy who almost killed him, just so he can help him out with directions. Paul shrugged. *I don't get these people at all.*

"Anyway," Paul said, "I told you before I don't want to see any palace. Just take me to the hotel.

The engine sputtered to a silent stop in the middle of the block on a dark street, seemingly in the heart of the old city. Paul glanced around, half expecting to be robbed by the driver's cohorts. A stray dog nosed through an empty lot piled with garbage, and across the road several rickshaws sat motionless, attached to bicycles—their drivers sleeping awkwardly on the small passenger seats.

"Where are we?" Paul asked.

"This is good hotel," he said. "Not so much lovely and gorgeous like JW Marriott, but is clean and good price for hardworking boss."

Hardworking boss? Who does this guy think I am?

Paul tentatively followed the driver into an alley where it seemed inconceivable a hotel could be. Noise and light faded the farther they walked from the mouth of the alley.

Paul continued on behind the man, his heart pounding with each step. Several narrow footpaths branched off in one direction or the other, snaking between buildings, and Paul caught glimpses of people sleeping on flat wooden carts. A rat scurried across the dirt between Paul's feet and disappeared over the lip of a trough that ran along the side of the alley. The trough, which was partially covered at some of the doorways, was mostly exposed and carried a putrid sludge out toward the larger road where they had parked. Paul's head already ached from clenching his teeth so hard on the ride from the airport, but the nauseating odor made it worse.

"Are you sure this is--?"

"Don't to worry, Boss." The man strode ahead. "It's good place. Not so much rupees to stay here, Boss. You can eat your cake and have some, also."

Paul's eyes squinted ahead through the darkness, to a weeping, red neon sign.

"Hotel Punjab Palace," the driver said, with a royal arm sweep.

At the dead end of the alley stood the hotel. Other than a lighted name above an etched glass door, the rickety stone building was indistinguishable from those surrounding it. A shiny man, whom Paul presumed was the doorman, jumped up from a lying position in the dirt, and held the door open for Paul. The man's hair was an unnatural pumpkin orange, and he was decked out in a powder blue military-type shirt with epaulets and a gold woven shoulder cord slung across his chest.

Inside the building was a tiny lobby. Two men stood up abruptly, one who had been asleep on a small sofa and another who had been slumped in a chair behind the counter. The one behind the counter slid a large registration book toward Paul and asked him, in broken but understandable English, to fill in his information and sign it.

As Paul turned to pay his driver, two more young men appeared from out of nowhere. The driver happily accepted another hundred-rupee note before departing. From the eager expressions on the men's faces, Paul's wad of Indian cash had guaranteed his room, irrespective of a credit card.

"These men will help you to your room," said the guy who registered him. The other three men, two of whom were just boys really, eagerly stepped forward; one pressing the elevator button for Paul, another holding the room key like an Olympic torch, and the third frantically looking for something to help with. He finally said something to the man behind the counter, who gave him a bottle of water, which he carried up to the room.

After showing Paul how to work the lights, TV, hot water, fan, and air conditioner, the three *helpers* loitered awkwardly at the door. Paul handed one of them another hundred-rupee note and motioned for them to split it between them.

Then Paul looked around and saw what he was paying for. It was a good size room, but disgustingly drab. He remembered once when he was 10 years old, sneaking into one of the stable hands' quarters behind the horse barn—and this room was worse. It even smelled worse. Sweaty and dark, the wooden clothes cabinet and heavy brown drapes reminded Paul of a funeral parlor, except with the heat on high. He pushed open the painted glass window only to find a musty black air vent about the dimensions of an elevator shaft. He gazed down into the black abyss and quickly shut and locked the window.

The bathroom was no more than a sink, a yellowed toilet, and a water hose with a plastic bucket. Paul surmised that it was intended to be some sort of shower. He used the bottled water and his finger to brush his teeth, and then rinsed himself off with the hose. The water never warmed, but it didn't matter. He just wanted to get it over with.

As the grime of his tuk-tuk ride washed down the floor drain, Paul patted himself dry with a towel. For the first time in the 31 hours since he left New York, Paul envisioned the home and surroundings to which he had become accustomed on Long Island. He had never longed for them as much as he did at that moment.

Paul laid on top of his bed, trying to figure out what to do. He hadn't been in this country more than a few hours and he hated everything about it. Missing his connection with the CRF bus had ruined everything. No, Paul thought, actually having his duffel bag, wallet and money stolen was worse.

Anger broiled inside him. How he wanted to get his hands on the son-of-a-bitch who took his things. Paul knew that some Indian thief had effectively destroyed any chance he had of getting through this on his own.

Without money, Paul felt trapped; he couldn't imagine staying in this backwards hellhole another day. Yet, to return home was out of the question. Since Paul hadn't fulfilled the judge's mandate that he complete the volunteer work, meant facing a certain prison sentence for hit and run.

And then there was Dad. As tempting as the money was, Paul knew he couldn't face asking his father to fix his screw-up. Again.

Thinking about the dismal alternatives drained him even more. Finally, exhausted from the trip and cooled by the Cessna-sounding fan blades over his head, Paul slept.

Eight

Abby's hard line toward Paul took time to soften after the early morning visit by Chicago's Finest. Eventually she ungraciously agreed to assist Paul with the church songbooks print job. "I don't know why I'm even talking to you," she said. "Much less helping you, after what you did."

"I'd do the same for you." Paul flashed an altar boy grin as he reached across to push the passenger door open for her. "And why are you making me park down the street?"

"Because my dad doesn't want you around."

Paul already knew the answer, but used the opportunity to look wounded by it. Abby got in and they drove back to the shop where he had already laid out the loose pages in tiny stacks on the floor.

Paul had found a generic rubber glue sold by the pint at a marine supply house on the Eastside. After purchasing two bottles of it, he used his bedroom as a laboratory to combine the glue with some of the epoxy he had stolen from the warehouse. Having no idea what it was he was mixing, he made several test batches. Over time Paul found a consistency that mimicked what he supposed was suitable for his binding needs. He tried the new compound on a test booklet and found that it held firmly. Paul's only hesitation was that it seemed to lose its strength when he heated it in the press. The adhesive wasn't quite perfect, but it was better than his first attempt with the Art Institute programs.

"We've got to do these by hand," he said to Abby as he flipped on the shop lights. "I've still got a little more experimenting to do."

"Experimenting tonight?" She stood facing the stacks of paper.

Paul laughed. "No, before I can use that hot press. Tonight we have to brush this stuff on by hand like we did the last time." He held the can up to show her.

SADHANA

Abby gazed into the ochre colored syrup. "I hope this glue won't spatter and harden all over the shop again."

Paul shrugged. "Shouldn't." He pointed toward one end of the row of stacks. "You start at that end while I finish printing the last batch."

He moved toward the printer then stopped suddenly. "Damn it!" He had forgotten the brushes at home. "We can't paste this adhesive on the pages without them."

Abby suggested they drive back to the house and get them, but Paul shook his head at the idea. "No time. I need to stay and print the last run." He dug in his pocket for the van keys. "Can you drive a stick?"

"Yes, I can drive a stick shift." Abby grimaced as she checked her watch. "But it's almost midnight and your house is twenty minutes away."

"Better hurry then." Paul tossed the keys to her. "They're in a bag under my bed. The other key will get you in the back door. My room is through the kitchen and downstairs."

* * *

Services for Tommy were held at the John J. Quinn Funeral Home in Erie, Pennsylvania. His fraternity brothers caravanned in three carloads. LJ was careful to avoid Lisa, who sat near the front with a group of her close friends. He wanted to say something comforting, but he couldn't bring himself to approach her. LJ knew he had ruined whatever friendship the two might have had, and that Lisa probably hated him for what must be the most awkward misunderstanding in recorded history—and on the night of her boyfriend's death, no less.

LJ's own feelings were more muddled. He had lost a best friend and a companion that he loved like family, and LJ couldn't begin to imagine what campus life would be like without him. Feeling as if he was somehow responsible for Tommy's death, LJ kept replaying the night Tommy sat at the foot of his bed asking for help. Perhaps the outcome would have been different if he had refused. LJ had gone against what he knew was right, and because of it karma had taken his best friend. He saw Lisa as simply another innocent casualty of his poor decision.

After Tommy's death LJ slept on one of the couches downstairs, unable to bear the agonizing memories alone in their room. He had spoken only briefly to Abby, telling her only about what happened to Tommy and of the services in Erie.

Thanksgiving break was the following week, but LJ had missed some important classes during the funeral and he wasn't sure he could make it home.

One-by-one his fraternity brothers headed out to spend the break with their families. As they did, LJ became convinced he could not bear the misery of Kappa House alone. At the last minute he hastily packed some clothes and books into a duffel bag, and as he left LJ wondered if he could ever bring himself to return to the house.

The train pulled away from the Battle Creek station and over the Kalamazoo River. He had been lost in thought since Ann Arbor, peering out the window into the murky lagoon of his future, his life, and of his own character. He looked at his watch and decided it was good that he hadn't called to ask Abby for a ride. The train was running twenty-minutes late already, and she'd probably be asleep by the time he would finally arrive in Chicago. Resigning himself to taking a cab home, LJ settled for seeing Abby first thing in the morning. He knew that the comfort of her arms and the reassurance of her love would help him figure things out and make his life whole again.

The 355 Wolverine pulled into Union Station five minutes after midnight.

* * *

Abby tiptoed in the back door and through the mudroom. The lights were all off, and the tapping of the heating furnace was the only sound in the house. Paul's aunt and uncle slept upstairs and Abby knew that Paul's mother had a small room off of the kitchen. Her door was closed, so Abby continued past it and down the stairs to the converted laundry room. She shuddered as a chill from the dank concrete walls permeated her cotton blouse.

Abby had been there only once before, but it was three years ago— the April before LJ went off to college. His mother had thrown a small Easter brunch and LJ had invited Abby to meet his family. While everyone sat chatting in the living room, she and LJ had slipped downstairs for a talk. It was there that he told Abby he loved her and would be faithful to her while he was away. Abby had promised him the same.

She felt her way in the dark, afraid to turn on the light for fear it would shine up the stairway. After a few seconds, her eyes became accustomed and she was able to make out the room's interior. Two single beds sat adjacent to each other, against opposite walls. The room was very small and only a narrow space separated the beds. Abby squatted and felt beneath one of them. After coming up empty, she moved to the opposite bed and climbed on top of it. To get a better angle, she hung her arm over the side—sweeping her hand back and forth along the dusty tiled floor beneath it.

The light in the stairway suddenly came on and Abby froze. She lay there splayed across the bed, too panicked to move. As if she were the paralyzed victim in a Hitchcock film, Abby listened as footsteps plodded slowly down the stairs. Unable to speak, she watched the growing shadow billowing against the wall. Abby was trapped. She covered her eyes as a hand reached around the threshold and flicked on the light switch.

"Abby?" a familiar voice said.

She peeked through her fingers to see LJ standing in the doorway with his duffel bag dangling from his shoulder. "Loring?"

Abby jumped off the bed, her arms open wide. "Loring! Oh Loring, I had no idea you were coming home."

"So I see." He took a step back as she went to hug him. "You want to tell me what you're doing here . . . on my brother's bed?"

"What?" Abby looked back at the bed and then at LJ. "You can't be serious, Loring."

"Serious? Yeah, I'm serious." LJ tossed his backpack on the other bed. "So where is he?"

Abby's eyes narrowed as her hands found her hips. "Your *brother* is working late at the print shop and he asked me to pick something up for him."

"Baloney! I saw his van parked out front."

Abby picked up a bag from the floor near where LJ was standing. "These are the brushes he needs," she said, showing them to LJ. "See? And it was *me* who drove the van here, not Paul."

"Oh, so now you're driving my brother's van around town? Abby, what's going on here?"

She looked at him through watery eyes. "I can't believe you really think--"

"Honestly, Abby, I don't know what to think." LJ's fingers coursed back through his wavy hair. "I come home unexpectedly in the middle of the night, and find you lying on my brother's bed. Now you're telling me that you two were together at the print shop, and I find out you're driving *his* van. How long has *all this* been going on?"

"All what?" Abby stepped closer and rested her hands softly on his chest. "I promise you, there's nothing going on between me and Paul. I can prove it. C'mon, let's bring his brushes to him at the shop. You'll see, he's just printing some songbooks for the church. He asked me to help him out, and that's it. It's a one-time thing."

They walked up the stairs and out to the van. Abby started it up and LJ took the passenger's seat. The only sound on North Kedzie Avenue was the rasp of the VW's engine. LJ gazed out the window as they drove along, wanting desperately to believe her but not knowing where to start or what to say. This was definitely not the homecoming he had hoped for.

A sudden *whoop* of a police siren shook the van and they were suddenly bathed in flashing red and blue lights. A blinding spotlight reflected into Abby's eyes as she tried to glance at the speedometer. Easing the VW over to the curb, she let out a sigh that matched one emitted by LJ. Before the cop even got out of his car, LJ had opened the glove box and was rifling through the jumbled mess of papers, fast food wrappers and 8-track tapes.

"License and registration, please." The voice at Abby's window was low and stern.

Paul found the van's registration and passed it to Abby. She slipped her driver's license from her purse and handed both documents to the officer.

"Did I do something wrong?" she asked.

The officer grunted about the tag stickers, and then moved to the rear of the van. LJ waited until the cop was well out of earshot before turning to Abby. "I hope that imbecile brother of mine doesn't have some weed in the car."

Abby's heart began pounding as she suddenly remembered the heating press under the blanket in the back of the van. Her face burned white hot and she felt her pulse in her neck. Abby didn't know which was more terrifying, having to tell Loring the truth about what she knew, or being arrested for possessing stolen property.

"Step out of the vehicle, please." The commanding voice was back at the window.

Abby and LJ got out and stood at the curb while the officer spoke into a handheld radio. Abby wasn't certain, but she thought the officer was one of the two who had dragged Paul to her house in the middle of the night. Abby closed her eyes in prayer as the cop walked in an arc around the van, peering through the windows with his flashlight. She held her breath as the beam stopped directly on the blanket in the back.

"Your vehicle?" the officer said to LJ.

"Uh, no." He took out his driver's license to show the cop. "It belongs to my brother, Paul."

The officer turned toward Abby. "Did you know *what* you were driving around?"

Beads of perspiration formed along her hairline. Abby realized the stolen press was probably traceable through a serial number. She decided it would be in her best interest to admit everything to the officer, from the beginning. Though learning of her involvement in the cover-up would further infuriate Loring, and probably break his heart, she couldn't protect Paul any longer.

The officer flashed his light in Abby's eyes. "Did you know you were driving a vehicle with expired registration tags?"

"No, sir." Abby thought back to the money Paul had borrowed under the pretext of registering his van. "I'm pretty sure he paid the registration fee," she said. "He borrowed the money from me over a month ago. Maybe he just forgot to put the new tags on."

LJ stared at her in disbelief. His face turned pale and his slack jaw hung open. He had no idea that his fiancé and his brother had become so close. And he was now certain that there was a lot more he didn't know.

The officer looked indifferent. "I've called for a tow truck. You kids are going to have to find another means of transportation."

"You're towing my brother's van?" LJ's response bordered on confrontational, and a sharp glare from the cop slapped him back into place.

"Computer shows his 1971 registration was never paid." The cop waved a hand as the tow truck pulled around to the front of Paul's van. "Impound yard is at 103rd and Doty. You can pick it up there once the fees are all paid up."

"I don't even know where that is," LJ muttered to nobody in particular.

Abby's heart was still fluttering from the scare over the stolen press. As it was, the thing was still sitting in the back of the van and could be discovered by Loring or the officer at any minute. If the blanket were to slide off, or if the police were to inventory the contents of the van, she knew it would only be a short leap for them to connect it to the break-in that Paul had committed. The break-in about which Abby had been questioned. The break-in that had occurred on a night in which she was now on record as having been with Paul.

LJ walked over and spoke with the tow driver while the police officer sat in his car filling out a report form. When LJ returned he told Abby that the driver had agreed to give them a lift to the impound yard.

The cop drove off in one direction and the two of them climbed into the tow truck with the greasy driver. Abby breathed a sigh of relief. She had dodged at least one bullet.

The sign above the gate read: Auto Pound #2. A small office just behind the fence held two Chicago cops. They sat behind a low counter drinking coffee, watching a portable TV, and warming themselves with an electric heater. One glanced up when LJ and Abby walked in, and then went back to the show.

LJ watched as Abby put a quarter in the payphone on the wall and dialed Carter's Print Shop. He could hear her telling Paul what had happened with his van. "No, they didn't find it," she said with a quick glance in LJ's direction. "I don't know that, either."

She hung up the phone, and turned to find LJ only inches away—his eyes slicing into her. "Don't know *what*, either?"

Abby steadied her breathing. "I told Paul that I don't know how much it'll cost to get the van out. Apparently he never paid the fee."

"Oh, you mean with the money *you* lent him?" LJ tilted his head back and gazed up at the ceiling. "And tell me, how is it that you've memorized the number to my brother's workplace? Just how often do you call him? And *what* didn't the cops find?"

"Shhh!" Abby's eyes flashed over toward the officers. "You're embarrassing yourself, Loring."

But LJ sensed there was something else. Beneath her assertive tone and haughty demeanor was fear. He took Abby's arm and drew her closer. "No, *you're* embarrassing *me!*"

He was boiling with rage and was about to demand some answers when one of the cops stood up.

"Everything alright over there?" The cop looked more annoyed that they had interrupted his TV show.

LJ released Abby's arm and turned toward the door. Abby answered the officer in a shaky voice, assuring him that everything was fine.

Stepping into the icy night didn't help to cool LJ's anger. He felt his body trembling and his chest heaving, as if he couldn't get enough air. After a few minutes he wandered back inside—still agitated, but at least under control.

Abby had written a check to cover the $77 license renewal fee. LJ sucked in a deep breath and let it out slowly as he watched her pay the fee. She turned back toward LJ while the officer tried to locate the report on his computer. Her eyes were softer now and her tone more soothing. "You have absolutely nothing to worry about, Loring. Obviously, I've stayed friends with Paul over the past couple of years, and yes, I have helped him out a few times." She stroked a hand along the lapel of his coat. "You know how he is. But there's nothing between us, and there never could be."

LJ felt her words dousing his fiery rage. They were the words he wanted to hear and wanted even more to believe. Abby, on the other hand, felt the guilt of omission strangling her as she spoke. She had *technically* told him the truth, but there was even more that she had left out. Abby assured herself that she would eventually explain the warehouse burglary to LJ, and of her *coerced* involvement in the cover-up. She would even tell him about the late nights alone at the shop with Paul, reading all about bookbinding techniques.

But she could never tell LJ of the conflicted feelings inside her—the ones she could barely admit to herself.

"What's the registered owner's name again?" the officer asked from behind his computer screen.

"Paul Griffiths," said LJ as he approached the counter.

"I've actually got two reports here," the officer said. "Can't tell which one was for the impound." He flipped a switch and a large dot matrix printer began noisily hacking letters onto a drum of paper. The cop then pushed a pair of reading glasses up the slope of his nose as he tore the perforated sheet from the printer. "Says here Mr. Griffiths was stopped about six weeks ago in the same vehicle, after a commercial burglary out by O'Hare."

"What?" LJ leaned over the counter, trying to get a look.

Abby felt like she was going to be sick, but she said nothing.

LJ craned his neck. "Did you say he was involved in--?"

"Never mind," said the cop. "Your brother was released without any charges being filed." He picked up the second report from the tray. "Okay, here we go. Expired vehicle registration impound. All the fees have been paid up now, so you can go ahead and take the car."

"Wait a minute," LJ said, clearing his throat. "Can I take a look at that other report? The one about a break-in."

"Don't see why not." The officer handed it to him.

LJ shook his head as his eyes scanned through the report. He knew his brother was a screw-up, but pulling off something like this was almost beyond LJ's comprehension. He was beginning to wonder if Paul had gotten into heavy drugs, when his eyes suddenly stopped halfway down the page. LJ swallowed, glanced up at Abby, and then continued reading—his face filled with fury and rage.

He reached the end of the page and his arms fell limp at his side, the papers fluttering to the concrete floor. LJ turned toward the door and Abby saw the tears in his eyes. She made an inept grasp at his sleeve, but he pulled away and continued out the door.

Abby dropped to the floor and sat there reading through the report LJ had discarded. Her eyes zeroed in on a paragraph near the middle of the page:

> Subj. Paul Griffiths admitted to being in the area of the warehouse on the date and time of the burglary, but refused to admit involvement in the crime. Griffiths claimed he was having sex in the back of the van with Subj. Abigail Townsend.
>
> Townsend was interviewed at the home of her parents and corroborated Griffiths' alibi. It should be noted that a blanket was located in the van, which tends to support Subj. Griffiths' claim. None of the stolen property was located.

"Everything alright, lady?" one of the cops asked as they stood there watching her from behind the counter. Abby sat cross-legged on the floor and didn't answer. They shrugged at one another and went back to watching their TV show.

Abby looked out the doors, but LJ had already disappeared into the night. She wanted to run out after him, though even if she found him she had no idea what she would say. Her face fell into her hands and she began to sob.

Eventually she gathered herself together, collected the van keys from the police officers, and drove it out of the impound lot. Abby crisscrossed back and forth through the area, trying to find Loring. She followed Doty Street to the intersection with 103rd, and then finally gave up.

SADHANA

Paul had finished the last run of printed sheets and was sitting against the wall, his eyes closed and the smell of pot in the air. He nodded to Abby as she came in, then looked behind her expecting to see his brother. "Lore decided not to come?"

Abby shook her head. Paul could see she'd been crying. "Does he know about the press I took?"

"I don't know . . . maybe." She put the car keys and the bag of brushes down and then sat on a stool. "He saw the report they wrote that night. He saw what you said *we* were doing in your van out by the airport. Why did you tell them that, Paul? You need to explain it to Loring."

"Yeah, yeah, I will." He grabbed the bag of brushes. "Let's get going on this stuff or we'll never get them done."

"I'm serious, Paul. You have to straighten this out!"

"I said, I will." Paul knelt down and started pasting the adhesive onto the first stack of hymn booklets. "Lore just needs to get over it. Give him time; he'll be fine. I know my brother."

Abby stared down at the floor. "I know him, too . . . and I don't think he'll be fine."

LJ took the Blue Line bus to Jefferson Park and then walked home from there. Paul's van was still gone, and LJ felt the hit of another crashing wave of anger. He wondered if the two of them were together now. And then an image flashed in his mind: Abby and Paul, under a blanket in the back of the van. He grabbed his duffel bag and walked out of the house. It was 2:30 a.m. and LJ had nowhere to go, but he knew he had to leave. Otherwise, he was afraid of what he would do to Paul when they finally ran into each other.

It was over a mile to the night owl bus stop, and though LJ would have preferred taking a cab, he had spent all his cash on the ride home. He thought about Abby as he walked, realizing that the night had been one of the worst in his life. Was she at home, feeling badly? He wondered if there could possibly be a version of the story he would accept. Was there anything Abby could say that would make him feel better?

LJ took the bus downtown and then walked toward the train station. He passed an all-night gas station on North Michigan, and decided to phone Abby. LJ had always considered himself a fair person, and after everything that he and Abby had meant to each other, he figured he owed her at least that. LJ would allow her to tell her side.

Abby was anything but her usual upbeat self, Paul thought, as she helped him carry the boxes of songbooks into the van. He caught glimpses of her distraught expression while she worked and as she sat down in the passenger seat.

"Wanna get something to eat?" Paul asked cheerfully.

"Just take me home, please." Even with her smeared makeup and bloodshot eyes, Paul's attraction to her was still as intense as it was hidden. He had no intention of explaining the police report to his brother, as it was not in Paul's best interest. He realized, in fact, that his objectives would be best served by Abby and LJ remaining apart. And any guilt about that, he quickly chased away by reminding himself that LJ was the one who left Abby and went off to college.

Paul headed down North Michigan, hoping to catch Lakeshore Drive up to Abby's neighborhood. Neither of them spoke; there was only the sound of Al Green's voice singing *Let's Stay Together*.

LJ stood at the pay phone as the blue Volkswagen van approached. He squinted into the headlights, realizing that it was his brother's car. Paul hadn't noticed the dark silhouette at first, but his brother was suddenly bathed in light when he closed the door of the booth. Abby had her head down and didn't see him, but Paul stared right at his twin.

The phone dropped from his hand as LJ stopped dialing and stared back.

Paul eased off the gas and the van slowed, just enough to make certain that LJ saw Abby sitting in the passenger seat beside him.

The receiver dangled in the air as LJ slid open the phone booth door and stepped into the night, following the van with his icy gaze. Like an invisible laser locked onto one another, the brothers spoke without words.

Nine

The sun had not yet risen, its smoky glow hovering just beneath the horizon line of the Atlantic.

There Mr. Griffiths was, standing outside, one hand in his pocket and the other cradling a steaming mug. The spirited nylon warm-ups my boss wore gave him a look that was not out of place in the early morning scene, as if he had just finished a workout. I knew he was thinking about Paul—wondering, imagining, and hoping for the best but anticipating the worst. There was still no word from him.

My boss paused near the stables and I watched as he took in the breadth of the structure. It had been a vibrant venue when Paul was younger; in its heyday the building held a dozen horses. The boy was actually a talented rider. But as his interests shifted into the social arena, his equestrian training became a blasé obligation.

Paul eventually lost interest in riding altogether, and Mr. Griffiths sold off all those beautiful horses. He had the building remodeled in the early 1990's, using a portion of it as a garage, and refurbishing the greater part of the structure as staff's living quarters.

It's where I've lived since I began my tenure here, serving Loring Griffiths. And it's through the window of my bungalow that I watched Mr. Griffiths on that September morning, as he stood alone pondering the fate of his son.

* * *

Paul's eyes sprung open at 4:30 in the morning. He instinctively glanced across the blackness to where the glowing cable box in his bedroom would normally show the time. For a few frantic seconds he didn't know where he was. Between the lengthy flight—the first leg of which he slept—and the 9½-hour time change, Paul's internal clock was as fractious and distorted as his fogged brain.

He rolled onto his back and stared up toward the sound of rotating fan blades, his sweat-soaked bed sheet gripping him like arms of remorse. India, he remembered. Acquiring his compass, Paul felt his way to the bathroom light switch. Standing on tiles—still wet from last night's shower—he peed and then splashed water on his face, before falling back onto the bed.

The streets had terrified Paul the night before, and now he would be without a driver to guide him. It would soon be daylight and Paul knew he had to figure some way out of his predicament. He needed to gather courage from somewhere in order to come up with a plan.

Daylight from the hallway crept under the door offering a muted contour of the room. As Paul lay there allowing his eyes to adjust, it occurred to him that his mind would have to adjust in the same way. In order to survive, at least long enough to figure out his next step, he would have to first accept his situation for what it was, and then permit himself to become accustomed to it. Paul realized that by some physical law of human anatomy, his eyes did it naturally. His mind would take more effort.

A deep humid breath filled his lungs and then slowly passed through his nose as he again considered his choices. Returning home or asking his father for money were not options; he had already decided that. Paul felt determined to find the resolve, somewhere inside himself, to gain control of his situation.

His stomach growled from hunger and his face itched beneath two days of unshaven stubble. Paul gazed across the room assessing his net worth: A small tote bag, a passport, an Indian storybook, and an expensive wristwatch. Then there was his wardrobe, the entirety of which consisted of a pair of hard soled loafers, a soiled dress shirt, and socks and underwear in dire need of laundering. He also owned a torn pair of Dockers, which he figured were in such poor shape that they didn't even count.

"First things first," he murmured. Paul got himself up off the bed and dressed in his ragged outfit. Realizing he couldn't do much without something to eat, he decided to check around for a coffee shop. It would require venturing outside though—he couldn't very well adapt to, or gain control over his situation until he knew exactly what that was.

"Sir, sir." The man behind the counter called to Paul as he crossed the lobby. "Complimentary breakfast for guest of our good hotel is on third floor."

Never before had the word *complimentary* meant so much or sounded so good. He stepped back into the elevator and wandered to the end of the 3rd floor hallway. There he found an unmarked door propped open with a portable box fan. A man greeted Paul and sat him at a small table facing a tiny window. Five other tables sat shoulder-to-shoulder in the room, all of them empty but one. A middle-aged Caucasian couple smiled at Paul from their spot just across from him.

The waiter poured coffee from a steaming pot, which he left with Paul. He then brought cream, sugar, and a single printed sheet with four breakfast options. Paul stirred some cream into his mug as he glanced over the menu. None of the dishes were recognizable. He was about to ask if they could just make some French toast or a simple omelet, when the woman at the other table spoke.

"Try the *puri bhaji*, it's quite good."

Paul offered her a smile that hid a grimace. "Sure, whatever," he said to the waiter. "I'll have what she said."

It was obvious that the couple wanted to talk, and it didn't take long for them to ask Paul where he was from. They told Paul they lived in Canada and were recently retired. Paul wanted to ask why, out of all the beautiful places to travel in the world, they would pick India. He resisted asking the question, and instead forced himself to look interested in the tale of their journey. They had been in Delhi for a week and planned to catch a train to Lucknow that afternoon.

"A train?" Paul suddenly wondered why he hadn't already thought of it. "Is there a train station around here?"

"Oh yes," said the man. "Everybody travels by train in this country. There are railroad stations in almost every city. Four or five right here in New Delhi."

The woman added, "There is a nice gentleman who runs a travel agency right next door. He can assist with reservations if you need help with tickets."

Breakfast came and Paul was surprised at how good it smelled. He spooned some kind of salted curry onto chunks of spicy potato and took a bite. Then Paul tore off a piece of a puffy pastry and heaped another spoonful onto it. "Hey, this isn't half bad."

Paul sipped his coffee and watched the rays of sun separate through the louvered pane, then stretch toward his table. He felt as if he had accomplished something momentous. Eating breakfast. After all that happened last night, he thought, I'll take my victories wherever I can get them.

Paul's next stop was the travel agent's tiny office across the alley from the hotel lobby.

A man about Paul's age sat behind the desk, smoking a cigarette and thumbing his iPhone. He set the phone aside when Paul entered through the smudged sliding glass door.

"Harshit Mann," he said, standing to extend his hand.

One of Paul's eyebrows cocked upward as he glanced down at the nameplate on the desk. *Sure enough, Harshit.*

Paul shook his hand and introduced himself. He told Harshit that the Canadian couple had referred him, and then Paul described the series of mishaps that had plagued him since his arrival. "I need to meet up with my group in Jaipur," Paul said. "Since I missed the bus, I'd like to take the train there."

Harshit stubbed out the rest of his cigarette and picked up his phone again. "Indian railroad ticket is difficult for American to buy, even with credit card. I buy ticket for you and you pay me, plus ten percent."

Paul asked about the cost of a ticket and found that there are several price levels, all dependent on the type of car you are seated in. A first class ticket on an air-conditioned train car to Jaipur, plus 10% for Harshit, would cost 1,127 rupees. Paul cringed. The price of the room, and the generous tips Paul had already dished out, left him with little in his pocket. But Paul had seen news photos of overcrowded Indian trains, of people hanging from the doors and clinging to the sides, and he wanted no part of that. "I'll take the first class ticket," he said.

As Mr. Mann counted the money and then printed out the itinerary, Paul convinced himself he had made the right decision. Once he got to Jaipur, Paul would connect with his CRF group and everything would be fine. Besides, he reasoned, I'll still have some rupees left over to get something to eat.

Harshit lit another cigarette and blew the smoke upwards out of the side of his mouth. "The ticket is confirmed for the afternoon Delhi-Jaisalmer Express from Sarai Rohilla station."

"Sarai what?" Paul said, turning the paper toward himself, as if seeing it printed would explain it any better. "Is that station around here?"

"Six kilometers distance. Only twenty minutes in bicycle rickshaw or fifteen if you ride in tuk-tuk."

SADHANA

Paul gathered what remained of his money and stuffed it into his tote bag. He glanced down at the nameplate on the desk and back up at the travel agent. "What kind of name is that?"

"Indian name." He seemed amused by the question. "Harshit is meaning joyful and happy person."

Paul shook the man's hand. "Well, thank you for the help. You have made me very, very *harshit* today."

The man smiled and put his palms together as if in prayer, then dipped his head slightly. Paul imitated the salutation.

Feeling rejuvenated after another small triumph, Paul left the office and headed out the alley toward the road. He had not only figured out how to get to Jaipur via the train, but he had cracked what he considered to be a pretty clever joke.

Paul's senses were immediately besieged by the surroundings outside; smothering aromas of waste and human sweat, animal dung and garbage, all tinged with an eye-watering medley of raw spices. A woman in a red saree lay curled near a bony dog, both of them asleep in the shade of an oxcart. Two men sat talking nearby, and stopped to watch Paul as he passed them. The air smelled strongly of urine and the street was littered with trash—mostly plastics. At the mouth of the alleyway, a man sat in a partially built wooden box, about the size of a bathtub, hammering slats together. Paul stopped to watch him, realizing that back home, machines built boxes such as that. He had never considered how difficult it would be to actually put one of them together by hand. Yet the man sat there in the blazing sun, judiciously tapping tiny nails into each board to create a box—plumb at each corner, as far as Paul could tell.

Dodging motorcycles and bicycle-led rickshaws, Paul found his way across the dirt road. Daylight had insinuated life and activity into the streets that had been relatively quiet when he had arrived the night before. Though nobody approached him or spoke to him, Paul felt as if a million eyes were all fixed on the white American tourist.

Stopping at a dirt berm in the center of the roadway, Paul looked around to assess his options. A few feet away, a man with a straight razor shaved the face of another man beneath a tree. A small mirror hung from a nail imbedded into the tree trunk, and two more *customers* sat cross-legged in the dirt waiting their turn. Paul rubbed a hand over his rough chin, wondered if he could trust his exposed neck to an Indian vagrant with a razor, then decided to pass on it.

On the far side of the road, a dirt lot had been transformed into an open-air market. Hundreds of stalls stretched for blocks, each separated by blue plastic tarps strung between trees, carts and tables. All of them were loaded down with goods. Most of the merchants offered clothing and footwear, some jewelry, and there were a couple of food vendors at the front of the lot where it intersected the road. A man stood next to a cart of fruit, menacingly rapping a switch against the side of his leg. He looked like an Indian version of a Manhattan dance club bouncer. Paul watched him in his peripheral view as he walked around the man, and headed further into the bustling marketplace.

"Here, good sir," a voice called from behind one of the carts. "We have just the thing for your good lady. Pashmina, one hundred percent wool," the man said, quickly unwrapping the plastic from one of the scarves and laying it atop a mound of pants.

Paul waved him off, but the man unwrapped another scarf. "Blue is your color, I think, yes? I give you best deal in Delhi."

"I don't need a scarf." Paul stopped at the cart, pushed the scarves aside and picked up a pair of the pajama pants. "How much for these?"

"For you? Special sale." The man tossed the pashminas onto the table behind him then waved a hand toward the pants. "One hundred rupee."

Paul shook his head. "Too much. I also need to buy a shirt, and I don't have a lot to spend."

"Excellent, good sir." The man bent to pull out a box of Indian tunics, ignoring Paul's comment about money. "We have *kurta* in just your size. Also too, many beautiful and colorful colors."

Frowning at the Sanskrit designs on the shirts, one resembling a Nazi swastika, Paul asked, "Don't you have anything better? Like, American?"

The guy flashed a mouthful of stained teeth. "Those pants you are wearing, they have hole on them. Made in America, yes? Indian clothes better, made stronger."

Paul picked up the white cotton pants; they *might* have fit him when he was 12. He remembered wearing pajamas as a kid that felt thicker than these. "Show me the biggest size you have in these pants and shirts."

While the vendor dug through boxes of clothing, Paul counted his measly wad of rupees. His funds were dwindling fast.

SADHANA

The salesman pulled out another pair of white pants and a tan kurta with thin black designs, handing them to Paul with a half bow.

Paul asked, "You got a dressing room anywhere around here?"

He looked at Paul as if he were crazy. "You go behind tent," he said, motioning to the backside of the blue tarp.

A minute later Paul emerged wearing more traditional Indian dress, and though he was still the whitest person for miles, at least his clothes tended not to draw so much attention to him.

"Two-hundred, fifty rupee." The man held his hand out as if it were a done deal.

"I only have one-hundred to spend," said Paul.

The man shook his head.

After a minute of contemplation, Paul looked down at his loafers. They looked absolutely ridiculous with the rest of his new outfit. "I'll tell you what," Paul said. "I'll pay one-hundred, and I'll also throw in my shoes, in return for the shirt, pants, and a pair of sandals."

The man eyed the shoes tentatively.

"These are Berluti loafers," Paul said. "Worth a couple thousand dollars. That's the equivalent of like, ten billion rupees!"

The guy took the deal, and immediately went to work wiping the mud off of his new loafers.

In return, Paul handed the man the money. "You can take these, too," Paul said, tossing the guy his soiled dress shirt and his torn slacks. Even though the man scowled at the pants, he did not reject them. Content with the negotiation, Paul slung his small tote bag across the breast of his new tunic.

The merchant held the hundred-rupee note between both his hands and made a prayer-like motion with it, first pressing it against his forehead, then his lips, and then his heart.

"What was that?" Paul asked.

"First sale of this day," the man said. "I pray my thanks and to bring me good fortune."

The new sandals slapped a peppy cadence as Paul strode back toward the road. He felt inflated by yet another in a succession of achievements that had begun with such demoralizing failure. "I think I can do this," he said aloud to himself. *Who needs my father's help?*

A flash of fur moved across the dirt in front of Paul, startling him to a stuttered stop. It was a brownish gray monkey about waist-high. The animal's narrow brown eyes were set deep into his pink face, and his long arms and legs swung wildly as he raced toward the fruit cart.

The *bouncer* with the stick spotted the monkey, who was already in midair on his desperate mission to snatch a free meal. The man spun, yelling unmistakably Hindi curse words and swinging the switch with practiced precision. Catching the monkey across the leg, the little thief let out an eerie-sounding yelp, but clung tightly to two figs he had snatched from the top of the cart. He darted off with his prize, though favoring the swatted leg, and leaving the angry merchant still muttering.

While checking out of the hotel, Paul paid the tariff and got directions to Sarai Rohilla train station. He could have bartered to have a rickshaw take him, but his money was running out fast, and Paul knew at the very least he would need a bottled water to make it through the day. Paul set out on foot for the train depot at 11 a.m., leaving himself plenty of time to navigate the labyrinth of Chandni Chowk.

At Qutab Road near the Sadar Bazaar, the streets became even more congested. Paul found it difficult to find road markings, and he was forced to stop and ask for directions. He asked one woman, but she would not speak to him. Avoiding eye contact with Paul, she lifted her hijab to cover her face and scurried on. Several men and boys were quick to grab his arm and offer to take Paul to the train station, but he figured they were only pandering for a nice tip from the mistakenly generous American.

Straining to get his bearings, Paul felt a weak tug on his sleeve.

"Baksheesh?" A young boy stood pleading with cupped hands. One eye was covered with gray scar tissue, leaving only a bit of the iris visible. But even that white part was oddly misshapen, and the entire eyeball was cocked upward. "Baksheesh?" the boy insisted, tilting his head back and blinking the bad eye to make certain Paul saw it.

A traffic jam blocked the street and Paul took the opportunity to cross between stopped taxis and rickshaws. He ran to the other side before glancing back to make sure the beggar boy hadn't followed. Paul didn't see him.

"Baksheesh?" The boy was suddenly at his side again, tugging on Paul's sleeve with renewed vigor. This time the boy pointed a finger into his bad eye—digging at it with his dirty fingernail. "Baksheesh!"

It was a creepy gesture, and the kid's lopsided stare only served to disturb Paul all the more.

"Beat it, kid!" Paul sped up his pace until he was nearly running from the boy. When he looked back, the beggar was still there—darting through the crowd with his hands still cupped.

Another busy street crossing and Paul was forced to stop. He fumbled into his tote bag, feeling for coins. He plunked a few into the kid's hands. "There, now go."

One of the boy's eyes counted the coins while the other stared freakishly up at Paul. The kid slowly tilted his head sideways, glaring at him with his seeing eye. His face retracted into a scowl as he gripped the coins. Letting out an angry chuff, he shook his head and walked off.

Paul arrived at the railway terminal in just over an hour. It was a crushing madhouse of families and blaring announcements over loudspeakers. Inside the main building, dozens of people funneled to a ticket window, as if they had never known the concept of a single-file line. Hundreds of them pushed and shoved toward a train stopped on a track outside, some climbing aboard through the windows.

The floors, both inside the station and outside on the platforms, were littered with individuals and families sleeping on blankets—literally thousands of them. Rats scurried from the tracks, across the platforms to the garbage cans, and back again. Beggars with missing limbs scooted and wiggled their way from group to group asking for *baksheesh*. A large cow had wandered onto the platform and meandered unbothered to one of the trashcans. Paul was amazed at how the cow managed to avoid stepping on any of those sleeping, and even more so, why nobody chased it away.

The place was huge. Sixteen different tracks ran on both sides of a half-dozen platforms—all accessible by overhead walkways at either end of the station. As Paul consulted with his printed ticket for the correct platform, the errant cow ambled past him. Then, just as it came within feet of Paul, it's tail lifted and the animal unleashed a heap of wet, plopping manure. Diving backwards, Paul was able to avoid most of it. But his new white pants, already saturated with dirt from the walk to the station, were now splattered with cow dung.

After cleaning off his feet with a napkin, Paul purchased a bottle of water at a snack counter. He then found a shady spot to wait for his train. Other than the heat and grime, Paul was beginning to feel pretty good about himself. Managing to buy some clothes and a train ticket had given him a real taste of self-confidence. He was starting to believe that he actually could make it to Jaipur and locate the group of volunteers.

Paul leaned back against a post and gazed up at the side of a snack counter, where a weathered map of India had been glued onto the green plywood siding. At the bottom corner was a legend, with measurements marked in kilometers. Paul estimated that Jaipur was somewhere around 300 kilometers southwest of Delhi.

Glancing around the platform to make sure the cow had left and there were no rats in his vicinity, Paul closed his eyes to rest.

The monotony of the recorded announcements and the stifling heat prevented Paul from actually sleeping though, and soon his eyes were open again. He took the book from his small satchel—the Indian storybook that had mysteriously showed up in his luggage.

Paul read the title. "Sadhana," he said with a smirk. He thumbed the pages from back to front, his eyes not fixed on any of the text. Paul saw that the book was laid out in short sections; some with drawings and some with some type of Hindu symbols, but most of it was written in English. Somewhere around the middle of the book, he stopped and read a paragraph—not really thinking as he grazed over the words.

It was a story. A parable, really, about a young boy named Rajeev who had left his home in search of great wealth.

> *The boy comes upon a wise man and asks, "How can I be certain to acquire all the things I really want in life?"*
>
> *The wise man pondered the question. "If I could guarantee you to live until you were 100 years old, what would you want for?" asked the wise man.*
>
> *"Great riches," answered the boy. "A big house, servants, and many animals."*
>
> *"If I could guarantee you to live only 10 years, what would you want for?" asked the wise man.*
>
> *The boy thought about it for a long time. "I would want to fall in love with a woman, get married and have children of my own."*
>
> *The wise man then asked, "What would you want for if you knew that you would live no longer than a single day?"*
>
> *The boy became saddened. He looked up at the wise man and said, "If this was my last day, I would go home to my mother and father, so that I could spend time with them while I am still alive."*

Paul rolled his eyes. He wondered how many rupees he could get for the book.

Thumbing through the rest of it, toward the front, he stopped suddenly on the title page. Paul leaned forward, squinting at the handwritten notation in disbelief:

Leigh Abigail Townsend—September 1982

Paul's mind raced as he studied the signature. His mother's name was Abby Griffiths, or so he had always been told. Abby would be short for Abigail. Paul touched the page, lightly coursing over the name as if absorbing it through his fingertips. It had to be her, he thought.

He had never seen his mother's penmanship, nothing she had ever written; in fact he had never seen anything of hers. Paul's mother, both her life and her death, had always been a mystery to him. A few times he had sought information about her on the Internet, but could never find anything about Abby Griffiths.

Now, the mystery deepened. Paul's curiosity had waned over the years, but now it was back, and with a grudge.

Paul was a child again, lying in his dark bedroom at night. Or on Christmas Eve, when he would wait up as long as he could, not wishing for a bicycle or a skateboard, but for his mother. The mother he never knew, and the mother he never even knew *about*. Now, here was her full name, in her own handwriting, in her own book.

Something suddenly felt wrong—a sickness in the pit of Paul's stomach, clawing at him like the beggar boy with the maimed eye. Paul's breathing had become rapid and shallow, as if an unseen threat were sneaking up on him at this very moment.

Paul's mind flashed to the plane, just before landing. He had been jostled by turbulence and dropped the book. It had fallen between the seats across the aisle.

Was it the man who's headdress he had bumped? Something about the woman whose legs he had crawled between? Anxiety somewhere inside was trying to tell Paul something was wrong. *But what was it?*

"The flight attendant!" he said aloud. She had found something that had fallen out of the book. Paul's mind replayed the entire scene, and he suddenly wished he had paid more attention to it. The flight attendant had thought the piece of paper was his, but he was told to sit down because the plane was landing. Paul remembered stuffing the folded sheet of paper into his pocket and zipping the book in his tote bag.

He instinctively thrust his hands into his pants pockets, but they were empty. Then Paul remembered, his pants were torn and he had given them to the merchant at the marketplace.

The piece of paper that had fallen from his mother's book was suddenly his most important possession in the world. Whatever it was, whatever it contained, Paul had to see it.

He dashed up the stairs, across the footbridge against oncoming passengers, and raced down the opposite side. Paul sprinted into the dusty, congested streets of New Delhi, as if he were meeting his mother, herself. Panicked now, everything outside the station looked different to him. He tried to remember each street, landmark and crossing roundabout, but he kept second-guessing himself.

He pictured the Dockers, dirty and torn and of no use to anyone. They were probably gone by now. It was clear the peddler didn't want them in the first place. Paul wanted to kick himself for not reading the piece of paper to see what it said, for not checking the pockets before getting rid of the pants. He wondered if the folded sheet had even come out of the book in the first place. But if it had, what could it be?

With lungs heaving, Paul stopped at a busy intersection, his hands gripping his knees. He felt the pants and tunic, drenched in sweat, clinging to him like cellophane. The air he inhaled was dank and yellow with exhaust fumes. Paul kept going, unsure if he had overshot the turn by a few streets. The buildings all looked the same.

He came to a bend in the road where several police or military men stood behind wooden barricades. Behind them was a huge arena built of deep reddish stones and surrounded by a high fence. I don't think I passed here, he thought. I would remember this.

Within seconds the street, already packed with people and vehicles, became clogged and impassible. More poured into the street from all directions, like hundreds of rivers into a stagnate sea.

Paul had gone several blocks past his street and now he was stuck. It was Friday afternoon and the Jama Masjid mosque—its courtyard able to hold 25,000 worshipers—had just finished the noon prayer. The gridlock extended for a half-mile in all directions, and would take hours to dissipate.

Nearly an hour passed before Paul was able to push and elbow his way free of the throng of worshipers, and then backtrack to find the neighborhood near his hotel. By then he was covered in tan dust that had congealed into every crease of his skin. His feet and toes were as black as his sandals, and he was exhausted.

Then, as Paul turned onto Matia Mahal Road, he recognized Karim's, a restaurant he had passed on the way. He knew he was close.

When he finally found his hotel, many of the vendors across the street had packed up and moved. With his last measure of energy, Paul darted across the road, past the cart where the monkey had stolen the figs, and into the marketplace. He scanned frantically for the merchant, with even more dread now than when his duffel bag went missing.

Paul recognized the Berluti loafers first. The man had buffed them to a mirrored sheen and was wearing them as he stood smartly at the front of his clothes cart. His prideful look turned to apprehension when he saw Paul barreling across the lot. Then to dread.

"My pants," Paul hollered. "Where are my pants?"

The seller retreated behind the cart. "You not getting a refunds." His peeked over the cart at the pajama pants he had sold Paul.

"Not these," said Paul. "The Dockers I gave you. The ones with a rip!"

The man seemed confused. Maybe he didn't understand the word *rip*, or perhaps he was not familiar with *Dockers*. But Paul was too impatient to explain further. He came around behind the cart and began digging through the stacks of clothes, looking for his old pants.

The merchant backed away further, yelling—first in broken English and then Hindi. Another man came from the next stall, smaller built and a bit younger. He had clearly come to help his friend, and began yelling at Paul, too.

Paul froze in place when he noticed the guy's pants. Paul's Dockers were cinched around the man's waist with some kind of cord and the cuffs had been rolled up several times to clear his bare feet. A lightning bolt of red thread zigzagged over the torn fabric in a crude but practical effort to keep them serviceable.

"I just need something out of the pocket," Paul pleaded, inching closer to the man as he spoke. "Important paper in the pocket."

Paul wasn't sure if the guy understood English. The merchant whom Paul had originally dealt with said something to the man and they both seemed to settle down some. The second man reached into his front pocket and pulled out a folded slip of paper—yellowed and tattered. He examined it curiously, and then handed it to Paul.

The two men stared at Paul with a strange expression that was neither angry nor aggressive. They smiled slightly, almost as if they empathized with Paul or could somehow understand the mysterious paper's importance to him.

Paul wanted to hug them. Instead, he placed his hands together just below his chin and bowed slightly, as if bestowing a blessing. The men returned the *Namaskar Mudra*, and then watched Paul dash away.

Time had passed too quickly, and the mosque fiasco had delayed Paul even further. He looked at his watch and knew he had to hurry if he had any hope of getting back to the railway station in time to catch his train. As much as Paul yearned to stop right there and read whatever was on that paper, it would have to wait. At least now he had possession of it.

The sun was starting to dip beneath the horizon by the time Paul made it back to the station. He had run or trotted most of the way, but he was physically spent and his feet ached from running in the flimsy sandals. Paul propelled himself up the stairway and across the footbridge. Somewhere in the center of the vast rail yard, Paul found platform #5, but it was too late. The Delhi-Jaisalmer Express had just pulled out. Paul collapsed against a concrete abutment and watched as the train's lights faded into hazy twilight.

He slumped into the pillar, gasping for air. "Nothing works in this entire pathetic, shit pile of a country, but *my* train had to be right on time."

When he recovered some of his strength, Paul went inside the terminal and stood at the back of a surging pack of travelers. He eventually worked his way to the front of the line where he presented his 1st class ticket to the agent. "I'd like to exchange this one for another ticket on the next train to Jaipur."

The agent shook his head before Paul had even finished asking the question. "Your train has already left."

"Yes, I know that." Paul could feel the day's frustration start to ooze out. "Hence why I asked you to exchange the ticket."

The agent shook his head with even more gusto this time. "Confirmed tickets cannot be exchanged or returned. Once the train leaves, it's worthless. You must purchase a new ticket."

Paul wanted to come across the counter and strangle the guy. He didn't have the money to pay for another 1st class ticket; in fact he hadn't enough for any of the ticket classes—with the exception of a *Sleeper car.*

For only 156 rupees, the man explained, Paul could buy space on a commoners' car. That left him with exactly 32 rupees—roughly the equivalent of 57 cents.

Paul shuddered away the images and noxious odors his mind had conjured up. "Can I at least get a window seat?"

"Seat?" The ticket agent laughed.

Paul bit hard and his jaw muscles twitched. "What time does the next train leave?"

"Nine-twenty," the agent said with a grin, pausing just long enough for Paul to look at his watch. Then his smile widened as he added, "Tomorrow morning."

Ten

Abby never saw LJ standing at the phone booth, and Paul wasn't about to point him out to her. He knew his twin well enough to recognize when he had the advantage. Seeing she and Paul together would take the last bit of fragrance off of the Abby bloom. Paul was right. LJ headed straight back to Ann Arbor without ever calling Abby.

In the week that followed, Abby kept to herself and Paul gave her plenty of space. He realized however, that it was only a matter of time before she would contact LJ to plead her case. Whether or not LJ would believe her was another story. So instead of playing the odds of probability, Paul took matters into his own hands.

Abby answered the phone on the first ring then sighed when she found out it wasn't LJ.

"Sorry to disappoint you," Paul said. "I wanted to let you know that I spoke with Lore last night. He called to wish my mom a happy Thanksgiving." Which was true to some extent—Loring had called his mother, but Paul never spoke with him.

"Did you explain everything to him?" Abby's tone was suddenly buoyant. "The truth about the police report and all that?

"I did."

"And?" Abby listened breathlessly.

"He doesn't feel the same anymore, Abby."

"About me? He doesn't feel the same about me anymore?"

Paul heard the desperation in her voice. "I'm sorry, Abby." Paul felt a tinge of contrition for hurting her further, yet not enough to stop. "Between you and me, I think he's met someone else."

The line was silent on the other end, and Paul was glad she didn't ask any questions. Eventually he heard light sniffles and then she hung up.

Abby tried to mend her broken heart by immersing herself in work at the pet shop. She steered clear of Paul for the most part, and during the year that followed, she even went out on a few dates. They were friends of friends, and none ever developed beyond the first meeting—primarily due to disinterest on Abby's part.

Paul continued experimenting with bonding adhesives, and began to have a measure of success. He discovered that one of the composites, a 3-to-1 mixture of rubber glue and epoxy—the same one he had used on the church programs—worked better when he combined it with an ethanol-based acetate.

The compound bonded perfectly in the paper press machine, especially when he rough cut the inside edge of the pages before feeding them into the hot press. They seemed to absorb the heated glue and adhere more firmly to the cover. Paul used this method almost exclusively, and his clandestine business was so busy that he could barely keep it from his boss.

The printing industry in general was beginning to show signs of distress however, and the once-vibrant Printer's Row was starting to languish. Ambrose Carter had seen the neighborhood in its prime, and he was now witnessing its decline. He had also seen his own heyday, and now found it more and more difficult to manage the work. He wanted to sell the business and retire.

LJ completed his senior year at Michigan, though not in Kappa House. He shared an apartment with two former housemates, just off campus, and his visits home to Chicago dwindled down to none. He had skillfully avoided his brother that year. Even when phoning home, he would hang up whenever Paul answered. LJ struggled to loathe Abby for what she had done behind his back, and all the while he wondered if she and Paul were together, and if so, how *together*.

With his graduation approaching, LJ enrolled in a masters program at University of Chicago's Booth School of Business. He told himself that his mother needed him closer to home, and that the tuition was only half of what he was paying at Michigan.

But he needed to somehow bring into focus his conflicted view of Abby, and he also knew he couldn't avoid Paul forever. Somewhere beneath LJ's anger was the core of his emotional yearning; he hoped Abby's path would eventually cross his again. Hand-in-hand with that was the hope that Abby's path hadn't been crossing Paul's.

He paid a visit home two weeks before the formal graduation.

"So, the man of mystery finally returns," Paul pulled himself out from under his van as LJ walked up the driveway. "Should have called, I could have met you at the station."

It irked LJ to no end that his brother could pick up after a year, as if absolutely nothing had ever happened between them. LJ wanted to respond with something clever, something stinging about loyalty and honesty. Something about Paul and Abby stabbing him in the back. But his fruitless search for the right words was cut short when his mother ran from the house, her arms open wide. She could hardly wait to tell him about her plan to drive up to Ann Arbor for the graduation ceremony.

"No, Mom." His labored tone was barely appeasing, bordering on irritated. "Please don't. You don't have to go to all that--"

Paul set down his ratchet and got up to watch the exchange. He stood with crossed arms and a smirk as his mother hugged LJ again.

"Nonsense," she said. "It's just going to be a small group of mostly family. Aunt Peg and Uncle Stuart are coming, Sally and the twins, and oh yes, I've invited that friend of yours, Abigail."

LJ's head reflexively snapped around to catch sight of Paul's reaction. Their eyes met and locked, and Paul stared back at LJ as if not a second had passed since that night in the phone booth on North Michigan Avenue.

"This ought to be interesting," Paul said, as he plucked a wrench from his toolbox. "Count me in." He then slid back under the van, leaving LJ smoldering under the guilt of his mother's excitement.

LJ tried in vain to prevent the trip from happening, or at least to somehow have Abby uninvited. But his mother, oblivious to all that had occurred between her two sons and the girl, held stubbornly.

"I thought you liked that young lady," she said. "Well regardless, I've already invited her to the graduation, and that's that."

"How did you even get a hold of her?" LJ asked, reaching for the front door. He turned back toward the van with eyes ablaze.

"I phoned her at that pet store where you used to work. Did you know she's a manager now?"

LJ grunted and followed his mother inside.

Two weeks later LJ was in the bedroom of his apartment at Ann Arbor, unwrapping his black graduation gown from its cellophane packaging, when he heard a weak knock at the door.

To LJ's surprise, Abby stood on the landing in front of him, holding a congratulations card in her hand. He was vaguely aware of his two roommates musing behind him, gazing over his shoulders to appraise the infamous Abby Townsend. LJ's heart felt as if it were dog paddling instead of pumping, and his mouth could barely form words to greet her, much less shoo his roommates away.

"Thanks," he finally managed to say, tugging the envelope loose from her nervous grip.

"Aren't you going to invite me in?"

One roommate pulled LJ backward by the shoulder, while the other shoved the door farther open. "Come in," they said in unison. The two of them introduced themselves to Abby, but her attention was fixed on LJ.

He stood there as if waiting to sign for the delivery—his face restrained and indecipherable.

Abby stepped tentatively past him into the cluttered apartment. "So how have you been, Loring?"

His roommates, neither of whom knew him by anything but LJ, eyed one another in astonishment. "*L-o-r-i-n-g?*"

LJ flashed them a piercing glare then quickly ushered Abby back through the doorway into the hall outside. "I'm sorry, Abby, I don't mean to be rude, but the apartment is a mess and my roommates are a couple of jerks."

"I shouldn't have surprised you, but your mom said--"

"I apologize for her, too." LJ saw that Abby was embarrassed, and guessed it must have taken a lot for her to come. He forced a smile and reached over with a single arm to hug her. "Good to see you, Abby. It really is."

Abby brought her arms up to return the embrace, but LJ was already stepping back. She teetered awkwardly then regained her balance, self-consciously thumbing a stray lock of hair off her face. "Do you have time for coffee?"

"Of course, yeah," LJ said uncomfortably. He had her wait in the hall while he went back inside to grab his keys and wallet. It only took a minute, but it gave them both a couple of seconds to think.

LJ caught his breath and steadied his emotions, but his mind conjured the hurt, distrust, and anger all over again. All the questions about Abby and Paul returned, and as bothered as he was, he knew it meant that he still had feelings for her.

Abby, on the other hand, seriously considered leaving before LJ returned with his wallet. For the past year, she had thought of little else than reuniting with LJ. But the reality of their stilted exchange in the doorway had fallen far short of the fantasy. She wished she hadn't come.

LJ suddenly sprang from the apartment. "There's a coffee shop downstairs."

They shared the elevator from the 8th floor with a trio of chattering young women, smelling strongly of patchouli perfume and marijuana smoke. Abby watched the girls, quietly wondering if LJ knew them. Remembering what Paul had told her about LJ having found someone else, Abby again felt foolish for coming. By the time they arrived at the lobby level, she was beset with doubt and was certain her visit was a mistake.

Abby stopped abruptly. "Listen, LJ, I shouldn't have come."

LJ eased a hand behind her elbow. "Let's just sit for a minute and get our bearings. It's been a year since we've even seen each other." They walked in silence around the corner onto South Forest, and sat at a tiny table in front of Biff's.

Abby watched his eyes avoid hers. "The last time we talked," she said, "I mean *really* talked, was the night your friend died."

"Tommy McDowell." LJ's head dropped slightly. "Worst night of my life." LJ kept his downward gaze. "Actually, it was the second worst night of my life." His eyes moved up to glare at her.

"What can I get you guys?" a young waiter asked, shattering the fragile stalemate.

LJ ordered two coffees, and they were left alone again.

"Your mom and your family are coming in today," she said, tactfully changing the path of the conversation. "I had the week off, so I thought I'd come a day earlier. It's really nice here."

"So, where are you staying?"

Abby shifted in her seat, trying to figure out directions. "The Campus Inn, on East Huron."

"Just across the Diag," he said. "Did you walk?"

She shook her head. "I didn't realize your apartment was so close, so I took a cab."

LJ absently watched an older woman pass by with a poodle on a leash. "So . . . is your room okay?" he asked Abby.

"Yes, very nice." She gazed up at the apartment building, then back to her hands. "Looks like it'll be a nice day for your graduation tomorrow."

"Yes," said LJ. "Should be very nice."

"Warm," Abby said.

"Yep, warm." LJ took in a breath and then cleared his throat. "I know it must have taken a lot for you to come here, Abby. Not just coming out for the graduation, but coming here to my apartment." A settling pause followed, and then LJ spoke again. "So, why did you come here?"

The waiter set two mugs on the table and disappeared. Abby watched him walk away as she pondered her answer. "You'd think after all this time, I would have a response for that." She took a sip of her drink. "I guess mainly, just to say that I'm sorry."

"That's nice to finally hear," said LJ. "Though I'm not sure what it actually means. Sorry you lied to me? Sorry you weren't there for me when my roommate died? Sorry you were too busy having sex with my brother in the back of his van?"

In her periphery, Abby saw a couple glancing over from their table. As embarrassed as she was, Abby kept her gaze fixed on LJ. "That's not fair, Loring. You've never even given me an opportunity to explain myself. That never happened."

LJ's head eased back as he stared up at the canopy of pink blossoms hanging over them. Spring was his favorite time of year in Ann Arbor, and the Flowering Dogwoods were the most beautiful. He knew his anger was ugly and out of character. It was also in crude contrast to the mellow setting. He dropped his head. There were so many things he wanted to ask, so much that he had imagined. In fact, LJ had envisioned these images with such detail and for so long, that he could no longer distinguish presumption from fact.

"I'm sorry for the anger, and I'm going to try to say this as respectfully as I can," he said. "I don't know what really happened that night in the van, because I wasn't there. All I know is what I read in an official police report." LJ paused for restraint. "And I also know what I saw with my own two eyes. And what I saw was you on my brother's bed when you thought I was away at school, and what I saw was you and my brother together in his van later that night . . . several hours later! Now I'm not a stupid man, Abby. And I won't be treated like one. I have never lied to you, and I think I have a right to expect honesty in return."

LJ was leaning forward like a spring about to snap. Abby saw that he was hurt, and still very angry. On one hand, she resented his accusations, or what were as close to accusations as one could get. Yet on the other hand, she knew *he* had done nothing wrong. Nothing to deserve the hurt she had caused him.

"It's my fault for not getting it all straight with you that night," she said, her eyes gazing down at her coffee mug. "I should have told you the entire truth right away."

LJ cocked his head. "The truth is always nice."

Abby ignored his sarcasm, choosing instead to respond to the issues he had brought up. She decided to address them out of order, saving the most difficult for last.

Abby did her best to explain how she had begun helping Paul with his new business, after hours and mostly whenever he had taken on a binding job that was too large for him to handle alone. She told LJ how devastated she was after leaving the police impound yard, and had to wait for a ride home from Paul. Abby said that she never saw LJ in the phone booth that night, and if she had, she would have gotten out right then to explain everything.

LJ knew he could live with the reasons she had given for helping Paul, if that was all that had happened between them. But that was not the case. He could feel it in his gut.

"And like I told you that night, I was in your room to pick up something for Paul," Abby said. "Some glue or brushes, something that he needed back at the shop. I had only been there once before, with you, and I wouldn't have known your bed from his."

LJ pushed his full cup of coffee away, as if disgusted by it and everything around him.

Abby sighed heavily before continuing. "As for what you saw in that police report . . ."

A long silence passed. LJ stared into Abby's eyes with lynch mob intensity, as she searched for the words of contrition.

"Paul . . . Paul had stolen some type of binding machine," she said. "I guess he did, I never really knew for sure. But he showed up at my house one night and wanted to hide it inside our garage, along with a bunch of cans and stuff."

LJ frowned. Though it didn't surprise him that his brother would make such a boneheaded move, the tale didn't begin to answer the one question that had plagued him for so long.

"The cops pulled Paul over in his van later that same night," Abby continued. "I think one of the cops knew he did it, that he had broken into the place. Paul must have told them he had been with me because they brought him to our door in the middle of the night. Woke up my parents and everything."

"Had you been with him? When he stole the thing, were you with him?"

Abby shook her head. "No way, absolutely not. But Paul was using me as his alibi. They had seen his van near the break-in, but the thing he took, it wasn't in the van when they stopped him. And when they asked what he was doing out there by the airport, he told the cops, right in front of my parents, that we had been together in the back of the van."

"But it wasn't true." LJ gazed warily at her.

Abby shook her head again. "I swear on my life."

"Then why the hell didn't you just deny it?"

A tear rolled down from the corner of her eye. "I don't know," she whispered. "I guess I just couldn't. I didn't want to be the one to get him in trouble."

LJ swallowed a lump of emotion. "Why didn't you ever tell me?"

"I tried to." Abby blotted her eyes with a napkin. "And then when he told me you had met someone else, I just--"

"Wait a minute." LJ sprung forward in his seat. "Who? Who said I met someone else?"

"Paul." Abby was confused. "It was right around Thanksgiving. Paul said he had talked to you on the phone and you told him--"

"That son-of-a . . ." LJ seethed, "The first time I even spoke to that idiot was last week. And no, there isn't someone else. Never has been." They sat silently, digesting the words that had been so long in coming.

He tossed a handful of coins onto the bill for the coffees—his still untouched—and the two began walking across the campus. For several minutes, neither one spoke.

LJ's mind was going back and forth, processing this new information Abby had provided, analyzing and crosschecking each purported fact. "So let me get this straight," he finally said. "You allow my brother to manipulate you into being an accomplice in some kind of burglary, you allow him to hide the stolen property in your parents' garage, and then you go along with him as he tarnishes your reputation—in front of your parents and in an official police report. Did I get that about right?"

They stopped walking near a quiet spot next to the applied physics building, where Abby stared off into space with two fingers pressed against her lips. Slowly, she nodded. "Yes, Loring. I guess I did all that."

"And I'm supposed to believe that? That you would do that, risk all that, for Paul, who you say you have no feelings for?"

Abby's eyes began to mist over again. She nodded without looking directly at LJ.

It was the end of the academic year; the air was warm and the mood light everywhere else on campus. Students rode bikes, threw Frisbees and lay shirtless on the grass. But in a shady alcove between the undergraduate library and Bert's Café, the two of them spoke with malignant intensity.

LJ shook his head in disgust. "Basically, while I'm falling apart over my best friend's death, a tragic death, you are aiding my brother in the commission of a felony."

Abby's head turned away from him. "I need to use the restroom," she whispered, her hand smearing a streak of eyeliner that had dribbled down her cheek.

LJ leaned against a large brick pillar outside the café while he waited, relieved to finally confront the anguish that had plagued him for the past year. He would miss Ann Arbor, he thought. But if he could ever believe Abby, it might be worth moving home where they could pick up again.

"Hello, LJ." The voice was vaguely familiar, soft but with a tinge of bitterness.

LJ glanced up. "Lisa."

"Haven't seen you in quite a while." Lisa spoke through pursed lips, and even though LJ couldn't see her eyes through the sunglasses she wore, he knew there was no smile in them.

"Since the funeral," LJ said. "How have you been?"

Abby could see the back of LJ's shoulder as she walked from the bathroom. He was leaning against the pillar talking to a woman. She was beautiful, Abby thought. Exotic and tanned, and shapely in her tank top, cutoff jeans, and sandals.

"How have I been?" Lisa repeated, mockingly. "You mean since the death of my fiancé?"

LJ stretched his neck uncomfortably. He wondered how she had now come to call herself Tommy's *fiancé*, though the point wasn't worth arguing. "You know," he said quietly. "Tommy was my best friend. I cared about him, too."

"Well you wouldn't have known it by the way you acted." Lisa's words were biting and loud. "You try to hit on your *best friend's* fiancé? That's what you call a best friend, LJ?"

"Lisa," he motioned for her to lower her volume. "I wasn't coming on to you. I just misunderstood--"

"You asked me to go to bed with you, LJ! Do you call that a misunderstanding? And not only did you proposition me behind Tommy's back, but you did it on the very night he died in a car accident!"

Abby felt a hollow pain in the pit of her stomach as she listened. She had heard enough—more than enough. Enough to know that LJ wasn't who she thought he was. He had sworn that there was nobody else, and she had been stupid enough to believe him. Certainly, he wasn't worthy of her tears and all her groveling. Abby quickly backed her way around the corner and into the restroom. She stood gazing into the mirror, numb and sickened. She splashed cool water on her face and tried to gather her composure.

Lisa, having said her piece—the monologue she had been waiting all this time to deliver—pivoted on her heals and stormed off. LJ stood there stunned and embarrassed. He glanced around, and though he knew a few people must have heard parts of Lisa's diatribe, they moved on their way without paying a lot of attention. He peered back toward the door. Thankfully, Abby was still in the bathroom.

Abby returned to find no sign of the woman in sunglasses. She and LJ walked in silence across the campus Diag, and up South State Street—both of them reeling privately from Lisa's words. The sick feeling in Abby's gut turned to burning anger, yet she pretended to have heard none of Lisa's scorching rebuke. She kept up the façade all the way back to the hotel. Abby, disgusted by what she had heard, only wanted to get away from LJ.

For the past couple of years, LJ had managed to avoid thinking about the humiliating misunderstanding with Lisa. Following their exchange that night outside her sorority, his friend's death had drained him of all his emotion. He hadn't the wherewithal to deal with Lisa or even attempt to straighten out the mix-up with her. But its importance had moved up on his priority list—not with Lisa, but with Abby. They had begun to clear the air between them and he wasn't about to dirty the slate because of an old mistake—less than a mistake even, a simple misinterpretation.

"Abby, there's something I need to tell you." LJ stopped and faced her, taking both her hands in his.

She closed her eyes, trying to shut out his sickening lies. Abby didn't want to look at LJ or hear anything he had to say.

"What's this?" boomed a voice from the balcony window above them. "A public display of affection?"

Abby and LJ looked up to see Paul's cheeky grin on the balcony above them. Their mother joined him on there. She waved wildly and held up her index finger for them to wait there.

"They're staying at the same hotel?" LJ asked sharply, his eyes narrowing as he glared up at the balcony. "Isn't *that* a cozy little arrangement."

Abby rolled her eyes. That figures, she thought. Then, just as quickly, she replaced LJ's malevolence with her own. *Wait just a minute, where does Loring get off doubting me? I'm done apologizing to him about his stupid brother!*

A moment later LJ's mother emerged from the hotel lobby, and greeted the graduate with a smothering hug. LJ made a stilted introduction to Abby, even though the two had met a few years prior and talked briefly on the phone once or twice.

With his mom there and Paul staring down from the balcony, it was no longer possible to explain the Lisa thing to Abby. LJ needed to talk more and in private, but Abby quickly excused herself and went up to her 3rd floor room. As his mom peppered LJ with questions about the upcoming graduation, his eyes searched the windows above trying to figure out how close Abby's room was to Paul's.

"I gotta go, Mom." LJ turned away when he saw Paul disappear off the balcony, back inside. "I'll try to come by later." LJ stormed off, back the way he had come, leaving his mother baffled as to what had transpired.

Abby tearfully packed her suitcase, and then peeked through the curtains to see if LJ had gone. When she was certain he was no longer there, Abby went down to the concierge's desk to ask for a cab then waited on a seat in the lobby.

"Leaving so soon?" Paul plopped himself on the couch directly across from her. "The big graduation isn't until tomorrow."

Abby rolled her eyes. "I don't want to discuss this with you, Paul. In fact, I'd rather we don't talk at all."

"Sure, have it your way," he said, picking up a travel guide and pretending to thumb through it. "But I tried to warn you."

Abby got up and carried her bag out to the portico. The cab pulled up a few minutes later and Paul watched from the lobby as Abby got in and rode away.

He slumped back against the cushions, wondering what had transpired between she and LJ, but more importantly, how he could capitalize on it.

The family had arranged for three rooms, side-by-side. Paul's room was on one end, his mother in the middle room, and Aunt Peg and Uncle Stuart, whom they lived with in Chicago, were on the other end. Sally, a cousin they rarely saw, had to cancel at the last minute because one of her twins had the flu.

At 6 o'clock that evening, Paul was having a beer in the lobby bar when LJ showed up looking for Abby. By that time she had already arrived at the train station, checked her suitcase and bought a sandwich at Zingerman's Deli, a block away.

LJ detested the idea of even talking to Paul about Abby, but he saw he had no choice. "Where is she?"

Paul turned nonchalantly on his barstool. "Lore?" he said with mock surprise. "Can I buy the graduate a drink?"

LJ dismissed the offer with a huff of air. "Where is she?"

"Mom? I assume she's in her room."

"Not Mom," LJ snapped. "*Abby*. Where is *Abby*?"

Paul shrugged. "I assume she's in *her* room." He pulled a key from his pocket and dangled it over the bar. "Here's the key to my room if you want to go up and search it."

LJ wanted to hit him. He was about to launch into another barrage of questions when his mother and his aunt and uncle stepped out of the elevator. Instead, LJ asked each of them if they had seen Abby. None of them had. It soon became apparent that none of them even knew which room Abby was staying in, which left LJ to wonder if the fact they were all staying at the same place was really a coincidence or a planned rendezvous known only to Abby and Paul.

Assuming Abby's room was right next to Paul's, LJ took the elevator to the second floor room, the number of which he had seen on Paul's key. He then knocked on the door of the room next to it, which unknown to LJ, belonged to his mother. When there was no answer, he tried the door on the other side. There was no answer at that door either, so LJ put his ear against it.

The elevator door suddenly opened, just across the hall from LJ. He quickly straightened and pulled back from the door, but it was too late.

"Who are you, the house detective?" Paul smirked.

LJ knocked loudly at the door, mistakenly assuming that the room was Abby's.

When nobody answered, Paul shrugged. "I thought she was still in her room. Must have gone out for a bite."

LJ pushed past him, taking the stairs back down. He took a position on the couch near the lobby entrance where he could see both elevators as well as anyone coming in from the street.

As he waited there, LJ became more and more certain that he should have accepted Paul's offer to search his room. LJ's mind was now flooded with images of Abby and Paul upstairs together, at that very moment, laughing at him.

He checked his watch: 7:20 p.m. LJ had waited there for over an hour already, and at that point decided to give up his sentry post. A minute later the 355 Wolverine, with Abby aboard, pulled out of Ann Arbor station. Once again, the distasteful recipe of LJ, Paul and Abby was a stew that left all three of them feeling nauseated—though each for different reasons.

Commencement exercises were held in Michigan Stadium at 10 o'clock the following morning. The 90-minute ceremony ended with throngs of rabid families with cameras and video recorders, trying to reunite with their kids. It took LJ a half-hour to find his family in the crowd.

He quickly surveyed the group, noticing that Abby was not with them. "Where's Abby?" he asked his mother.

"We thought she was with you." His mother turned toward Aunt Peg for corroboration. "Maybe she got lost in this crowd."

Paul gazed around, as if he had only now realized that Abby had not been with them all morning. His dramatics were not lost on LJ.

Paul was somehow involved in Abby's absence, LJ thought as he steadied his eyes on his brother. LJ was now even more certain that there was still something between them. They waited awhile, but Abby never materialized. Paul complained the entire time that he was hungry and needed to eat, which only infuriated LJ more.

Uncle Stuart offered to buy lunch for all of them at an Ethiopian restaurant close to the hotel. It was the only place in town that hadn't been booked months in advance for a graduation party.

Everyone at the table talked and laughed, but LJ sat quietly wondering what could have occurred to keep Abby from showing up.

Aunt Peg said, "I think it's great, what you've done."

LJ sat forward to thank her, but it became apparent that his aunt was addressing Paul, not him.

"What's *he* done?" LJ asked with disgust.

"His patent," said Aunt Peg. "Didn't you know? Paul invented his own glue for books. He had to pay an attorney and everything."

LJ mumbled under his breath, "That's good because he's going to need an attorney." While everybody talked happily, LJ poked a chunk of flatbread into a pool of reddish-brown stew. He was not interested in the meal and ended up leaving most of it on his plate.

"Good portions, don't you think?" Paul asked him.

"What?"

"The portions," said Paul in an overly spirited, carefree tone. "The documentaries always show people starving in Ethiopia. You know, with those big bellies? I just figured we'd end up being served a twig and a couple of nuts for an entrée, and maybe a fly or a beetle or something like that for dessert."

The rest of the table laughed heartily and his mother swatted at him in feigned embarrassment, but LJ could only turn his narrowing eyes toward the window in irritation. Paul was intentionally hamming it up just to bug LJ, and they both knew it.

Patent on glue. Who's he kidding?

When they got back to the hotel, LJ checked at the front desk for any word from Abby. He learned that she had checked out the previous day.

LJ convinced himself that Abby had hid out upstairs until he left the lobby at 7:20 last night, and then she must have checked out and stayed the night in Paul's room. *Probably couldn't face me after that,* he thought.

There would be no more chances for her, LJ thought. He swore he would never speak with Abby again or ever allow himself to care about her. She and Paul had gone too far this time.

Eleven

Though Mr. Griffiths still hadn't heard from him, we all wondered how Paul was making out in India. The subject dominated the staff break room, and there was a fair amount of wagering about it. Better-than-even odds were that Paul would not make it a month, while most had bet he would be back within a week. On this issue, I would have bet against them, had I partaken in such frivolous speculation.

Then, sometime toward the end of that first week, Mr. Griffiths received a phone call from Sheryl Beckham, Executive Director of Children's Relief Foundation International. He stayed alone in his office for a long time afterward, as rumors rained down upon the estate like a volcano's acrid ash. Nothing can describe the feeling I had when the news finally broke: Paul had never shown up for his assigned stint with CRF.

It was the last thing any of us expected to hear, mainly because Paul would be the last person on earth to try to go it alone.

Until now, the image of the spoiled heir to the Griffiths fortune volunteering in a third-world country was a source of mild humor among the staff. But the banter and levity quickly died down with the realization that Paul would be relying on a toolbox of life skills that was all but empty. Most in the house felt that his survival capabilities were tantamount to a toy poodle in a kennel full of pit bulls.

We couldn't comprehend the possibility that Paul had intentionally ducked the CRF group, and the only thing left for us to believe was that he had been robbed and killed, or possibly kidnapped for ransom.

Mr. Griffiths took it hard, regretting that he ever sent Paul on the sham mission. Even more, he blamed himself for raising a son with such immaturity and dearth of self-reliance.

* * *

Paul tried to ignore the hollow pangs in his stomach. Filthy odors wafting through the station helped suppress his hunger some, and then there was the lack of money. He couldn't afford to buy a meal anyway, though at least he had eaten a decent breakfast.

He stood there surveying the platform, gazing out over a sea of families and children, some asleep on blankets. There were people of all hues on the color spectrum, all types of religions, wearing all manner of clothing. There were old people and cripples, holy men, and women—some sheathed in colorful sarees and others covered in black from head to toe.

As he glanced up and down the tracks, Paul easily spotted 100 people who were clearly hungrier than he was—some who probably hadn't eaten in days. He had never seen or experienced such poverty. Paul wondered how so many people could live in one place without a source of income. Then he realized that he couldn't really claim any income as his own; he had never actually held a job. That realization also helped to stifle his cravings.

Wandering further down the platform, past the security office, Paul caught a glimpse of his own reflection in the window. He stopped to marvel at it in disbelief. It wasn't Paul Griffiths he saw, and it wasn't the privileged boy who had never wanted for anything. It was as if he were watching a street corner beggar—gaunt, disheveled and dirty. Paul brushed a fly from the sweaty crease of his neck and tried to rake back his tousled hair. He had wondered why nobody at the station had approached him for *baksheesh*, bothered him for money or asked if he needed a ride, and now he knew. He looked like one of them.

The stairway rose steeply over the tracks. He crossed the elevated footbridge, where several people had claimed space. Two women with matted hair and tiny babies in their arms held out their hands for money—though not to Paul, but to others who were more neatly dressed. Stepping past them, Paul beheld children, elderly people and disfigured cripples, all of whom lay rotting in the sun. He couldn't bear to lock eyes with any of them, for fear they would be able to see something inside him. Something he feared but could not identify.

Paul found a spot near a track that was under construction. Except for the blaring announcements, it was quiet and there was a light overhead. Enough for him to read the mysterious writings he had worked so hard to recover. His throat tightened with the anticipation that he was about to read a letter from his mother. Possibly written to him.

Slowly unfolding the wrinkled sheet of paper, Paul carefully straightened the folds and creases, as one might handle the Dead Sea Scrolls. The page was weathered and the bottom of it was badly frayed. Its obvious age encouraged Paul that it was indeed a message from his mother. But his spirits crashed when he recognized his father's handwriting—he'd seen it a million times. Probably some perverse love letter, he thought.

Abby,

It's probably too late for me to tell you this, or for you to hear it, but I'll say it anyway. I'm sorry.

I suppose by now you realize how I've always felt about you. For those feelings however, I can't apologize.

My brother and I having fallen in love with the same woman is just an unfortunate fact of life. I only wish I'd said something sooner or found a better way to show you. Maybe then things would have been different. But none of it really matters anyway—now that you're pregnant.

I know it's my brother's baby you're carrying, and I'm not sure I'll ever be able to get past that. I guess it's something I will just have to face. Maybe in time.

In any case, it's too late for my brother and me— what has happened between us . . . and you, has torn my brother and me apart forever. There is no way to mend something like this.

I now regret all the mistakes I've made in my life. I can't change any of what's happened, but neither can I change how I feel about you. Believe it or not, all I really want to do at this point is make up for all I've done and try to set things right.

I hope you can find it in your heart to forgive me, and maybe someday my brother will, too.

The signature at the bottom of the page was torn ragged, but Paul was certain of the handwriting—it was definitely Loring's. Not that it made any difference anyway, now that Paul's *father* wasn't really his father. He was his uncle. And his mother . . . who knows what she was?

Paul felt sick, but he had nothing inside his stomach to throw up. He struggled to his feet and walked aimlessly along the platform, his legs feeling asleep beneath him. He stumbled along the cracked and scuffed tiles, over blankets and sleeping families.

It wasn't just one truth that had been pulled out from under Paul, but several. It was his whole life—his entire foundation—everything he had always believed in. He despised his father even more now—or more accurately, *Uncle Loring*. Not only did Paul not know his mother, but now his real father was an equal mystery.

The revelation sucked the life out of Paul—he didn't know what he was, who he was, or why he was. The world he had left in New York now felt shallow and meaningless, yet it paled in comparison to the abyss he had fallen into here. Alone and penniless in this vile country, Paul wanted to throw himself onto the tracks, in front of the next train he saw.

As the hour grew late, activity lessened on the platforms and there were fewer people to contend with. But there were a lot more rats. It never really got any quieter or any cooler though. By then Paul's bladder was at high tide, which finally convinced him to get up again. He searched around the station until he spotted what looked like a restroom. It was at the far end of the main platform.

Several men stood peeing into a stained cinder block trough, their backs fully exposed to anyone walking past. The acidic odor made Paul's eyes sting. As he started to step up onto the cracked tile precipice to join the men, a boy who couldn't have been more than twelve or thirteen stopped him with a thin brown elbow.

"Five rupee," he said, holding out his hand.

Another beggar, Paul thought. But then he saw that the kid had set up a small wooden table and a seat made from an overturned paint drum. "You gotta be kidd'n me."

"Five rupee." The boy's face was dark and it was obvious that he took himself seriously.

Maybe Paul could have afforded the five rupees or maybe not, but it didn't matter. It was the principle of the thing. He had been through enough, and there was no way he was going to diminish his meager holdings in order to urinate into a dirty trough.

"Five rupee," Paul mimicked back. "Five rupee to piss? What do you charge someone to take a shit?"

The boy's expression didn't change. "Five rupee."

Paul walked through the terminal and out to an open area where some of the tracks dead-ended into concrete blocks with rebar jutting out of them. It was darker there, and he saw fewer people. He stepped carefully along the uneven pavement, just beyond the glow of the terminal. He came upon a tiny clump of bushes next to the track. Suddenly there was movement near him and Paul saw that somebody else had the same idea. The person—Paul couldn't tell if it was a young man or woman—squatted with grunting determination. Paul quickly went around to the other side of the tracks, behind a stationary boxcar. As he stood in the dark, peeing onto the track a few feet below, a grunting sound below sent Paul stumbling backwards. A huge pig emerged from beneath the boxcar and looked up at him. The sow then continued rooting through the debris along the tracks.

Paul finished his business and hurried back into the terminal.

Between eyeing the marauding rats, and listening to the man snorting and spitting behind him, Paul found no rest. He waited there through the night, through a thousand recorded announcements, through a dozen rereads of the letter Loring had written to his mother. It was the lowest and most miserable night of Paul's life, and it moved as if he were watching the second hand of a clock.

The orange sun rising over the Himalayas finally brought a lethargic, sweltering end to the eternal night. The brown morning air tasted as if it was being sucked out of a rickshaw's tailpipe. But with the new day came a fresh legion of *Chola Tikki* and *Bread Pakoda* vendors. Paul struggled to his feet—every muscle cramped from the pavement and the metal benches, both of which he had used at one time or another in a tortured attempt at sleep.

Paul tormented himself by watching the aromatic mounds of spiced chickpeas and potato being deep-fried to crispy wedges. He shouldered amongst the newly arrived travelers, his mouth watering for something he would have scoffed at when he first arrived. Now he watched for a dropped piece he could seize.

Paul's sudden sense that he was being watched caused him to pivot around, at which he came face-to-face with a frowning gray-haired man. He was a good measure shorter than Paul, and something about his dress; his brown skullcap perhaps, or the all white tunic and pajamas, gave the impression the man was Muslim. Paul stepped out of his way granting the old guy passage toward the food cart, but the man just glared back. Images of the 9-11 hijackers flooded Paul's mind, and he was certain that the man's eyes swore *death to the infidel.*

SADHANA

As Paul's departure time approached, he thought he heard an announcement about his train: the #12215 to Mumbai. Except that the 12215 was supposed to take Paul to Jaipur, not Mumbai. He checked his receipt again to confirm the train number, then immediately began to panic as the engine's single white headlamp came into view at the north end of the station. Paul had missed his connection at the airport already, and this was the only chance he would have to fix things. He couldn't afford to screw this up as well.

A hand suddenly reached out from the crowd, grabbing Paul's and pulling the receipt with it. The Muslim man stooped slightly to read the numbers from Paul's ticket, never releasing his hand. The old man nodded at Paul, and then pointed to the approaching train, and nodded again. Paul sheepishly dipped his head in thanks.

The teeming platform surged toward the rumbling *Garib Rath* as it slowed to a stop in front of Paul. He had prepared himself for the footrace to find a seat, and was intent on staking his claim to one—preferably next to one of the barred windows.

Though the mad dash into the train felt like a fondle and grope fest, the competitors were all smiles. Unlike the New York subway, none of the passengers seemed angry or aggressive. Paul bolted through the narrow car toward the first space he could find. Surprisingly, it was much cooler inside than outside. His mind was processing the conditioned air, wondering if he had accidentally stumbled into 1st class instead of a Sleeper, when someone behind Paul nudged him into a small alcove of empty seats. Rather than two rows facing each other as he had expected, the benches were stacked three rows high. They looked like narrow bunk beds.

"Quickly!" said a younger man who nudged Paul. Then as passengers poured in from the other direction, the young man dove past Paul onto the lowest bench. Another, who had been behind them, took Paul's hand in his and guided him toward the same bench.

Several people tried to jam themselves onto the bench, but Paul's two companions defended the spot with raised arms and sharply spoken words. It was then that Paul realized the older man was the frowning Muslim who had helped him on the platform. The man, whom Paul had feared might shove him in front of the train, had actually helped him get on the right train, and then secure a seat on it.

"Thank you," Paul said, taking a seat between them.

The gray-haired man nodded, his face still set in a scowl.

"You're American." The younger man scooted so close that he was nearly on top of Paul. "I am fan to Justin Bieber."

A slight chuckle escaped Paul's grin. Then Paul leaned back to make room for three men wearing yellow and orange robes, as they climbed a tiny foothold to the bunk above him. Several more people, including a young family, crammed into the remaining seats of the alcove until it was clear there was no more room.

Turning to the younger man who had removed a schoolbook from his knapsack, Paul asked, "This train has air conditioning?"

"Yes, A/C." His eyes searched for more to offer. "Very good and modern technology."

Paul raised his eyebrows. "Yeah."

"Indian Railways train, Garib Rath," he added. "It is translated to mean: *Poor Man's Chariot*."

Paul glanced around at the cramped quarters appreciating the *"poor man's"* piece of the translation.

The young student continued, "This train was made for Indian people who cannot be able to afford the 1st class ticket. This coach car are not so spacious. Very crowded like regular Sleeper car, but have good and nice A/C air condition."

The Muslim man finally smiled, and nodded as if he understood what was being said. But he soon settled back with his head against the metal wall, and fell asleep.

Occasionally the dangling foot of one of the robed men seated above them smacked against Paul's head, but he could tell by their spirited conversation that it was neither malicious nor conscious. After a while one of the men climbed down to remove a foil bundle from a small paper sack he had placed on the floor. He set it on a foldout tray under the window, and gently unwrapped its contents. There he set about dividing the ingredients of his lunch onto the open piece of foil.

Paul felt like a dog with slobbery jowls as he watched the man scoop mashed chickpeas onto pieces of flatbread. The man then took a small pocketknife, quartering a blood-red tomato and cutting half-inch slices of a tender, dew-covered cucumber.

It was the simplest of meals, but as the cramped car swayed rhythmically along the clacking tracks, Paul felt as if he was witness to a Thanksgiving feast. The man passed some of the food up to his two robed companions, one of whom declined.

"Holy men," said the student next to Paul. "They travel to pilgrimage for Hindu holiday."

Paul nodded, wondering how it was that Hindu holy men could eat so casually and a Muslim man could sleep so comfortably, all within inches of one another. *Aren't they supposed to be some kind of enemies?*

Another bump against his shoulder and Paul looked up, expecting to see the pilgrim's swinging foot again. Instead, the robed man who had judiciously prepared the feast now stood before Paul offering a small portion of his lunch to him.

"Thank you," Paul said, taking it from the man and cradling it against his chest. "Thank you so much." Paul tried to place his hands together, but afraid his meal might drop onto the floor, he managed only a half-baked salaam before shoving the teetering morsel into his mouth. Despite that Paul's particular salutation was most often used in Islamic cultures, its meaning was clear and the Hindu holy man returned to his bunk with a smile.

Food had never tasted so good. As he licked the pasty remnants from his fingers, Paul wanted to thank the man again and offer him something for his generosity. He took the few remaining rupees from his pocket as he leaned out of his bunk, but the student seated next to him suddenly grabbed hold of Paul's arm.

The young man's bobbling face grinned a soft admonishment. "The meal was the holy man's gift to you," he said. "Accepting it is your gift to him."

Paul gazed out at the small villages while the train headed south. Between clusters of mud homes were miles of open space—some cultivated farmland and some untamed jungle. Sometimes the dried earth stretched as far as the eye could see, with only a random leafless tree to intrude on the dust. Occasionally, a clearing would reveal a woman laboring in a field. Paul knew that the cruel heat outside was unbearable, yet these women carried long bundled stalks of grain or water buckets, or worked to gouge shallow rows into the scorched red dirt—the entire time cloistered beneath their colorful fabric.

None of the passengers seemed to notice them, but Paul watched in amazement. It wasn't as if these women were working for a paycheck. Their punishing toils served only to provide life-sustaining nourishment for their families. Nothing more.

He continued watching from the window as the train sped over primitive wooden bridges, past people riding upon camels, donkeys and bicycles. Past sleeping men, playing children, and women washing clothes in a muddy stream.

Paul saw an old man herding goats, who had stopped next to the tracks to urinate. Suddenly Paul wished he had found the time and a place to do the same before boarding the train in Delhi. He had read in his guidebook that some travelers recommended padlocking your suitcase or backpack to the seat while moving about the train. Since Paul had neither a suitcase nor backpack, he was more concerned about losing his spot to another passenger.

As the train stopped and then pulled out of Rewari Junction, Paul figured it was a good time to go—now that there would be no new passengers vying for empty seats. At the end of the car Paul caught the stench of the restroom, even before he saw it. He edged the door open, making sure it was vacant, stepped inside and secured it with a flimsily nailed clasp.

The window inside had been painted yellow, casting a mustard glow into the tiny space. Two metal pads in the shape of shoes were affixed to either side of a hole that had been cut through the floor. Paul peered downward through the hole and saw the tracks racing by. No toilet, no water, just a hole in the floor—well spattered, he noted, with feces and urine, no doubt left from passengers trying to balance themselves against the jarring movement of the train.

Paul did his best to aim into the encrusted perforation, thusly relieving himself before weaving his way back toward his seat. He edged passed a chai wallah selling small cups of tea for 1 rupee, and wished the man were selling hand sanitizer instead.

When the wallah finally made it to their small compartment, the Muslim man had woken up and was digging through a small coin purse. The tea man poured from a large steel pot, holding it chest high as the stream made a wide, downward arc. And without a single drop falling elsewhere, he filled the plastic cup right to the brim.

"Much better to drink from clay cup," said the student to Paul. "Traditional Indian way."

The old Muslim sipped his tea, and when he was finished he passed the cup across from person to person until it reached a mother with two young children seated closest to the window. She maneuvered the sliding window open, tossed the plastic cup out, and slid it closed again.

"Indian government made law to prevent railroad chai wallahs from using plastic cups." The young man smiled and wagged his head slightly. "They still use them."

122

Paul imagined the reaction of passengers on the LIRR if one of them discarded garbage out the train window. Then he figured, compared to the feces and urine pouring onto the rails from the trains' bathrooms, the plastic cups weren't such a big deal after all.

They arrived at Jaipur Junction station at 2:10 p.m. and Paul nodded his farewells to the frowning Muslim, the student and the three holy men. The woman seated by the window with her children tucked her saree across the lower half of her face, pretending to pay no attention. Her husband, who had read the newspaper for most of the nearly five-hour trip, continued reading without ever looking up.

Paul stepped into the glaring midday sun, and if not for the huge *JAIPUR JUNCTION* sign on top of the broad pink terminal building, he would have thought he was still in New Delhi. The place was teeming. Paul realized he had badly misjudged the situation, assuming that Jaipur was a small place. Now he felt stupid. The city was large and overwhelming—certainly not a place he could simply ask somebody, "Hey, do you happen to know where one might find the Children's Relief Foundation group?"

The street outside the station was filled with dust and noise, and was gridlocked with animals that Paul judged to be better off behind a fence somewhere. A cluster of tuk-tuk drivers swarmed toward the arriving passengers, regarding Paul for a brief second before moving on. His tattered clothing, ragged beard and general disheveled appearance had effectively taken him off everyone's radar. He no longer had the look or smell of a wealthy American.

Having freed himself by taking a route leading away from the train station, Paul was suddenly accosted by a dog. The mutt ran out from across the dirt road, heading right at him. He was soon joined by a second, and then a third—all barking and growling, as if arguing over which of them would feast on Paul before the others. Facing the pack, Paul backed slowly down the road. Occasionally one would make an insincere charge, at which Paul would raise a foot in readiness to kick. But the dogs never actually made good on their threats.

At one point, Paul noticed a figure watching from a raised sidewalk next to a bank. The man wore a uniform and held a double-barrel weapon of some sort across his chest. The thing looked old enough to be a Civil War musket, and for a moment Paul actually wanted the guy to shoot at the dogs—maybe just to scare them off. But the guard only watched with mild amusement before finally strolling back to his post near the bank doorway.

Then, just as the three mutts turned and strutted back to their driveway, a rattling rickshaw came up next to Paul and stopped. A dark haired boy wearing a loose fitting blue work shirt sat grinning from the driver's seat. Paul thought he couldn't have been more than eighteen or nineteen years old.

"You want ride?" The boy's chipped front tooth gave additional innocence to his youthful face.

"No thanks," Paul answered, patting his pockets. "No rupees."

As he began walking again, the lawnmower-sized engine started up and the rickshaw eased forward. It kept pace next to Paul. "It's okay," said the boy. "Not so much work for tuk-tuk driver in Jaipur today. I give you ride."

Paul climbed into the back seat, doubting the sincerity of the gesture. Had the driver been older, Paul would have been more certain it was a scam, and he would have declined the *free* ride. Either way, the boy clearly posed no threat.

"I try to practicing English," he said, turning back to Paul. "What you name?"

"Paul." He extended his hand over the seat. "Paul Griffiths."

The boy awkwardly took it. "I am Juber Kazi."

"You speak pretty well," Paul said. "Did you take English classes in school?"

Juber flashed a timid grin in the rearview mirror. "I not go to school. This I learn from driving English people and also some Australia peoples, too."

"Wow, that's pretty good." Then Paul caught a glimpse of his own pitiful reflection. "Then you understand that I have no money to pay you for the ride."

"Is okay, Mr. Paul. Where you want to go?"

He tried to envision the paperwork he'd received from CRF. "It's a classroom, I think. A place where they do training."

Juber wrinkled his brow, and his deep brown eyes stared back in the mirror. "For study for school?"

"Yes, yes!" Paul hunched forward over the seat. "For school. My group is called Children's Relief Foundation . . . CRF International. Do you know of them?"

"Sorry, Mr. Paul. I not know him." Juber turned sharply and the tuk-tuk's engine sputtered to a halt. The rickshaw silently rolled the last six feet up a small embankment. When its movement ceased, Juber set the parking brake and got out. "But I find out for you."

Paul waited in the shade of the back seat while Juber slid open one side of a double metal gate. Behind it was the Sunder Palace, a four-story hotel hidden behind a thick canopy of palms, white magnolias, and purple flowering orchid trees. After a few minutes, Juber returned holding a scrap of paper bearing handwritten notes.

"My father say he know a school for to learn American English." Juber held up the paper. "I take you."

Paul tried to explain that he was trying to find a training class for Americans, not English classes, but Juber didn't seem to understand the difference. Then Paul asked him if his father owned the hotel.

"Oh no, Mr. Paul." Juber started the rickshaw and backed down the incline. "My father work at Sunder Palace. My brother, he also work at Sunder Palace. And I also sometimes drive tuk-tuk for customers at Sunder Palace, for taking sightseeing and tours, also."

With about 100% certainty, Paul figured this place Juber was taking him was a complete waste of time. But his options were few, actually none, and at the very least there would be English-speakers there with whom Paul might be able to converse. With any luck, he might actually find someone familiar with CRF's training location.

"How far is this place, anyway?" Paul asked.

Juber shrugged. "I never go to Malviya Nagar before. Maybe fifteen minutes, I think so."

A spark of enthusiasm flashed through Paul. "Malviya Nagar. That sounds really familiar to me. I think I might have seen it on the paperwork they sent me."

Juber glanced back in the mirror, but his expression showed no hint of understanding. "I think yes."

Malviya Nagar was a bustling district of street vendors, offices and older buildings that looked like leftovers from British rule. A lot of colonial detail, but many were in dire need of landscaping and a coat of paint. Then there were the new buildings—more modern, built of steel and glass. They looked like an attempt at the Jaipur version of Silicon Valley, yet not even coming close.

ARCH Institute of English Language was in the latter group: a stylish, two-story structure painted cream and pink, with angular concrete outcroppings of aqua and bright orange. Although kindergarten students could have easily been responsible for the color selection, Paul suspected the architect had probably won an award for the thing's design. In any case, Paul saw no sign of the CRF bus or American volunteers.

When their rickshaw stopped at the gate, Juber stepped out and eagerly approached the painted sign on the wall. He pointed proudly to the word *ENGLISH*, as if all things English are somehow related.

Paul stretched and rubbed his legs. The jarring ride through southern Jaipur had pulverized his backside. He found a shady spot in to sit while Juber walked over and had a word with the gate guard.

As Paul waited, a bright yellow cart rolled along the road next to the curb, weaving in and out of traffic. As it came closer, Paul saw that the driver was severely deformed. His legs were short stubs—fish flippers, really, with only the slightest resemblance of a toe or two at the end of them. The man used his hands to push and pull at pedals mounted on the topside, propelling the gizmo at a fairly decent clip. It was the second such cycle Paul had seen—the first had been earlier during the drive, and he hadn't noticed the driver's deformities.

"The guard, he know of your school." Juber's grin was wide upon his return. "The CRF is near to this place."

Paul jumped to his feet. "You're sure? The guy said 'CRF,' right? Children's Relief Foundation?"

Juber's head wobbled a bit, which Paul took as uncertainty. But after coming all this way, and with no other leads, Paul's spirits soared at the prospect of actually reconnecting with his group.

Paul gripped the underside of his seat as the rickshaw sped across oncoming traffic to the left side of the street. Two men ambled down the road, one walked with the aid of a wooden crutch and a prosthetic leg. The other man had no legs, and slid alongside the first, with his torso balanced on something akin to a wide skateboard. Paul was about to ask Juber about all the people with mobility problems, when the tuk-tuk suddenly veered back across the road and into a long driveway.

The short white bus was facing in, so Paul couldn't see a logo, but he was sure they had found the training center. It was a gray building about the size of a small hotel, with tiny porthole-like windows along the front wall.

"Thank you, Juber!" Paul gripped the boy's shoulders and shook them. "This is it. This is the place I've been trying to find." Paul rambled about his lost luggage, his missing wallet and his broken phone, but Juber just grinned and nodded. "I can't thank you enough," Paul finally said.

Paul dug into his pocket, cupping the remaining rupees in his hand.

"No, Mr. Paul." Juber was quick to press his palms together and bow his head. "You are a visitor in my country. To helping for you, it is my honor and my duty."

Paul wanted to hug Juber, but he sensed the boy's discomfort with the shoulder massage a second prior. Paul got out and returned the salutation. He watched in deep introspection as the green and yellow tuk-tuk darted back into traffic and disappeared.

This boy, Paul thought, is a saint. I'll never see him again, but he did more to help me than any stranger ever has. More than any friend ever has. And for what? *He has nothing, and yet he wants nothing.*

Paul tried to brush the dirt from his rumpled tunic and thumb the greasy hair off his face as he walked toward the doors. The CRF International logo was printed on the side of the bus, and Paul was certain it was the same vehicle he had ineptly chased through the New Delhi airport.

Inside the building, two young men sat at a table to the right of a small receiving area. One was Indian and the other Caucasian, both about Paul's age or a little younger.

"Hi," Paul said, easing the glass door closed behind him. "I'm Paul Griffiths, part of the volunteer group."

The two men, both wearing CRF nametags, stared blankly back at him. Paul noticed their eyes drift slowly downward to his filthy clothes and blackened feet.

"My wallet was stolen at the airport," he said. "It's a long story. Anyway, I'm sure I'm on your list there. How about signing me in and getting my nametag and--"

"How can we help you, sir?" the woman's voice behind him spoke with confident authority.

As Paul turned back, he felt as if all the blood in his body had suddenly congealed in his veins. His back stiffened and his arms and face went slack. "You . . ."

The young woman with short blond hair squinted slightly at the faintest wisps of recognition.

Paul smiled. "It's me," he said, holding his hand to cover his gnarled beard. "Remember? Paul. I'm the American guy from the airport in Helsinki. You also saw me on the plane. You're . . ."

"Gwyneth Eichler." As full recognition came to her, an amused smile edged slowly across her lips. Eichler stepped back to take in his disheveled look and then guardedly extended her hand. "I'm CRF's deputy director of volunteer and community partnerships."

Twelve

"Fucking assholes!"

The executive assistant heard the CEO through the heavy door separating his outer office from the Boss's.

The red brick building on West Roscoe Street had served as headquarters for Bind-Chem Industries since its inception. Paul had bought out Ambrose Carter in 1975 and converted the majority of the Dearborn Street shop into his bookbinding facility. A year later Paul changed the company name to Bind-Chem and expanded into the top two floors of the M. A. Donohue building. He discontinued printing at that location altogether, focusing instead on the production of binding adhesives and glues.

After several successful patents and several profitable contracts, Paul's fledgling company had become a notable presence in the industry. He was able to purchase the 19,000 square foot Roscoe building, with a ground floor warehouse, 2nd level R&D space and offices on the top level.

In January 1976, the U.S. Office of Personnel Management adopted TS-23, an entirely new classification schedule for all federal employee positions. Bind-Chem was awarded the contract for printing and binding the 25-page *Research Grade Evaluation Guide* for each and every member of the 5,005,000 federal employee workforce. Paul's company subsequently leased another large industrial facility in Winchester, Virginia.

Paul successfully acquired a second federal contract in 1977, when the Military Personnel Records Center—a branch of the National Personnel Records Center—named Bind-Chem their sole supplier of binding adhesives for the entire federal government printing office. That contract required Bind-Chem to lease another 28,000 square foot site in Spanish Lake, Missouri.

His dream had turned into a lucrative but complex venture. Paul cursed again as he dialed the phone. "Fucking assholes are trying to close me down!" He tossed the EPA's letter onto his desk.

When the other end of the phone was answered, Paul tempered his language slightly but his tone was clear. "Charles, this is Paul Griffiths." He continued before the congressman was even able to acknowledge. "This EPA thing is getting out of hand. They've just placed my Virginia plant on their hit list of hazardous waste management facilities."

The Illinois congressman was mildly annoyed, but more amused than anything. "Idiots. That's John Quarles' acting administration; they're just trying to make a name for themselves. The president has already picked Doug Costle to replace him, though I doubt he'll be any easier on you guys."

"That's just great."

A thought suddenly occurred to the legislator. "Your Spanish Lake operation is bigger than Virginia, isn't it?"

"Yeah, by about ten-thousand square feet. Why?"

"But nobody's mentioned anything about that facility, right?" The congressman mumbled to someone in his office, then got back on the line. "They've only focused on your Virginia plant because it's close to D.C. That'll generate more press, which means more White House attention on them. It's what they're looking for—a big splash."

"Should I be worried?" Paul asked.

The congressman's pause was foretelling. "I think you're alright for now; Quarles won't have the position much longer. But to be perfectly frank, I see a few obstacles on the horizon."

"What obstacles are we talking about?"

"The Resource Conservation and Recovery Act," he said. "The Senate passed it in June and the House in September."

"What the hell is it?" Paul eyed a bottle of Johnnie Walker and a tumbler on the credenza across the room. The phone cord stretched, pulling the phone to the edge of the desk, as Paul reached to pour himself a drink.

"The White House is really getting serious about dangerous chemicals, Paul. It's all the stuff you probably use in your binding adhesives."

"They're not dangerous," Paul said. "In fact we've never had so much as a single industrial accident. Go ahead and check it out; my OSHA record is clean!"

"Cancer, Paul. Studies are finding that a lot of these compounds cause all kinds of long-term issues. We're talking, things that might not show up for years, even decades. Anyway, I'm just warning you that stiffer government regulations are not too far off. This RCRA Act was only the first shot across the bow."

Paul took another good swing. "You wanna hear the shit of it?"

"What's that?"

"The EPA gave us the contract to print their goddamn hazardous waste report. *We* printed their fucking report about us!"

The congressman let out a robust laugh. "That's rich. I told you they were idiots. Anyway, come by next time you're in town and we'll have dinner."

Paul hung up the phone. The idea of outsourcing had never occurred to him before. But, as he downed his Scotch and poured himself another, he became more intrigued with the idea. It was something he'd have his staff start looking into.

* * *

It took nearly two years to relocate operations out from under federal EPA jurisdiction. With 90% of his labor force overseas, Paul had scaled back his domestic managers to only a handful. The company moved again, selling off the old brick building on West Roscoe. They began operating out of a high-rise office in New York, but the address was largely a façade, maintained to satisfy the government contracts. It created the illusion that Bind-Chem's products were still *American-made.*

By August of 1979 Paul had sold his loft in Chicago and moved to a flat in Manhattan's Upper Eastside. With the exception of his lucrative federal printing contracts, Bind-Chem's revenue source had transitioned to production of their uniquely formulated bookbinding adhesives and glues. In that market, Bind-Chem now held exclusive dominance.

During that time, Paul made intermittent trips back to Chicago—all of them business-related. He often thought about Abby, and wondered what she would think of his success. Paul had even tried to seek her out during some of his visits, but was never successful. He had learned that Abby no longer worked at the pet shop, and she had moved out of her parents' home in Wicker Park. But Paul's mushrooming business eventually consumed all of his time, and his obsession with Abby was put in storage.

130

SADHANA

A sub-tropical weather front had turned an otherwise beautiful summer morning into a stifling downpour. Paul held his raincoat over his head with one arm as he ducked into the cab. The company's legal counsel waited for him inside. "LaGuardia," Paul said to the driver.

The attorney flipped the clasps of his briefcase and opened it on his lap. "I've got to warn you, Paul. This thing is getting pretty risky."

"I know what I'm doing." Paul shook the rain from his coat and smoothed his hair with a wet hand. "Just tell me what you found out."

Nathan slid a file out and handed it to Paul. "You can skip through the wording of the bill itself. The index of chemicals is on the second page of the addendum; you'll notice that bisphenol and ethylene glycol methyl ether are at the top of the list.

Paul ran a finger down the page. "I don't see--"

"It's listed as *EGME; 2-methoxyethanol*," he said. "Same thing."

Paul closed the file and handed it back. "So what's the rest of it?"

The attorney fingered another file out of the briefcase. "The federal government contracts. We're playing fast and loose with the spec agreements."

Paul backhanded the air dismissively. "They can't pay me to make the adhesives for them, only to outlaw the ingredients. And then have me promise not to make the stuff anywhere else but in the good old U.S. of A. It's total horseshit!"

"That may well be, Paul." His counselor tapped nervously beneath his bottom lip. It was a conversation they had had before. "The issue is that you signed a contractual agreement, under penalty of perjury. This is potentially serious stuff. We're talking federal prison."

"I thought that's why we kept the New York office," Paul said, as he glanced through the contract. "They can assume what they want, but in the end, how are they ever going to know that our production plant is in India? They have no idea where we produce it or what we put in it, now do they?"

"Paul, the feds can track these things at the borders. Your passport is probably already on a watch list. They'll know when you travel out of the country."

Paul stared out the car window, tired and fed up with the entire conversation.

The attorney pressed, "It says right there on page 12 of the contract. Unless otherwise specified, all work and materials shall conform to and comply with the American National HazMat Standards, and Federal Hazardous Chemical--"

"Yeah, yeah. I know what I signed." Paul tossed the file onto the top of his attorney's briefcase. "Is there anything else you want to kick me in the nuts about before I leave this morning?"

The lawyer took off his glasses and massaged the bridge of his nose. "Just the India thing."

Paul sighed.

"It's not just this government that's hypersensitive, but the entire international community. Industrial carcinogens are turning into a hot button issue."

The cab exited the Brooklyn Queens Expressway onto Grand Central Parkway. "That's exactly *why* we built the plant in India. They've got so many issues, they're just happy to have work." Paul suddenly noticed the brown rectangle of the driver's face in the rearview mirror—his black eyes glaring back at him. He leaned toward Nathan and in a lowered voice continued, "Besides, neither the Philippines nor South America would have worked for us. We didn't just need the cheap labor, we had to have access to a good rail system."

The attorney was quick to the counterpoint. "Not to mention, almost zero environmental regulations, lax enforcement, and plenty of graft when we need a workaround. I should really go with you to the hearings."

The cab pulled to a jerky stop at the departures curb.

"Once this deal is in place it will all be academic anyway." Paul patted the top of the attorney's briefcase. "Just find out when either of the buyers will be ready to move. I'll be staying at the Georgetown Hilton; give me a call when you hear back."

The man tried his best to offer a confident smile. "Whatever you say, boss."

"Pay the man, will you? I've got a plane to catch." Paul jumped out and took his suitcase from the open trunk. "It'll be fine; you just worry yourself too much."

"I thought that's what you pay me for." The attorney closed the door and the cab took him back into the city.

The 1-hour and 20-minute flight to DC was a flash. Paul barely had enough time to order his Bloody Mary before being told to fasten his seatbelt and dump his plastic cup of ice.

It was the first in a series of Senate subcommittee hearings into the illegal procurement of government contracts. Paul checked his watch to see that he still had plenty of time.

He sprayed a generous dousing of the *Dry Look* onto his hair and pressed a hand over the double-breasted buttons of his blue suit. The red, white and blue *'power tie'* was a nice touch, he thought. But his attorney's words gnawed at him. The noose was getting tighter, and a bleak future for Bind-Chem was beginning to come into view. Paul would have to sell the company and get out of the business altogether if he were to avoid government penalties. Or in a worse case, he would be involved in a protracted legal battle and possibly even go to jail.

The testimony today would be his 'Swan Song,' Paul decided. He would provide the subcommittee with all the assurances they wanted to hear, though not a word of it would be the truth. They would believe him of course, because they and their colleagues had voted to give Bind-Chem the government contracts. By implicating Paul, they would essentially be implicating themselves.

Paul believed that as long as he and his company stayed under the radar, he was golden. In the unlikely chance that things went badly however, Paul needed some kind of insurance. He realized the complicity of a couple of senators was not enough. And Paul knew the Washington heavyweights always had a way of hanging the blame on someone else. He needed more protection—a way to move in and out of the country freely, without being tracked.

In the meantime, Paul had lined up two interested parties—both potential buyers for Bind-Chem, and both foreign owned.

Paul's hotel phone rang and it was his attorney. "Give me some good news," Paul answered.

"Wish I could." The man let out a lawyerly sigh. "Neither buyer will be able to put together a deal for at least a year."

Paul cursed into the phone. "I can't wait a year. What about Börse Einsatz? I thought Hoffmann's people were onboard."

"Well, yes, the German's are cash-ready, but they have multiple financial backers. These people are punctilious."

"What the shit does that mean?" Paul looked at the phone as if he could see through it. "Stop talking like an attorney."

"They're anal as hell, Paul. The investors all have their own accountants, and they all want to go over the books with a fine tooth."

"What happened with the Ottawa Group? I thought they were chomping at the bit."

His counselor cleared his throat. "They have issues, too. Canada didn't sign the GATT agreement."

Paul was silent except for a sigh, and the attorney took it to mean he was losing patience.

"The General Agreement on Tariffs and Trade," Nathan quickly explained. "It was signed into effect by the WTO in Geneva three months ago and the Canadians were one of only 14 countries that refused to sign."

"Why? What does that mean to us?"

"Their reluctance to sign had something to do with an agricultural commodities exception in the agreement."

Paul snapped. "Bind-Chem doesn't produce or use agricultural goods in our facilities!"

"I know that, Paul. They know that, too." The attorney paused a beat to let Paul settle down. "Ottawa Investment Group just needs time to determine the GATT agreement's impact on the sale. That's all, Paul. Between them and Hoffmann's people, it'll happen. We just have to be patient."

The message light on the hotel phone was blinking. "Somebody else is calling me. I'll have to get back to you later."

* * *

The invitation was addressed to LJ and guest, but there was nobody at the present time he cared to bring.

The windows were down on his new Buick Lesabre as he headed onto I-55 toward Darien. The mostly Latino Pilsen neighborhood passed by just across the river, looking like a gigantic flea market on this scorcher of a day. LJ had paid extra for the model with air conditioning, a feature he had been excited to show his mother, but he was reluctant to turn it on now for fear of lowered gas mileage and the possibility it might overheat the engine.

Parking on the far end of the lot, away from the cart path and safe from door dings, LJ grabbed the gift-wrapped sugar and creamer set and headed into the country club.

The air inside was a cool and refreshing change from outside. LJ thought about taking off his sport coat, but he knew the short walk from the parking lot had turned the shirt beneath into a mottled mess. He set the gift onto the gift table, and as he turned to sign the guest book, they stood face-to-face. Each more surprised than the other, and too late to pretend they hadn't seen one another.

"Abby . . . hi."

"Loring." Abigail smiled warmly. Her hair was shorter and maybe a little lighter than he remembered; it looked good against her tanned skin and bright, smiling eyes. "How are you?"

"Good, real good." LJ couldn't help eyeing her pink summer dress, long legs and platform sandals. She had grown into herself, a real woman with her own look. And there was something else. It took a second to define it—self-confidence. "You're different," he said. "In a good way, I mean. You look great."

Abby grinned, enjoying for the moment watching LJ stumble over his own words. "So what are *you* up to these days?"

"Not much, really." He stepped around a lady who was waiting to sign the guest book. "Investing, mostly," *he lied*. "And you? Probably married by now with a houseful of kids, huh?"

Abby reached past him to set her wedding gift on the table. "I'm downtown now." She intentionally ignored the crux of his question. "Bought a condo in the Wells Street Towers. Great view of the river."

LJ nodded. "Good investment, condominiums." He was familiar enough with the place to know she couldn't have afforded it on a pet shop manager's salary. Though he wanted to delve deeper, LJ tried to appear only politely interested. Besides, he had heard that his brother had purchased a loft in a downtown building close to the Towers, and he didn't even want to think about that topic.

"How's your mom?" Abby was making small talk now. She accepted a glass of champagne from a waiter with a tray of them, handing it to LJ and then taking another for herself.

"She's doing okay." LJ didn't want to get into all her medical issues. He still lived in the basement of his uncle's home and wasn't about to admit that to Abby.

Though he would have liked to move into his own place, his mother's forgetfulness was getting to be problematic. The state had finally revoked her driver's license, and she now depended on LJ to get to and from her appointments. Uncle Stuart wasn't in the best of health either, and LJ had taken on helping him around the aging family home.

"And Paul? How's he doing?"

LJ couldn't believe she had actually brought *him* up. *What in the hell was she thinking?* He wanted to tell Abby that because of her, he and Paul hadn't spoken in 5 years. That for all he knew, she and Paul might be living together, or even married. Then it occurred to LJ that Abby might have even asked the question just to throw him off, pretend she hasn't been in touch with Paul in all this time.

LJ callously shrugged his answer. "Don't hear much from Paul these days. Couldn't really care less, anyway."

They ended up sitting together at a table near a large wall of windows. After a couple of more flutes of champagne, LJ and Abby settled into a looser exchange, one with a few restorative laughs that hinted at what they once felt.

Eventually, LJ opened up about his mom. He came clean about his living arrangement and told Abby about his mother's dementia. His aunt Peg had also broken her hip in a fall and was now in an assisted living facility in Schaumburg. LJ confided that he was considering moving his mother there as well. Abby on the other hand, revealed that she had lost her father to cancer.

"What about grad school?" Abby asked.

Paul shook his head. "Had to stop learning and start working. I'm actually an accountant for a financial advisor firm."

As evening approached and the drinks had numbed years of restraint, the two left the reception and strolled along the fairways of Carriage Greens. They held hands and talked about old times working together at the pet shop. Abby had gone back to school after leaving her job there and was now working as a secretary at a law firm in the city. She admitted to LJ that she lived in her condo alone and had never gotten married. LJ was surprised at how relieved he was to hear that.

They both avoided any further talk about Paul. As a result, the conversation stayed light and easy. When they stepped back inside, the reception was in full swing. LJ asked Abby if she wanted to dance, and they headed onto the dance floor—just as the 5-piece band began playing the hit song by Peaches and Herb, *Reunited*.

It felt good to hold Abby again. LJ's promise to himself never to care about her again started to dissolve into regret as they pressed into one another. The lyrics seemed prophetic, and LJ wondered if their meeting like this was destiny. Some sort of message, perhaps.

The scene on the Michigan campus the weekend of LJ's graduation had hurt Abby and had forced her to separate herself from him. Time and maturity had dulled the pain however, and it was now difficult to find the same resolve she felt that day. After all these years, dancing with LJ and feeling her head resting against his strong chest, Abby could barely recall the particulars. Her mind was clouded with memories, emotion, and champagne, and she knew this was not the time to make any decisions, either encouraging or discouraging. For now, she simply wanted to enjoy the moment.

SADHANA

Somewhere during the evening, LJ made a decision. He wasn't going to let this wedding of a mutual friend, this serendipitous event, catapult he and Abby back into love. Abby was equally as guarded, and refused to allow a spark to ignite feelings that had been extinguished so many years ago.

But neither of them realized how life enjoyed mocking those most self-assured.

"Are you okay to drive?" LJ asked Abby, as they walked out to the parking lot after the reception. She had parked a few stalls away from him. "Wow, I don't believe it," he said, circling around her car. "A '79 Mustang convertible." LJ looked back at her, trying to find the young girl who he once worked with.

She flipped her hair blithely and raised her eyebrows. "A lot has changed about me in the last five years," her playful but sluggish words running together.

LJ's head buzzed as he watched Abby flop down behind the Mustang's wheel. "Slide over," he said. "You're in no condition to drive."

Abby laughed. "And you are?"

LJ nuzzled her into the passenger's side and started her car. Abby reclined contently against the headrest with her eyes closed. A few minutes later they were stopped and the engine was silent.

"Where are we?" Abby looked around, trying to focus her eyes. "The Holiday Inn." She grinned at LJ. "Aren't you the sly dog. Get a girl sloshed and then make your move."

LJ rolled his eyes and laughed. "We'll get separate rooms if you like. It's just that neither one of us should be on the road tonight."

Abby smirked. "Oh, is that the reason you brought me here?"

LJ registered at the front desk while Abby sat in the lobby. She used the time to sharpen her mind, but all she could do was chuckle at the irony of the situation. She led LJ up the stairs, during which he stared at how the pink dress clung to her shapely butt. He couldn't figure out if the sway in Abby's step was intentional or a result of the drinks—not that it really mattered.

"I know we've both had a lot to drink," LJ said, slipping the key into the door. "Like I said, we could get two separate--"

"No that's fine," Abby said. "Save your money. But I better warn you; I didn't think to bring my pajamas. Hope that's okay."

LJ eased the door closed behind them.

Abby awoke to find LJ watching her from only inches away. They had fallen asleep entwined in one another—his arm wrapped beneath her shoulder and her head resting on his chest.

"How long have you been looking at me?"

LJ kissed her on the forehead. "Just a little bit. Do you feel okay?"

"Other than my pounding headache?"

"You know what I mean." LJ adjusted himself so he could see her eyes. "About what we did. You feeling any regrets?"

"Not yet." Abby smiled lightly. "You?"

LJ shook his head. He smiled back, but behind it was the nagging question of whether she and Paul had ever known each other in the same way. It was still the single obstacle blocking his path back to her. He wondered if it always would be, or if he was capable of having enough faith in Abby to move past it.

She reached up and cradled his face, as if somehow sensing the rival emotions grappling for position inside him. "You don't have to worry, LJ," Abby stared into his eyes. "I wouldn't lie to you."

They both understood the sub-context without Abby having to actually say Paul's name. He settled back into the pillow and they enjoyed the pleasure of one another again—this time more clearly and with more intensity. Their passion was a full surrender of emotion denounced, denied and bridled for years.

LJ gazed out at the trees as Abby drove him back to his car. The neighborhoods bordering the golf course were expansive and beautifully landscaped, shaded beneath towering oaks. One gated home after another passed as he imagined settling down with Abby and raising a family in one of them. So many good years had been wasted, he thought.

The Mustang pulled into the parking area next to the clubhouse. Abby stopped abruptly when she saw LJ's car, a disheartened gasp escaping her lips. LJ sat up and followed her line of sight to the far end of the lot. A sledgehammer of bad memories crushed his gut, rendering him weak and incapable of saying anything.

Paul stood there, leaning against the driver's door, arms folded across his chest and a face devoid of expression. His glassy, lifeless eyes stared back at LJ, who threw open the car door and slowly stepped out. They stood staring at one another across the lot.

Abby grasped the wheel; unsure of what was happening between the twins, and of what part she played. Was this some new hostility, or was it ongoing bloodshed from a war that has never ended?

SADHANA

LJ clenched his teeth as Paul eased himself off of the car and stepped toward them. LJ looked back at Abby, and for a second his eyes locked on hers in silent scrutiny. His expression begged Abby for an answer—some explanation as to what was going on.

She looked back at Paul and his eyes pleaded for the same answer.

Thirteen

A decision was made at some point to hire a private investigator—a man named Curtis Tam. The Hong Kong detective had done work in the past for Nathan Geerts, the Griffiths family attorney, and had a respected reputation with both sensitive cases and in conducting investigations with international features.

After only a few days, Tam got back to Geerts with an important, yet even more upsetting piece of information. Paul's connecting flight from Helsinki to New Delhi had been cancelled, raising the possibility that Paul had never even made it out of Finland.

Adding credibility to that scenario, the airline had no information that Paul had taken their later flight.

* * *

"Paul Griffiths." He extended his hand to meet Eichler's. "If you're the person in charge, then you're who I need to talk to."

She looked him up and down. "Paul Griffiths? The no-show we *had* on our list of volunteers?"

"Well, yeah." Paul brushed some of the remaining dust from his tunic. "I ran into a few problems. You see, my luggage was--"

"Yes, I see that, Paul." Eichler took the clipboard from one of the young men seated behind the table. "But you've missed all the training. We're shipping out today and we've already reassigned your slot."

"What does that mean?"

Eichler shook her head. "Another volunteer has been assigned to stay with your host family. Somebody who actually showed up and went through the training."

Paul turned his palms up like one of the beggars outside, his mouth hanging partially open. "You can't just leave me here."

"Look," she said, turning to him with little compassion in her eyes. "Not everybody is cut out for this kind of thing. It takes a little bit of commitment, ya know? Like, to a cause? Anyway, we're on a tight schedule here, so if I were you I'd jump on the first flight back to the states."

"That's not an option." Paul lowered his voice suddenly, as if the federal government might be listening in. "I can't go back, is what I'm trying to tell you. Even if I had the money, which I don't, I'd be signing my own death warrant. I can't show my face back home."

"I'm sure you're just being overly dramatic."

"No, I'm not. Besides, like I said, I have no money. I'll probably starve if you leave me alone here."

"I seriously doubt that," Eichler said with a chuckle. Then, after a few seconds of deliberation, she looked up from her clipboard. "Tell you what, Mr. Griffiths . . . you can ride in the bus with my group as far as Vrindavan."

"That's it? I don't even know where that is?" Paul leaned to look past her, out through the glass doors and onto the street. "What am I supposed to do then?"

Eichler shrugged. "Look, it's the best I can do. You can either take it or leave it."

"No, no, I'll take it." Paul lifted a submissive hand. "I'll take it."

"Vrindavan is a holy city," she said. "There are lots of ashrams— shelters that help people in your *situation*."

She seemed to get added pleasure in her choice of words. Paul suspected it was because he had come off as some kind of wealthy jerk when they met at the airport. In fact he was certain of it. But who could blame her, he thought. The woman was probably just savoring the comeuppance he deserved for his arrogance. He said nothing.

"Mostly religious retreats." She wrote on the clipboard now, only half attentive to the conversation. "Some of them run by charitable organizations. I'm sure you'll be able to find the help you need."

Paul wanted to apologize for his behavior, to explain that he had never been away from home or without the trappings of his family's money. He wanted to tell her of the people who had helped him, and of what they had meant to him, and to ask her for the same kindness. But he couldn't prostrate himself like that, bearing all in front of a total stranger. Instead, he simply nodded.

"Thank you, Ms. Eichler." Paul gripped her hand between both of his. "I *do* appreciate your giving me a ride. I really do."

The road to Vrindavan was long and hot. Hours and hours of barren land and hazy asphalt punctuated by small, congested towns. The bus stopped after two hours in a place called Mahwa—an intersection of three highways along the main route to the Taj Mahal. A cluster of charter busses huddled around a roadside market, where mostly Europeans bartered for cheap replicas while avoiding dozens of young beggars.

Paul milled around on the shady side of the bus and watched the tourists turn up their noses at the food vendors.

"Reminds me of your *Karelian pie*."

Paul turned back to find Gwyneth Eichler leaning against a tree a few feet away. He gave her a half-smile. "You mean the meal I didn't even bother to try?"

"Exactly." She held out an icy bottle of guava juice. "Thought you could use some energy."

He thanked her several times over, in between breathless gulps of the pulpy sweetness. It felt as if whatever nourishment the drink held was being absorbed into every cell in his body. Eichler smiled as they walked to the door of the bus.

Paul had taken a seat in the very back during the first leg of the journey, mostly because he didn't know any of the other volunteers and partly because of how badly he knew he smelled. Eichler was seated at the front, just behind the driver, where she stood at the trip's onset to welcome the group and make some basic safety and procedural announcements. Now, as Paul stepped back onto the bus, she moved her things and motioned for him to sit on the seat next to her.

"So, Mr. Griffiths . . . explain to me what a privileged guy from the Hamptons is doing in India." Eichler thought about making another crack—something like correcting herself to say, *former* privileged guy, but she saw the worn look on Paul's face and decided better of it. She had already had enough fun with him.

Paul told her about his missing suitcase and broken cell phone, somehow dancing around the specifics of his coerced volunteerism. Then, his eyebrows came together in puzzlement. "Wait, how did you know I live in the Hamptons?"

She thought for a second. "Sheryl told me about you. She's my boss, the foundation's director. I think she said she's good friends with your father, and your mother is a big donor."

"I doubt that. My mom died when I was an infant," he said. "I don't really know much about her. Is that all your boss told you?"

Eichler shrugged. "There was some hush-hush discussion about squeezing you onto the list at the last minute, but I wasn't privy. So what's the deal? You need some brownie points for an employment resume or something?"

Paul glanced around to make sure nobody else was listening. "I got myself into a little trouble back home. Nothing *really* bad, more like a minor misunderstanding. Anyway, I was sort of forced into coming here in order to avoid, well, something worse."

"What a pity." She playfully punched him in the shoulder. "Catch a break and you even managed to screw that up."

Paul tried to smile, but the joke cut too close to the bone. "Listen, Ms. Eichler, I'm going to fix this thing. And I'm going to do it without my father's help . . . I mean, without my uncle's help."

"Gwyn." She looked at him though a lifted eyebrow. "Call me Gwyn. And what the hell are you talking about?"

Paul's hand came up unconsciously, as he dug a finger into the creases of his forehead. "Yeah." The bus stopped and Paul gazed out at a few dozen goats being herded down the middle of the road. "It was just an added little surprise for my trip."

She waited without saying anything, sensing a hurtful tone in his words.

He unzipped his tote bag and slipped the letter out of the book. "Here," he said, handing it to Gwyneth. "Check this out."

She read the note in silence then reread it once before handing it back.

"What do you think?" Paul tucked the letter back into the book.

She gazed out the window for a minute before answering. "I can't say I know who all the players are, but I can see that it's some pretty powerful stuff." Gwyn watched him zip the book back into his bag. "Your mom and dad?"

Paul nodded. "And my uncle, who I thought was my dad."

She could see the anguish in his eyes. Her surprise at Paul's candor was transcended only by her amazement that she actually felt bad for the guy. "You mean, not only don't you know about your mom, but you're not even sure who your dad is?"

Paul said nothing.

"That'd drive me nuts." She shook her head. "I'd have to get to the bottom of that, like, yesterday."

"Not much I can do from India," he said. "Just found this out when I got here."

It was late in the day when the bus stopped in front of a giant white temple. The black gates were closed, but Indians crowded for position, their faces pressed between the metal bars, looking in at the place. The orange rays of the setting sun glinted off the huge marble tiles surrounding the temple. A lone woman wearing a red saree sat cross-legged in the center of the polished plaza, arms outstretched in prayer.

"That place is the Prem Mandir," Gwyn announced to the group as they gathered their things. "It's the temple of divine love, inaugurated in February 2012. Thousands of devotees of *Jagat Guru Kripaluji Maharaj* carried water from the holy river, Yamuna, to cleanse the temple and make it pure."

"Are we staying there?" someone asked from the back of the bus.

Gwyn laughed. "Not quite. Our lodgings are less imposing, but I'm sure you'll all get a lot out of the experience. I'm getting out here, and the rest of you will be driven to your host residences here and there around the city. We'll be meeting up again at the medical clinic in the morning; you each have a map of the city, with directions to the clinic."

The driver climbed onto the roof and took her suitcase down from a rack above the bus. Gwyn motioned to Paul to follow her out as she stepped onto the muddy road.

"If you walk further up about a quarter mile," she said, indicating with her chin, "you'll see an alleyway off to the left." Gwyn slung her pink carry-on over one shoulder, and then set her suitcase upright on its wheels just out of the mud. "Turn down the alley and you'll see the Krishna Balaram Temple. Keep walking to the end of the road and you'll run into the ashram." She touched a forefinger to her head in a mock salute. "Good luck, Paul."

"Wait!" He sounded like a child on the first day of kindergarten. "Where are *you* going to be?"

"I'm headquartered right here at the health care building," she said.

Paul scanned across the street to a gated stone archway. Behind it sat a temple-like façade of pinkish masonry. Though it was obviously intended to look like a place of worship, a more modern building of metal and glass stretched out behind it in odd disharmony. "Asha Heath Care and Research Centre," Paul read the lighted sign on the archway. "What will you be doing there?"

SADHANA

"The Vrindavan volunteers work primarily out of the Asha complex," she said. "I coordinate their housing, transportation, and their integration within the health care outreach programs. I'm only here for a couple of months, just to get everyone started, then I go back to New York."

He gazed listlessly at the building. "Isn't there any way I can work with you guys?"

She shook her head. "You're going to have your hands full just trying to get back on your feet." The bus pulled away, leaving her barely visible through a haze of dust. Gwyn called over her shoulder as she started across the road. "Check in with me in a week or so to let me know how you're doing."

A guard at the gate greeted her warmly, as if she held a position of some importance. She waved back at Paul as the guard lifted the crossing arm under the archway, then she rolled her suitcase up the walk and into the building.

Paul started in the direction Gwyn had indicated. Darkness was fast approaching, and hunger thrashed inside him. He felt defeated, as if he had been cruelly abandoned.

Pausing to eye a fruit cart off to his left, Paul gaped at a pile of brown bananas mulching beneath a cluster of circling flies. He stood there, facing toward what he thought was oncoming traffic, as he ogled at the fruit. A sharp horn blast from a flatbed truck quickly reminded him that vehicles traveled on the left in this country. He veered further over, away from the road, and stepped into a mucky puddle that smelled of urine. Paul shook his foot and continued on in a kind of limp, trying to keep the sludge from spattering onto his other leg. Then, feeling a little foolish, he wondered why it even mattered. His clothes were already covered in dirt and soot, and he smelled like a cesspool.

The man behind the cart, whom Paul hadn't even noticed, suddenly spoke. "A green stem on a rotten banana hardly makes a difference."

Paul acknowledged him with a simper then continued on in the paling light.

The roadsides became more congested the further Paul went; yet nobody else paid the slightest attention to him. He weaved his way through the crowds, taking in the exhilarating smell of food cooking on oiled grills. There were flowers, incense, savory spices, sweet fruits, mottled with briny waves of body odor and the stench of human waste.

At a corner where several rickshaw drivers rested beneath a tree, Paul turned into the alleyway—the one Gwyn had told him of. It was narrow—barely the width of a car—and unevenly paved with brick. Several monkeys were perched on top of a high wall on one side of the road. On the other side were smaller structures, doorways and a low cement block wall. An open sewage canal ran along the right side, several inches from the back of a temple.

Paul edged around a cow at the far end of the road, noticing the temple's entrance, monitored by two armed guards. They were posted on either side of an open gate, and people seemed to move freely in and out of the building. An old man shuffled past them, removing his thin black shoes and placing them on a wooden rack overflowing with identical pairs. Then the man went inside the temple, apparently unconcerned as to whether someone might take his shoes by mistake or whether he might end up wearing someone else's home.

A woman squatted in the darkness just beyond the temple entrance, where another even smaller alleyway branched off to the right. She wore a plain white saree, which was the only thing visible— her raven features hidden deep beneath the fabric covering. As Paul passed the smaller alley, he noticed several more women in white, moving in groups of two or three. Their flimsy outlines drifted in ghostlike silence through the dark. The distant sound of chanting hung in the air, but Paul couldn't make out the direction of its origin.

He continued to the end of the alley, where a man in white pajama pants and a blue uniform shirt sat on a plastic chair. His job might have been that of a security guard, though he was armed with nothing but a stick. Paul wondered if he was a doorman. The man bowed and gestured with his palms together. "Hare Krishna."

Paul returned the gesture. "Hare Krishna." Though other than lyrics used in a couple of songs, Paul had no idea what the words actually meant. "Is this the ashram?"

The man repeated the gesture, and Paul did the same. There was no way to know how much the grinning guard understood.

Continuing past him and up the marble steps, Paul saw that the interior was a well-lit lobby. Another man, younger and dressed in a long orange robe, sat behind a counter talking on a cell phone. The young man had long, braided hair and painted markings on his forehead. As Paul stood there waiting, he noticed a framed placard on the wall. It was written in Hindu with the English translation printed beneath it:

SADHANA

Since its inception in 1916, the Ashram has not charged fees because our founder believed it should be accessible to everyone, regardless of income. We continue this practice to maintain an atmosphere of service. The Ashram is supported by generous donations from participants and volunteers who clean, cook, and provide care for the sick and ailing guests.
Our doors are open to all.

"Good evening, sir." The clerk set the phone down. "I am Swami Chalah. Welcome to Bhakti Seva."

Paul indicated toward the placard. "I read your philosophy there on the wall." Suddenly feeling surprised by the choke of emotion, Paul had to pause and swallow. "I'm . . . I guess I'm asking for your help. I'm hungry and I have no place to sleep."

The Swami showed no expression of skepticism or judgment. He simply smiled and dipped his head slightly. "If you can sign your name here, good sir." He turned the registration book toward Paul and handed him a pen.

As Paul wrote his name and his home address, the man tilted his head slightly to view the page. "New York City," he said. "You have traveled a long way."

Paul nodded, and the man spoke again. "Bhakti is the path to salvation through love and devotion." He motioned toward the ashram's name behind him. "Seva simply means service. Our belief in the good of those who stay here, that they will serve others who are in greater need."

"I can cook, or I'll do whatever you want me to do. I'm a very hard worker."

The man's eyes were warm and clearly seasoned with knowledge beyond his years. "Many guests at Bhakti Seva are sick and are on special diets."

Probably eat only Indian food, too, Paul realized.

"This is a special ashram where the sick and aged come," he said. "Many want to be in this holy place at the end of their lives."

"They come here to die?"

The Swami nodded. "Every one of us will die, that is for certain. But not every one of us will have the chance to comfort another, a stranger perhaps, and hold their hand as they pass into death."

Paul said nothing. His mind ruminated on whether he was even strong enough to deal with something like that. He had never actually seen a dead person before. The closest he had come was a couple of years prior, while taking the Long Island Railroad home from college. The train had stuck and killed a vagrant, but the only thing Paul was able to see from the window of his stopped coach were flashing lights of the emergency crews.

"Is that what you need me to do?" Paul asked. "Hold someone's hand?"

The Swami laughed lightly. "We'll discuss all that in the morning." He handed Paul a room key. "You can stay in room #10; it's on the second level, all the way to the back of the building." Then he glanced at the clock. "And we will serve a modest meal in the basement dining room in thirty minutes time."

Paul's room was up the stairs and down a long concrete hallway of narrow doorways spaced only feet apart. The floor was painted deep rust, and one side of the hallway looked out on a small green courtyard below. Above him were several more levels, which had fewer doors and Paul guessed they were to larger accommodations.

He found his room small and stuffy, though there was a locking wood-framed screen door over a hardwood door. The barren space was barely wide enough for a single bed. A light bulb hung from a long brown cord, and there was a brightly colored print on the wall, of a deity with several arms. Paul supposed a common bathroom was somewhere down the hall.

He pushed open a small window at the foot of his bed, and heard the chanting voices again—this time more surely. He still could not make out the genesis of the sounds, yet they were at the same time sweet and sad, with a hallow resonance, as if reflecting off of tile or stone.

The dinner, which was really more like a snack, consisted of vegetable *pulao, khichdi* (a rice and lentils dish) and *lapsi* (cracked wheat cereal with cardamom and sugar). Paul had been one of the first to arrive in the dining area, and it gave him an opportunity to view the other guests. They came in waves, moving slowly, many with the aid of crutches, a walking stick or a caregiver. Paul guzzled a glass of water, not caring whether it was filtered or had come from a bottle. He looked at his bare plate and wondered if he dare get back into line for a second helping.

SADHANA

An elderly man shuffled in, wearing a red windbreaker over his drab cotton *kurta*. It was warm inside the dank dining room, yet the man quivered as if blasted by an arctic wind only he could feel. A younger man about Paul's age gently guided the old man by the elbow. They got their plates and sat at a small table next to Paul. The two men prayed together then the sickly old man ate his meal while his younger companion sat quietly watching.

Others came, frail and alone. Some so weak, so close to death, that their gaunt bodies had begun to reject food. They sipped from cups of chai, clear broth, or warm water. As Paul watched, his thoughts of wangling more food for himself disappeared. He suddenly felt badly—guilty for his gluttonous, self-serving thoughts.

After the meal, Paul cleared his plate. He went to other tables and cleared dishes and cups as well, taking these to the kitchen. Not sure what to do with them, Paul stacked them on the counter next to a plastic tub of tepid water. As he turned to leave, another man joined him—the young man who had been dining with the elderly man near Paul.

The man took up a wiry pad from the counter and began scrubbing the plates with it. "You are American." He spoke softly, as if whispering to someone during church. He dunked a plate into the tub and handed it to Paul.

"Yes," Paul said. "I'm from Long Island, New York."

The man nodded as if he knew of the place. "My name is Praneel."

"Paul." Paul found a piece of cloth and began drying the plate. "You speak English very well."

"I studied it when I attended school." He passed another plate to Paul. "Do you have family?"

Paul wasn't sure how to respond. Until recently, his answer would have been a simple one. "Just my father," he finally said.

Praneel glanced toward the door and nodded again, giving Paul the impression that he was referring to the old man at the table.

"Your father?" Paul asked.

"Yes." Praneel's eyes moistened, but at the same time he smiled with pride. "I have had many teachers, but none who have taught me as much as my father."

A bite of remorse took hold and an image of Loring Sr. emerged in Paul's head. Whether his father or his uncle, Paul had learned as much from the man as any father could tech a son. "It must be hard for him," Paul said. "With the sickness and all."

Praneel stared off. "It's difficult for both of us, but yes, my father is struggling."

The two men finished cleaning. When Paul got back to his room he opened the door and locked the screen door. With the window also open, a mild cross-breeze took the slap out of the heat. A tan rhesus stood on the tiled roof, glaring in at Paul. They watched each other suspiciously, but the monkey stood his ground as if waiting for Paul to toss him something to eat. Paul had nothing to offer.

The music, the voices of what sounded like many women, wasn't the same as earlier. Paul lay there in the darkness of his tiny room, listening. Their chanting sounded more sorrowful. He realized that it might have seemed that way because of the painful throes of nausea he was hearing in the next room. The misery was unimaginable, and it pierced Paul to the core. He wanted to go next-door and help, but he had no skills and knew he was only an awkward American who could not speak the language and did not understand the culture.

Paul's room and bed was a respite from sleeping at the train station or on the treacherous streets, but they came with a heavy price. Hearing the private suffering of a dying person was almost more than Paul could bear. In the morning, Paul lingered in the hallway, trying to figure out whether to knock on the door and ask if the person wanted breakfast or some tea.

Soon the door opened. The old man from the previous night's dinner hobbled out on his walking stick, followed by his son, who had washed dishes with Paul. They nodded as they passed, and Paul felt as if he had been caught peeking through a keyhole.

Dark bags of exhaustion moiled beneath their weary eyes. The two men looked as if it hurt them just to walk. Paul wondered if he was even capable of caring for his own father, or whoever Loring Griffiths was to him, if he were on his deathbed. It was at that moment that Paul realized he had to know the truth about it. He needed to find out who his father was, sooner rather than later.

The next few nights were the same: majestic hymns echoing from somewhere beyond the fence line. The songs seemed a colorful parody of the lifeless virtuoso being performed in the next room.

In the meantime, the Swami with his long, braided hair had approached Paul about his "service" in lieu of paying a tariff while staying at the ashram. "I have seen you help clear the tables at the end of mealtime."

"I have never cleaned dishes before," Paul said.

SADHANA

"You do it well." The man pressed his fingertips together lightly. "But there is work for which I believe you are even better suited."

Paul was eager for his assignment. "Anything you need me to do."

"On the third floor are two dormitories, one for men and the other for women—all of the occupants very ill. And on the other side of the temple there is a small chamber, something like hospice," he said. "It is part of the Bhakti Seva ashram. The infirm lodged there are bedridden and in need of constant care. We bring them to that room when they are in the lap of death and the light of heaven shines upon them."

Paul's face went blank as he tried to imagine the kind of care these patients required. "What would I have to do?"

"Feed and bathe them," he said. "Sometimes just sit with them or read to them."

"But I don't even speak the lang--"

"None of that matters." The man closed his eyes and paused. "It is companionship and comforting they need."

"I'm not sure I can deal with death." Paul sounded panicky and immature, even to his own ear. "Why don't these people go to a hospital? Why don't they just get some medicines to help them?"

Swami Chalah offered a knowing nod of his head. "These people do not fear death, they embrace it as part of life. Taking medicines to prolong the process is like adding rungs to a ten-foot ladder. In the end, it is still only ten feet.

"I've never . . ." Paul hung his head. "I can't do it."

Swami gently kneaded Paul's shoulder with the palm of his hand. "A man cannot give more than he is able to give."

Paul took in a breath and straightened himself back up.

"Likewise," Swami continued, "a man does not truly know how much he can give until he gives it."

That night was particularly difficult. Carried on the heavy, stagnate air were sounds of the old man in the next room getting sicker. Forgoing further attempts to sleep, Paul sat near the open window at the bottom of his bed. The gentle melody from the unknown chorus hung in the night, and for a time transcend the misery next door. But around 3 a.m. Paul heard them leave the room, slowly and with the help of someone, possibly Swami Chalah. Paul presumed the old man was in the final stages of his illness—the last rung of his ladder—and they were probably headed to the hospice room on the other side of the temple.

Paul wanted to go outside and help the man. He bit down hard and tensed his muscles, willing himself to be strong and to give something beyond his own comfort. Paul knew that this time his family's wealth didn't matter. It meant nothing to the dying old man and his son. It couldn't fix their problems, and it certainly couldn't buy Paul out of this. He turned on the dangling light and took the book from his small tote bag.

Under the dim glow of the bulb, Paul opened the book at random. He challenged himself to apply the message to his situation and follow the writings as best he was able. Paul had turned to a parable called *The Mustard Seed*.

> *A young woman was married and gave birth to a son. Just after his first birthday, the boy took ill and died. The distraught mother carried him from house to house looking for medicine to make the boy well again. She was told to go to the Buddha, and that he would give her the medicine she sought. The grieving mother found the Buddha and told him of her plight. He said, "All I need to make the boy well is mustard seed from a house that has seen no death."*
>
> *The woman rushed out to obtain the seed he needed. Surely, she thought, such a common spice will be easy to find. But at each house that provided her mustard seed, the occupant told her that the living are few and the dead are many. Each had suffered the death of a son, daughter, spouse or parent.*
>
> *Returning to the Buddha, she was asked if she acquired the mustard seed. The woman told the Buddha that each home had experienced death and there was no mustard seed to be had. It was then that the Buddha told the woman of the impermanence of all things, until her doubt was cleared away. She finally accepted her lot and accepted the boy's death.*

Paul shook his head in frustration. Sure, the subject matter of the parable seemed like an uncanny coincidence, but after reading it a second time Paul concluded that the story was lame and unrealistic. *Mustard seeds, Buddhas . . . how does any of this help me?*

Sadhana

He flipped back to the front of the book. Until now Paul had picked pages at random. The first chapter was called *Sadhana*. Paul read that its meaning had to do with a spiritual path toward self-realization. Sadhana, it said, is a discipline undertaken each day in pursuit of a goal. According to the book, the practice can be successful in guarding one's self against lust, anger, egoism and selfishness. He read aloud, "Sadhana is the path to overcoming life's obstacles."

A discipline, Paul thought, undertaken each day in pursuit of a goal. That's me, trying to find something to eat or drink ever since I've been in this screwed up country. As he stuffed the book back into his tote bag, Paul noticed the candle he had bought from the legless man at the airport. It crossed his mind that the damn thing was probably cursed; after all, it was soon after he bought the candle that Paul's luggage was stolen and all his problems began.

He turned out the light and lay on the bed, allowing the chanting to mesmerize him. It was the middle of the night, and women somewhere were singing—or was it a recording piped over a loudspeaker?

Either way, sleep did not come. The tiny room felt as if it were closing in on Paul. He tossed and turned as he thought about the poor old man from the next room. It made him reflect on his own father, uncle, or whoever Loring was. Regardless, the man had been a loving role model who had given Paul everything he could. Paul wondered why he had wasted so much effort feeling anger toward him. His resentment used to be so clear, so easy to identify. Now he couldn't even put a finger on it—like the depressing mood leftover from a dream that you can't actually remember.

He sat up abruptly. Feeling for his tote bag in the dark, Paul took out the candle and a book of matches and set them on the windowsill.

"Sadhana is the path to overcoming life's obstacles, huh?" Paul sat there, alone in the dark, thinking about his *life's obstacles*. It was a conversation he had never had with himself. Nothing had ever compelled him to. His privileged life had made it unnecessary and his ego would never have allowed it. But somehow now, stripped of his wealth and his identity, Paul could no longer mislead himself and hide behind a veil of prestige. Here he had no standing, no stature to fall back upon. In India a man's worth is measured only by his character. Nothing more.

Paul knelt before the windowsill and lit the candle. He watched its flame flicker in the tiniest breath of air, carrying upon it a delicate melody. This would be the first night of his Sadhana.

He bowed his head and thought of the things in his life that were important to him: his lineage, and finding out who he was—who his parents were, his capacity to serve and his capacity to be strong in the face of death. Paul also realized his goal was to be kind. To be nothing like he was back in New York, but an honest man, with heartfelt kindness toward others. Paul knew he had become a shallow person— judgmental and focused on superficial things.

"I practice this Sadhana with the intention of living an honest, ethical life, and to reach enlightenment through offering myself as a servant to others."

Paul blew out the candle and the room went dark again. A weak gust of air funneled through the tiny window, cooling him and causing the flimsy curtains to flutter. He got up and slipped into his sandals. Paul walked out into the early morning air, knowing that caring for the old man would be his greatest test.

Across the courtyard and a few steps down, the walkway led to an open hall. It reminded Paul of the parish house at St. Luke's, where he had spent many a Sunday morning. Unlike the church bingo games, the first thing Paul noticed here was the smell: a rotting odor that reeked of despair, only partially masked by burning incense. The lights were low and the tiny room was a sanctum of flowers, shrines and images of exotic gods.

A woman cloaked in what looked like a white bed sheet, gently sponged the head of a patient. Another man, possibly a doctor, stood next to her. Glancing around, Paul saw that the two other beds in the room were empty and had been pushed against the wall. It was a crowded little space, dark and quiet, nothing like the American-style hospice Paul had imagined.

"Please help me," the woman in white pleaded in a frail voice.

Paul glanced around to see who else was there to assist. There was no one. The man beside her stood helpless—clearly now, not a doctor. Reticently, Paul stepped over to help.

"He's having difficulty breathing." Her tattered saree was tucked across her face, exposing only deep almond-shaped eyes. They flashed with urgency.

Looking past the woman, Paul suddenly stopped. He recognized both the man standing next to her and the patient dying on the bed. They were from the room next door. Only it was the old man who stood beside the woman, and it was the younger man, Praneel, who lay dying before them.

Fourteen

"What's he doing here?" LJ leaned into the car—his eyes searching Abby's for a logical explanation for how Paul was able to find them. A logical reason as to why Paul would even come looking for them in the first place.

"I don't know what you're thinking, Loring." Abby's words were unconvincing. In reality, she knew exactly what he was thinking. "But whatever it is, you're wrong. This isn't what it looks like."

Where have I heard that line before? The words were on LJ's face, though he restrained himself from asking the chafing question.

Paul stepped toward them, his eyes fixed on Abby's. It wasn't until he got to the front of her car that he stopped and turned his attention to the brother he hadn't spoken to in five years. "It's Mom," he said in a tone bereft of expression. "She was taken to the hospital yesterday afternoon. She's in a coma."

LJ took an unconscious step backward, steadying himself against the open door. Paul watched him, but said nothing more. It was several awkward seconds before LJ was able to focus his mind back to the *here and now.*

"How?" he said. "What happened?"

"They think it's a stroke." Paul cocked his head around the glare of the windshield to better view Abby. Then with a slight smirk, looked back at his brother. "Uncle Stuart called me last night when he couldn't find you."

"We were . . . I was at a wedding."

"So I see." Paul glanced into Abby's car again. "Anyway, while I was at the house I checked your room and found the invitation. Since you never made it home from *the wedding* . . . I mean, I figured you'd want to know about the stroke, what with her being your mother and all."

LJ's eyes narrowed at the blistering jab. If Paul was looking for thanks, he wasn't going to get it. "Okay, after years of nothing you suddenly swing back into the picture to save the day, you ransack my room, and show up here. So fine, you passed on the message. Is there anything else?"

Paul stared back at LJ, perhaps for the first time really sensing the depth of LJ's contempt for him. He glanced at Abby. She probably hates me just as much, he thought. A smoldering ache bore deep into him—a white-hot iron that had branded his heart since that first year LJ was away at college. Like many times before, Paul repelled his emotions with a bitter show of indifference.

He strode past LJ with the regard one would give a parking attendant. Then, as he came even with the open car door, Paul spoke without actually stopping. "Abigail," he nodded a side-glance as he continued past. "You're looking well."

A minute after Paul disappeared around the building, a black Lincoln Town Car pulled onto Carriage Green Drive toward the interstate. A man with a hat was driving, and LJ thought he could see Paul glancing out at him from the back seat.

"Oh my God, Loring." Abby got out and hugged LJ. "I'm so sorry about your mom. You'd better get back to the city."

They talked for a few minutes before getting into separate cars, never bringing up Paul or the suspicions his unexpected presence had awakened in LJ. It seemed that avoiding the mere mention of his brother had become status quo for most conversations between LJ and Abby. If there was more to Paul's surprise visit, LJ couldn't know for sure—Abby would never admit it and LJ had promised himself he would never ask her about Paul again. Especially after last night.

As he drove to the hospital, LJ's heart ached for his mother. He felt smothered under the guilt of not having been there for her when she needed him. And Paul, of all people, had to be the one who showed up. The son-of-a-bitch who never lifted a finger for anyone but himself. The one who had poisoned his relationship with Abby, had robbed them of years together. Then LJ thought of how Abby had felt in his arms, the comfort of her body and the soothing sound of her voice.

The seesaw emotions of his mother and Abby gripped LJ's heart, making him feel dizzy. But through the darkness of his anguish came the light that he would now have Abby to help him through anything that happened in his life.

SADHANA

As Paul's driver headed into the city, Paul leaned back and thought about his mother. He had barely kept in touch—spoke with her every couple of weeks on the phone, but hadn't taken the time to visit in over a year. He had the dark presage that it was too late now.

Abby suddenly flashed into Paul's mind, staring at him from inside the car. He had fumbled that relationship as well, clumsily missing opportunities to tell her how he felt and never doing the right things to show her. Sure, Lore had fallen for her first, but they had broken up. Paul tried to rationalize in his mind, as if he had no hand in their separation. He ultimately conceded that whatever he *should* have done or *could* have done to win Abby's attention, he never did. Whatever the case, it was clear that it was now too late for that as well.

He had to refocus. Paul was in the middle of a chess match against the U.S. government and knew he had to play each move using every advantage at his disposal.

Paul glanced at LJ's invitation on the vinyl seat next to him—the fancy scroll of the words inviting LJ and a guest to the wedding. Paul slid it aside, and then he reached beneath it to the more important of the belongings he had taken from LJ's bedroom. Fanning the pages of the small blue booklet like a deck of cards, Paul stopped on the first page. His twin brother had aged a little better than he had, but not enough to arouse anyone's suspicion. The 2-inch square photograph was close enough to be a dead ringer.

As he mulled over his plan, Paul slipped LJ's passport into his breast pocket. He wondered if his brother would notice that it was missing. But Paul had planned for that contingency as well.

Patricia Ruth Griffiths' graveside service was held at Chicago's Rosehill Cemetery six weeks later. She had never regained consciousness, and over the course of the days that followed the stroke, she had declined steadily. It wasn't her wish to be buried in Chicago, but Uncle Stuart had insisted. He had worked with one of the gardening and irrigation specialists at Rosehill, and thought he could acquire the plot at a discount.

The burial itself evoked only a small collection of family and friends. Aunt Peg, though confined to a wheelchair, was guided in by one of Sally's twin daughters. The other twin was there with her boyfriend, a cab driver who also played base guitar in a rock band. And one of their mother's former co-workers had driven out from Cicero to pay her respects.

Their old boss from the bakery had sent a card from Florida, featuring a watercolor image of a bird flying into the sunset over the top of a palm tree. Another friend sent a wreath of flowers, which was propped up next to white roses that LJ had ordered. There were only the two flower arrangements. The whole affair seemed odd, and LJ didn't feel that it was really much of a final tribute.

He sat next to Abby on folding camp chairs that were arranged in a semi-circle around the burial plot. LJ's dark suit and tie were nicely pressed, and he held hands with Abby throughout the service. Paul stood across from them in black slacks, a two-toned gabardine shirt and dark sunglasses. LJ thought his brother looked like he was late for a bowling tournament. Neither of them spoke.

Back at the house, neighbors who barely knew the deceased flocked through the door, bearing an assortment of casseroles, bean dips and potato salads. Cousin Sally had arranged for catered sandwiches along with another huge bucket of potato salad. A large plastic thing, resembling a roulette wheel with carrots and celery and tomatoes, sat in the middle of the table. The center of the wheel held a dish of ranch dressing. Next to the table someone had placed an old photograph of their mother on an easel. LJ paused at the picture, thinking about the difficult life his mother had led.

Paul, meanwhile, slipped away as the others were busy talking and eating. He descended the stairway into the basement room he used to share with his brother. When he was certain he was alone, Paul slid a plastic bin out from beneath the bed. Inside it he found a large, clasped accordion file containing LJ's important papers. It was the same file from which he had stolen LJ's passport the night his mother had the stroke. Paul slipped his own passport out of his pocket and placed it into the file, then back into the bin.

After all, Paul wasn't about to use his real passport now, knowing that it would leave a paper trail for the federal government. And in the unlikely event that LJ opened the bin for something, or even for the file itself, he'd see a passport that he would assume was his own.

A whispering voice from the top of the stairs suddenly startled Paul. As footsteps began down the steps, he quickly put the lid onto the plastic container and slid it back under the bed. Rolling onto his back, he folded his arms behind his head as if it were his own room. Paul recognized Abby's voice right away, and assumed that she and LJ were coming down the stairs. He expected the two of them to come around the corner at any moment, at which time he would act cool and aloof.

Paul knew that would anger LJ as much or more than finding Paul in his room. Or, Paul thought, he could pretend to be asleep, tired after a late night out. Paul realized that either way, it would irritate LJ to no end and give Paul the opportunity he was looking for to interact with Abby—even if it was just to say hello. Although he doubted she would have anything nice to say back.

But the footsteps ceased as abruptly as they started. Paul froze in place, straining to hear if they were still in the stairwell. After a tense silence, the hushed conversation resumed. As Paul listened, he realized Abby was alone. She had taken the wall phone from the kitchen, and stretching the cord into the stairway, she was now whispering into the receiver.

"I know it's only been a couple of days," she said. "How much time does the lab take? I mean, when can the doctor give me a definite answer?"

She must have been put on hold, because Paul couldn't hear anything for several minutes. His heart raced at the thought that Abby might be seriously sick. He also wondered if LJ knew of her illness.

Her mumbled voice started up again, and Paul strained to make out the words. It sounded like she was talking with the doctor now.

" . . . Are you sure?" Abby's voice was quivering. "You're certain it was positive?" Abby was sniffing, and it sounded to Paul as if she might be crying. "Yes, I've missed two periods. I'm usually like clockwork."

Paul's eyes widened at the implications of the conversation. He couldn't believe what he was hearing. Dozens of conflicting thoughts flooded his head, along with the sound of his blood pulsing loudly in his ears. *This can't be happening.*

"No," said Abby. "The father doesn't know yet."

If what he was hearing was what it sounded like, brother LJ had finally slipped up—stumbled on the primrose path of righteousness. He wasn't perfect after all. That is, Paul thought, if Abby *is* actually pregnant, and if Lore is in fact the father.

He listened as Abby cracked open the door at the top of the steps and reached into the kitchen to hang up the phone. The door quickly closed again and Paul heard her moving in the stairwell. He listened to see if she was coming down to the bedroom, but she had stopped and taken a seat on one of the steps. Paul listened as Abby sobbed quietly there in the darkness. He battled to restrain his own stampeding emotions and to keep his breathing quiet.

Abby sat alone in the stairway for what seemed like an eternity. Paul was certain that at any moment she would decide to leave her perch and find him there, eavesdropping. Or worse, his brother would find Abby there and Paul hiding nearby. Suddenly, after having listened in on the big news, screwing with Loring's head no longer had the same appeal that it used to.

Seconds turned to minutes and time passed with little more than hushed sniffles from the stairwell. After 35 or 40 minutes, Paul had made up his mind to throw in the towel. He could pretend he had been asleep and didn't hear her phone conversation, or he could drop all the bullshit and act like a normal person. Paul weighed that concept; he could actually apologize to Abby for unintentionally overhearing such a personal conversation. He debated the sincerity of doing that, but as it turned out it didn't matter. Paul heard the door open and Abby tiptoe back into the collection of mourners, closing the door behind her.

Paul took in a deep breath and let it out slowly. He sat at the edge of his brother's bed pressing his face into both hands. "I gotta get the hell outta here."

LJ was busy playing host to the folks who had stuck around to eat, but mostly talk and drink. A funeral always seemed as good an excuse as any for a midday cocktail or two, especially for Uncle Stuart and a few of his neighborhood buddies.

At one point LJ tapped an empty glass and said a few words about his mother. He intended to introduce Abby during his talk, and it was then that he noticed her missing from the group. At first, he thought she had gone outside for some fresh air. Not long after that, LJ realized that Paul was also missing.

Peering out the windows, LJ wasn't able to spot either of them in the front or backyards. He was becoming more concerned as time wore on and neither one of them reappeared. He began to feel the heat rising up beneath a necktie that was suddenly too tight. About the time LJ was ready to completely lose it, Uncle Stuart cornered him at the card table bar they'd set up in the dining room.

He and his war buddies were eager to regale LJ with their exaggerated stories that involved people he didn't even know. The drinks started flowing and LJ was in no mood to resist. He downed a couple of shots in a row. His face tingled, his head buzzed and his mood soured even more.

SADHANA

LJ tuned back into the conversation, a debate about Jane Byrne—Chicago's newly elected, first ever "lady mayor." Uncle Stuart, more outspoken than usual, insisted that woman didn't have a mind for politics, and in fact weren't good for much other than cooking and making babies. It got a hardy laugh from his pals.

Then, in what seemed to be a clumsy afterthought, he assured LJ that his mother would have enjoyed the funeral service.

"Nobody enjoys their own funeral," LJ said. But then he thanked his uncle just the same.

"I'll tell you this," boasted Uncle Stuart, "Patricia is lucky I was able to get her into Rosehill. You know they have veterans of every war buried there, including some from the American Revolution."

LJ had heard the list before. So had his buddies, yet they seemed more willing than LJ to listen to it again.

"Did you know there are twelve Civil War Generals laid to rest at that cemetery?" Uncle Stuart slurped his gin and tonic down to the ice, spitting a wedge of lime back into the plastic cup.

LJ scanned over the heads of the neighbors and boozed old men, now feeling the punch of the third shot he had drunk. He spotted Abby as she emerged from the basement stairway, her eyes watery and her face puffy and red. She avoided eye contact with LJ as she grabbed her coat and purse, and then headed for the door without saying goodbye. He moved to go after her, but Uncle Stuart hooked LJ's arm with a sweaty bear paw.

"And not only that, but four Illinois governors are buried in the ground there, too. Your mother would like that."

"I'm sure she's comforted by that fact." LJ slugged down another burning shot, eyeing the basement door the entire time.

When Paul emerged from the stairwell a few seconds later the burning spread through LJ's entire body, producing a violent eruption.

"You!" LJ screamed across the room. "I ought to kick your ass!"

The air was suddenly sucked from the room as everyone turned to watch, their mouths half open.

Paul glared back at his brother, not as a threat or a challenge, but more in surprise. He saw the half-drunken bottle in front of LJ, and his newfound bravado suddenly made sense. Still, he said nothing.

"How much of your shit am I supposed to take?" LJ brushed Uncle Stuart's hand off him and stepped around the bar. "You've driven a wedge between me and Abby since day-one. You've gone behind my back with her and done . . . who knows what?"

Not much, really. Paul's mind answered LJ's allegations, but he remained silent.

"Every time we start to get close, there you are to screw things up again!" LJ stood wobbling in the living room, his fists balled at his sides. "But this . . . this is the final needle in a . . . the last straw."

"I don't think you really know what you're talking about, Lore." Paul back stepped to the far side of the buffet table. "Besides, I'm thinking that mom's funeral might not be the best time to have this discussion?"

LJ ambled toward Paul, his eyes glazed over and his neck and head pitched forward at an odd angle. "No, asshole. This *is* the best time. It's gonna happen right now!"

A collective gasp arose from the mourners as LJ dove toward his brother, leading with a wild, roundhouse swing.

Paul parried to the side, causing LJ to miss badly. He stumbled forward, sending a bowl of potato salad crashing to the floor.

With both hands outstretched, Paul tried to calm him. "You need to maintain, buddy. How 'bout we just try to mellow out a little?"

"You'd like that wouldn't you?" LJ regained his balance, but stepped into the potato salad in the process and tracked it across the hardwood floor. "Then you could sleep with *my* girlfriend, *again*! Or is that what you two were doing together downstairs?" LJ turned to address the group. "Yeah, didn't Paul tell you? At his own mother's funeral, he went downstairs and got it on with Abby!"

One of the neighbor ladies whispered to another, "Which one is Abby?"

LJ turned back to Paul, his own words having made him even wilder with rage. He reared back again with his fist and made a second dive at his brother. But this time Paul was against the wall and had nowhere to go.

LJ's sloppy swing threw him off balance and his feet slipped out from under him on the potato sheen. His arm smacked the easel on his way down, knocking his mother's photograph onto the floor. The momentum of LJ's clumsy follow-through carried him into the table of food again, this time propelling a green bean casserole into the air—the contents of which landed all over Aunt Peg. LJ ended up on his back, while Aunt Peg sat there stunned in her wheelchair.

"Damn it, boy!" Uncle Stuart swigged down the rest of his drink and rushed across the room to help his bean-covered wife.

SADHANA

Paul bent down to pick up the photograph of his mother, wiped it off, righted the easel and set the picture on it. He carefully stepped over LJ and across the debris field of potato salad, then left without a word to anyone.

Fifteen

Several quiet meetings took place over the next few days, with the elder Griffiths appearing as if his son had gone missing in the war. We later heard that Tam's investigation was beginning to focus on the very real possibility that something had happened to Paul while in Finland.

According to Paul's bank, his credit cards had not been used since his layover at the airport in Helsinki. The investigator was quick to point out that the information was not necessarily negative. His hypothesis was that the lack of activity was a good sign. Typically, a flurry of high-value purchases and cash withdrawals would have been seen if Paul had fallen victim of *"foul-play."* But there was no such credit card activity.

We figured that it was little more than an investigator's theory, speculative at best, yet we all clung to it for hope. Truth was, nobody had the slightest idea where Paul was, or what had happened to him.

* * *

"Please, come and help me." The woman spoke softly from behind a white *chuddar* that covered her face. "He can't breathe."

"Praneel!" Paul stood in shock, looking from the young man on the bed to his father standing beside him. "I, I thought . . ."

His father's red and weeping eyes pleaded.

Paul gathered himself together and moved quickly to Praneel's bedside. "What should I do?"

"Help me turn him on his side," the woman said.

Praneel was ashen. He gasped and then let out a moan as Paul helped the woman roll the young man onto his side. It seemed to relieve some of Praneel's distress, but he continued to wheeze through cracked lips and a mouth caked with silty residue. Praneel gripped Paul's hand as his lungs struggled to take in air.

SADHANA

The woman folded a blanket tightly, like an accordion, and then used it to prop Praneel in that position.

"He's thirsty," Paul said. "He needs something to eat."

The woman left and came back with a small clay bowl filled with water. She handed Paul a piece of cloth. "You can dab the water on his mouth, but his body can no longer tolerate fluids."

Paul's expression was one of bewildered doubt.

"Praneel has been sick for a long time," she said. "He hasn't been able to keep down solid food for two months. It is in this way that a body surrenders to death. We can only try to make him comfortable."

Praneel's father knelt on the floor near his son's head and lit a lantern next to him. The sweet scent of oil hovered in the air above the flickering lamp. In hushed tones, his father hummed some kind of prayer or mantra into Praneel's right ear. "*Aum Namo Narayana*," he repeated over and over.

Together, the woman and Praneel's father rotated the bed so that the head faced east. It was some kind of Hindu practice, which Paul could only watch in fascination.

As Paul sat beside his friend, holding his hand and wiping his lips with a moist rag, he wondered how it happened that this part of life had escaped him for thirty years. He had not experienced real sickness or suffering, and never death. The cloistered environs of Long Island had never permitted it. But here in India, shorn of his nobility and unguarded by wealth, Paul felt the pangs of true anguish and heartache. Unsure of himself, he felt as if he were stepping into a pool of black water and couldn't see the bottom. And even though Paul was now surrounded by death, he felt startlingly alive. It was the first time in his life that he felt relevant. What was happening was real and true.

Paul saw Praneel staring up at him with thankful eyes. He smiled and squeezed Paul's hand. At that moment Paul knew that even though his life may have been insignificant to everybody else, at this place and at this moment, his life had meaning—at least to his dying friend.

Sometime just before dawn, Praneel slipped into a fitful sleep. He began shaking uncontrollably, his eyes rolled back in his head and his mouth and nose oozed mucous. The woman in the white saree rushed over to help. She asked Paul to hold Praneel's arms and body so he wouldn't fall onto the floor. As Paul wrapped Praneel in a bear hug, the woman eased a cotton cloth into Praneel's mouth to keep him from biting his tongue. After several minutes, the spastic motions ceased and slowly Praneel began breathing normally again.

Paul glanced up to see that Praneel's father had closed his eyes and continued whispering the mantra without pause. The Indian woman's chuddar had slipped off her face, exposing it fully for the first time. She appeared to be a few years older than Paul, but then again, he found it difficult to gauge the age of the people here. Regardless, Paul thought her looks surprisingly pleasant and unworthy of being covered by fabric.

Daybreak crept through the shuttered windows, falling like a radiant hand across Praneel's withered body. Paul sat on one side of him while the boy's father stayed crouched near his head. The woman came and went, bringing water and fresh bedding.

Swami Chalah came in sometime during the morning. Paul was holding Praneel's hand, and both he and Praneel had fallen asleep. Paul was in a delusive, fragmented dream state, in which he was still vaguely aware of his surroundings. He imagined possessing mystical powers to heal and bring the dead back to life. Consciousness came back slowly, and he remembered having the same dream when he was a child.

Stirring himself fully awake, Paul opened his eyes to find Swami standing beside him. He was performing a prayer over the sick man, which Paul surmised was the Hindu equivalent of the last rites. At the conclusion Swami smiled knowingly at Paul and placed his hand on Paul's forehead. Paul nodded. It was a silent acknowledgement that the Swami was right: *A man does not truly know how much he can give until he gives it.*

The day grinded on. Even without any training or experience, Paul sensed that Praneel's condition was rapidly growing worse. The Indian woman was gone for several hours, but returned around noon. By then, Praneel's breathing had changed, digressed into short, rattling inhalations through the mouth, followed by long pauses. His skin was devoid of color, save for its ghostly gray hue.

The afternoon receded like a tide over a muddy shoal. All that remained in the room was the shell of a once-healthy man. Paul could tell that the water-soaked rag on Praneel's lips was of little help. The young man had lapsed into a coma and each new breath was an epic struggle. Paul had left only twice: once to use the restroom, and once to drink a glass of water and take in some fresh air.

Daylight had completely disappeared from the sky, yet the air was stale and warm inside the hospice chamber. As Paul sat there holding Praneel's hand, he found his own breathing mirroring his sick friend's.

They had somehow become joined together in an ethereal stage play, in which Paul was supporting actor to the leading character. But it was a dark tragedy in which Paul knew there would be no good ending.

Suddenly, the pause after Praneel's breathing grew long, and then longer still. After a particularly impassive, shuttering exhale, there was no follow-on. Only a lingering silence.

Paul was overwhelmed by emotion. He felt his throat tighten and the sticky trail of tears snaking down his cheeks. Surprised by the sudden sensitivity, he was content that his friend had known little suffering and was free of his pain. Almost immediately, Praneel's father and the Indian woman rotated the bed a quarter turn. Swami Chalah came in with a plain silver chalice and dribbled its contents into Praneel's flaccid mouth.

"What is that?" Paul asked the woman in the white saree.

"*Ganga*. It is the holiest of water, from the Ganges River." The woman studied Paul for a moment. "We have turned him to face south, into the lap of Mother Earth."

The Swami assisted Praneel's father in wrapping a cloth around the top of the corpse's head and tying it beneath his chin. They also wrapped and tied his thumbs together and then did the same with his big toes. Paul watched in rapt fascination.

It was still dark when Paul left. He stepped down to the rutted dirt road in front of the Bhakti Seva ashram, noting for the first time a soft breeze that bellowed his tunic and evaporated the sweat from his torso. Two men in orange cloaks walked arm-in-arm, laughing, toward the temple next door. Paul looked on with a serene acceptance that life goes on. It was a forgiveness of sorts, to a world that Paul used to blame for things that he did not like or understand. But this was different.

"You were a good friend to Praneel."

Paul turned to see the floating image of white fabric emerge from the darkness. She was the woman who had also cared for his friend—a nurse perhaps, working with Swami Chalah to help the sick and dying.

"Thank you." Paul sat down on a wooden cart at the side of the road.

The woman stood off to the side, subordinate, Paul thought, to the moral conventions of her culture. "You are from America?"

"Yes." Paul's answer was ambivalent, lacking the same starch he had arrived in the country with. "I was here to . . ." He was going to continue, but lost his train of thought.

"You are with international health care?"

Paul thought about his answer and shrugged. "I suppose so. I was part of the Children's Relief Foundation group, and--"

"Oh yes, a volunteer worker." The woman inched a step closer. "Such a noble thing."

"Can I ask, what will happen with Praneel's body now? Will his family hold a funeral to bury him?"

"He will be brought home by his father," she said. "A *homa* is performed to bless nine brass *kumbhas* and one clay pot."

Paul's forehead wrinkled as he repeated, " . . . and one clay pot."

"The family, they will wash Praneel's body and dress him in white," she said. "This is when they will rub sesame oil onto his head and place puffed rice into his mouth."

"Whose mouth?" Paul sat straight and turned to face the woman. "Praneel's mouth? He's dead, for Christ sakes."

She took a step back. "It is our custom. This is done with great care and respect, to provide nourishment for the journey ahead."

"Journey ahead," Paul repeated.

"If he is a married man, Praneel's widow will place her *tali*—her wedding pendant—around his neck. This demonstrates her eternal tie to him."

"Are you going to attend the funeral services?"

The woman hesitated. "Only men are permitted at the cremation site."

Paul lifted his eyebrows. For several minutes there was only silence. Then Paul asked, "How did you learn to speak English so well?"

"My father." Then she quickly added, "I must go now."

He lifted his hand in a western-style wave.

The woman ran off down the alley, as if being chased. Paul had no way of knowing that in the Indian culture, his side-to-side hand gesture was a signal to *go away*.

Returning to his room, Paul fell onto his bed, emotionally and physically exhausted. He sat at the window gazing into the alleyway below. There were so many things he needed to sort out, to understand. Paul had to find out who he really was and why he had become the way he was. He needed to learn about his mother, and to uncover the truth about his *real* father.

And amidst those life-altering discoveries, he couldn't help but wonder about the source of this mystical singing. The music that echoed through his window day and night, never ceasing.

SADHANA

He eyed the candle on the windowsill and then pulled himself up to a sitting position in front of it. He found a book of matches and lit the candle. In the flickering light of his room, Paul replicated his actions of the previous night.

"I practice this Sadhana with the intention of living my life as meaningful as possible, and reaching enlightenment by being of benefit to others." They weren't exactly the same words he had used the night before, but Paul knew his meaning had not differed.

He sat there, his eyes fixed far beyond the cracked green wall he stared into. Paul's jumbled thoughts were on Praneel and the young man's father—an old man who had been left alone to grieve a son that died too young. He thought of his own father, or the man who Paul had always believed was his father, and of their strained relationship.

Paul had led a privileged life; one he imagined was much more abundant than Praneel's, yet Praneel had gone to his death happy, fulfilled, and with the love of his father. Paul couldn't make sense of it.

He picked up his book and opened it on his lap. The candlelight danced on the page titled, *The Burning Houses*.

> *A wealthy aristocrat lived with his family in a fine house with many rooms. On his property, very close by, was the meager home of his lowly servant. One night during a thunderstorm, a bolt of lightening struck a tree between them and its burning branches ignited both homes. The two fathers both escaped safely. But their children remained inside the two houses, laughing and playing, unaware of the fire.*
>
> *The two fathers called to their children, begging them to come out. They were too busy playing to take their fathers seriously. Then the two fathers pleaded with their children, promising to buy them wonderful gifts, fancy clothes and exciting toys if they came outside.*
>
> *The poor servant's children ran outside, for they had never known such riches. But the children of the wealthy man already owned everything their father had promised, and they remained inside. The aristocrat had nothing left to tempt his children with, and they perished in the blaze.*

Paul blew out the flame. His eyes, unable to focus in the dark, saw only the characters in the story of the burning houses. Paul thought it an amusing fable, heavy with symbolism, yet in many ways it seemed to epitomize his life—possibly even the contrast between his and Praneel's lives. It made Paul wonder about material things—the things that had always taken up so much room in his life. He reflected on his past and his upbringing and how he had been predisposed to view wealth and abundance in *traditional* terms.

Until coming here, Paul never gave these things any thought. Now he was seeing himself in a distorted mirror. Or, he wondered, is this reflection genuine and the old view of myself was the one distorted?

It was 8 p.m., and somewhere in the night the angelic voices began to sing again. He sat at the window listening, then he lay back, then he closed his eyes . . .

Paul awoke very early the following morning feeling refreshed, yet famished. He walked to the hospice quarters in the dark and found that Praneel's body had been removed. There were no other patients in the room. It was earlier than usual and Paul knew the dining room would be empty. Even when guests of the ashram would later filter in with the daylight, it would feel barren this morning without Praneel and his father. The two men had become a comfortable fixture, and though they never talked much with Paul, he enjoyed seeing them together.

The dank air had cooled just a bit during the night, and it felt good to be outside before the streets turned hot and dusty and chaotic. Paul wandered around the grounds, taking in the silence.

A wooden gate stood at the far end of the courtyard, almost undetectable in the dark. Paul opened it and stuck his head around the cinderblock wall. On the other side of the gate was a dirt alley that ran behind the ashram. Paul closed the gate behind him and stepped across the sewage trough, onto the road.

A flimsy image dashed across the alleyway, almost ghostlike in the blue-gray morning. A yellow wedge of light suddenly stretched out from the stone wall onto the dirt, illuminating a frail woman, and then she disappeared along with the light, into the building. A melodic euphony rose from inside the walls, and Paul knew he had found the source of the mysterious music. He stood outside the heavy wooden door, listening to the voices—thin and piping sopranos. It was the rear entrance to a temple. A temple, Paul realized, of only women.

Breakfast on this morning was to be leavened wheat bread called *samovar*, essentially biscuits made in different ways. Paul had arrived in the kitchen early enough to watch how the *bakirkhani* was made.

The dough had already been mixed and kneaded by the cook, a quiet gentleman named Sree. The dark-skinned man smiled with perfect teeth as he began the process of adding blanched almond slivers and sunflower seeds to the doughy mix.

He was thin, as wiry as his eyeglasses, and he moved about the kitchen with purpose—as if it were the one place in the world he could wield his quiet power. Sree spoke little English, but he demonstrated to Paul how he wanted the loaf separated into balls and then pressed flat. Paul washed his hands and then followed Sree's directions with studious intent. When Paul was finished, Sree slid the tray into the oven and baked the disks for 12 minutes and then brushed each one with ghee.

Paul carried the tray into the dining area and served the biscuits warm. By the time he finished passing them around and sat down to eat his, the biscuit had grown cold and the crust had become hard. Paul took his usual spot, but it lacked the fullness of spirit without the father and son seated at the table near him.

Sree emerged from the kitchen with a new tray and made his way to Paul. He stood beside the table, motioning for Paul to sample one. "Foods," he said in a soft voice.

Paul selected a smaller one, just in case.

"*Tsachvaru*," said Sree with a grin.

Paul set the *tsachvaru* on his plate and nodded appreciatively to the cook. It was a sesame-sprinkled biscuit, still warm, and softer than the other. Paul savored each bite. He repeated the name to himself in the futile hope that he might remember it later.

Swami Chalah appeared from the kitchen with two simple water glasses filled with a sludgy liquid. He handed one to Paul.

"It is *kavah*," he said, taking a seat across from him. "Sugar, cardamom and ground almonds added to normal tea."

Paul thanked him then took a tentative sip. It was very good.

"You have given of yourself very generously." Swami caressed the warm glass between his hands. "I have noticed you also clearing the dishes, and scrubbing pots and pans in the kitchen."

"It makes me feel good about myself." Paul smiled. "Like I'm earning my keep."

Swami gazed back, maybe not fully understanding the term. "You have also brought food and tea upstairs to patients too ill to leave their rooms. Some, you have even taken the time to sit with and read to."

"It's just a storybook I brought with me." Paul shrugged out a chuckle. "Since none of the guests here understand English, they have no idea how poorly I read."

"Understanding goes beyond the spoken word," Swami said, as he sipped from his glass. "Your company, your patience, and the kindness you showed to Praneel . . . these things . . . they are worth more than one can measure."

They sat together in silence, enjoying the *kavah*. Paul thought it curiously ironic that Swami would use terms associated with wealth. He figured Swami Chalah was an intuitive man, and though Paul didn't know exactly what earned the title, *Swami*, he imagined it had quite a bit to do with personal enlightenment and an awareness of life. Paul's thoughts and words were suddenly too intertwined to separate.

"I'm not what you think," Paul finally said. "I used to be . . ."

Swami tilted his head slightly as he gazed back at Paul then slowly shook his head. "We all used to be somebody else." He ran a finger around the rim of his *kavah* glass for several seconds. "It is said that no man ever steps in the same river twice, for it is not the same river and he is not the same man."

Paul felt a sudden and surprising rush of emotion. Swallowing hard to tamp it down, he closed his eyes. Swami's words struck at his core, a marrow muddled with a weighty desire to know the truth about his past, so he could better know himself.

Opening his eyes again, Paul looked across at Swami. "I need to find the truth about my parents—my mother and about my *real* father. How can I even begin to know me if I don't even know them? I feel like I'm lost right now."

Paul immediately realized he had blurted out his feelings with no background, no context from which Swami Chalah could draw, no way to understand. But Swami's expression was unchanged, showing no hint of a struggle for discernment or insight.

"Guests of Bhakti Seva come to us for many different reasons," he said. "Sometimes when a man is lost, he is in the best place to find himself. It is not only important that you learn who you are, but also who you want to be. Once you can do that, everything else will follow."

Swami's talk had left Paul with an inspired contentment. He felt as though he had already embarked on the journey to figure out who it was he wanted to be, but Swami's advice had somehow taken some of the anxiety and urgency out of his quest for information about his lineage.

SADHANA

Paul had stayed at the table later than he had on other mornings, and since most of the others had already gone, there were fewer plates to clear. As Paul carried them into the kitchen he was surprised to find Sree still there, cooking several more trays of *samovar*.

The kitchen's back door was open and several women huddled in the alleyway outside. Paul set the dishes next to a bucket of soapy water and moved toward the door. The women who were clustered there hurriedly covered their faces with the white fabric of their sarees—their black eyes peering out at Paul's every move. Paul glanced out over the women to see a line of fifty or more, standing along the shaded side of the alley.

Sree motioned for Paul to take a tray, and they both began serving. The women were as silent as mourners, moving quickly and gracefully as the line snaked forward. Each would drop a coin onto the tray, gingerly take a biscuit, clasp it between their hands as if in prayer, and then touch it to their forehead and lips in thanks before moving off.

When the group had dwindled to nothing, Paul gazed down at his tray covered with copper colored coins. He stepped out into the deserted alley. Having been fed, the singing women from the temple had disappeared as quickly and mysteriously as they had appeared. He looked to Sree for an explanation.

"Vee-dow Voo-mons." Sree turned back to his kitchen, as if the matter-of-fact response had answered Paul's question. In actuality, his foreign and heavily accented words made no sense to Paul.

He finished cleaning up and spent the day helping out with the patients at Bhakti Seva. A sickly old man named Mr. Gopal, wanted to sit outside in the sun. He communicated this through the woman whom Paul had assisted the night Praneel died. She asked Paul to help transfer Gopal from his bed into a rickety wheelchair—one of only three on the ashram grounds.

The late afternoon sun beat down at a steep angle, throwing long shadows across the small grassy courtyard. Mr. Gopal dined on the last slice of daylight, soaking it into his leathery skin as if it were a life-prolonging salve.

Paul moved off of the muggy lawn to sit on a shaded walkway nearby. The woman who had pushed the wheelchair had also sought out a sheltered area, but had shrunk quietly away to a spot a respectable distance from Paul. Instead of sitting however, she squatted on arched legs—her sinuous body, wrapped in white cloth, making the taut position appear effortless.

When the last of the daylight ebbed up and over the courtyard wall, Paul and the crouching woman assisted the elderly man back to the 3rd floor dormitory room. Mr. Gopal conversed with the woman in their native tongue, none of which Paul understood.

As Paul turned to leave, the old man put his hands together in a prayer of thanks, and nodded.

"This gentleman wishes to thank you for your kindness," the woman said to Paul.

Before he responded, Mr. Gopal raised his hands again in blessing. *"Kharman ki tenishaha khuni badi dauno jaay umto chal chal Swaha."*

Paul grinned back at him with folded hands. "Wow," he turned to the woman. "That was quite a thank you."

She covered her mouth, exposing tiny smile lines at the corners of her brown eyes. "It's a Hindu mantra, a special blessing."

"What does it mean?" Paul's grin widened to match hers.

"It is a blessing to cure piles."

"Piles?" Paul's smile dropped. "Like, hemorrhoids? Why would he think I need a prayer for that?"

The woman spoke to Mr. Gopal in rapid parlance, and after he responded she turned back to Paul. "You were seated on the walkway."

"Yeah, it was hot out."

"Indian people rarely sit directly on the ground. Mr. Gopal thought the coolness of the concrete was to soothe your suffering."

The comedy of the situation finally eased its way through Paul's embarrassment and he began to laugh. The woman, who was afraid she had offended him, was now relieved and laughed as well. Mr. Gopal, who understood none of it, chuckled along with them.

Paul sat in the calm of the courtyard, enjoying the whisper of a twilight breeze. He watched two gray monkeys—a mother and a baby—lying on the stone wall next to the gate at the far end of the garden. They eyed Paul as he hesitatingly inched toward them to get a better look. At the last second they squawked and clamored down the other side of the wall. Paul jumped.

"Hey, Mr. Hamptons," a woman's voice called out from behind him, causing Paul to jump again.

He swung around to see who it was, as she took another step into the courtyard.

"I see you're still with us. Didn't die of starvation yet?"

Şixteen

Paul caught a flight back to New York that night, having left the funeral gathering without so much as goodbye to anyone. By 6 o'clock the following evening he was boarding the redeye to London's Heathrow Airport.

American Airlines flight 100 was on time for its 6:20 p.m. departure. That pleased Paul, since it meant he would make his connecting flight to New Delhi.

The Boeing 747 had been part of American Airlines' optimistic venture toward larger aircraft on transatlantic routes. That was before the oil crisis of 1973, when the company had difficulty filling the behemoths to capacity. In an effort to woo the more upscale traveler, the airline replaced several of its forward seats on the plane to make room for onboard piano bars.

The airline company had transitioned the rest of the large bodies into cargo aircraft, favoring the smaller DC-10s for commercial routes. But Paul's flight was the last remaining 747 in the fleet, causing pilots and flight attendants to affectionately refer to the plane as *'Gulliver.'*

When the seatbelt light went out, Paul took advantage of the relic by gathering the company production reports he was reading, and moving to a padded chair in the lounge. He ordered a glass of bourbon, lit a cigarette, and listened to the Wurlitzer piano.

This would only be Paul's second trip to check out the India operation; his first being 16 months earlier when Bind-Chem opened the plant. He didn't like India. It was hot and crowded, and Paul found the food disgusting. Until now, he had no real reason or need to return there. But things had changed. Paul wanted to ensure the plant was in condition to sell, and maybe even more importantly, he wanted to get his mind off of Abby and her pregnancy.

Paul browsed the paperwork, hoping the charts and graphs would replace the humiliating images of the performance he and LJ put on at his mother's funeral. *Pathetic* was the only word he could think of to describe it.

The production reports were thorough enough, indicating a strong profit-margin ratio. There were few personnel problems, thanks in large part to a third world economy that endeared the workers to anyone who would pay them. The India operation had also benefitted from a bi-lingual foreman who quite ably bridged the communication and cultural gap between American management and Indian workers.

According to the report, the plant's infrastructure was the only issue in need of attention. If he were going to continue the operation for another 10 years, it might be worth the investment. But Paul saw major repairs as a costly and questionable undertaking at this stage of the game. Though he hadn't completely made up his mind about it, Paul planned to wait to hear what the manager had to say during his visit to the plant.

Norm O'Bryan was the plant manager—hand picked by Paul at the time of the move out of the states. O'Bryan had been an up and comer during the company's early years. A young man with piercing eyes and a crew cut military hairstyle, his short, athletic stature had reminded Paul of a collegiate wrestler. Among other things, O'Bryan had been credited with tenaciously fulfilling the requirements of the Military Personnel Records Center contract, and making the Spanish Lake, Missouri operation a success.

Now, as Paul emerged from the front of the terminal, O'Bryan was there to greet him. The man looked nothing like he had only two years prior, in fact Paul barely recognized him. Though he still wore his hair short, the man had gained a lot of weight—the kind that settles in the chest and stomach and hints of too many gin and tonics.

O'Bryan waved to Paul with one hand while swabbing a handkerchief across his sweaty forehead with the other. The skin around his eyes was tight, pinched at the corners by his swollen cheeks.

"Good to see ya, Mr. Griffiths." O'Bryan clasped Paul's hand in his clammy paw. "How was the flight? Take your bag?"

"Yeah, thanks." Paul handed his suitcase to O'Bryan. "So what's going on with you? You look a little off your game."

"Whadda ya mean?" O'Bryan padded the handkerchief on the back of his neck.

"I've taken ling cod off my fishing hook that looked better."

"Oh, that." O'Bryan forced a laugh. "I'm not much for the heat."

Paul gave him a sideways glance. Clearly, O'Bryan had no clue as to how bad he looked.

A dark-skinned Indian driver pulled to the curb in a tan Hindustan Ambassador. He got out and helped O'Bryan heft the suitcase into the trunk. Paul slid into the back seat and pulled the door shut behind him. O'Bryan paused at the closed door and then took a seat in the front, next to the driver.

O'Bryan turned in his seat. "So, ya got dinner plans tonight, Mr. Griffiths?"

Paul let out a deflating breath. "Hadn't gotten that far yet, Norm. Thought maybe I'd get checked into the hotel? Perhaps take a shower and shave after the 14-hour flight?"

"Yeah, sure, of course," said O'Bryan, the collar of his tweed jacket digging into his neck. "It's just that one of our employees asked if his family could host a dinner tonight in your honor."

Paul's eyes rolled back. "That's not . . . no, not necessary. I'm just here for a few days to check on the plant. I don't need all that."

The car was silent for a minute. O'Bryan glanced over at the driver, who continued staring straight ahead. O'Bryan propped an elbow on the seatback as he turned again toward Paul—his squinty eyes darting over at the driver.

Paul got the hint. He let out another sigh and said, "Yeah, okay, dinner will be fine."

The driver's face broke into a broad grin.

"I'm not sure you've met our foreman," O'Bryan said, indicating the driver. "This is Bhupinder Magar. He's kind of like the plant supervisor, slash translator. Magar speaks pretty good English, and he can also get our point across to the employees. He lives just outside Aligarh, near the facility."

"Good to know you, Magar." Paul palmed the air in the general direction of the driver.

"The pleasure is exceptionally mine, Mr. Paul Griffiths, sahib." Magar's grinning face kept watch in the mirror. "It will be an honor to have you attend dinner with my family and I."

"Yep, thanks." Paul lifted a chin toward the mirror in a kind of nod. "Looking forward to it, Magar."

"Sometimes I let Bhupinder drive me around in the company car," O'Bryan said. "He knows this town better than me, and frankly these streets are like driving through a monkey's dick."

Paul looked at his watch, thinking it's going to be a long couple of days.

O'Bryan added, "B'sides, Magar is a better driver than me."

A grimace was Paul's only response. *That's probably because he's sober and you're not.*

Paul checked into the Hotel Royal, showered and shaved and then fell asleep watching a televised cricket game. He woke in mid-afternoon, dressed and went down to the restaurant to wait for O'Bryan and Magar to meet him. Paul had a cup of coffee and read the international news while he waited.

During the ride to the hotel, Paul had mentioned that he wanted to see the operation before dinner. When the two employees arrived back at the hotel to pick him up, the plant was the first stop on the agenda.

Bind-Chem's India division was a ten-minute drive south, just outside the city of Aligarh. Small pockets of homes and small grazing fields were interspersed with industrial warehouses—the latter increasing in number the farther outside of Aligarh they drove. A single rusted train track ran alongside the main road, and was overgrown with high yellow grass. The cyclone fence-enclosed Bind-Chem facility bordered an open field, just south of Kasba Kol—a neighborhood of small mud-brick houses, or lesser quality residences made of thatch, with corrugated plastic or tarpaulins. The community consisted of mostly poor farmers or employees at the Bind-Chem plant.

The two men escorted Paul around the facility, O'Bryan talking the entire time and Magar walking silently a pace or two behind. Many of the workers they passed stopped to bow or clasp their hands together as if praying to Paul. The attention was disturbing to him, partly because he didn't know how to respond and partly because he didn't care about them nearly as much as they did him.

At one point Magar asked if it would be permissible to have a photograph taken of he, Paul and O'Bryan all together. Paul rolled his eyes as one of the workers fiddled with the antiquated camera, leaving the three men squinting into the sunlight. He finally figured out where the button was, took the picture, and then bowed along with Magar as if capturing the boss's image were some great honor.

Paul pulled O'Bryan aside after walking the grounds, and the two spoke alone in O'Bryan's office. The place was crammed with stacks of folders and loose papers that looked as if they probably should be filed somewhere. As Paul gazed around, he saw trash bins that hadn't been emptied, and the whole place smelled of stale cigarettes. Something about the place, the entire operation in fact, bellowed to Paul of shoddy management.

"So tell me about the infrastructure problems, Norm." Paul picked a glass tumbler off the chair and sniffed it. He put it on the desk as he sat down.

"Yeah, it should all be in the report," O'Bryan said. "You know, well, because of the corrosive nature of what we use, the lines, well let's just say they're not in the best shape."

Paul lifted an eyebrow. "Then replace them. Isn't maintenance and replacement part of our fixed costs? We've budgeted for it."

O'Bryan tilted his head like a dog getting water out of his ear. "You have to look at the marginal revenue, marginal cost perspective," he said. From that point on Paul was lost. O'Bryan started talking in mathematic terms that Paul recognized as nothing more than doubletalk. He hadn't the patience for it, and Paul found the advice condescending to hear this from an underling. "You take marginal profit . . ." O'Bryan began penning an equation on the back of a piece of paper that looked like it had been something important. "Which equals marginal revenue, minus marginal costs--"

"Stop right there!" said Paul. "Is this your way of telling me that you cooked the books to show more profits? Tell me you didn't eliminate our maintenance and replacement funds?"

"With all due respect, Mr. Griffiths, that's pretty much how things are done over here." O'Bryan waved a hand through the air as if indicating the entire nation of India. "Those funds just sit there, kind of like an insurance policy, but they're kind of like a waste because we've never used them."

"That's because we haven't needed them," said Paul. "That money *is* an insurance policy, Norm. Only now, thanks to you, there is no maintenance and replacement money." He rubbed the bridge of his nose. "What else?"

O'Bryan was eager to move off the subject, but the next issue wasn't much better. "There are eighty-three chemical storage tanks, each able to hold up to 12,000 gallons. You saw them outside behind the fence."

Paul nodded then tapped the report in his hand.

"I guess you already read that." O'Bryan licked his lips like a man who can hardly wait to pour himself a drink. "Anywho, they're all pump-fed. That means we have to maintain containment pools in case there's a leak, problem with the pumps, or if the electricity goes out—which it does here in India from time to time."

Paul shifted in his seat. "I got all that in the report, Norm. So where is the problem?"

"Not really a problem," said O'Bryan. "It's just that the workers have to clean the tanks every month, and, well, we've been using the containment pools as holding tanks while we do it. In addition to that, we average a couple of good power outages each month."

"So?" Paul flipped through the report, not finding any of this information.

"Well, we've noticed that each time this happens—either because of power loss or from cleaning the tanks—we're short several hundred gallons. Sometimes even thousands."

Paul frowned. "Okay, what's that mean? Somebody is stealing our chemicals? Selling them on the Indian black market?"

O'Bryan laughed. "No, no. These workers are as loyal as they come. Besides, I wouldn't let something like that happen. Not on my watch."

"Then, what?"

"Ground contamination." O'Bryan wiped sweat from his brow. "What would be nice, what we really need are below-ground containment *tanks*, not pools."

"Holy shit, Norm. Do you know what that would cost?" Paul thought about it then fanned himself with the report. "We passed a petroleum company less than a half-mile from here."

"O'Bryan nodded. "Shivra Petrol and Durga HP. They're both just down that way." He pointed toward the dusty brown wall.

"They've all got the same issues, right? Every company here does. I mean, that's why we built the plant out here, Norm. Because there are no requirements for containment tanks."

"I'm just saying, if we're going to keep the current pace of production, it's going to cost the company to upgrade."

"You know this stuff isn't cheap," Paul said. "There's a hell of a price tag attached to these 'upgrades.' It's not like we'd just be buying the tanks. We'd have to excavate, do groundwater testing, permits, the whole enchilada."

"Exactly what I was thinking," said O'Bryan. "I'm not say'n we do all this stuff right now, it's just, I don't want anything to go wrong on--"

"On my watch, yeah, I know." Paul shook his head in frustration. "How come the repair and replacement budget was eliminated *on your watch*? And why the hell was all of this information left out of the quarterly *on your watch?*"

O'Bryan's face was blotchy and without an answer. It crossed Paul's mind as he looked at the guy, that it was unlikely O'Bryan had actually gotten dumber. True, the drinking could have pickled his brain some. But there was something else. Something wasn't right, and Paul's gut told him that this wasn't the same Norm O'Bryan he had handpicked to lead the Aligarh operation. There was definitely something else going on with the guy.

Sure, the equipment repairs and replacements were all probably worth doing. But in the time it would take to get them done, the plant will already be on the market. The sooner we sell—the better, Paul thought. Because nobody will even think of making an offer if those kinds of problems, or even potential problems, are anywhere on the radar. Any serious buyer would certainly run for the hills.

By the time they finished their meeting, Paul was hungry and O'Bryan needed a beer with a whiskey chaser.

Paul stood and stretched. "So, what's this Bippino guy having for dinner anyway?"

"Not sure," said O'Bryan. "I know Bhupinder's wife and daughter have been preparing the meal all day. These people like to do things like this. It's like their custom or something."

"You wanna know what my custom is?" said Paul. "It's having a New York steak, medium-rare, smothered in mushrooms. And washing it down with a nice 72 Vosne-Romanée Pinot."

"I'm pretty sure it's not going to be that." O'Bryan hesitated at the credenza. "Care for a quick snort before we head out?"

Paul rolled his eyes. It figured; that's why O'Bryan had been eyeing the overcrowded cabinet throughout the meeting. "Sure, what the hell?" Paul knew he could use one after all the bad news O'Bryan had just pummeled him with.

They had a drink and then another, as Magar waited patiently for them outside.

Bhupinder Magar was a proud man, though he had little to be proud of by prevailing American standards. He tooted the Hindustan's horn as he pulled to a stop in front of the single-story clay brick house.

His wife, Pooja, stood with their daughter at the door to greet them—having waited there for some time, even before the car's horn sounded. Pooja wore a saree of yellow silk with gold thread woven into the trim. It was a symbol of wealth, which even though Magar's family had none, they wanted to acknowledge that the little they did have was due to Paul. A vertical slash of red turmeric powder adorned the woman's forehead—a decorative symbol worn by married women.

A goat, tethered to a tree, tugged at its bindings and bleated noisily as Magar introduced his family. Paul thought the daughter to be nine or ten, as she hid, smiling, behind her mother. The little girl stepped forward and extended her hand, as if coached ahead of time on the western custom. Paul shook the girl's hand and did his best to smile.

Ducking beneath a nylon cord anchored to a tree and weighted with drying clothes, Paul followed Magar and O'Bryan up the two steps, over a putrid stream, and into the dwelling.

The house smelled of spices and freshly prepared food, and Paul was thankful that at least the goat didn't appear to be the main course.

Magar motioned for them to sit, though there were no chairs and the floor was a woven mat on top of hard-packed dirt. There the men talked, mostly about the weather and an upcoming cricket test match between England and Australia. It was to be played at Lord's, which Paul gathered was in England. He knew little about the game of cricket, and for that matter knew little about the weather—other than it was miserably hot and muggy.

Before dinner, Magar's daughter performed a *Natya* dance for the guests. She was a cute little girl with big brown eyes, and it was apparent she had been made to practice the bouncy, oscillating dance movements and gestures. But Paul found the music high-pitched and monotonous, and his legs were cramping from sitting on the floor.

The dinner was served without silverware. It was, according to their host, a festive *Mughlai* recipe for vegetable *biryani*—a seasoned rice dish served with a toasted flatbread they called *naan*. Paul picked through the rust-colored grain, trying to figure out what was in it. He saw nuts, peas, coconut, and even raisins. He figured they crammed just about every known food group into it, and that somehow made it more "festive." Paul didn't care for peas, and he would have just as soon had something with beef or pork in it.

Other vegetarian dishes were served, and though Magar spooned ample helpings onto Paul's plate, he managed to avoid eating any of it. The food was just too different looking and the aroma too pungent for him. Any concern Paul might have had that the Magar's wife would be offended turned out to be pointless. Both Pooja and her daughter made themselves scarce while the men ate, only returning to offer more food and to clear their plates.

The dinner conversation between the three men felt like a struggle to Paul. "Hey," he said at one point, breaking an awkward silence. "This reminds me of an old joke: an Indian, an Irishman and an Englishman were having dinner..."

He looked at the two men, waiting for a laugh, but neither of them seemed to get the humor. O'Bryan sat waiting for the rest of the joke, and Magar cocked his head in puzzlement.

"Oh, you are of British ancestry?" Magar's head bobbled like a smiling dashboard decoration. "Has any of your family spent time here in India?"

Paul's shoulders dropped at the tepid reaction. "No. Yeah, I don't know." He yawned. "I think my father had some old statue he got from his dad. My grandfather's father, or great-grandfather might have been here, I'm not sure."

O'Bryan's head swiveled back and forth, as if he too was learning new, worthwhile information.

"Great-grandfather," Magar repeated thoughtfully. "A statue, you say?"

Paul nodded, completely bored with the conversation.

"This statue. It is a likeness of your great-grandfather?"

"No, no. Some other guy." Paul rubbed his eyes. "I didn't even know my grandfather. Barely even knew my dad. He died in Vietnam."

O'Bryan's eyes grew wide. It was the most personal information he had ever heard about his boss. Magar bowed his head, clearly a gesture of posthumous reverence.

"Yeah," Paul continued. "The statue is of some English soldier my grandfather's father fought under. Havelock, I think is the name."

"Sir Henry Havelock," Magar announced. "This man your great-grandfather fought under is a famous general. He is an important figure in our history."

"That so?" Paul grabbed his knee with both hands. "An Indian war hero, eh?" He glanced at O'Bryan with a satisfied expression.

"Oh no," said Magar. "Sir Havelock killed many Indians in 1857, during the uprising against British colonization. It was right here in this state of Uttar Pradesh that it happened." Magar had expressed this in a matter-of-fact way, almost happy to share the piece of history. There was no animosity in his words—no blame or judgment that Paul's relative had slaughtered Magar's countrymen. Yet Paul suddenly felt as if he himself were the invading force.

Magar sensed his discomfort and smiled. "The past is like a road, each stone laid by someone else. And though much of it was put in place before either of us were even born, it is the route over which we both came to be who we are and where we are at this place and time."

"Here, here!" O'Bryan raised a glass of water, wishing it was something much stronger.

Paul stayed in Aligarh another two days, visiting the plant again to go over the books himself. The office was a disaster, but at least O'Bryan kept meticulous financial accountings. Not that any of it was good news. On the contrary, the records reflected cost overruns and projected expenses in excess of what the company had budgeted. Even more troubling to Paul was that none of this negative information had been disclosed in the quarterly report.

His hotel had a restaurant on the premises. It offered a variety of Asian cuisine, which much to Paul's relief included Chinese and chicken dishes. Other than the dinner with Magar's family and the two outings to the plant, Paul was determined to confine the remainder of his 78-hour India visit to the hotel lounge and restaurant.

While there, Paul tried several times to call back to the company's accountant and the attorney. But international phone service was unreliable and the 9½-hour time difference from the East Coast only complicated the undertaking. When he was finally able to get through on Nathan's line, Paul was forced to leave a recording.

"Nathan, Paul." He disliked leaving messages—always imagining the person sitting right there, listening and making the decision not to pick up the phone. "Still here in India. Checked out the plant, went over the books, and ate some weird dinner at a worker's house. Can't figure out which of those was the most painful; all I know is that fucking O'Bryan needs to be yanked out of here by the short hairs. We'll talk when I get back. And I hope you have some good news from the Germans or the Canadians."

Magar drove Paul to the airport, and this time O'Bryan sat in the back seat with him. It was midday and the road was dusty, crowded and hot. Paul couldn't wait to get out of there, and he barely spoke during the ride.

"Sooooo," O'Bryan ran a hand over his spiky flattop. "Looks like another scorcher."

Paul wrinkled his face as if he had just bit his tongue. Ignoring the weather report, he turned his head toward the window.

"Bad luck about all the unforeseen expenses, eh, Mr. Griffiths?" O'Bryan leaned forward to gage his boss's expression. "I mean, who needs that headache, especially right now?"

The airport departure terminal was suddenly in front of them. Magar unloaded Paul's bag at the curb. O'Bryan leaned over to shake hands with Paul, but he had already jumped out and taken the suitcase from Magar. O'Bryan's last comment was the most telling disclosure of the entire trip, Paul thought. Except that O'Bryan was too stupid to realize what he had just said.

Especially right now? Paul's eyes were ice cold when he looked back into the car. *What else could he have meant by that? How would O'Bryan know that the company was going to be sold?*

"We'll be in touch," was as much civility as Paul could muster.

The flight was long, but it gave Paul time to put some of the pieces together in his mind.

A company Town Car was waiting for Paul at the Arrivals curb when he came out. His attorney, Nathan Geerts, was in the backseat beneath an open briefcase and a stack of folders.

"How was the trip?" Nathan asked, as Paul handed the driver his suitcase and slid in.

"The shits." Paul tossed his head back against the seat. "I couldn't have gotten outta that hell hole any faster if my ass was on fire."

"There's an image." The car pulled into traffic. "Flight back went okay?"

"Never mind that," said Paul. "We've got a serious problem."

Nathan removed his eyeglasses, slipping them into his coat pocket. "You mentioned something about O'Bryan on the phone."

"He knows we're trying to sell the company." Paul squinted out the window into the morning sun, still trying to figure it out. "Not to mention, he's been pencil whipping the books to make things appear better than they are. Or worse than they are, I'm not sure which."

"We'll have an in-house audit done right away." Nathan scribbled into his notebook.

Paul turned back from the window. "Yeah, O'Bryan is a mess. He's got everything screwed up over there—telling me about problems that aren't mentioned anywhere in the quarterly; cost overruns, rotting containment tanks, infrastructure issues. I don't know what to believe. That little jerkoff is up to something."

Nathan stopped writing and stared down at his pad, quick-frozen in place.

Paul eyed him. "What is it?"

"Börse Einsatz." The attorney looked up slowly. "I didn't pick up on it at the time, but it's the Germans. They've gotten to O'Bryan."

"Back up," said Paul. "What . . . How do you know?"

"I called Hoffmann while you were gone." Nathan rested the end of his pen against his lip. "Wanted to see where they were with their financing. Anyway, Hoffmann must have been told there was a call holding from Bind-Chem."

Paul's eyebrows twisted in confusion. "And?"

"Hoffmann answered the phone expecting that it was O'Bryan calling him." Nathan slapped his notebook closed. "He picked up and said, 'Hello Norm.' Don't you see? Why would Hoffmann think O'Bryan was calling him?"

"They don't even know each other," said Paul.

"They shouldn't. I mean, how would they?"

The two men sat in silence, and then suddenly the same thought struck them.

"They're paying him off," said Nathan.

Paul snapped his fingers. "All that bullshit about equipment and maintenance costs. Hoffmann is using Norm O'Bryan to devalue the company."

Nathan nodded as the concept jelled in his mind. "At least on paper. And when *you* get desperate enough, thinking you're going to have to spend a fortune on infrastructure upgrades, the Germans swoop in and buy it for--"

"Some bratwurst and a Heineken." Paul balled his right hand into a fist.

"Actually, Paul, Heineken is a Dutch beer."

"Irregardless," barked Paul. "Anyway, I wonder what the bastards promised O'Bryan."

Nathan considered for a second advising Paul that 'irregardless' wasn't really a word, but thought better of it. His boss was already spitting nails.

"We've got to get O'Bryan out of there, and fast."

"He could do you a lot of harm," said Nathan. "Have you got anyone who could step in on short notice?"

"Maybe." Paul sighed. "There are a couple of young managers at the Winchester plant, but I'm not sure either of them are ready for India. I should probably do it myself, but the thought of actually staying there for any length of time . . ."

"Well whatever you decide to do, you had better do it soon."

"Thank you for stating the obvious," said Paul.

They sat in silence, both gazing out opposite windows as the car rode along the Queens Midtown Expressway. They passed Grand Central Terminal and turned right onto Madison Avenue.

Paul cocked his head toward Nathan. "I've got an idea," he said. "There's an Indian guy . . . I ate dinner at his house . . . Magoo something or other. He seems to have a following among the workers."

"But can he manage the *entire* Aligarh operation?"

Paul shrugged. "I guess we'll find out." He paused a few beats before finally saying, "There's something else I need you to do, Nathan."

The attorney gave Paul a sideways glance.

"I want you to get me a current address for Abigail Townsend."

Şėvėņtėėņ

The location from which Mr. Tam was conducting his investigation wasn't clear to me. Regardless, there seemed to be a steady flow of information as to the case's progress, much of it passed along through Geerts, the attorney.

Unfortunately none of the updates sounded positive. Finnish police had broken up a human trafficking ring at the Helsinki-Vantaa Airport on the day Paul would have been there, and from what I gathered, the incident caused quite a hoo-ha in the terminal. Several law enforcement agencies were involved and a big splash appeared on the national news. It apparently had something to do with a Jet Airways flight originating in Hanoi, Vietnam.

Nothing about the incident sounded even remotely like something Paul would be involved in, but Tam was looking into it just the same. When Paul's name didn't surface as either a suspect or a witness, Tam advised that it was no more than a coincidence, and the raid and arrests didn't appear to be a factor in Paul's disappearance. The news, however, caused more wild talk around the estate—some employees actually speculating that Paul was really a criminal kingpin.

According to Tam's overseas contacts in the police department, no crime victims with Paul's description had surfaced and thankfully, no unidentified bodies had been recovered of late. There were no records of police contacts with Paul Griffiths anywhere in Finland.

They continued to check storage caches from the airport video surveillance cameras, but each of the tapes still had to be viewed by a real person—someone familiar with Paul, it would stand to reason.

Mr. Geerts wired several additional photos of Paul to Curtis Tam. Meanwhile, we kept our fingers crossed that Paul would turn up soon.

* * *

Paul turned away from the two fleeing monkeys. "Gwyneth Eichler. I certainly didn't expect to see you here."

She surveyed the manicured grounds around her. "Please, just call me Gwyn. And what are you doing out here? Scaring the monkeys?"

He motioned toward the wall. "I don't think that female liked me getting too close."

"Smart girl." Gwyn's face had seen some sun since arriving in India. Paul noticed the tanned skin and a smattering of freckles across the bridge of her nose. Gwyn's sparkling blue eyes matched the color of her cotton *shalwar kameez*. It was a traditional style long pant, tapered tight at the ankles and worn under a long, loose-fitting tunic. She seemed more relaxed than when he saw her last; as if it was the first day off she'd had since they landed in India.

"Turns out I'm an integral part of the operation here," Paul said, getting a laugh out of her. "Seriously. In fact, just this morning I was promoted from busboy and dishwasher to the samovar sous-chef. I've already made a whole tray of them."

"I'm impressed." An uncomfortable moment passed, during which neither of them could think of anything to say. "So, I just thought I'd come by to see how you're getting along."

"Good, I think." Paul smiled, unconsciously brushing the wrinkles from his tunic. "The ashram has been very interesting. Wonderful people, really. But then, of course, there's also the sadness that goes along with seeing all the sickness and death here."

Gwyn saw the sudden turn in their light-hearted banter. She also sensed a change in Paul—this wasn't the same arrogant guy she had met a few weeks ago.

"Anyway, I'm glad you came by." Paul sauntered absently across the grass and Gwyn joined him. "Remember the letter I showed you? The one from my mother?"

She nodded, her eyes continuing to study him.

"It's really got me thinking. I'd like to do some checking into this situation with my family, you know, try to find out where I come from. But I can't do it alone. Not over here in India."

"And you think I can somehow help you?"

"Maybe. I need to get access to the Internet." He swept his hand toward the ashram. "They've got no Wi-Fi connection here; it's like they're still in the Jurassic era. Which is okay; in fact, it's probably a good thing—especially for someone like me."

"Sure." Gwyn sounded relieved, as if she had expected Paul to ask her to partake in espionage. "You can use the desktop in my office."

Paul pointed the way through the back gate, out toward the alley. "I found a shortcut to the main road," he said. "Through an alleyway, past some kind of temple. Which reminds me, do you know what *Vee-dow Voo-mons* means?"

Gwyn repeated it to herself then shook her head. "Doesn't sound familiar. Should I know it?"

"They're a bunch of ladies we fed breakfast to this morning," he said. "Just another thing I'm trying to figure out."

Paul and Gwyn left the ashram grounds and walked down the alleyway together in the dark. Colorful lights from the street ahead reflected on the road to illuminate their path.

"You seem different than you did before," Gwyn said, more or less out of the blue.

"Yeah," Paul laughed. "Well I've showered, for one thing."

He could see her watching him, as if she were making an appraisal.

"I may have misjudged you," she said.

"Were you judging me?"

They emerged into a steamy marketplace that seemingly belched the smells of people and bustling stalls around them. Squeezing past food vendors and shoppers, the two navigated over uneven ground and putrid puddles. The din of the crowd made it difficult to hear one another, so they didn't speak. It gave Gwyn time to think. The cluster of merchants thinned as they followed the roadway toward the Asha Heath Care complex where Gwyn was housed. She turned toward him when she had finally found the words.

"You're like one of those bottles of wine you find at a discount store or at the bottom of your wine rack, and you don't know what to expect."

"I'm a bottle of wine." Paul said, mockingly.

"Sort of." She stepped around a huge black and white cow as it foraged through a trash heap. "Like, a nice bottle with a fancy label. But then when you open it, the cork is corroded and it smells bad."

Paul frowned. "Not sure I like the direction this comparison is heading."

"Well, not really." Gwyn took his arm to steady herself as they stepped up to a raised sidewalk. "Then you let it sit for awhile, you know? You let it breathe a little bit, and it turns out to be different than you thought. A pleasant surprise."

190

Paul liked the analogy.

They greeted the guard as they passed through the gate in front of the health care complex. Gwyn's office was in a small outbuilding down a long driveway at the rear of the hospital. The sign over the doorway read, CHILDREN'S RELIEF FOUNDATION INTERNATIONAL – *Volunteer and Community Partnerships.*

It was a pleasant little building, more modern than Paul had expected, with a small glass-enclosed atrium in the center of it. Gwyn's office sat off to the side of the entryway, with a view of the palm and fern garden.

She escorted Paul around the grounds, explaining some of the foundation's initiatives. "We oversee about two-dozen outreach clinics," she said, indicating a map of India on the wall. "Most of the children we serve come from families too poor to travel any distance to get medical care. So, we try to bring healthcare to them."

"The outreach clinics," he said. "Those are where the other CRF volunteers were assigned?"

"Exactly. You might have ended up in some jungle outpost, had you made it here on time."

Paul wondered if he could have handled that. Perhaps now he would be able to, but not when he first arrived.

"We also network with doctors, hospitals and specialists; helping parents navigate the whole healthcare system here, and we try to put the families in touch with the right people."

He stopped to look at a collage of photographs—mostly smiling children. "These are your patients?"

Gwyn nodded. "Many of them are." She moved to one of the photos, a little boy seated on a metal chair. His denim pants had been bunched up at his thighs to expose two legs, which had both been amputated just below the knees. "This little boy was one of mine," she said. "My first trip over here."

Paul stood next to Gwyn for a closer look. The boy wore a red and blue, American soccer shirt. He had the saddest look on his face, and huge tears streamed down his cheeks.

"Is he in pain?" Paul asked.

"Embarrassed," she said. "He came from a small village in Tamil Nadu. A truck had run over his legs as he tried to cross a road, and there was no medical help in the area. Well, none with any state-of-the-art knowledge or equipment. And by state-of-the-art, I mean an osteopathic physician or simple bone-setting techniques."

Paul leaned toward the photo, examining the boy's savagely uneven amputation scars. He shuttered as a tinge of pain coursed through him. "Poor kid."

"In the states, a metal plate and a couple of pins could have saved his legs." Gwyn turned away from the picture. "Anyhow, by the time we got involved all we could do was put the family in touch with a special hospital in Jaipur."

They walked back toward the front of the building and into Gwyn's office. Paul slumped into a folding chair, deflated by the young boy's plight. The consequences of the life one is born into had never occurred to Paul. He wondered what the boy's life might have been like had he been the son of Loring Griffiths. He'd have had no more of an inconvenience than six-weeks of splinted legs, and his life would have been perfect. How one person is born into wealth and another into poverty was a philosophical abstraction, the depth to which Paul had never delved. Maybe it's just the luck of the draw, he thought. Nothing more complex than that.

The luck of the draw.

"Here," Gwyn said, having booted her computer. "There's an Indian version of Yahoo that connects to their general database."

"Do you mind doing it?" Paul's hesitance was a mix of sorrow for the young boy in the photograph, and fear of what he may learn about his own past.

"Let's check your email first," she said. "What's your password?"

"October 28; my birthday."

Gwyn laughed and shook her head, "I was kidding, Paul. Who tells someone their password?" She began typing into the computer. "So, you have a birthday coming up."

"No!" Paul lunged across the desk. "Wait a minute! We can't do that."

"Relax," she said. "I don't even know who your service provider is. I was only joking around--"

"Nothing personal." Paul settled back onto the chair. "It's just that I can't . . . don't want to log in anywhere it can be traced."

"Traced?" Gwyn raised an eyebrow. "A little paranoid, are we?"

He grimaced. Paul was certain that by now the judge knew he hadn't made good on his commitment with CRF. Which meant that Paul was now in violation of the court ordered volunteer work.

"It's kind of complicated," said Paul. "There's a real possibility that the FBI may have some kind of tap on my email. That's why I told you that I can't go home."

She tried to suppress a laugh, which ultimately escaped. "You don't really believe that, do you?"

"It's true, Gwyn." Paul was not smiling. His head dropped to his chest. "Anyway, I just need you to find out about my parents."

Gwyn took a pen out of the desk. "Okay then, what was your mom's name?"

"Leigh Griffiths."

She tapped the letters into her keyboard. "Nothing. When did she pass away?"

"Shortly after I was born, I think. Probably, like, about 30 years ago, maybe more."

Gwyn smirked then raised her eyebrows. "So you're an old guy."

Paul watched Gwyn scroll down the page. He thought she couldn't be too much younger.

"Do you know where she died?"

Paul shook his head. "Wait, hold on a minute. I just remembered, she signed the book with her maiden name—her whole name. Try it with Leigh Abigail Townsend."

Gwyn typed the name into the search request. Suddenly, the overhead lights flickered and everything in the office went black.

"C'mon," Paul groaned. "You gotta be kidding me."

He could hear Gwyn laughing in the dark. "Maybe it's a sign," she said. "Somebody upstairs doesn't want you to go snooping around into her life."

Paul stood up and felt his way along the wall. "More likely it's the Karma God, paying me back for all of the technology I took for granted during my lifetime. And now, when I need it most--"

"Hello?" a weak voice called out from the hallway. "Is somebody there?" It was a woman's voice, soft and with an Indian accent.

Gwyn answered, "Is that you, Tatleen?"

"Yes, ma'am. I was just finishing up out back when the electrical current lost power."

Gwyn saw out the window that the entire complex was without lights. "The emergency backup should kick on soon."

The woman groped cautiously in the dark as she stepped into the room. "Unfortunately ma'am, the generator isn't working. Repairs are scheduled for tomorrow."

"Well, I guess that won't help us much tonight." Gwyn laughed.

Suddenly there was a short, high-pitched screech. The woman—her arms outstretched in front of her—had run into Paul. Her pawing hands had managed to land around Paul's waist, propelling the two of them into each other. The full-body swaddling had lasted but a second, and both quickly retreated in total blackness.

"I'm so sorry," he said, stumbling backward, knocking into a chair. "I'm right here, in the room also. I'm a, a friend of Gwyn's. I didn't mean to startle you."

It took a second for the woman to catch her breath. Touching a man in such a way was beyond humiliating for her, not to mention a fundamental violation of cultural and social mores and a profound breach of propriety. Her only hope, although quite unlikely, was that it had all happened so quickly that the man hadn't noticed.

"What is going on over there between you two?" Gwyn jokingly asked, as she fumbled through her desk drawers in the dark.

Paul had indeed felt the contact between them. It was a glimpse into the world of the blind. Without having ever seen this woman, he knew the sound of her voice, the touch of her body, and the earthy scent of her skin. Paul had even felt her warm breath on his neck.

He had only been in this country a short time, but it had been long enough to recognize the difference between women at the Sloppy Tuna in Montauk, and women here in India. Grinding up against this poor woman must have embarrassed her to no end.

"Are you alright?" he asked her.

"Fine," answered Gwyn. "Just trying to find a flashlight."

The woman to whom Paul had intended the question stayed silent.

"Okay, then." Paul deliberately rustled his clothing to telegraph his whereabouts. "I guess I'll be heading back. Making my way to the door now."

The woman compressed her body against the wall, clearing her throat to let Paul know she was there. Paul squeezed against the doorframe to avoid a second contact in the dark.

"Here it is," announced Gwyn.

A faded yellow light flashed wildly on the ceiling as Gwyn switched on the flashlight.

Paul was in the middle of the doorway when the beam found him. As he raised an arm to shield his eyes, he heard a frail gasp.

SADHANA

The light bounced off the floor and then onto the stunned and cringing woman. Paul immediately let out a hardy laugh. The woman, somewhat relieved at his reaction, smiled shyly.

"Do you two know each other?" Gwyn asked.

"Yes," said Paul. "She is an employee at my ashram, too. We've worked together, helping some of the patients."

"Imagine that." Gwyn aimed the light directly into Paul's face.

"Well, guess I'd better be heading back." Paul turned to leave.

"I am also going toward Bhakti Seva," said the Indian woman. "Might I impose my company on you?"

"You want to walk back with me?" Paul said. "Sure, of course."

Gwyn stood and made her way around the desk, lighting the way to the front doors for them.

Paul turned back as he held the door for the other woman. "Thanks for the help, Gwyn. Maybe we can try running the names again when the Internet gods are more hospitable."

Gwyn struggled a tight smile, but neither woman laughed. Gwyn turned out the flashlight and watched the two of them disappear into the night together.

Paul labored to find neutral dialogue, but it wasn't as easy as he hoped it would be. For starters, every time he turned to say something, Paul found the woman several steps behind him. Another axiom of Indian morality, he thought.

"Can I ask you something?" Paul said, turning all the way around to face her as they reached the front gate of the Health Care complex. He asked the question before she had time to respond. "Did I hear Gwyn call you Tatleen?"

She paused, unsure of how to answer. From a literal perspective, an Indian perspective, she wondered how she could possibly know what he heard. It took only a few seconds to Americanize her interpretation. "Yes, that is my name."

Paul was excited to introduce himself and tell her all about his experiences in India. "I have met many nice people here."

Tatleen offered a strained head bow. Chitchat between a man and a woman wasn't part of the lifestyle here, unless they were married to one another.

"Hey, have you ever heard of a thing called Sadhana?" Paul smiled eagerly with his eyes.

What an odd topic, she thought. Lingering embarrassment from their earlier encounter had finally begun to subside, and now they stood at the curb, facing one another again. "Yes, Sadhana comes from the Hindu practice of fulfillment through sacrifice and worship."

"Yes, exactly," Paul spouted. "It's like a meditation practice, right? I practice Sadhana every night!" *Finally, a subject of mutual interest.*

Her expression was curiously pleased. "You are Hindu, yes?"

"Oh, well no." He shifted his sandaled feet. "I'm just, actually, I'm trying to figure some things out. Sadhana is . . . well this practice of self-sacrifice, seems to be helping me."

They stood awkwardly in the little bit of light from a wood-fired kettle. The aroma of *Chaat Papdi* swept between them, but neither had rupees needed to buy any of it. Paul instinctively felt for his wallet, eager to flip out a wad of bills and play the benevolent Lothario. It was a habit that had served him well in his former life. A life to which he felt less and less connected.

"In Indian astrology, Sadhana also means a strong sense of religion. A pathway to God."

A space opened up in the vehicle traffic and they quickly stepped across the roadway.

"Wow, you know a lot. The schooling for your profession must have been pretty intense." Paul slowed to make sure she was well out of the way of an approaching tuk-tuk.

In truth, she hadn't attended school since her father's death and had never worked in any *profession*. Even the use of the terms shamed her. Tatleen's life, her situation, was too complex to even try to explain, so she avoided it altogether. "I wanted to become a dancer," she said out of expediency. "But that was a long time ago, when I was just a girl."

"A dancer, huh?" Paul turned down the alley leading to the rear of the ashram, pleased with himself for navigating the way back at night. "I don't even know what I wanted to become. Probably nothing."

Tatleen looked at him in the dark. "May I ask you, what is your good name?"

"I'm sorry," he said. "I didn't realize we have never actually been introduced. My name is Paul. Paul Griffiths."

Tatleen continued looking at him as they came to the end of the alley. "In America, you have many names used in common?"

"I guess so," he said. "Never really thought about it."

SADHANA

"In India, there are many, many people named Gupta, and Patel, and others. For example, a boy given the name Manish Singh will be one of many." She stopped at the gate. "It is the same way in America?"

"Sure, probably. I'm guessing there are about a million guys named Joe Smith or Bob Johnson."

The conversation had come to a stilted conclusion—neither of them fully understanding what the other was talking about.

"Thank you for allowing me to walk with you."

"You're not coming in?" Paul swung the gate open.

"Not now," she said. "There is something I must do. Goodnight, sir."

"Paul Griffiths," he said, closing the gate behind him. Tatleen's footsteps on the stones faded away on the other side.

As he reached the door, softly chanting voices rose from the temple. Paul stopped to listen before going inside for the night.

Electricity was out in the ashram, and Swami Chalah and the door guard sat together in the lobby—both holding flickering candles.

The men greeted Paul with prayerful hands as he passed them on his way up to his room. Like Paul had done every night previous, he lit a candle and recited his Sadhana—a prayer for personal growth through self-sacrifice. This time there was more meaning to it, having spoken with the Indian woman, Tatleen, who also knew of it.

He had missed dinner. Able to access the Internet for the first time, Paul had chosen his genealogy search over eating. Now, as his stomach called to him like a neglected friend, he regretted the decision.

Without the ceiling fan to push the warm air around his kiln-like quarters, Paul's sleep took a long time to arrive. It was approaching midnight when he woke with a start. Something had stirred his senses, perhaps a noise or pains of hunger inside him. Maybe it was the musical voices rising from the alleyway below his window. Then, feeling the air stirring around him now, Paul knew what it was that had woken him—the electricity had come back on.

He wore only his boxer shorts, and it felt good to lie on his back with the breeze consoling his scorched skin. His mind turned circles in his head, sweeping through the dark like the fan blades above him, shoving his thoughts around at random: his relationship with Loring, the uncle who had created a world of riddles for Paul to unravel. And then there was Leigh, Abigail, or Abby—whoever his mother was. This woman who had cheated on her husband with his twin brother, and who had given birth to Paul and then mysteriously died. Paul took solace in a deep breath, trying to exhale the weight of his past.

197

Gwyn's image came into his mind, and he wondered what she thought of him. Paul was certain that he had created a miserable first impression. Even his second impression was a disaster, showing up several days late at the CRF office. But she seems to be changing her opinion, Paul thought. That whole thing about the wine bottle, and even the way she had looked at him—Paul was convinced there was hope. After all, she was exactly the type of woman he had always been attracted to—blond hair, sparkling eyes and a tight athletic figure. She was outgoing, confident, and had an intriguing style that any man would find captivating. She was an all-American girl.

Charming a beautiful woman was a familiar scenario. He pictured the pool back home, and how many women had partaken in the routine—the slippery anticipation of his room in the pool house, a bowl of good weed, some cognac, a jazz CD playing softly in the background . . . and Gwyn. Paul imagined her body, the feel of it in bed with him. Suddenly he felt himself getting aroused.

He sat up abruptly, frowning into the night. Something about the facsimile hadn't transmitted well. It was blotchy, artificial, or maybe superficial—like a one-dimensional image that didn't do justice to the real thing. Was it about Gwyn or his own, *new* reality? Whatever the case, there was a hollowness to the picture that definitely detracted from it. Something about the fantasy felt in conflict with his Sadhana practices and who he was trying to be. It wasn't that Paul didn't want her, he did. It was more about the *wanting* that debased him—almost the same feeling that came with his continued reliance on his father's money.

Paul stood at the tiny window, facing out into the darkness but only seeing himself. It was a picture that he didn't want to look at. He closed his eyes and tried to focus on the mystical voices outside, but after a while even they faded into silence. As hard as Paul tried, he couldn't avoid being alone with himself.

"What in the hell is wrong with me?" His voice sounded weak in the hallow room. Paul sat at the bottom of his bed, pressing his palms into his eyes.

It was midnight, and Paul's thoughts had rallied him to the point that any further attempt at sleep would be futile. He picked up *Sadhana*, shoved his soiled clothes off of the chair, and sat down to read. It was a story called, *The Old Carpenter*.

SADHANA

The old carpenter finally decided to retire after many years of dedication and hard work. He told his employer/contractor of his decision. The carpenter had worked for the contractor for a long time, and the contractor was saddened to see his loyal employee go.

The carpenter said that he was eager to enjoy time with his family, and though he would miss the income he had made his decision.

His employer asked the carpenter to help build one last house, as a final favor. The carpenter reluctantly agreed, but his heart was not in the job. He cut corners, performed shoddy craftsmanship and used substandard equipment.

When the contractor came to inspect the house, the carpenter handed him the key to the front door. The contractor handed it back and said, "This is your house. For the years of loyal work you have given me, the house is my gift to you."

It was a shock to the carpenter, who now had to live in the home he had built. Had he known he was building his own house he would have done so very differently.

He realized too late that everything you do in life, every nail you drive, each board you put in place, and every wall you build is something you will have to live with. Therefore it is important to construct your life as you would your own home.

Paul sat in the room, eyes closed, absorbing the story's meaning. It wasn't difficult to do. His own life had been poorly constructed, with little thought given to long-term consequences of its craftsmanship.

An unpleasant smell permeated his momentary introspection. Paul glanced down at the heap of clothing he had tossed on the floor and realized his hygiene was also in need of attention. In a country where deodorant was a rarity and a pressed tunic only invited beggars, he had become complacent. The smell of his own clothes was no longer possible to ignore.

Paul carried his clothing into the bathroom, but the tiny bar of soap that had been there since his arrival was now paper thin—not more than a postage stamp.

He slipped back into his musty top and stale pants and headed downstairs. Though he hoped to locate some detergent with which to wash his garments, in the back of Paul's mind lingered the competing motivation to find something to eat.

The kitchen was dark and empty when Paul flipped on the light. He foraged around and the best he was able to come up with was a large, Capri Sun-type juice pouch that said Pitambari Dishwash Liquid. After a little more searching, Paul found a metal mop bucket and filled it with water. He was about to take off his clothes and toss them into the bucket when he heard someone coming from the office.

When Paul saw the pair of almond eyes hesitatingly peek around the doorframe, he was thankful the woman hadn't come in just a couple of minutes later. He would have been standing there in his boxers, or perhaps nothing at all.

"Hello, Tatleen." For reasons Paul was unable to understand, he was surprisingly happy to see her.

"Good morning, Mr. Paul Griffiths."

He explained that he had come down to wash his clothes. And though she did not question Paul about the oddness of his actions, her expression was one of intense curiosity.

"It would be my honor to wash them for you," she said.

"Some honor." Paul glanced down at the brown stains on the knees and thighs of his pants.

Tatleen suddenly realized he was talking about the garments he was presently wearing. "If you will place them outside your room, I can--"

Paul quickly held up a hand. "That's so kind of you, but I couldn't." A ghost of an inclination inside him actually considered it for a second, but Paul recognized the old habit for what it was. "But thank you," he repeated.

So there they stood, separated by a restless silence, under the stark light of the kitchen. Tatleen glanced around the room, avoiding eye contact with Paul. "I was going to prepare some tea for Mr. Gopal on the third floor. Would you like some?"

"That, I will gladly accept."

Tatleen smiled as she filled a pot with water.

The sound of women singing began again. As on previous nights, it began as a chant, low and barely audible, and then grew into an earthy paean. Paul nodded in the direction of the voices, as if to point out something that she may not have heard.

Tatleen smiled again.

"Vee-dow Voo-mons," said Paul, knowingly.

Tatleen stopped smiling.

It was obvious that the term Sree had used, and Paul had tried to repeat, was somehow wrong. Or worse, it was in some way offensive.

"I wasn't trying to . . . I mean, so, who are those ladies?"

"Widows," said Tatleen. "They have all lost their husbands."

"Widow women," Paul said under his breath. *Of course. That was what Sree was trying to say.* Paul's eyes rolled back in embarrassment as he realized the mocking ignorance of his mimicry.

Paul wanted to explain, or at least apologize, but Tatleen was going about making the tea, and no longer seemed bothered by it. Paul elected to move the conversation forward.

"Can I ask, why do they sing?"

Her thick eyebrows came together as she thought about her answer. "It is how they honor their departed husbands. They show devotion through prayer and song and chanting *bhajan.*"

"Do they ever take breaks? I hear these poor women singing all night long."

Tatleen covered a smile with her tiny hand. "Yes, of course. They are not always the same women. Many, many widow women come to the temple. They worship in groups, four hours at a time, twice daily."

"Eight hours a day?" Paul's question had come out a little louder than he intended, and he quickly tried to temper his awe with concern. "I mean, that seems very difficult. Almost like a job."

"In return for their devotion, every woman is given a meal token at the conclusion of each prayer gathering. These are exchanged for food. In that way they are also fed twice daily."

"Then it really is like a job." Paul grinned. "So, I guess this is the night shift on duty now."

Tatleen handed him his tea. "Yes, the night shift. I will bring the rest of the pot upstairs to the patient. Goodnight Mr. Paul Griffiths."

Beneath her contrasting white saree, Tatleen's brown skin loomed rich and smooth and flawless. Paul watched her leave, wondering how she had come to know so much about the widow women.

Tatleen's bare feet padded up the steps to the third floor, where she stopped at the landing and set the teapot on the railing. Gazing down to the grassy courtyard below, at night only a black circle in the center of the horseshoe-shaped ashram, she saw a narrow shard of light edging out from the kitchen window.

Tatleen stood there reflecting about the American man—a man who did not know her, yet had spoken to her with such respect. He had shown her such dignity.

She wondered why she had not told him that she, too, was one of the singing widows.

Eighteen

Restaurant Kwality sat on a moon-shaped curve along a busy stretch of Railway Road. The newly painted, yellow brick building was the most popular eatery in Aligarh, and it was Norm O'Bryan's favorite haunt. It beckoned to the sweaty, red-faced American like a bull's-eye in the center of the route between Bind-Chem's plant and his house. And through the place had no bar, they would serve him beer upon request. So, Norm O'Bryan's presence that afternoon, hunched over his bottle in a corner booth, didn't really muster anyone's attention.

The CEO of Börse Einsatz had wanted to send an underling to handle Bind-Chem's Aligarh plant manager, but O'Bryan had insisted, once again, on dealing only with the company's "top dog." And as he had on the three previous face-to-face meetings with Sig Hoffmann, O'Bryan chose to meet at the Kwality.

"Griffiths spent three days here last month," said O'Bryan. "And I fed him all of the stuff you guys told me to—about how expensive replacing everything will be, and whatnot. He didn't like it, but I think he bought it. So we're good, right?"

Hoffmann managed to appear comfortable, even cool, despite the smothering heat. "We'll be 'good,' as you say, when Paul Griffiths accepts our below market value offer to purchase his company. Until then, you need to continue feeding him the rhetoric about failing infrastructure. Just follow the script."

O'Bryan dragged a sleeve across his shiny forehead. "I'm taking a huge risk here. And on top of which, Mr. Griffiths was none too happy with my report, I'll tell you that. He's got me pegged as some idiot who can't even keep the records straight. For all I know, he's already figured out what we're doing."

"Nobody has figured out anything." Hoffmann sipped his Club Soda. "Unless of course, you got nervous and said something that concerned him."

"No way. Absolutely not," said O'Bryan. "But I'm getting the feeling they're trying to put the squeeze on me."

"What is this, 'squeezing on me'? What does this mean?"

They're trying to get rid of me." O'Bryan barked. Then, lowering his voice, he continued. "I think they're going to fire me."

"Why do you say this?"

"For starters, I've been told to start showing Bhupinder Magar how to do my job. He's some Indian worker, a plant foreman we use every so often to help translate to the locals. Now what does that sound like? And another thing, Griffiths has ordered an audit of the books. A couple of his budget people are supposedly coming here within a few weeks to check things out."

Hoffmann nodded then worked his glass around in a stationary circle on the table. He stared into the bubbly water, thinking. "Not to worry. As long as the deal is made, you'll be well compensated. And if you lose your position, get the squeeze out, as you say, we will simply hire you back to your old position once Bind-Chem is in our hands."

O'Bryan gulped the end of his beer. "That's all well and good. But I just don't want to be left holding the bag at the end of this little game."

Hoffmann didn't fully get the slang, but smiled dryly as if he did. "Do yourself a favor, O'Bryan. Go along with whatever they ask of you, and try not to look so guilty."

"But what if things don't go the way we want them to?" O'Bryan cleared his phlegmy throat. "Maybe I should get something in writing, just to cover my ass."

"Let me tell you something, O'Bryan. I don't care for India. It's hot, and smelly, and I have a multi-billion dollar company to run back home." Hoffmann paused as his waxy smile melted into a solemn glare. "Now, I just flew here from Frankfurt just to hold your hand. Make no mistake, this will not happen again. Do we understand each other?"

"Yes, but--"

Hoffmann silenced him with a flat palm in the air. He rose from the table and left the Kwality, as if he was walking out of a bad movie.

Receding further into the muggy booth, O'Bryan watched the starchy German step into a waiting car and leave. Several beers later, O'Bryan's posture had deteriorated along with his disposition. It was nighttime now, and he sat slumped in the corner muttering to himself.

"Who in the hell does Hoffmann think he is, trying to muscle me around?"

O'Bryan waved the waiter over for a fresh beer, snatching it from the young Indian's hand as if to validate his own potency. The scrawny kid grinned and backed away submissively. The American had a reputation for bizarre and erratic moodiness.

"They're not going to run me out like that," O'Bryan slurred. "I'll blow this thing wide open before I'll let that happen. I could destroy everything for them. For shit sakes, I could sabotage the whole plant, if I wanted to. " He slurped the foamy head from the fresh bottle. "They better make this deal, that's all I can say. Griffiths and Hoffmann had better make this deal."

* * *

The Rogers Park Women's Health Center was set back from the street, sheltered behind a stand of maple trees. The small brick clinic operated as part of the larger Mercy Medical Center downtown, yet sat inconspicuously on a quiet block of old tree-shaded homes. Even so, Abby was fearful that someone she knew might recognize her car, and had parked on West Greenleaf Avenue four blocks from the clinic. She had still not told anyone that she was pregnant.

In the restroom outside her doctor's office, Abby dabbed at her red eyes and stared at herself in the mirror, unable to believe she was really pregnant. And still unmarried, to boot. But now she had a sonogram image to prove it. Strangely, the grainy, black and white picture made it seem even more real than the positive blood test. That, and heaving heard the tiny heartbeat for the first time. According to the doctor, Abby was going to have a boy.

Under any other circumstances, this baby would have been a gift. It would have felt like the reward for a lifetime of goodness, a blessing. But these weren't *other* circumstances. This misadventure with LJ . . . this whole thing was a huge mistake, a mistake with a man who didn't even know about the baby.

The changes taking place in Abby's body, felt suffocating—the result of a careless lapse in judgment that would change her life forever. It seemed her future would be a life sentence of regret.

A week after Abby's doctor visit, the deskman in her apartment building motioned her over as she passed through the lobby. He stopped his phone conversation long enough to bury the receiver into his large neck and whisper that he hadn't been able to fit a box in her mail slot.

Abby studied the small brown parcel on the elevator ride up. It bore a New York City postmark and a Madison Avenue return address.

She read the accompanying letter as she closed the door of her apartment, then crumpled onto the couch as if her legs had suddenly lost the strength to support her.

Setting the letter on her lap, she gazed off into a perplexing void. "How could Paul have possibly known I was pregnant?"

He must have spotted me at the clinic, she thought. Paul must have seen me going into my appointment last week. Abby quickly realized that LJ would also know by now. Paul couldn't keep a priceless gem like her pregnancy to himself; the humiliation value against LJ would be too much for him to resist.

Abby's eyes misted over with anguish and sorrow. She had wanted to tell LJ herself. Though she didn't know where or when she was going to do it, or how he would take it, the news was hers to share. She realized that this whole thing had now gone from bad to worse.

Abby picked up the letter and read one of the lines again. *"The fact that my brother and I fell in love with the same woman is just an unfortunate fact of life."*

There was more. He had finally come clean with how he felt about her. Abby had never really thought about his feelings for her, never considered what lay beneath Paul's bitter sarcasm. Now it all made sense—the acidic rivalry with LJ, the rebelliousness, the divisiveness. Paul was hurt; she could feel it in every line of the letter. He had been in love with her all this time.

Abby's thoughts flashed back to that day behind the print shop, when she swatted Paul on the shoulder after catching him in a lie. Alone in the alleyway, the two had playfully wrestled one another into an ardent embrace. Their eyes had met, if only for a tense moment, yet the mutual heat generated during the contact had both stirred and confused her. Reading Paul's note now for the third time, Abby was immersed in guilt. Carelessly, even selfishly, she had buried that incident away—pretending for years as if it had never happened.

She wondered now if she had always been able to sense Paul's feelings for her. The thought of it made her sick inside. Sick for what she had done to Paul, sick about deceiving herself, and equally as badly for deceiving LJ. He had always recognized something there between her and Paul. Now Abby realized that behind her vehement denials was fear. Fear that at the core of LJ's unfounded suspicions and wild accusations there lay a tiny particle of truth.

SADHANA

The package Paul had sent contained something else—a book, *Sadhana*. Abby slid it onto her lap and studied the ornate fig tree with heart-shaped leaves on the cover. The gift was perplexing, not only because Paul had never given her anything, but also because the book itself seemed oddly unlike him. Definitely not the type of publication she could imagine Paul reading—Playboy or Penthouse, she could see. The whole thing, the letter and the book, was a bizarre enigma in a life already replete with complications.

Days passed and there was no contact from LJ. Abby had been certain he would seek her out after hearing about her pregnancy from Paul. But he never did. Days turned to weeks. A month passed, and then two. Abby was convinced that LJ had turned his back on her, wanted nothing to do with she or her unborn child.

In the meantime, Abby began reading the book Paul had sent her. It seemed an odd little collection of stories, but it became a source of calm in her abstruse and often confusing life. At times she identified with the book's proverbs and parables, finding in them some semblance of harmony and balance.

Every day Abby would wonder what LJ thought, or if he even cared. She could understand his not wanting to start a family with her—he was a young man beginning a career—but to cut off all communication baffled Abby. Even though something still compelled her to confront LJ, she didn't think she could face being rebuffed by him again. Their seesaw relationship had begun to erode Abby's self-respect, and her pride was now weighing in on the issue.

She fought a battle inside herself, constantly debating the pros and cons of contacting him. The thought of love scared her, but the thought of not being loved in return worried her more. Still, the one thing that terrified Abby more than all else was raising a child alone.

Then she read about the practice of Sadhana: *"A means whereby bondage becomes liberation."* She related it to her feelings of being burdened by the baby.

Whether a result of the confusion in her life, or perhaps merely out of despair, Abby began the ritual of lighting the candle each night. She asked for clarity and understanding, and for direction. She imagined the Sadhana flame as a beacon, guiding her toward enlightenment.

Slowly, her view began to change. Abby realized that embracing the concept of "serving," also meant fully embracing the child she was bringing into the world.

Abby was approaching the end of her first trimester. Her clothes fit tightly, especially around her hips, stomach and breasts, and she could no longer squeeze into some of her things. Thankfully, the cooler weather had allowed for loose fitting coats, otherwise a sharply tuned eye would have spotted the changes. Abby still hadn't told a soul, and had no intention of doing so—at least until she knew for sure how Loring felt.

Though she had long since decided to keep the baby, until now Abby hadn't thought clearly about her role. Time alone, meditating, helped bring these things into focus and galvanize her spirit. Abby realized she would be a sentinel in her son's life, standing guard against anyone who would bring him harm. She would be there for him, regardless of whether or not his father was in his life. Like the Sadhana candle, she would help her son find his way if he ever became lost.

The quarrel inside Abby had become a distraction, as she debated how best to handle LJ. The dilemma continued to vex her until a particular incisive line from her book caught her eye: *"When you fight with yourself, someone is always going to be the loser. It will inevitably be you."*

She made the decision to contact LJ and ask him to meet her. Despite her certainty that Paul had already told LJ about the pregnancy, Abby wanted to make her position known. And she wanted to do it, face-to-face.

The phone number Abby had, went to a recording—one of those automated voices that sounded like a librarian, with words that were taped together without regard for modulation.

"Hello, Loring." She paused a second for effect. "This is Abby. It's obvious that you don't care to hear what I have to say about this, but I'd like to meet with you. I think you owe the *two of us* that much."

LJ stood in his room staring at the wood grained answering machine. He took off his coat and loosened his tie before turning the dial and rewinding the tape to listen to it again.

He had made a fool of himself, yet again. The day of his mother's funeral had ended in disaster, and the only upshot was that Abby had already left, and wasn't there to see the result of her own handiwork.

It was not in LJ's character to be out of control. It felt even more humiliating to know that Abby had that control over his actions. But LJ also realized that whenever it happened, it always smelled of Paul.

SADHANA

LJ had seen with his own eyes that she and Paul had snuck off to the bedroom downstairs—to do, who knows what? LJ hadn't trusted Paul from the start, but now his faith in Abby was also gone. For good.

LJ stared at the recorder, incredulous at her gall. *Now she's telling me, I owe the two of them?* He decided he *would* meet with her, if only to say it to her, face-to-face.

The Ambassador East was only a few blocks from the law firm on East Goethe Street. Abby thought that the walk after work would do she and the baby some good, as long as the rain held off. So when LJ called back, Abby did not have to think about it. "The Pump Room is a nice place; we'll meet there." Her brazen decree referred to the flashy restaurant inside the landmark hotel. It was a well-known hangout for celebrities and Chicago elites. Abby figured the place would create the image she desired—one in which she would appear financially capable, with an air of independence. "The stroll and the fresh air will be good for us" she added.

LJ was caught off balance by the determination in her voice. Before he could even think, he heard himself agreeing to the place. As he hung up, he replayed the one-sided proposition—directive, really. Then his eyes squinted in anger. Did she say that the stroll and fresh air will do *us* good? Who the hell is *us*?

She better not be bringing Paul with her.

"Abby." LJ slid into the booth across from her. "Glad to see you came alone."

She let the strange comment pass. "Hello, Loring. Thank you for agreeing to talk."

"I'm not sure I have much to say." LJ took a gulp from his water glass. "Anyway, you sounded so insistent. Nonetheless, I'm here."

"I hoped you might have wanted to come." Abby regarded him intently, waiting for a response that seemed stalled behind his clenched teeth. "I know you heard the news. I'm sure Paul couldn't wait to tell you."

"He didn't have to," said LJ. "I already knew. I knew it when you came up from downstairs the day of my mom's funeral."

Abby's mouth dropped open, thinking LJ must have somehow heard her talking to her doctor on the phone. "You knew all the time? And you never said anything?"

"What was I supposed to say? Congratulations? I hope you two will be happy together?"

Her eyes blazed at him. "I don't even know you anymore, Loring."

"I don't know you!" LJ sneered in disgust. "I'm sure you just made yourself comfortable, taking care of business in *my* bedroom!"

"I didn't think you would really care. Besides, I was on the stairs anyway."

"Oh, really nice." LJ could barely catch his breath "On the stairs? Right there on the stairs of my Uncle Stuart's house? We had a house full of people. Did you ever think of what it might have looked like had someone opened the door and looked down there?"

Abby shook her head. "No, not really."

LJ rubbed his head with the palm of his hand.

"Anyway, Loring," Abby said, leaning forward in her seat. "Like it or not, he'll always be part of you. I need to know if you are even the slightest bit interested in participating in his life?"

LJ shuttered. "No, I'm not. I thought I'd already made that pretty clear."

Abby's eyes welled up and she looked away. She sniffed lightly and dabbed her eyes with the corner of the cloth napkin. "I don't know how you could feel that way."

"How am I supposed to feel?" LJ couldn't imagine how she would possibly expect him to feel otherwise. Paul had finally succeeded in doing what he had set out to do. He had stolen Abby from him.

"This changes everything for me, Loring. He's my life now."

LJ rolled his eyes and let out a snicker. "Half expected the little bastard to make an appearance here tonight."

"Oh my God, Loring." Abby's expression was one of horrific shock.

"What?" he glanced behind him, around the room then back at Abby. "He's here, isn't he? I knew it."

"What's wrong with you?" Her eyes narrowed. "How could you look at me and say something so thoughtless as that?"

LJ sighed, frustrated with Abby's erratic emotions. "Sorry, you'll have to excuse me for not being as excited about this little affair as you seem to be. It's just not quite that easy for me."

"What are you saying?"

"I'm saying I had feelings for you. I'm saying . . . I even thought that I loved you." LJ's head dropped and his voice quivered. "But this. You're right, you and him, it changes everything."

Abby was quiet. She stared across the table, tears running down her cheeks. "Well, I guess if that's how you feel."

LJ slid to the side of the booth seat. A waiter came and LJ shook his head, sending him on his way.

"Goodbye Abby," LJ said, standing now with his coat tucked under his arm. "The best I can do is wish you two a happy life together."

She gazed at him with a mixture of regret and pity. "You'll never know what you missed."

He turned to leave and she called out after him. "You'll never be able to play with him, teach him things, toss a ball--"

LJ stopped a few steps away and wheeled around to face her. His face contorted as his eyebrows dipped together. "Abby, what the hell are you talking about?"

They stared at one another in confusion. LJ finally said, "I haven't played with Paul since we were kids. And who cares about that, anyway?"

Now her brow twisted. "Who said anything about Paul? I'm talking about the baby."

"Baby. What baby?"

"What baby?" Abby glanced around at the other diners. Her frown deepened as she spoke in a lowered voice, "This baby. My baby."

"You're pregnant?" LJ's words came out several decibels louder than the surrounding din. "Now you're going to have a baby?"

Dozens of conversations were suddenly halted and the room around them grew quiet.

Abby's head did not move, but her eyes flashed back and forth to the surrounding tables. In a hushed tone she answered, "Yes, Loring. That's what we're, or at least that's what I'm talking about. What are you talking about?"

He ignored the question. "You and Paul," LJ said, more to himself in realization. "I knew it."

"Again with Paul?" Abby shook her head. "What is it with you two?"

He ignored her again. "That day! The day we buried my mother. You and Paul were downstairs together. That's when it happened."

Now Abby was thoroughly perplexed. "Loring, I don't know what you're talking about. I was never downstairs with Paul, that day or any other day."

"Oh yes you were. I saw you." He sat back on the seat, numbly. "I saw you come up and then a minute later I saw Paul come up."

She gazed into space, thinking back. "So that's how Paul knew."

With the soap opera now over, the other diners returned to their meals.

"Loring, I never went all the way down the steps." Abby was putting it all together now. "I stood in the stairway talking on the telephone to my doctor. The kitchen phone cord could only stretch so far."

"And?"

"Don't you see?" Abby rested her palms on the table in front of her. "That's how Paul knew I was pregnant. He was down there, listening."

"Wait a minute, Abby." LJ was rigid on the seat, still holding his coat. "I'm not following this at all. You're saying it's not Paul's baby?"

"Don't be ridiculous—of course it's not."

"If it's not Paul's, then whose baby is it?"

"Loring!" Her hands were now planted solidly on her hips. "What do you think? It's your baby!"

The room fell silent again.

Nineteen

The investigator, Tam, had flown to Helsinki.

None of us knew what it meant exactly, but it sounded as if things were beginning to happen. We speculated that the police had matched Paul's photo to someone on a surveillance video. A good lead, perhaps.

As it turned out, the Finnish police had found absolutely nothing. No matches on their surveillance monitors and still no new activity detected on Paul's bank cards.

Tam assured Mr. Griffiths that Paul was "*probably okay.*" According to the investigator, Finland's crime statistics were comparatively very low, and foreigners traveling there were *generally* quite safe. He made it a point to emphasize that Paul was more likely to become a crime victim in the United States than in Finland.

Then where is he? I said to myself. *Paul didn't just disappear.*

* * *

Naagesh crawled across the room, pulling himself over the dirt like a serpent with arms. Propped on his side at the opening, he swept back the cloth door with one hand and turned to smile at Tatleen.

The dancers outside jumped and spun in the narrow street. Painted in bright colors and moving wildly to the beat of a double-headed *Dhol* drum, the celebrants gathered strength as neighbors poured from the scrappy shanties that lined the road.

"It is the beginning of *Radhastami*," she told the boy, "anniversary of the appearance of *Srimati Radharani*, Krishna's greatest devotee. Tonight when I return I will take you with me to the temple."

The boy was captivated. Other children in the orphanage had joined Naagesh at the doorway. With wide eyes, they leaned across the worn wooden threshold. "Hare Krishna!" they yelled out to the people as they passed. "Hare Krishna!"

The portly guard sat on a white plastic chair at the gates of the Asha Health Care and Research Centre. Dressed in a powder blue uniform with dark disks of perspiration under his arms, the man greeted Paul with clasped hands. "Hare Krishna."

Returning the acknowledgement of the holiday, Paul then said, "I am a friend of Gwyneth Eichler. May I go inside to see her?"

The guard's head bobbled slightly as he grinned back at Paul. "Miss Gwyn not at clinic today. Not at clinic. She come back, two days more."

Paul looked past the guard, at the tree-shaded building with the pink façade. "Left, where? Where did she go?"

"Hinganghat." The man's grin seemed glued in place. His answer meant nothing to Paul, but the guard was clearly pleased with his own helpfulness.

The sunlight had diminished into narrow splinters reaching out from behind the clinic buildings, but the day's heat still hung heavy in the air. Paul thanked the guard then walked back toward the road. He had hoped to use the desktop computer in Gwyn's office again, and since the electricity seemed to be working with more reliability of late, he was eager to research his mother's death—especially now, aware of her maiden name.

Paul cupped a hand over his squinting eyes to view the long procession moving slowly toward him up the road from the west. He assumed it had something to do with the religious holiday.

For several days Paul had noticed preparations underway, as temples and streets were decorated with flowers, candles and incense. He had learned from Swami Chalah that the town of Vrindavan is believed by Hindus to have once been the site of an ancient forest where the deity Krishna spent his childhood days, and that is the reason followers flock by the thousands each year to celebrate.

Waiting as the devotees slowly passed, Paul wondered how far they had traveled. Some wore orange robes and were painted like the holy men he had met on the train, while others were dirty and threadbare. An old lady, one of the last to pass, was withered and bent, and walked with one dominant leg, while her trailing leg drug in the dirt like the axle of a car with a missing wheel. Her bare feet were cracked and calloused, and covered in tan dust. She carried a small paper bag from which she gummed pieces of dried fruit. The woman glanced at Paul with tired eyes then bowed her head slightly before continuing.

SADHANA

Paul crossed the street behind the procession, pausing at the mouth of an alleyway where a small shrine had been erected. Inhaling the sweet scents, he stared into a flickering candle. Music had started to play through speakers strung high upon utility poles throughout the town. Paul turned into the alley, one through which he had never traveled. It was dark and narrow, yet its mystical lure provoked more curiosity than fear.

He walked past several huts, many with nothing more than a tarp or curtain covering the doorway. At the end of the alley Paul came upon a stone-faced temple. He could see inside, as there was no door and only a wide opening in the stone veneer wall. Dozens of men were huddled there, in the light of a fire and what appeared to be heated stones. Most were stripped of clothing, save for a single cloth strung around their waists to cover their genitals. Paul had the impression that it was some type of sweat lodge ritual.

A large, white Malvi cow meandered out of the shadows at the end of the alleyway and Paul stepped back against the wall to allow ample leeway. The beast stopped and swung his big head around to gaze into the temple, and then ambled inside without concern. Paul watched for startled reactions from the celebrants, but there were none. A few even paused to gesticulate a blessing upon it.

As Paul continued back toward the light of the street, he saw the silhouette of a woman walking in his direction. She wore a white saree, but beyond that Paul was unable to distinguish her features. Midway down the alley, the woman turned into one of the ramshackle shelters. As she lifted back the curtain that covered the doorway opening, a light from within bathed her face in a golden glow. It was Tatleen, the woman with whom he had cared for his dying friend, Praneel. An uncanny coincidence, Paul thought, that their paths had crossed several times since that night.

Paul wasn't quite sure why, but he abruptly stepped back into the shadows. From his concealed spot in the alley he watched the tiny doorway with restless anticipation, wondering what this place was and why Tatleen had gone there. For reasons unknown to Paul, the woman provoked in him a curious allure that fell somewhere between sympathy and enchantment. She was soft and quiet and generous, but something in her deep brown eyes hinted at an unfathomable burden.

After several minutes Tatleen emerged from the hut with a young boy in her arms. His gaunt frame rested upon her hip, and his arms were slung around her neck like a cumbrous shoulder bag.

"Remember," she whispered to Naagesh in Hindi, "never refer to me as your mother in front of others. It is an important secret that nobody can ever know."

Following from a distance, Paul saw Tatleen speaking softly into the boy's ear. He appeared to be older than a toddler, yet his age was difficult for Paul to gauge in the dark, and without moving up to get a closer look.

Perhaps he is a patient of the health centre, Paul thought. He knew Tatleen's work at both the ashram and the clinic involved patient care, so moonlighting in the same field made perfect sense. He guessed she was a physical therapist, but wondered if she was a nurse, or possibly even a doctor. In any case, the boy seemed old enough to walk, so the fact that Tatleen carried him convinced Paul that the boy's mobility was impaired and that he was under Tatleen's care.

They came to the road and turned left, toward the center of town. The shops, stalls and sidewalks were choked with people, making it easier for Paul to follow Tatleen unnoticed. But he was fearful she might turn and see him, or just as easily be swallowed up and lost in the massive crowds. Not that there was any real point to his skulking surveillance, in fact he felt almost as if he were following a junior high school crush, to find the location of her homeroom class. It was stupid, he knew, yet he felt compelled to continue.

At times they were compressed by the mob, drawing Paul close enough to reach out and touch Tatleen. He could see her thin body, leaning to one side to compensate for the child's weight. Paul saw the boy's legs, oddly twisted and ending at the knees.

Tatleen was unnoticed in the noisy crowd. They pushed and shoved and brushed her aside as if she were no more than a bothersome cobweb. She stepped along quickly, her bare feet zigzagging around potholes and mud puddles, her head lowered so as not to make eye contact with anyone.

Darting onto a quiet side street not too far from the ashram, the two quickly disappeared from view. Paul turned up the alley after them, but Tatleen and the crippled boy were gone.

He wandered further up the dark roadway to a brightly lit temple, bustling with people and vibrating with music. Two shotgun-toting men in ragtag, mismatched uniforms guarded the open gate in front. Paul clasped his hands together, offering them a solemn blessing as he passed.

SADHANA

As Paul's foot landed on the first of the temple's three marble steps, one of the guards grunted something at him. To Paul's ear, it did not sound like the *Hare Krishna* blessing he expected to hear in response. Paul stopped and looked back, afraid he had been made; a white, non-Hindu American, trying to assimilate with the locals. He was probably just what those lawmen were guarding against.

Paul turned around, expecting to see one of their antique shotguns pointing at him.

"Pssst!" one of the guards hissed, pointing at Paul's feet. "*Juta.*"

"Oh, sorry." Paul slipped off his sandals and set them in the dirt next to a rack filled with shoes. "Dammit," he said to himself. "And I knew that one from the travel book."

Paul ascended the steps into the temple, stopping suddenly just inside the doors as the scene struck him like a headlight in the eyes. He wilted against the wall as the colors, noise and dance engulfed his senses. Gasping in sweet, fragrant flowers and spicy wisps of incense smoke that hung over the percolating worshipers, Paul was almost dizzied by the carousel of activity surrounding him.

His eyes scanned the huge room, the center of which was a full five or six feet below him and filled with hundreds of celebrants. Some prayed, some sat cross-legged and watched, while others danced and sang with outstretched hands that waited for sweets. At intervals around the room, holy men tossed candy into the frenzied crowd.

Paul spotted one of the ashram's patients sitting against a pillar at the back of the temple. He was Mr. Gopal, from the third floor dormitory. Paul waved and the man nodded solemnly. Gopal was very ill, but he had somehow trudged his feeble body there to worship.

A pair of almond eyes suddenly caught Paul's from across the floor. Buried beneath a cloth *chuddar*, the small rectangle of the woman's face was unmistakably that of Tatleen. Paul quickly turned his head, pretending not to have seen her, and then immediately wondered why.

As he watched a man bang wildly on a tambourine, Paul realized he hadn't noticed if the boy was with Tatleen. He casually ventured a second glance, only to find that yes—the boy was still with her, and yes—Tatleen's eyes were still on Paul.

To pretend not to see her a second time would be foolish, he thought, so Paul stepped down the marble stairs onto the main floor and made his way over to them. It was only when he was halfway there that Tatleen's head lowered slightly and her eyes dipped to the boy in her lap.

"Hello, Tatleen." Paul folded himself onto a space on the floor next to them. "May I join you?"

She nodded, but a look of dread flashed in her eyes. She quickly glanced around, then down at the boy, who smiled at Paul with the same almond-shaped eyes as Tatleen.

"Is this your son?" Paul asked, trying to avert his gaze from the boy's disfigured legs.

She glanced around again before answering. "Naagesh lives in an orphanage a short distance from here. I take him to and from the clinic each week."

Paul playfully tousled the boy's hair, to which Tatleen instinctively retracted her arms, pulling the boy with her. Both she and Naagesh looked at Paul curiously, causing him to wonder if they somehow found the innocent *Western* gesture insulting.

In a poorly planned demonstration that there had been no ill intent, Paul reached up and rumpled his own hair. Tatleen's expression turned to fearful apprehension as she watched the odd display, but then Naagesh suddenly began to laugh. A great relief to Paul, he grinned at Tatleen in reassurance—as if it were a *guy thing*, beyond her understanding.

To the delight of Naagesh, Paul mussed his own hair again, but then stopped when he noticed others around him staring. Even across the cultural and language rift, Paul could see that the orphan was unacquainted with men. The glint in Naagesh's eyes was evidence enough that it was something he craved.

Paul winked at him and Naagesh tried to wink back, but Tatleen's gentle hands turned the boy's face back toward the activity at the front of the temple.

"How old is he?" Paul asked.

Tatleen shifted nervously. "Ten years and one half."

Paul would have guessed he was half that age. Cautiously, he glanced down at Naagesh's disfigured legs—both of which ended in misshapen nubs where the knees should have been.

The noise made it difficult to carry on a conversation, so Paul found contentment in the subdued company of the woman and her orphan charge. As Paul pretended to watch the goings on around him, he was aware that Naagesh's eyes constantly watched him.

Tatleen's eyes were on Paul, too.

As the ceremony began to wind down, Tatleen and Naagesh got up to leave. Paul offered to walk with them, and even though Tatleen seemed hesitant about the idea, she consented to it.

Paul retrieved his sandals and slipped them on. Since Tatleen did not own a pair, she had none to retrieve.

They squeezed through the teeming crowds that clogged temple entrances, food stalls and shops. Paul followed Tatleen as she carried the boy along on her hip. "That's wonderful," Paul said, motioning to the boy. "What you're doing in your spare time. I think it's fantastic to help orphan children. A very kind and giving thing to do."

She looked into Paul's eyes with a mixture of admiration and shame. Naagesh was not her charity patient. And though she wouldn't even know where to start, Tatleen wanted very much to tell Paul that the boy was her son and not an orphan. She wanted to explain it, to try to tell him her story in a way he might understand. She hated deceiving anyone, especially the kind-hearted American man. But her situation had become too complex to share. Once a beautiful garden full of colorful flowers, life's monsoons and fate's pulverizing winds had eroded Tatleen to her core. There was nothing left in her soul to cultivate. Nothing except Naagesh, the only thing keeping her alive.

But how could she even begin to explain all this to Paul? A man who had shown she and her son such kindness. A man who actually *did* volunteer to care for the sick. Who had come all the way from the United States of America to help those less fortunate than himself. And he did it for no other reason than the kindness inside his heart.

Tatleen knew her plight could not be appreciated or even understood by merely glimpsing the dried weed she had become. No, Tatleen would find another time to explain her life to this man.

Paul waited in the alley while Tatleen carried Naagesh through the flimsy doorway of the orphanage. She kissed her son gently on the face, out of view of anyone else, and then quietly reminded him not to ever tell others that she was his mother.

She emerged after a few minutes appearing more relaxed.

"He's a good boy," Paul said.

Tatleen's eyes smiled from behind the cloth that covered the lower half of her face. Then after a minute of walking in silence, she asked, "You celebrate *Radhastami*?"

"I just sort of wandered into the temple," Paul said. Her mystic eyes stared back at him and he was unable to shade the truth. "Actually, I saw you walking and, well, I wondered where you were going."

"You follow me?"

Paul swallowed and a long pause followed it. Her question hadn't been asked in annoyance or objection. In fact, Tatleen didn't seem offended at all. "Yes, I guess I did."

"Thank you, Mr. Paul Griffiths," she said. "It can be dangerous for a woman to be out at night. Especially when unescorted."

Paul leaned back, his chest inflating with a fresh breath. "Oh sure, sure, not a problem."

It got quiet again. They stepped gingerly over the dark and uneven cobblestones, as they headed back toward the ashram.

Paul turned to her. "Can I ask you a question?"

Tatleen stared back at him in confusion. His question *was* a question.

"I noticed that you call me by my full name," Paul said. "And I remember one of the first times we spoke, you asked me about my name . . . if Americans had a lot of common names."

She stared at Paul, again confused. This *question* was not a question. He was telling her something she already knew.

Paul raised an eyebrow, trying to work his way through whatever miscommunication was going on. "So, I was wondering, why did you ask me that?"

Tatleen unwrapped the fabric from her face and let it hang down the front of her saree. Her face was at ease now, exotic and warm in the muted light of the alleyway. Her white teeth glinted as she answered him. "I once met a man with your name."

A chuckle escaped Paul's lips. "Oh, is that all. Yeah, Paul is fairly common as far as American names go."

"Yes," she said with a nod. "The man I speak of, Paul Griffiths, he was a friend of my father's."

Paul stopped mid-stride and stood motionless in the dark. "His name, this friend of your fathers, it was Paul *Griffiths*?"

"Yes." Tatleen's eyes flashed confusion again. "The man was my father's boss. But that was many years ago."

With frenzied eyes, the only things visible on Paul's otherwise dark face, he reached out and took Tatleen's arm. "Paul Griffiths is the name of my uncle. I have to talk to your father. I need to find out if they are one in the same."

"My father died many years ago." She stared back at him, gently easing her arm free of his grasp. "I don't understand. You said the name was a common one."

"I meant *Paul*. Paul is a common name in the U.S., Tatleen." His hand grazed through his scraggly beard. "Paul Griffiths, not so common." He took a step in the other direction and then whirled back around. "Is there anybody else? Someone who might have worked for him?"

She thought. "Yes. I think, yes, there was another . . . the man my father replaced. His name was O'Bryan."

"This O'Bryan guy, please tell me he's still around."

Tatleen shook her head. "He was not a good man."

"Anybody else? Anybody you can think of who can describe Paul Griffiths for me?"

"He came to our house for dinner one night. My mother, she would remember, but she has also died." Tatleen squinted into the darkness at Paul. "I was just a little girl, but I also saw Mr. Paul Griffiths. He was a big man, larger than my father."

"Big, like fat?"

She shook her head again. "No, he seemed very tall to me, and he had strong hands."

"When was this?" Paul took both her hands in his. "Think back, how old was this man?"

"September of 1983." She knew the date without even thinking. "I was only nine years when he came to visit. Adults all seemed old to me back then, and I had never seen an American Caucasian person before." Tatleen tilted her head back, gazing into the night sky. "I think his age was about thirty years."

"The year I was born," he said. "So, that would be just about right. My dad is sixty-two, I think."

"Your father?" Tatleen was confused again.

"Well both, my father and my uncle. They're twins. And to be honest, I'm not sure which is my father and which is my uncle."

It made no sense to Tatleen, so she said nothing. They walked the rest of the way without talking. When they arrived at the ashram, she turned abruptly to Paul.

"There was a photograph," she said with some enthusiasm. "I remember seeing it once. It was of my father and Mr. Paul Griffiths, and the other man, Mr. O'Bryan. It may be with my father's things."

"You have it? A photograph of the man, you have it?"

Tatleen nodded with apprehension. "It just now occurred to me. I kept a small pouch of my father's when he died; perhaps the photograph is there with his treasured belongings."

"Can we go to your house now?" Paul's eager expression stunned her. "I'd like to see the picture right away."

House? There is no house. Tatleen shook her head vehemently. She lived in a squalid dormitory where dozens of women slept in a dank room, on jute sacks or directly on the cracked tiled floors. It was a safe haven from thieves, rapists and the harsh monsoon rains, but little more than that.

"Perhaps I could bring the photograph to you later?" She asked. "There is something I have to do first."

"I'll meet you right here," he said, indicating the ashram's grass courtyard. "What do you think, an hour?"

"Longer," she said. "Perhaps in four hours."

Paul watched her hurry off down the alley into the darkness. Minutes later, the nightshift of angelic widows began to sing. He still hadn't made the connection that Tatleen was one of them, and for reasons she did not fully understand, she still had not told him.

* * *

Gwyn Eichler had her hands full at CRF International's satellite clinic in Hinganghat. A late monsoon rain lasting several days had flooded a broad area of the Dham River, 26 kilometers north of the town. A massive breach had occurred in the Narmada canal, which runs between the villages of Sujatpura and Balsara, leaving homes and crop fields under several feet of water.

The flood itself was directly responsible for only 39 deaths—an almost amazingly low number given that the canal breach had occurred just after midnight in October, during one of the darkest nights of the year. Fortunately, the villagers were celebrating *Lakshmi Puja*—a Hindu ritual known as festival of lights, held after sunset on the third day of Diwali.

Despite recovery efforts, stagnate runoff had concealed rotting corpses and dead animals for days, until their bloated carcasses floated to the surface. By then the *vibrio cholerae bacterium*-filled water had saturated aquifers and contaminated local irrigation and drinking water.

So after giving thanks to the gods who had protected them from drowning, hundreds of villagers began falling ill. Watery diarrhea and dehydration caused by the cholera outbreak had overwhelmed local clinics with dead and dying villagers, as many more, not knowing the cause of the illness, continued drinking the polluted well water.

SADHANA

Gwyn and her crew of volunteers had been sent into the area with drinking water, hygiene and survival kits, floor mats and solar lamps, and had worked nearly around the clock for five days. But as busy as she was, Gwyn couldn't stop thinking about Paul.

The spoiled rich kid from the Hamptons had surprised her. He had forged ahead after the theft of his belongings and had prevailed, penniless and alone, in one of the most formidable countries in the world. Paul had impressed her with his ability to adapt and overcome. Whether Paul Griffiths had reinvented himself or had finally found himself, Gwyn didn't know. What she did know was that whoever he was, whoever he had become, he intrigued her. This was a guy she could actually see herself with.

"Stop here," Gwyn said to the college intern driving the CRF bus. They were on their way back to the satellite clinic in Hinganghat when she spotted the silver shop. "I'll only be a few minutes."

The others in the bus groaned, exhausted from the past week.

Gwyn bounded into the shop and was immediately swarmed by the owner, his wife and their teenage son—all offering the American woman *the best deal in all of India.* She smiled politely and moved away to browse alone; she had something special in mind, more or less. Gwyn had wanted to buy Paul a set of silver cufflinks. She had seen them in shops like this before, and they seemed like a birthday gift that would convey a message that she was mildly interested, yet they weren't personal enough to make her look like a stalker.

But this shop didn't have any cufflinks.

The owner barked out something to his son who clambered onto his belly and scrambled under a small religious shrine at the back of the shop. He backed out with a cardboard box filled with rumpled newsprint. The owner reached past his son and pulled out a small silver tray mounted on the backs of three tiny temple elephants. It was no bigger than an ashtray, and the little silver elephants wore hand-painted caparisons and tassels. It was a cute little trinket that stood only a few inches off the table. Though it wasn't what Gwyn had hoped to buy Paul, it would serve the same purpose.

* * *

Paul went up to his room after Tatleen left, wondering what he would do for the next four hours while he waited for her. Normally it wouldn't be an issue, but with the new information about his uncle, or his father, whichever Paul Griffiths was, he was itching to find out more. Reclining on his rigid bed, Paul stared up at the circulating fan.

223

He couldn't help but feel anger toward the man, Loring John Griffiths, whom he had always known as his father. Whether or not he even was his father, it infuriated Paul that the man had disowned his own brother. Uncle or dad, Paul felt he had been robbed of the opportunity to know the man. And why had Paul been kept in the dark about his mother's life as well as her death?

He sneered at the thought of Loring Griffiths—a man who tosses the truth around like a game of keep away, and withholds knowledge like it's his divine power to do so. Paul felt as if his life had been stolen from him. He cursed aloud—his words quashing the serenity of the ashram and sounding contrary to what he was trying to find in his life.

Knowing there was little he could do until Tatleen returned with the photograph, Paul went down and sat under a light in the courtyard with his book, *Sadhana*.

He opened it to a parable called, *The Blind Men and the Elephant*.

> *Three blind men were walking along when they came upon an elephant in the road. They each placed a hand upon the beast and felt its body. The men had never encountered an elephant before and were curious as to what it looked like.*
>
> *The man with his hand on the stomach said, "The elephant is solid like a rock wall."*
>
> *Another man held the elephant's tusk. "No, it is long and rigid like a tree branch."*
>
> *The third blind man felt the tail. "The elephant is like a rope."*
>
> *Their debate turned heated, each man certain that his description of the elephant was the most accurate.*
>
> *A wise man soon encountered the group and asked why they were fighting. The men each told the wise man what they had felt, and asked that he tell them which one was correct.*
>
> *"You are each right and you are each wrong," he answered. "All three of you felt a different part of the animal and were accurate in your description. But it requires patience and cooperation to communicate with one another, and only then will each of you understand the context of the others' description. And together each of you will see the whole elephant.*

SADHANA

It was half past midnight. Paul reclined against the side of the building, watching a large moth flutter in the light above him. He tried to understand the meaning of the story, struggling to apply it to his own situation. He wondered if it had to do with his limited view of the Indian culture. If he were to experience more of it, or see it though the eyes of others, perhaps he could better understand and appreciate it.

Swami Chalah had been meditating in his small room on the ground floor of the ashram. At the conclusion of his *Hare Rama* mantra prayer, he glanced out the window. Just beyond the garden he saw Paul sitting against the wall. He walked out and across the dim courtyard to join the American.

Paul started to stand. "Hello, Swami Chalah."

"Please don't get up," he said. "I only wish to enjoy this beautiful evening with you. I see you are reading." The swami eased himself into a squatting position against the wall.

Paul held the book up under the light. He considered describing to the swami how mysteriously the old manuscript had come to be in his possession, and of the significance it held. He wanted to tell the holy man about the letter found tucked inside it—unopened for years, and bearing his mother's full name. Paul's mind scrambled to organize his epic story into something logical, something that would make sense.

But Swami's understanding expression rendered any explanation Paul would come up with, irrelevant. The swami nodded graciously. "Tell me which of *Sadhana's* stories you have read."

"I've read about three blind men and an elephant," Paul said. "I'm trying to find a meaning I can use in my life."

Swami nodded again. "It is an ancient proverb."

"You've heard of it?"

"There are many versions of the story," said the swami. "Jaina dharma, Buddhist, Sufi, Hindu . . . but its message is the same."

Paul looked at the swami, waiting for him to unveil the proverb's hidden meaning, but Swami Chalah just smiled back.

Finally Swami said, "A person in your life perhaps? Someone who has hurt you . . . someone who you have not forgiven."

Paul realized that he may have taken the story too literally; he had not explored or considered its deeper meaning. Slowly nodding to Swami, Paul immediately thought about Loring and about the anger and resentment he had for the man. He wondered if there was any way to apply the proverb to his feelings about the man who had raised him as his son.

Eased slightly after releasing a long, tension-filled breath, Paul knew the answer was there. Still too full of angst to delve into it any further, he recognized that he might have judged his father without knowing all the facts. *Without taking time to see the whole elephant.*

Swami Chalah got up and stretched under the hanging lamp above them. "Goodnight," he said to Paul. "Sleep well."

Paul continued sitting against the wall, thinking. Several minutes had passed when the hinges creaked across the courtyard as the wooden door from the alley inched open.

"Tatleen?" Paul stood, pushing himself off the wall.

"Hello, Mr. Paul Griffiths." Tatleen's eyes were downcast and she spoke in a quiet, almost shame-filled tone.

"What's the matter?" Paul met her halfway across the grassy area. "And by the way, you can just call me Paul."

"I was not able to find the photograph," her voice trailed off. After a few seconds she spoke again without looking up. "I'm very sorry to disappoint you."

"Is that what's bothering you?" Although Paul was disappointed, it was not at Tatleen. And she seemed to be taking it much worse than him. "No worries. None whatsoever."

Finally, Paul saw the flickering reflection of light in Tatleen's deep brown eyes. They were warm and moist and inviting. "Then you are not angry with me?"

"Of course not," he said. "Not one iota."

Tatleen stared at him curiously. "What is iota?"

Paul laughed. "That's a good question. Actually, I haven't the slightest idea. Some form of measurement, I suspect. And they must only come in ones because I have never heard of two iotas."

Tatleen smiled, though she was completely puzzled by the conversation. At least he was not upset, she thought.

They walked quietly back toward the light of the ashram, as Paul thought about what steps he might take to learn more about this man Tatleen's father worked for—a man to whom Paul may be related.

He suddenly became aware that Tatleen had stopped. When Paul turned back, she was frozen a few feet behind him. She stared, as if in a daze, at the book in his hand.

"What is it?" Paul looked from Tatleen to the book and back at her again.

"That book." Tatleen didn't move.

"What about it?"

"I know that book."

"Sadhana?"

"Yes," she nodded. "The Sadhana. It was a gift."

Paul glanced down at the old manuscript again and shrugged. "Yeah, I guess it was."

Tatleen moved toward him and gently slipped her hand over the spine of the book, caressing it. Paul released it and Tatleen brought it to her chest. She held it to her cheek, closed her eyes and felt it as if she were one of the blind men in the story. After a minute, Tatleen opened the book. She read the Hindi handwriting on the bottom of the title page, and then pressed her fingertips onto the coiled script. "This was my father's book."

Paul took a step toward her. "This book? This exact book?"

"The night of the dinner at our house . . ." She stared at the yellowed page as if it were a window into her past. "My father gave this book as a gift to his boss, Paul Griffiths."

Twenty

December 12, 1983

Bhupinder Magar awoke early Monday morning and dressed for work. It was still dark as he felt his way about the small house, gathering his things. He noticed Tatleen peering up at him through one eye as she snuggled against her mother, and he patted her gently on the head.

"Be good and help *Mataji* until *Baba* gets home tonight."

The little girl nodded and smiled at her father.

It was more than three hours before Magar's workday would begin, but he had made this a practice since his promotion to plant manager. He was now assigned the company's Hindustan Ambassador, which had previously been driven by Norm O'Bryan. Magar was the only person in Kasba Kol who had a car; most of his neighbors either rode bicycles, or in some cases shared the small seat of a *family* motorcycle.

His good fortune was not taken lightly, and Magar felt the call to impart this blessing on those who worked for him. So every morning he would leave the house at 4:30 a.m. and shuttle his employees from their homes to the plant. Magar would drive as far as Hathras, 33 kilometers to the south, then to Sangor Village, another hour north, and then back again. Prior to Magar's appointment as manager, these same employees had either spent hours walking, or taking the bus, or simply stayed at the plant during the week, sleeping on the warehouse floor between shifts.

As he drove north along NH-91 toward Sangor, Magar had a bad feeling about what this day would bring. It was the day he would deliver a message to Mr. Norm O'Bryan from the big bosses in America—the message that O'Bryan's employment with Bind-Chem was being terminated. Magar had never had to sack anyone before.

SADHANA

The last several months with O'Bryan had not been easy. The man was drinking even more often, and with that he had become more sullen and ill tempered. O'Bryan had put little effort into training his replacement, often leaving Magar to figure out the books for himself, while O'Bryan spent entire shifts tucked into his dark booth in the back of Kwality.

The official party line from Bind-Chem management in America was that Magar was taking the reins from O'Bryan, who was needed back home at Bind-Chem's military records operation in Spanish Lake. O'Bryan didn't believe it for a minute, and only hoped that the German firm, with whom he had collaborated to devalue Bind-Chem, would keep true to their word. And when the day came that they finally bought out Griffiths' company, O'Bryan would be back in the driver's seat—making double what he was making now.

Listening to his two employees, his two friends, talking quietly in the backseat of the Hindustan, Magar thought about what he would say to O'Bryan. Perhaps he would first offer O'Bryan a glass of tea.

The national highway broadened as it snaked through towns and villages, and concrete medians would bisect the center of the roadway. They were just wide enough for garbage to accumulate, a cow to graze, or homeless persons to curl up and sleep upon their rumpled bedding. Then, just as quickly, the cement islands would disappear and the street would narrow again—as if surrendering to the dried grasses and cracked red earth they called farmland.

This was Grand Trunk Road, South Asia's longest and most historic roadway. It is said to have been a path before modern times, originally built during the Mauryan Empire. Though Magar had never ventured farther than the confines of his home state of Uttar Pradesh, he had heard that Grand Trunk actually traversed all of India, from Kolkata, through Delhi, across Pakistan, and ending in Kabul, Afghanistan.

The breadth of the massive byway gave Magar an idea.

When he met with O'Bryan at the plant that day, the tea service was laid out on a tiny table. After delivering the message to O'Bryan that his *"services are no longer required,"* Magar took out a map of India. He ran his finger over it, tracing Grand Trunk's route along the Ganges.

"This roadway is like the course of a man's life," Magar said. "Perhaps like your life. It evolves over time, changing direction, taking on new features and--"

"Save the bullshit, Magar."

"I beg your pardon, sir?" Magar was unflustered, used to O'Bryan's impulsive and sometimes drunken outbursts. "My thought is that you may find a new perspective from which to view this change in your career. An opportunity, perhaps."

O'Bryan's jaw was tightly clenched. Though none of this had been completely unforeseen, it angered him just the same. And not that he blamed Magar—in fact he had always found the guy honest and hard working—but O'Bryan didn't care to hear his cliché Hindu ideologies. What he needed was for the sale to Börse Einsatz to go through and for Hoffmann to honor his word.

Magar poured O'Bryan a cup of chai. "If there is anything I can ever do--"

"It's fucking done already, Bhupinder. Let's just get on with it."

Magar wrote out a check from the payroll book, which included a modest severance payout that the company attorney, Mr. Geerts, had authorized. O'Bryan snatched the check and left.

When he had spoken with Hoffmann last, the deal was close to being made—a week, maybe ten days at the most. At least that's what Hoffmann had told him. Now that he was officially unemployed, O'Bryan wouldn't wait long. He walked out of the plant, down the unmarked road to its intersection with State Highway 39. There at the dusty corner, O'Bryan waved down a bicycle rickshaw, telling the driver to take him to Restaurant Kwality in Aligarh.

The 5-kilometer ride should have taken only ten minutes, but the driver turned onto the longer Mathura Bypass Road, stopping at a bike shop to fix a loose chain. By the time O'Bryan was finally delivered to the restaurant, he was furious and refused to pay the impoverished driver. The man yelled at O'Bryan's sweaty backside as he turned and swaggered into Kwality, but the driver's pleas had little effect. Finally the exhausted driver climbed back onto his rickshaw and peddled off.

As sunlight faded that evening, Norm O'Bryan didn't notice the changing hues and then the finality of night. He had spent the entire afternoon drinking, playing out a worst-case scenario in his head, and convincing himself that these scenarios had actually already occurred. "They're not going to pay me for my help," he muttered to himself between gulps. "The Krauts probably aren't even going to buy the company in the first place. The only thing that's going to happen for sure is ol' Norm's going to get fucked again."

And then he drank some more. It was close to midnight when O'Bryan finally stumbled out of Kwality. He searched his pockets for the keys to the Hindustan and then remembered that he had been fired and no longer had access to the company car. But he had patted a key ring in his pocket.

"Ha!" He pulled them out, then fingered through them with his meaty paws. He started laughing, howling wildly until he coughed, then gagged, then spit. "That dumbass forgot to take back the keys."

O'Bryan tripped over a curb and stumbled against the wall. He rested there, breathing hard—his face pressed against the cool bricks. As he steadied himself, an inkling crept into his addled mind. It was a fuzzy idea that spun in circles around him as if it were a brass ring he needed to reach out and grab. When the spinning slowed, O'Bryan realized he had grabbed it. "I have the keys to the plant," he slurred into the wall. "Those cocksuckers are going to pay for screwing me over."

He arrived at the plant somewhere close to 2 a.m., though he was too drunk to read his watch. In any case, O'Bryan knew it was dark and none of the workers would be there. The lone security guard was asleep inside, on the floor of one of the offices, just as O'Bryan figured he would be.

With the exception of a single halogen light aimed at the chain link fence, there was nothing to illuminate the grounds. O'Bryan dropped the gate key and the ring jingled loudly as it bounced off his knee and into the dirt. He had to fumble around to find them, then he froze to see if the guard had heard the noise.

After a few tense but woozy seconds, O'Bryan unlocked the gate and slipped inside. He stumbled down the path toward the chemical tanks, keeping an eye on the dark office building where the guard slept.

O'Bryan buttressed his ebbing determination by constantly reminding himself of all he had done for Hoffmann, and for Griffiths as well, and of what little respect had come his way as a result. Plucked from his comfortable home in Ladue—only 20 minutes from the Spanish Lake plant, O'Bryan had been exiled to this third-world hellhole. He hated India, hated the heat, and hated the isolation he felt from the rest of the developed world. Most of all O'Bryan hated what he had become: a fat drunk. And he blamed all of them for it.

He opened the gray metal box next to the first row of tanks and switched off the alarm. Waiting a second for the system to shutdown, O'Bryan watched as the tiny row of LED lights cycled from green to red, and then to dark. Bypassing the audible release warning, O'Bryan steadied himself with a shoulder against the housing for a final few deep breaths.

He held his inflated lungs, and with bulging cheeks and tightly clenched lips, he reached down to the pipeline and turned the red throttle control wheel as far as it would go.

Slowly at first, O'Bryan heard the trickle of liquid escaping from the five chemical tanks in that row. Then, the maniacal splashing as hundreds of gallons poured into the faulty containment pools.

He held his breath as he ran. Angry, gnashing strides toward the gate. Behind him, O'Bryan heard loud hissing as the liquid compounds commingled into vapors, forming a huge toxic cloud.

* * *

"Are you sure you want to do this?" Geerts' voice was dubious, yet resigned to his boss's inclinations.

"It's November already and we wanted to seal this by the end of the year." Paul had obviously made up his mind. "And yes, I'm sure this is what I want. Go ahead and make the name change and fax me the contract. I'll sign it over to Hoffmann in the morning."

The line disconnected. Nathan Geerts looked at his watch; it was 5:40 p.m. where he was in Bind-Chem's New York office, which meant it was 2:40 a.m. in Frankfurt. He printed out the 39-page sales contract and proofread it one more time. As instructed, he had changed the payee's name for receipt of proceeds. The entirety of the capital earned from the sale of Bind-Chem would now be deposited into the bank account of his boss's twin brother, Loring John Griffiths.

Geerts faxed it to Le Meridien Parkhotel where Paul was staying. Less than a mile away was Börse Einsatz, the multinational corporation that was positioned to purchase Paul's company far beneath its market value. And though Paul was well aware he was being lowballed by Hoffmann's firm, he was also mindful that the infrastructure upgrades required to keep the Aligarh plant running would be huge—comparable to, and perhaps even eclipsing, his company's diminished value.

In any case, Paul had tired of the unwieldy conglomerate he had created, the federal regulations, the foreign headaches, the unreliable personnel and all the issues that begat them.

232

Paul didn't sleep well. He had waited in the hotel's business center for Nathan's fax to arrive, well into the early morning. It took Paul until sometime after 4 a.m. to finish reading over the contract.

It was now 9 a.m., and Paul sat on the sunny terrace of Restaurant Le Parc, feeling the warm morning breeze and watching the traffic on the street below. He hoped to be on his way home by the afternoon, assuming that everything would go through without a hitch. Paul closed his eyes, tilted his head back to take in the sun's reassuring rays, and took a deep breath. He opened the leather folder and glanced over the sales contract one last time. It was all there.

Paul got a cab in front of the hotel and took it the short distance to Hoffmann's office. When he saw how close it was, Paul realized he could have walked. The multinational corporation was headquartered in the 28-story Park Tower building on Goetheplatz, only a half-dozen blocks away. The meeting with Hoffmann and his attorneys wasn't scheduled for another hour, but Paul had arrived plenty early, and though he knew he didn't need it, he drank another cup of coffee.

He figured there would be enough time to relax once the deal was over and done with.

"Mr. Griffiths?" The administrative assistant called out dryly. "Siegfried will see you now."

It took Paul a second to compute. Odd show of familiarity, he thought, her referring to the CEO by his first name. As Paul walked past the terse blond in a tight gray pantsuit, he wondered if Hoffmann was banging her.

The room full of cigarette-smoking men emptied out abruptly when Paul stepped through the doorway—a few of the men stealing furtive glances at him, but most avoiding eye contact altogether.

"Come in," Hoffmann called from his seat at the far end of an oval table. "I must say I'm surprised to see you here."

Paul assumed he meant to say, surprised to see you here *so early*.

A television set on a rolling metal stand played off to Hoffmann's right, its volume turned down low. Paul paid no attention to it as he took a seat at the table.

Hoffmann studied Paul with an odd gaze. A probing, curious look that fell somewhere short of distrust. Amusement, perhaps.

Paul shifted in his seat. "Are we waiting for your attorneys?"

"Uh, no." Hoffmann finally reached for the TV remote, and with a pained expression said, "You haven't seen this morning's news, I take it."

He turned up the volume without waiting for an answer, and Paul swung around in his chair. A condom commercial was playing and Hoffmann frowned, quickly changing the station.

Frankfurt Morning news was being televised on Hessen Drei public network. The main story flashed on the screen in German, but it was obvious that the images being displayed were foreign—perhaps somewhere in Southeast Asia. Clips showing sick people, some obviously dead, apparently a disaster of some kind that had occurred at night, clearly overwhelming the government's ability to render aid.

Paul figured it must be one of Börse Einsatz's overseas interests. "What is it?" He tried to sound curious, but in truth he was ready to get on with the sale.

"This was filmed last night," Hoffmann said, glancing at his watch. "It's now 2:07 p.m. local time there, and this thing has gotten a lot worse. Dozens of victims dead and injured, maybe into the hundreds."

"Local time, where?"

"Local time in Aligarh," Hoffmann said flatly. "There was a chemical spill at *your* Bind-Chem plant."

* * *

Loring sat on the end of his bed, tying his shoes as he watched TV. He and Abby had moved from the basement into his mother's old room once the baby came. It was better, much better, but still not what LJ wanted for his new family. In the meantime, while he and Abby saved their money, it was the best they could do.

LJ glanced over the top of the cradle next to the bed and watched his tiny son as he slept. Abby's shower was running, and her clothes were laid out on the bed. LJ smiled at the thought of how drastically his life had changed—all for the better. These were the happiest times he had known, and it was obvious to him that Abby felt the same way.

They had been married in August by a Cook County Circuit Court judge. It was a weekday morning, and they had been one of the first couples in line for the *first come, first served* licensing at the Marriage and Civil Union Division. Afterwards, the newlyweds walked three blocks to Macy's on State Street, where LJ had reserved a table near the window in the Walnut Room. They celebrated with an expensive lunch of iceberg lettuce salad, chicken potpies, and Frango mint cheesecake.

SADHANA

LJ had wanted to give Abby a "real wedding," but by then she was already into her third trimester. Besides, so few relatives were left on either side of their families that a traditional ceremony would have been pointless. Abby had moved her mother to an assisted living facility upstate and LJ had only his elderly Uncle Stuart and his twin cousins left. Of course there was Paul, a veritable stranger who no longer had a place in his life.

He glanced in again at his son's peaceful face, and thought back. Loring John Griffiths Jr. had been born on a breezy, unseasonably warm, fall afternoon on Chicago's West Side. Abby's room at Mount Sinai Medical Center looked over West 15th Place, a quiet residential street lined with white ash trees. Outside her window, leaves swirled and blew flat against fences and settled under cars parked bumper to bumper along the curb.

LJ sat next to Abby's bed that day, holding his tiny son in a tight cocoon of blankets and wondering what kind of person he would become.

"He's beautiful," Abby whispered, her throat rough from fatigue. "And I know you'll make a great father, Loring."

He grinned without taking his eyes off the baby. "Hard to believe. A few months ago you and I were living two separate lives; now all of a sudden, in the blink of an eye, we have a son."

Abby offered a weak smile as she placed a hand on her tender mid-section. "Not sure I would exactly call it a 'blink of an eye.' For a time there, I wasn't sure our little guy was ever going to come out."

He knew she had been through a lot. Probably more than he could imagine. She had shouldered the first few months of the pregnancy alone, not knowing if she and her baby even mattered to LJ. Actually believing that they didn't. And then the delivery itself was a long one, definitely no walk in the park.

LJ felt badly for all the distress he had caused Abby, but then quickly replaced it with a less doleful thought. "And don't forget," LJ said to Abby as he adjusted the baby in his arms, "I still owe you a honeymoon."

"Don't worry, I won't forget. And believe me, I won't let *you* forget."

As LJ sat on his bed now in his uncle's house, he found it hard to believe Loring Jr. was two months old. He was already tracking with his eyes, and had started reaching for the colorful mobile hanging over his cradle.

LJ finally tore his gaze from his son at the sound of his wife's footsteps on the gray and white tile. He glanced at Abby as she stepped from the bathroom, wrapped in a towel and looking as beautiful and stunning as ever.

He thought of how sad their situation had been—years wasted on stubborn jealousy. In the preceding months LJ and Abby had had a chance to discuss their pasts at length, and finally listened to one another with open hearts. They had come to visualize with clarity, the comedy of errors, ironies, and misconceptions that had come between them. It had taken a good deal of faith on both their parts to move beyond suspicion, and they both realized that Paul's constant innuendoes and manipulation of events had played a significant role in their dissonance.

The baby stirred and LJ quickly and happily picked him up. "I think he was about to cry," he said with a sheepish expression.

Abby gave him a chiding look. "Do you ever feel badly that our son won't know any family?" She bent forward over the bed to towel-dry her hair. "I mean, our fathers are gone, your mom is gone, and my mom is fading fast. Who else will be there? Uncle Stuart? Your brother?"

"I was just thinking about him." LJ wrinkled the corner of his mouth, like a silent growl. "Paul."

Abby wrapped her hair in the towel and flipped it to the back. "Uncle Paul, now."

"Hardly." LJ looked back down at his son. "We don't want to meet him, do we? No we don't. Uncle Paul's an asshole."

"Loring." Abby rolled her eyes. "Is that what we really want our son to grow up hearing?"

He shrugged, as if that wouldn't be so bad. But inside he wondered if he had what it would take to reach out to his brother.

LJ had quietly kept current on Paul's whereabouts, having seen in a business magazine that his brother was now living in New York and was a successful bigwig of his own company.

A tinge of sadness had passed through LJ as he thought of his brother. "You think I should call him."

Abby shrugged. "I didn't say that." She turned away and slipped into her clothes. LJ couldn't see her sassy smirk, but he knew it was as big as life on her face.

"I don't know . . . someday." LJ propped the baby against his chest. "Maybe after we get back from our trip."

236

SADHANA

A knock at the front door brought all three of them downstairs to answer it—Abby and LJ, with the baby held tightly in his arms. It was one of the twins; there to take care of Loring Jr. while Abby and LJ celebrated their belated honeymoon at Niagara Falls.

"Which one is she?" LJ whispered to Abby as they reached the door. "Marian or Harriet? I can never tell them apart."

"The one without the boyfriend," she said with a grimace.

Their suitcases were already packed and set on the landing next to the door. Uncle Stuart had wandered out from the kitchen with a cup of coffee. He offered LJ several unsolicited tips on how to best view the falls, insisting that they travel to the Canadian side. Abby meanwhile, went over her list of instructions with the twin.

The baby went to her easily, drinking his bottle and glancing around at everybody as if he enjoyed being the center of attention. LJ was thankful it would not be a painful goodbye.

Abby ran upstairs to do a final check, making certain she had left nothing behind. The morning news chattered away, the TV screen immersed in ghastly images of a chemical disaster in India.

She paused long enough to see the horrific scene—a row of dead laid out in a temporary morgue—before flipping the TV off and going back downstairs.

LJ lifted the suitcases. "All ready?"

Abby nodded and kissed the baby again.

The couple got into Abby's Mustang and waved to their son as they drove off.

LJ had brought along his collection of cassette tapes, and they listened to one after another of them as they cruised along I-90. He had hoped to make it all the way to Niagara Falls, but by late afternoon the weather was getting ugly and they were both tired and hungry. Signs for the city of Erie had raced by their fogged window some time ago, reminding LJ of Tommy's funeral. They decided to push on another hour to Buffalo, New York.

The couple checked into a Motel 6 just off of the interstate, and then drove a mile further up the road to Uncle Joe's Diner. LJ bought a newspaper from a vending machine as they entered the restaurant, then studied the front-page story of an American Embassy bombing in Kuwait. He shook his head, then set the paper aside.

"Mmmm," Abby murmured as she looked over the menu. "I'm thinking double decker club melt with fries."

The waitress showed up just then. "Good choice," she said to Abby, then turning to LJ, "And what can I get you?"

"I'll try the lasagna."

"Grandma Gargano's famous recipe," the waitress said with a laugh. "You won't be disappointed."

"And two beers," Abby added. "It's our honeymoon."

"Congrats." The waitress smiled. "Sorry we're fresh out of our Dom Pérignon, but a couple of beers I can do."

The diner was decorated with tiny colored Christmas lights. It was warm inside and the smells of home cooked food comforted LJ and Abby, helping to temper their thoughts of missing Loring Jr.

"It's only for a few days," LJ said, placing his hand on hers.

"We can call when we get back to the motel, right?" Abby asked. "Just to make sure he's okay?"

"Of course," he said, "I was thinking the same thing."

The darkness had settled in along with a thick fog. Gusts of wind blew against the window, and LJ was glad their traveling was done for the day. The weather was definitely looking worse instead of better.

The meals came and they talked and laughed as they ate. When they were finished, LJ slid the bulk of the newspaper to Abby and kept the sports section for himself.

Abby glanced over the entertainment page, reading about the second child born to the Governor of Kentucky and his wife, a former Miss America.

LJ read about the Bears win over the Vikings, which he had watched on Sunday, and of Chicago's upcoming game against Green Bay—their final regular season game.

"A win on Sunday will end us with an eight-and-eight record," he said over the top of the paper. "No playoffs this year."

Abby mocked a sad face. "Did you know that Yves Saint Laurent is turning forty-seven?"

"Uh huh." It took a second before he glanced up, and then they both started laughing.

LJ paid their bill and they left the diner, hand-in-hand. Their newspaper sat among their dinner plates and empty drink glasses—an unread article about a massive chemical spill in India lying open on the table.

Back at the motel Abby couldn't wait to phone the house and see how Little Loring was getting along without them. LJ kicked off his shoes and stretched out on the bed while Abby dialed the phone.

"Hi Uncle Stuart . . ." Abby's face suddenly went slack. "What is it? What's wrong?"

LJ sat up, his heart suddenly pounding so hard that he felt he might lose his entire lasagna dinner. "What?"

Finally, after a protracted editorial, LJ heard his uncle pause. Abby's face relaxed a bit as she covered the mouthpiece with her hand. "The baby is fine, it's your brother."

"Let me talk to him," LJ said. Abby handed him the phone. "Uncle Stuart, it's LJ. Are you sure the baby is alright?"

"I told Abby, yes, the baby is fine. It's your brother, *Paul*."

LJ rolled his eyes—partly because he didn't care, but mostly because of the way Stuart said it. As if LJ needed clarification about which brother he was talking about.

"He's in some kind of trouble," Stuart continued. "It's all over the news—an international incident of some sort. People have been left homeless, gone blind, some have even been killed."

"That's ridiculous. Paul wouldn't kill anyone," LJ said. "Stuart, what are you talking about? I didn't hear anything about this. Are you sure?"

Once his uncle settled down, he related the news as best he could in his usual haphazard manner. Though it sounded as if Stuart had already downed a couple of cocktails, LJ found his story containing enough compelling facts to cause concern.

LJ ended the call with his uncle. "It has something to do with Paul's company," he said to Abby while turning on the news.

"Well," Abby sighed. "While you figure out what Paul's gotten himself into now, I'm going to call back and talk to Marian. Regardless of Uncle Stuart's news, I still have a baby to check on."

She stretched the phone cord into the bathroom so as not to be drowned out by the TV. Abby was relieved to actually speak to the twin and learn that Little Loring was okay. When she came out of the bathroom LJ was hunched over the TV.

"Look at this!" he said. "Paul's company is responsible for this."

The prerecorded footage, now over 48-hours old, showed Indian women and children crying next to the dead. It was nighttime and the scene was chaotic.

Abby sat at the end of the bed in stunned silence.

Daylight images now flashed on the screen. Ambulances, a hospital, and police barricades around a commercial plant. A riotous crowd storming a gate, and a young Indian man pointing angrily at a sign mounted behind the fence: BIND-CHEM, LTD.

"This is horrible," Abby murmured.

A reporter cut in, a British woman with her hair coiffured around a face that appeared to be melting from the humidity. She read from a notepad: "Reports have confirmed that chemical contaminants in the water system have spread to a hospital, two schools, and several small villages. The Indian government has mounted an all out investigation to find those responsible for this terrible tragedy. Thus far we have been able to learn that this is a U.S. company, owned by Paul James Griffiths of New York City."

LJ turned away from the set. "He's so screwed."

Abby turned down the volume. "Do you know where he is, how to reach him?"

He shook his head. "Paul will probably go to prison because of this. He'll lose everything he's worked for. And what about those poor people who breathed that poisonous stuff? How will he ever be able to live with that?" LJ shook his head again. "This is the worst thing I can imagine . . . He's got nobody. I need to help him."

They packed the car and checked out of the motel. LJ and Abby had come within 30 miles of their destination. For the second time, the couple's honeymoon trip had been postponed—this time for something much less pleasant than the birth of their son.

"Are you sure this is a good idea?" asked Abby. "Maybe it would be safer to stay the night and head back tomorrow."

LJ thought about it for a moment. He imagined his brother, alone and afraid. "They'll seize his house, freeze his bank accounts. This thing will build and they'll want answers—someone they can blame for all of it. Paul will be hunted like an animal."

They sat in the idling car, listening to the pounding wind and waiting for the heater to warm them. In the headlights, tiny flecks of white dropped from the darkness and swirled frantically in front of them. "If we drive straight through, we'll get to Chicago by morning."

LJ aimed the Mustang onto the I-90 onramp—unaware that an icy storm was rolling over Lake Erie, headed directly into their path.

Twenty-one

Mr. Griffiths had sent several emails to Paul during that first month, none of which had been answered. Apparently Paul had also shut off his cell phone, as all of Mr. Griffiths' calls went directly to voicemail and were not returned. He hoped his son's silence was a consequence of his busy schedule, or a lack of access in such a remote part of the world. He probably would have gladly accepted that his son was angry with him, and that Paul's not calling was just more passive aggressive behavior. But privately Mr. Griffiths was becoming more concerned that something tragic had happened to his son.

Mr. Tam's progress was as dismal. He had learned from the cellular carrier that Paul's phone had not been used since he left New York. Of equal concern was that he had not logged into his email account.

The fact that it was Paul's birthday only served to sadden Mr. Griffiths all the more. It didn't take a genius to see that he was beating himself up for forcing his son to go on this trip.

Nonetheless, my boss continued to call and send messages to Paul.

* * *

The old woman's eyes had lost their color. It was as if gray scars had formed on them to shield the woman from the pain of her years.

Paul took her gently around the waist as she leaned into his shoulder. He lifted her a few inches off the bed while Tatleen changed the soiled sheet beneath her. As he set her back down, the woman reached up and caressed Paul's face with her gnarled brown hand.

Social mores no longer mattered to her. She was beyond self-consciousness and embarrassment; only a serene gratefulness dwelled in her expression. She was near death, and no doctor needed to confirm it to any of the three of them. It was there with them in the room like another presence.

They had moved the woman from the dormitory into the chapel room that afternoon. She could not move the left side of her body and had lost her ability to speak. The paralysis in her throat had also made it impossible for the woman to swallow food or liquids.

Tatleen left sometime after sunset. By the time she returned it was well after midnight and the old woman had given herself over to unconsciousness. Paul sat on a chair next to her bed, holding the woman's hand and wetting her parched lips with a wet cloth. Tatleen watched from the doorway before joining him at the woman's bedside.

"You are a gentle man," Tatleen said. "A very kind man. I had a different image of the culture in America."

Paul wrinkled his nose and brushed an itch with the sleeve on his upper arm. "I'm not sure America has a culture anymore." He gazed at the dying woman beside him and thought back to who he was at home in New York. "I don't think I'm part of it anyway, but thank you."

"You said you are uncertain of who your father is." Tatleen paused to gauge the appropriateness of her question. "Is this why you so urgently want to find the other Mr. Paul Griffiths?"

Paul nodded. "My mother died when I was just a baby. I have never been told about her, or about my uncle. My father, well, the man who raised me, he . . . it's hard to explain. Anyway, I just learned that there was something going on between my uncle, Paul Griffiths, and my mother."

She guessed at the subtext and her expression tried to mask the shock behind it. "A married woman's infidelity in this country is harshly punished, sometimes by death. There are very strict rules in India society."

"I don't know anything for sure," he said. "But I do know that I'll never learn anything from the man who says he's my father. That's why I need to research these things for myself."

The old woman lying in the bed between them lingered throughout the night, her breathing quietly settling into a shallow cadence. The two caretakers sat with her, much of the time in thoughtful silence.

"About your parents," Paul said, breaking a long lull. "Are they both gone?"

"Yes," she said.

Tatleen had already told Paul that, but he hoped the question would prompt her to open up a bit more. Her silence was another cultural thing, he figured, so he tried again with a more direct approach. "Can I ask, how?"

She mused over the double question again. "My mother became very ill from the water. Many people in our village were affected by it and many died."

"The water?"

"Yes." Tatleen lowered her eyes as her voice lost ground to her thoughts. "There were chemicals . . . in the soil and in the wells. They had spilled out from tanks at my father's plant."

"The company that my uncle owned?"

Tatleen took a shaky breath and nodded. "My father . . . he was the one held responsible."

Paul watched her without saying anything. Tatleen's sadness was profound; her eyes were devoid of tears but fixed on the worn floor below her.

"My father was a good man, an honest man. They took him to jail and I never saw him again." Tatleen's voice weakened, and she spoke as if she had forgotten that Paul was even there. "He died at the Naini Central Prison in Allahabad."

"You never got an chance to see him again?" Paul's heart broke.

"We had no means to get there." Tatleen wiped a strand of hair from her face and tucked it under her *chaddar*. "Allahabad is eight hours travel by train from our home."

Paul leaned his head back and stared at the ceiling, overwhelmed by Tatleen's sadness and wracked by his own guilt. The Griffiths family and their wealth repulsed him. *Was this incident the source of Loring Griffiths' distain towards his brother? Is that why they are estranged?*

"I'm so sorry, Tatleen." Paul reached for her, but a tense stillness suddenly permeated the room.

"She's not breathing," said Tatleen.

Paul looked down at the old woman. A look of contentment was imprinted on her ashen face. Her struggles were finally over.

Tatleen lit a stick of Tara incense—an herbal recipe created at the Sakya Monastery to ease the dead into the next life. It was a peaceful departure that neither frightened nor saddened Paul. It was somehow different than the passing of his friend, Praneel—a young man in his prime, no older than Paul. This woman was ready, even eager to go forward. Paul had seen it in her eyes. Understood it.

"I'll prepare her body," said Tatleen softly as she stoked the woman's graying hair.

"Will you meet me in the dining room when you are finished?" he asked. "I'd like to talk with you more."

Tatleen gave Paul a lingering look as if two opposing thoughts fought for position in her mind. She finally agreed to meet him.

Paul nodded and left the room. He sat on a bench just across from the covered hallway, watching the burnt sky as it lightened over the mountains of Nepal. In the distance, a baying *muezzin* echoed a call to prayer from the top of a minaret.

* * *

The CRF bus stopped at the gate of the Asha Heath Care complex. The rest of the group, exhausted from the long journey back, went toward their dormitory. But Gwyn was eager to give Paul the gift she had bought for him during the trip to Hinganghat. Waiting until the other volunteers had left the bus, she grabbed the trinket she had purchased for Paul and moved off in the other direction.

She crossed the street; there was little traffic this early, as the stalls and shops were not yet open. Stepping into the Bhakti Seva lobby, Gwyn found Swami Chalah praying in front of a small shrine. She waited impatiently for him to finish, tapping her foot on the tile in case he wasn't aware she was there. When he finished, the swami turned and bowed to Gwyn.

"I'm a friend of Paul Griffiths," she said. "I'd like to leave something for him in his room."

He smiled and took a set of keys from behind the counter. She followed him up the stairs to the tiny room at the end of the hall. The swami knocked first and then opened the door, but continued to watch Gwyn from the doorway.

"It's just a little gift," she told him as she set the trinket on the bed. Gwyn had hoped Swami Chalah would have left her alone there so she could look around. Not that Gwyn wanted to nose into anything private, but the week away had done much to stimulate her curiosity. Given the chance, Gwyn might have even left a note. But the swami's hovering presence outside in the hallway made her nervous. She emerged from the room and Swami locked the door—assuming Gwyn had left whatever it was she had brought for Paul.

She walked back downstairs, wondering where Paul could be at this early hour. As Gwyn passed back through the lobby, she heard the sound of utensils clinking from the dining room down the stairs. She walked down and to the doorway, standing just outside looking in.

At a table in the corner, Paul and Tatleen sat quietly together talking over glasses of tea.

SADHANA

They didn't notice Gwyn, so she continued to watch them. Something unsettling gnawed at her as she observed their hushed conversation. There was a palpable intimacy to it that struck Gwyn like a blast of icy air. It was the last thing she would have suspected. Paul was a wealthy playboy from New York and Tatleen was a poor Indian widow—an outcast in her own country. Her social status was less than nothing. Yet there they were, staring across the table at one another, whispering about . . . *who knows what?*

All at once she felt like a fool. Humiliated about giving Paul a birthday gift, she darted back through the lobby, looking for Swami Chalah. He had just set the keys back on a hook behind the counter when Gwyn rushed up.

"Excuse me!" She leaned over the counter toward him until they were face-to-face. Then in a lowered voice she said, "I'm sorry, but I need to get back into Paul's room."

The swami was slow to respond. After a few seconds, he reached down and took the key ring from the hook.

"I made a mistake," Gwyn told him. "It seemed like a good idea at the moment, but it was stupid and impulsive."

Swami Chalah looked at her through warm eyes that held not a hint of judgment. And though Gwyn knew there was no way he could possibly understand what she was talking about, his perceptive smile comforted her.

Had the swami simply given Gwyn the keys, she would have raced up the stairs and taken the ridiculous trinket out of Paul's room. But the holy man moved with a tranquil patience that made her feel like a Greyhound tugging on a leash.

As Gwyn bounded up the stairs ahead of Swami, she heard voices in the stairwell below them. Cringing at the thought that it might be Paul, or worse, Paul and Tatleen, Gwyn motioned for Swami to hurry.

He strode calmly to the door with his keys in hand, and then thumbed through each key, one-by-one. Footsteps ascending the stairwell made Gwyn's heart race.

The swami put the key into the lock, and as soon as the door opened, Gwyn bolted past him. She dove across the bed, grabbed the round tray mounted on tiny temple elephants, and stuffed it into her shoulder bag. The swami still did not see what it was that was so important for the woman to deposit in the room, and then retrieve again with such haste.

She left the room and quickly closed the door. Swami turned the key to lock it, and no sooner did they start back down the hall than two people appeared at the top of the stairs.

Gwyn saw that it was Paul and Tatleen, so she tactfully stepped in front of the swami so they wouldn't see the keys.

"Paul, hi!" Gwyn reached behind her and pawed at the key ring in Swami's hand. He slowly placed them into the pocket of his robe.

"Gwyn?" Paul seemed perplexed as to why she was at the ashram with Swami Chalah. "Hey, what's up? Thought you were out of town."

Gwyn tried to think of a plausible answer, but nothing clicked. Anything she came up with would surely sound pathetic. Tatleen stood off to Paul's right and slightly behind him. Her eyes were downcast, as if she wanted nothing more than to melt into the background.

The foursome stood bunched in the narrow hallway, only three of them uncomfortable with the silence. Swami Chalah not so much. His serene expression and knowing eyes gazed back and forth among the group as if he had choreographed the entire meeting. Again, there was no judgment in his eyes, only a contemplative look of amusement.

"I just returned from a cholera outbreak near Hinganghat." Gwyn knew she was only delaying the inevitable. "And, well, actually I was looking for Tatleen."

"Yes?" Tatleen pulled the thin veil of fabric across the bottom half of her face as she took a step forward.

"There are two large bags of dirty clothes in the back of the bus," Gwyn said. "We'll need them laundered as soon as possible."

"Certainly, Miss Gwyn. Right away." Tatleen moved quickly to the stairway and then out of sight.

Paul's eyes followed Tatleen as she scampered away, then he turned back toward Gwyn with a confused expression. *Dirty clothes? Laundered?*

His perplexed look was not lost on Gwyn. It was clear that Paul had no idea that Tatleen's work at the health care complex was that of a servant, merely to do laundry and other odd jobs.

"Oh yeah," she said to Paul, nudging the genial swami on his way. "I also wanted to let you know that you're welcome to use my desktop, if you still want to."

"You sure?" Paul perked up. "This is really good timing, because I just found out that my uncle was involved in some kind of business over here in India. Do you have time now?"

Gwyn thought over her options and decided later would be better. If they could meet up in the afternoon, Gwyn might be able to parlay the rendezvous into a dinner. Besides, she was exhausted from the long journey back and would need time to rest, shower, and primp for their date.

Paul was tired as well, from his night providing care to the elderly woman. But he welcomed the opportunity to do some more Internet research. He had to unravel the mystery about Paul Griffiths—the twin his father had always refused to speak about.

"How about you come by around five this afternoon?" Gwyn said. "The clinic will be a lot quieter then, and there won't be the usual interruptions." She rolled her eyes in the direction Tatleen had just gone, making Paul wonder if that was the reference.

Gwyn left Paul on the landing outside his room and hurried down the steps. She passed the swami in the lobby, offering him a curt wave as she headed out to the narrow roadway in front of the ashram. About 50 meters beyond the gate, Gwyn reached inside her shoulder bag and tossed the tiny trinket into the brush.

That afternoon Paul appeared at Gwyn's office in the rear of the sprawling Asha Heath Care and Research Centre. Something about her seemed different, Paul thought. Certainly it was a contrast to her fatigued appearance this morning at the ashram.

Gwyn wore a silky, loose fitting top that had an Indian print of blues and pinks. It was long—almost like a short dress—and she wore it over matching stretch pants and sandals. Her short hair was damp, as if she had just showered, and it was swept back off of her face. A light pink tint glossed her lips, matching the color in her top.

She booted up her desktop computer when she saw him come in. "Ready to do some investigating?"

Paul laughed. "But I still don't want to risk logging into my email account--"

"Yeah, yeah, I know," Gwyn said. "You're afraid INTERPOL or the CIA will come after you."

He raised his eyebrows. "It's no joke, Gwyn. I don't know if I've told you this, but I'm a wanted man."

She wrinkled her face questioningly.

"Seriously, I can't even think about going back to the U.S. There's probably a price on my head."

"Doubtful," Gwyn said. "CRF does a background check on all of our overseas volunteers. Mrs. Beckham wouldn't have assigned you to my group if there were a problem. What the hell did you do anyway?"

"It's complicated—too much to try to explain now. How about we just try to find out about my uncle?"

She slid a small notepad next to her computer. "You don't want to look up Abigail Townsend?"

Paul shook his head. "We'll try that after. Search for Paul Griffiths."

Gwyn frowned.

"It's my uncle's name, too."

She typed in the name and waited for the results. "Here's something," Gwyn said, picking up a pen. "Paul Griffiths of New York University's swim team was ranked by CSCAA--"

"Forget that one," Paul said. "That's not my uncle."

"It's you," she said flatly while reading on. "Ranked number one by the College Swimming Coaches Association of America?"

"Yeah well, I had a good year." Paul came around the desk and stood beside Gwyn's chair. "Put in *India* after his name. See if that narrows it down."

She glanced up at Paul, giving him a long look before going back to the keyboard. As he lingered over her, Paul could smell the flowery scent of her lotion, or powder, or whatever soap she'd used.

"Okay, here's something." Gwyn tilted the viewing screen so he could see it. "December 13, 1983. Indian authorities are seeking Paul James Griffiths, the American owner of Bind-Chem, Ltd., after a deadly chemical spill at the facility in Aligarh. The plant's foreman, Bhupinder Magar, a Kasba Kol resident, was arrested and is being held in the deaths of dozens of residents who live near the facility. Fatalities are estimated to be in the--"

"Stop." Paul backed away from the computer and collapsed on a chair across from Gwyn. "I can't hear this. It's horrible."

Gwyn scrolled down the series of news reports in silence. "Paul, this was thirty years ago. I only found it because they reprinted the original article in 2003 for the twenty-year anniversary of the incident. Most people probably don't even remember it."

"Some will remember. The poor people who breathed in that chemical cloud and drank the water, and the families of the injured and dead will remember. Poor Tatleen remembers."

Gwyn stopped abruptly. She leaned back in her seat, glaring at Paul. "Tatleen." She squinted until the blue of her eyes no longer showed. "What in the hell does *she* have to do with anything?"

He was startled by Gwyn's tone. "I think that was her father—the guy who went to jail because of this. Tatleen told me that he died in prison. She was just a young girl, and she never saw him after that day."

Gwyn rolled her eyes, but then recovered quickly. "Poor little thing. Must be tough to live with something like that."

Paul sat there in stunned silence.

"There's a photo," Gwyn said.

Paul jumped up and went around behind her again. "Yep, that's got to be him. He looks just like old pictures I've seen of my dad. This is insane. I need some time to wrap my head around this whole thing."

Paul started for the door but Gwyn got up and took his arm. "I'm so sorry, Paul." She clutched him close, as if she were as broken up about it as he was. "Let's do something to shake this off."

She felt good against him, sweet and comforting. Paul hadn't been with a woman in a long time, and Gwyn seemed to understand him. She cared about him. He rested his chin on the top of her damp blond hair and they were a perfect fit. She was shapely and clean and wholesome.

"Don't you have a birthday coming up?" she asked.

"Tomorrow."

"How about we go out tonight and celebrate?" She pulled her head back so she faced up at him. "My treat."

Paul rubbed his eyes with his thumb and forefinger. "I'm really not going to be very good company tonight, Gwyn. How about I take a rain check?"

He stepped backwards, slowly releasing himself from her grasp. She gazed at Paul in disbelief as he gave her a placating smile and left her office.

Gwyn glanced at the clock. It was 6:20 p.m., which meant it was 10:50 in the morning in New York. She dialed the number for CRF's executive director. The secretary put Gwyn right through to her boss.

"Ms. Beckham speaking."

"Sheryl, it's Gwyn." She looked out the window as Paul disappeared from view. "Tell me about this Paul Griffiths guy. Why is he here, and why does he think the cops are after him?"

The afternoon air carried upon it the scent of boiled cauliflower. Swami Chalah ducked his head into the kitchen to inquire of the cook, Sree, what was to be served during the evening meal.

It would be *Bandh Gobhi Ki Sabzi*, Swami's favorite. Sree held up a basket of onions and garlic cloves, showing Swami that they would be included in the meal.

That was a delight to Swami Chalah, as they had intentionally been left out of the dish when it was served three weeks prior. Sree had last prepared *Bandh Gobhi Ki Sabzi* during the nine nights of the *Navratri* festival. It was a time when the faithful demonstrated their devotion to the Hindu deity, *Durga*, following strict rules on fasting. During the festival period, certain foods, grains and spices are prohibited from consumption—garlic and onion being among them.

In any case, the dish had lacked its traditional flavor as far as Swami was concerned, and he was grateful to have the original version on tonight's menu.

The swami boiled a pot of Masala Chai for the patients and carried it up the stairs to the dormitories, along with a double rack of small drinking glasses.

The first to be served was Mr. Gopal. His cancer was progressing rapidly, and it was apparent that he was in a great deal of discomfort.

Swami had just set the glass of Chai next to the bed when he felt a hand grip his own. Swami recognized the look of sad eyes, rimmed in redness and filled with regret. Gopal was a man close to death.

The swami stroked the man's cheek with his other hand. "Are you in pain?"

Gopal forced a smile. "The cancer inside my body causes me great suffering, but it is a penalty I must pay. I am comforted to know that it is but a temporary condition of this life," he said, struggling to envision his reincarnation.

Swami released his hand and sat down on the bed next to him. "*Atman*—the universal self—will attain *moksha* (release) from the bonds of existence. As *Bhagwad Gita*, our sacred scripture has told us, '*death is certain for the one who is born, and birth is certain for the one who dies.*'"

Mr. Gopal opened his eyes and gripped the swami's hand again, this time with the fervor of a man slipping over the edge of a cliff. "Swami Chalah, I have tried to live a credible life."

"Your rebirth in a level of enlightenment will make you one with Brahman—the highest reality."

"My deeds during this lifetime," he tightened his grip on Swami, "I fear they will prevent me from attaining *moksha*."

"You have been a non-violent man," Swami said. "And you have practiced vegetarianism with great dedication. What is it that you fear?"

"My eyes," he said. "My eyes were cursed with a sight that I should not have seen. A thing I should have spoken up about, but did nothing."

Swami nodded warmly, but stayed silent.

"It was many years ago." Mr. Gopal closed his eyes. "I was the night watchman at the company that spilled chemicals into the drinking water at Aligarh."

Twenty-two

Mr. Tam's investigation had fallen flat. Any leads we had thought might pan out had all dried up. Nobody had seen or heard of Paul since he used his bankcard to gather several hundred dollars from an ATM during a layover at the Helsinki Airport.

Tam wasn't willing to admit that the case was dead, but the fact he had flown back to Hong Kong was telling. There was obviously nothing left for him to follow-up on in Finland.

It was an exasperating time around the estate. Mr. Griffiths spent most of his days on the phone in his office, while the staff tried to keep out of his way. We didn't know what to say to him.

As if we had all resigned ourselves to the probability that Paul was dead, the house became a morbid vigil—waiting for a call from the State Department.

* * *

The street was a blur of activity, yet Paul paid attention to none of it. He felt like a pinball, glancing off of people as he ambled past bustling stalls, food carts and open cooking fires. His mind was somewhere else; it was on Tatleen and her father, and whoever else had been affected by the horrific tragedy caused by his uncle's company.

Paul wanted to talk to Tatleen, to apologize to her. People in her village had died because of his uncle, and Tatleen's father had gone to jail. Now more than ever Paul wanted to know the truth about his family, especially about his uncle. What had become of him? Had he gone to prison as well? But before Paul could continue on with his research, he needed to find Tatleen.

He checked the ashram, the kitchen, the dormitory where the infirm lay in rotting rows, and the temple-like room that served as a hospice for those closest to the end of life. Tatleen was nowhere.

SADHANA

The courtyard behind the ashram was dark, and the hushed voices of the women singing began to rise in the dusty alley, reverberating from inside the walls of the widow women temple.

Paul sat down in the center of the grassy clearing and tried to calm his turbulent mind. After all, it wasn't as if the chemical spill was an intentional act. And thirty years had already passed since it happened. Maybe Gwyn was right; it was reasonable to assume that most people had forgotten about it by now.

But something deep inside Paul continued to batter him with guilt. He closed his eyes, refusing to turn away from the sickening thought trying to form itself in his mind. Then he realized what it was: his life had been so toxic, so self-absorbed, so narrow and egocentric that the blood might as well be on his own hands. He had become part of the whole malignant racket—he was an heir, in fact the sole heir, to the Griffiths monarchy. Whether the person responsible for the disaster was his father or his uncle didn't really make any difference— arrogance and entitlement were enmeshed in Paul's DNA. And for that he hated both of the Griffiths brothers.

"Another wonderful evening," said a voice from the darkness on the other side of the courtyard.

"Swami Chalah," Paul said, squinting into the night. "I didn't see you there."

The swami sat quietly looking up at the night sky. He took in a deep breath as if cleansing his soul. "Whatever is troubling you . . . it has many features," Swami continued. "Not unlike the elephant in your story. Very often we sense only part of the thing; an initial perception through our own narrow perspective."

Paul wondered how the swami could know what he was thinking. But the holy man was right; Paul only knew a piece of the story.

"I want to show you something." Swami stepped from the darkness onto the grass, extending his hand out to Paul. "Deepak, the security doorman, found this in the brush near the road in front of the ashram. He thought one of our guests might have lost it, but its presence cannot be explained by any of our residents."

Paul examined the tiny trinket, holding it up to the dim light. "It's beautiful." He ran his hand over the garnet colored jewels inlaid in the elephants' headdress.

"It reminded me of the story in your book," Swami said. "Perhaps a symbol of your journey." He smiled thoughtfully. "It is yours to do with as you please."

The holy man then placed his hands on Paul's shoulders and embraced him. The warm, fatherly feel of it surprised Paul. He had not experienced expressions of affection from men in his life, ever. Yet this felt somehow satisfying, even familiar.

Swami left Paul in the garden holding the small figurine, peaceful now as he realized there are more dimensions to everything in his life. He was still drawn to Tatleen, and for reasons Paul couldn't articulate, even to himself, he felt the need to talk with her.

Paul walked down a narrow side passage behind the ashram, back out to a main street teeming with people. He was trying to remember which of the side roads led to the orphanage. It was dark the night he had followed Tatleen there, and he hadn't paid enough attention to landmarks. Everywhere there were side streets branching into smaller alleys, and each one looked exactly the same as the next.

It took him awhile to find the corner, as the small shrine that marked its location the first time had been dismantled. Paul headed into the dark alleyway, wandering past many of the huts that were similar in appearance. Paul recognized one in particular, shabby, with a weathered burlap cloth covering the entrance.

Uncertain if it was customary or even appropriate to knock, Paul tapped lightly on the wall and called out, *"Namaste"*. It was an all-purpose greeting—one of the first he had learned upon arriving in India.

Seconds later a scuffing sound came from within and a tiny hand yanked back the fabric covering. Naagesh lay on his side, halfway over the threshold, gazing up at Paul.

Paul motioned past him into the room. "Tatleen?"

The boy smiled brightly and bobbed his head, but Paul couldn't tell if he really understood. He leaned his head in over the top of Naagesh and glanced around the dingy quarters. "Tatleen?"

An old woman suddenly appeared through a labyrinth of narrow passages, and rattled off an angry Hindi diatribe. It was unclear to Paul how much was directed at him and how much at Naagesh.

The boy appeared unruffled by the woman, and responded to her in a soft and even, matter-of-fact tone. Whatever it was Naagesh said seemed to be an antidote to her venom, and the woman regressed back into the room from which she had emerged. In his native tongue, Naagesh had told his caretaker that the American man worked with Tatleen at the health care clinic.

SADHANA

A total of thirteen children resided at the orphanage—eight fulltime, including Naagesh, and another five who stayed only during the evening hours. They were children of prostitutes working red light districts in the nearby town of Mathura. Naagesh, being the only child there with impaired mobility, spent most of his time slithering in the dirt near the doorway. From there he watched activity on the road in front of the orphanage, while the other children played in the rear of the shanty.

Paul soon realized that Tatleen was not there, yet he continued to be charmed by the boy. Naagesh's bright eyes and infectious smile kept Paul perched there on the narrow wooden threshold entertaining the young orphan. Their communication consisted of little more than drawing stick figures in the dirt, mimicking each other's comedic facial expressions, and exchanging the few Hindi words that Paul knew. Naagesh was introduced to the vaunted *high-five* hand slap, which the two exchanged with gusto.

Other children, residents of the orphanage, drifted in and out of the room to view the stranger that had befriended Naagesh. They quickly tired of their dull games and meandered back to their own, more challenging activities.

Paul could see the intelligence in Naagesh's eyes. He was quick to pick up on Paul's subtle humor and wit. Though there was a great deal the boy was unable to do because of his malformed legs, he seemed to find happiness in everything.

A thought occurred to Paul, and he pulled the small figurine from his trouser pocket. Naagesh's eyes ignited with excitement as Paul set the painted elephant on the wooden threshold between them. At first Paul's intent was only to show the boy his odd little trinket, but Naagesh's fascination was immense. It was as if Paul had suddenly produced the Hope Diamond or King Tut's golden sarcophagus. It was clear to Paul that the impoverished young orphan had never been exposed to anything of value—even as inconsequential as this meager knickknack.

Paul had planned to use it during his evening Sadhana rituals, but he could not resist his young admirer's engaging smile. He motioned to Naagesh that he could take it, sliding it across the dirt to the boy's eager hands. Naagesh sat there stunned for a moment, and then grasped it into his chest. He propped himself against the wall so he could use both hands and then kissed the figurine, touched it to his forehead in prayer, and then kissed it again.

Paul saw that he had made a good decision, as he could never have appreciated the cheap memento as anything more than a souvenir of his trip to India. To Naagesh on the other hand, it clearly meant something very special.

The hour was late, and though Paul hadn't actually entered the shabby orphanage, he didn't want to overstay his welcome. He patted his little friend on the head and motioned that it was time for him to go. Paul had been up over 24-hours straight, and he needed to rest.

Paul's ashram duties included serving tea to those too ill to receive it in the dining room. He had hoped to meet Tatleen during his rounds that next morning, but he didn't see her anywhere on the premises.

By mid-afternoon he had also cleaned the dining area and swept the hallways, completing most of the tasks that required his attention. The swami had a small list of medical supplies he needed from Asha Health Care Centre, and after Paul retrieved them for Swami, he would be free to do as he pleased with the remainder of his day.

He had slept well the night before. So well in fact, that he had missed the morning meal. Now, as the afternoon sun struggled through a smoky brown haze, Paul's empty stomach gnawed at him. He was also angry with himself for snoozing through a potential opportunity to run into Tatleen in the kitchen.

He was thinking of her when a brown rat suddenly darted across the alley in front of him, then ducked over the lip of the sewage trough. Stepping more cautiously now, Paul wondered if the rodent had pals lurking somewhere in the shadows nearby. The route he had taken was the shortest one to the health care centre, which would also take him past the temple where Paul had seen Tatleen on prior occasions.

He did not find her at the temple, and did not see her anywhere along the way. Paul moved on, deciding it would be a good idea to use his visit to the health centre to ask Gwyn if she knew where he might find Tatleen.

Gwyneth Eichler had just stepped out of her office for some fresh air. By now she was nearly accustomed to the annoying humming sound that emanated from the sprawling electrical substation on the other side of the fence, but for some reason the noise seemed particularly irritating today. For that reason, Gwyn decided to take her afternoon walk around the backside of the health centre grounds this afternoon, ending at the front of the building.

SADHANA

Just past Asha's pink façade entryway, Gwyn took a seat at a bench tucked against the wall under a dwarf willow tree. It was her favorite spot to sit and sometimes read, or just watch people walking by.

Paul ducked his head into Gwyn's building, but the lights were out and her office was empty. He walked across the driveway to the main building where plant maintenance was located. Back behind a maze of hospital beds and other apparatuses, Paul found the facility supplies section. The concept was a spinoff of the 1946 Bhore Committee hearings and the Sokhey report of 1948, both of which found medical care in India lacking "standardized affordable, accountable and appropriate medical health services of assured quality". To Paul, the dank room filled with boxes of gauze, bandages and tape still looked like a battlefield first aid tent, but as long as they had what the swami needed it didn't matter to him.

At the corner of Gandhi Marg, Tatleen waited for a break in traffic. When it was clear, she darted across the highway between a camel-drawn cart and a motorcycle carrying a family of four. Just as she made it to the far curb, Tatleen saw Paul walking toward her from inside the health care complex. He carried with him a bag of supplies.

"Hello, Mr. Paul Griffiths," Tatleen called out to him. "I was hoping to find you today."

Her eager words induced a warm rush, exciting and embarrassing Paul at the same time. "And me, you."

Tatleen studied him, wondering what words he had left out to render his sentence so meaningless to her.

"I was hoping I'd run into you too, because I wanted to apologize again," Paul said. "This whole thing that happened to your father, to all those people in your village. I feel somehow responsible--"

She frowned in confusion and then held up her hand. Then, with a gentle and respectful nod of her head she said, "Hindus believe that children are a gift from God. The son is an extension of a father's life—his rebirth."

"I don't know about that," he said. "My family, maybe even my own father, did this terrible thing to you."

Tatleen shook her head. "According to the Brahma rite, if a son performs a righteous act, he liberates from sin ten ancestors."

Paul looked into her kind eyes and smiled. "It might take more than just one 'righteous act' to atone for all those sins," he said. "But I'm definitely trying."

"Now I must tell you something, Mr. Paul Griffiths." Tatleen's eyes dropped and did not come up to meet his. "The gift that you gave to Naagesh . . . I'm very sorry, but he cannot accept it."

Paul's face looked puzzled—partly because they were talking about such an insignificant trinket, but also because Tatleen was speaking as if she was the boy's guardian. Paul could only ask, "Why?"

"A thing of such value . . . it is not possible for him to keep it."

"You gotta be kidding," Paul said. "It's just a little incense burner with painted elephants. I think he really liked it."

"I'm certain that he did," she said. "But in an orphanage such as his, where the other children have nothing . . . it would appear boastful and could possibly bring him karma."

"What, like bad karma?" Paul frowned in frustration. "You mean, like, someone could steal the thing from him?"

Tatleen's eyes finally rose to meet Paul's. "Karma is neither punishment nor retribution, but simply a consequence of natural acts. God does not make one suffer for no reason--"

"Then we're all good." Paul grinned, clasping his hands together triumphantly.

Tatleen paused before continuing. "But neither does God make one happy for no reason. God is very fair and gives us *exactly* what we deserve in this life."

She handed the elephant trinket to Paul. "An undeserved gift such as this can only disrupt the natural harmony of Naagesh's life."

Gwyneth Eichler sat silently watching Paul and Tatleen, her jaw clenched and her eyebrows as straight and taught as her lips. Gwyn's expression grew even more venomous when she spotted the elephant incense burner, her birthday gift to Paul, now being presented to him by Tatleen. Gwyn wondered how in the world she had managed to find the stupid figurine that had been discarded in the bushes.

"Do you have time for tea?" Paul asked Tatleen. "I'd really like to talk with you some more." He wanted to learn about her past, her family and whatever she remembered about Paul's uncle. And he was curious, now more than ever, about the boy he had become so fond of.

Tatleen motioned toward the health centre. "I have my duties here at the clinic. It will take one hour for me to complete them, and then I will be able to take tea with you."

258

"Okay, good." Paul slipped the trinket into his pocket. "And we can discuss this thing, too. I'll meet you back here in an hour."

Tatleen laundered soiled bedding and emptied trash, finishing up her responsibilities at the clinic as quickly as possible. She arrived back at the front gate several minutes early, and Paul was not yet there to meet her. Instead, Gwyneth Eichler called to her from a bench in the shadows of the building.

"Oh, hello Miss Gwyneth, Tatleen said as she walked over to her. "I did not see you sitting there."

"You seem to be in something of a hurry, Tatleen." Gwyn crossed her legs and leaned her head back. "Meeting someone?"

"Yes, Miss Gwyneth." Tatleen hesitated. "Mr. Paul Griffiths said he would meet me in front of the gates."

"Paul is a nice guy, isn't he?"

"Yes," Tatleen said. "He is very kind and compassionate."

"Hard to believe he's gotten himself into so much trouble."

Tatleen squinted in confusion. "I don't understand, Miss--"

"Surely, Paul must have told you." Gwyn gave her a lamenting pout. "He was forced to come here in order to avoid going to prison."

"No, Miss Gwyneth." Tatleen shook her head as if there had been a misunderstanding. "Mr. Paul Griffiths is a giving man. He has sacrificed much for the benefit of others. He couldn't have been forced to come."

Gwyn smiled as she shook her head. "I'm so sorry, Tatleen. My superior back in New York knows Paul's father. A judge ordered Paul to come here, and believe me, it was anything but voluntary."

"But I thought." Tatleen dropped her gaze. "I think that I would like to hear his own words before I--"

"Unfortunately Tatleen, I need you to clean the floors in my office building, and there's some more laundry. It's very important that it gets done right away."

Tatleen glanced back toward the street before turning back. "Yes, of course, Miss Gwyneth." Tatleen's cracked brown feet padded off around the side of the building.

Paul zigzagged across the street a few minutes after Tatleen had left. He waved to the guard seated stoically at his post in front of the gate.

"Well, isn't this a pleasant surprise." Gwyn suddenly appeared, stepping around the guard and into Paul's path. "Where are you headed, Mr. New York?"

Paul smiled cordially and leaned into Gwyn's assertive embrace. "I actually stopped by to see you earlier."

"Did you?"

"Uh-huh." Paul glanced around casually to see if Tatleen was there to meet him.

"Looking for something?"

Paul hesitated. "I was supposed to meet--"

"Let me guess," Gwyn said with a hint of mockery. "My cleaning woman, Tatleen?"

Paul studied Gwyn, trying to decipher the sarcasm.

"She's gone," Gwyn said. "I have no idea where she is. Probably had to go see her kid."

Paul's expression turned to confusion. "Her kid?"

"Her son."

"You mean the orphan?" Paul's voice went up an octave. "Tatleen adopted Naagesh?"

"Other way around," Gwyn said. "He was her son to begin with, and she gave him up for adoption. Tatleen is the one who made the boy an orphan."

The energy drained from Paul's body as he stood there trying to make sense of it. He stared down at his feet, as if all his strength had pooled there in the dirt beneath him.

"You knew she was married at one time, right?" Gwyn leaned her head in front of Paul's vacant stare. "That's why she sings with all the other *widowed* women."

All of a sudden Tatleen's 4-hour disappearances each evening made sense. Paul realized that was why he always seemed to run into Tatleen in or around the alleyway near the temple. It was almost too much for Paul to grasp; yet it had been so obvious.

"I'm sorry, Paul. I thought you knew."

Paul slowly shook his head.

"Would have thought the white saree was a clue." Gwyn shoved him playfully. "All of the widow women wear the same garb."

"She never told me," Paul said. "How do you know about Naagesh?"

"Tatleen works for me," Gwyn said. "It wasn't hard to figure out. Besides, all you have to do is look at the kid to see that he belongs to her."

"Why would she lie to me?"

Gwyn shrugged. "Maybe it's a cultural thing. Widows don't have any standing in the Indian culture. They're sort of like vagrants, just a few rungs below nothing."

Paul stood there in silence. He wondered why Tatleen hadn't told him that she had been married. He couldn't even imagine how she could have given up her own son, a deformed little boy whose needs had to be enormous.

"Anyway, Tatleen is gone for today." Gwyn threw her arm around Paul's waist. "Now, how about you let me buy you a birthday dinner?"

Paul's spirit had been depleted by Gwyn's news. He felt foolish for being tricked. Maybe Tatleen was working an angle to get some money, he thought. He was suddenly sure that she was only using him.

Now he felt really stupid.

"I haven't eaten all day," Paul said. He glanced around, checking again to see if Tatleen had come to meet him. Seeing no one, his shoulders dropped as he turned back to Gwyn.

She slipped her arm through his. "C'mon, I know of a nice spot just down the road."

Gwyn ushered Paul down bustling Bhaktivedanta Swami Marg, just past the Vrindavan Research Institute. Krishna Balaram Restaurant was set back from the street in the Krishna-Balaram Mandir temple complex.

Paul looked up at the ornate *sikhara.* "What is this place?"

"This temple is a 24-hour kirtan—a place where devoted people come to chant."

"And they have a restaurant?"

She shrugged. "Maybe the flock gets hungry from all the chanting."

They walked into the restaurant, a long narrow rectangle with small tables lining both sides of the room. The tables were only large enough for one person, so Paul and Gwyn slid theirs against one another so they could sit side-by-side.

Strangely enough, their male server was obviously not from India. His Caucasian head was shaved, except for a long blond ponytail sprouting from the back of it. He wore a camel colored robe and acted as if he was an ethnic Indian, or at least like he wanted everyone to believe he was. Yet his accent sounded curiously of Nordic origin.

Not so much as a smile crossed his face, just a sober expression that said: I loathe American, non-Hindus. *Either eat your Moong Dal or go somewhere else, and no, we don't serve meat!*

"I know a place near the clinic where we could get something to drink," Gwyn said as they emerged from the driveway after their meal.

For once the evening was warm, not hot. Paul had enjoyed his food, finding it more bountiful and spicier than he was used to. "I'd die for a cold beer."

She smiled and took his hand. Down a narrow alley, next door to an Internet café, Gwyn led Paul into a small sundries shop. From a man who seemed to recognize her, Gwyn bought four large bottles of Kingfisher Premium beer.

They took their time walking back to the clinic. It was dark, and the pungent aromas of food and filth and the clatter of people and traffic all blanched behind them as a warm rain began to fall.

Gwyn leaned a shoulder into Paul as they walked—playful, light-hearted, and seductive. The conversation was easy and the taste of it was familiar to Paul.

They flounced down the driveway next to the hospital, and Gwyn used her keys to open the CRF building. Her office and the rest of the building were dark. She took Paul by the hand and led him through a glass door into a small, enclosed atrium. A few of the other offices had windows looking out into it, but they were all empty and the lights were off. A wrought iron bench stood in the center of the space, surrounded by a tiny landscaped garden and a couple of ornamental bamboo trees.

Steamy drops of rain tapped on the clear plastic covering overhead as they talked and sipped from the cool bottles.

Paul found himself telling Gwyn about his new car, his pool house apartment behind the family's estate, about the riding stables and about the money. The well rehearsed rhetoric flowed, cozy and about as familiar as an old pair of slippers. This scenario wasn't new to Paul—he knew how it was done.

Paul saw the sex in her eyes. She wanted to be with him, and why not? They were the same. They were intelligent and good-looking. They knew the same music, the taste of a good martini, the experience of a Broadway play. They bathed and flossed and wore deodorant. They were Americans; they understood the culture and played by the same rules. And they were both away from home.

Gwyn raked her fingers back through her damp hair, leaving her sparkling eyes and moist lips speaking silently to him. He kissed her and she kissed him back. Then, sharing the heady taste of yeast and the wet fizz of the beer between them, they kissed deeper and longer.

Her hand caressed along Paul's thigh and he reached up to the back of her neck, pulling her even closer into him.

"I stay in a small apartment up on the second floor," Gwyn's hot breath whispered into his ear.

Closing his eyes, Paul breathed in the gardenia scent of Gwyn's hair and the clean balm of her soapy skin. How many times he had whispered similar words into a woman's ear.

They stood, melded together like the wind and rain buffeting the covering overhead. Gwyn stepped first back into the dark hallway, holding Paul's hand, guiding him as if he were a blind man. They were woozy from the Kingfishers, and neither of them noticed the creaking hinge of a door somewhere deeper inside the building.

"This way," Gwyn said, turning into yet another dark hallway. "The stairs are in the back."

As they approached the rear portion of the clinic, the rhythmic hum of an appliance crept into their consciousness. A small crack of light reached out from beneath a closed door, illuminating their two silhouettes in the hall.

Paul leaned close to Gwyn. "Is someone else here?"

Through her frothy buzz and haze of desire, it dawned on Gwyn who the only person could be in the laundry room at that time of night. "It's nothing," she said, grabbing hold of Paul's hand again, the tenderness suddenly replaced with an off-key potency. She slung Paul ahead of her, shoving him toward the stairway.

A harsh wedge of light grew abruptly as the laundry room door eased open. Bright yellow glared and battered the couple, as if they stood stunned in front of a movie screen.

"Good evening, Ms. Gwyneth." Tatleen's words were clear and measured, yet as graceful as a song. "I have finished the laundry you asked me to do tonight."

A final shove of Paul's lower back propelled him to the end of the hall. "Thank you, Tatleen." Gwyn quickly followed him.

Paul turned back to see her, but Tatleen had shut off the light and was already moving toward the opposite end of the corridor. Gwyn stood firmly in front of him, preventing any attempt to go after her.

"My room is at the top of the stairs," Gwyn said, holding her position. She reached her hand onto the center of his chest with a caressing touch, and her face slackened to that of a saint. "I'm heading back to the states in a couple of weeks and we may not have another chance. Isn't this what we both want?"

Paul turned back to the stairs, placing a foot on the bottom step. He paused there for a second. "I thought you said earlier that you didn't know where Tatleen was?"

"Did I?" Gwyn glanced over her shoulder down the empty hallway and shrugged. "To tell you the truth, I don't pay that much attention to where Tatleen is at any given time. She's just a--"

"I know," Paul said. "She's just a *cleaning woman*."

"I never meant it that way."

Paul hesitated again. "Why did you tell me all those things about her?"

"Honestly, I thought you already knew." Gwyn let out a sigh. "Either way, you should know what Tatleen's all about."

"Why's that?"

"You seem to have some kind of . . . soft spot for her." Gwyn took Paul's hand. "And I think that's really sweet, I do. You just don't know how some of these people can be, and I wouldn't want to see you get taken."

"And you think that's what Tatleen's trying to do—get over on me somehow?"

"From what I've seen, she pretends to be this innocent little lamb when she's around you. I'm just saying; why would she hide the fact that she was married and has a kid?"

Paul shook his head slowly. "I don't know."

Gwyn's expression implored him to let it go. But Gwyn could no longer continue Tatleen's verbal flogging. The chafing guilt was beginning to make her feel like a shit. Somewhere in Gwyn's heart she knew the badmouthing was underserved. Whatever Tatleen's motives, she couldn't be nearly as calculating as Gwyn was making her sound.

The mood had definitely taken a turn, and the enticement of Gwyn's room was evaporating fast. She thought of trying to revive the night with another offer, but she had her pride. Anyway, Gwyn could see that *passion* had left the building.

Distractions of any sort had never been a problem for Paul, especially when it came to women. But this encounter between Gwyn and Tatleen had left him confused. It had knocked him off a horse that he now had no desire to climb back onto. At least not until he could figure out what was really going on here. Paul wondered if Tatleen had seen he and Gwyn in the atrium. And if it even mattered.

Gwyn said nothing when Paul kissed her on the forehead and thanked her for dinner.

SADHANA

Swami Chalah sat on a chair on the landing in front of the ashram. He sipped his chai and nodded to Paul as he passed—Swami's wise expression an inviting confessional. The gentle glow from the lobby seemed to envelop him there on his seat.

Paul paused, wondering if he should even bother. It was probably written all over his face anyway, Paul thought, as he schlepped past the swami. Paul felt like a man with a pronounced limp—his Achilles heel now on display for all to see. He had come face-to-face with it tonight, realizing he was a fraud, unchanged at any real depth from the shallow Paul Griffiths who was empowered by his daddy's money and who picked up wanton girls at the Sloppy Tuna in Montauk.

"Yet another troubled evening for my friend." The honey warmth of Swami's voice immediately calmed Paul. He felt himself sitting down on the steps just below the glowing holy man.

"You seek that which you cannot find," Swami said.

Paul hadn't thought of it that way, but soon relented to Swami's appraisement. "I guess that's right," he said. "I'm not sure what to believe. There are these two women--"

Swami gently swiped a hand through the air to quiet Paul. "The specifics, like the seeds a farmer plants when monsoons have passed, are not as important as how the crop grows." He sipped his chai, then set the glass down. "Whatever your troubles, you must not dwell on the early stages of a sapling. The true bounty of a tree always reveals itself during harvest."

Swami gazed out into the darkness.

Paul watched him. "You seem to already know what worries me. Sometimes I think you understand me better than I even understand myself."

Swami smiled. "I understand the nature of man—Noble Truths that are the root of all things."

"Truth," Paul repeated. "There's the problem, right there."

The swami sipped slowly from his mug. "There is an old story about a man named Nasrudin who had lost a key. A friend happened upon Nasrudin, who was searching for the key on his hands and knees under a streetlight. When the friend asked where he had lost the key, Nasrudin answered, "I lost it inside my house, but the light is much better out here."

Paul forced a chuckle. "That's a good one."

"Some see it as a joke," said the swami. "But the story has a deeper meaning."

Paul shook his head. "I don't get it."

"We all search in the easy places for the things we want to find," Swami said. "Not necessarily in the right places. You seek truth in your life, but you are looking to others to find it. You must first find it inside yourself." Swami leaned back into the cup of his chair, head tilted toward the night sky. "You have spoken to me about your life—a life you left behind to come here."

Paul shook his head, angry with himself. "I thought that I had left it behind. I'm realizing that I'm not capable of making any real changes in my life. Who I've always been is just who I am."

Swami smiled. "Life has a funny way of letting you know who you *really* are."

"I've tried to change, I honestly have. But then I think it's all fake— like I'm just living a big lie."

Swami gazed into a dream, somewhere in his own mind. "We are all capable of change," he finally said. "Mohandas Karamchand Gandhi once said, 'To believe in something and not to live it, that is dishonest.' That would be fake." He paused again. "Find what it is *you* believe in."

Paul wasn't sure what he believed in. He reflected on his efforts toward selflessness and the progress he'd made since coming to India. But frustration always accompanied a relapse back to what was comfortable. His old life was still comfortable. Gwyn was comfortable.

He thought about explaining his problems to the swami. Describing how Tatleen had lied to him about who she was, and that she had been married and has a child. And then there was Gwyn—she was just as bad. She'd told him terrible things about Tatleen. And then she'd lied about not knowing where Tatleen was, when the whole time Tatleen was washing the laundry that Gwyn had given her. Both women were manipulative and distrustful in different ways, but both were liars.

None of it made sense, and yet it all felt very familiar—like the lies Loring Griffiths had told him about his mother and about his uncle. No matter which way he turned in his world, Paul believed no one anymore. He felt he had lost the capacity to trust.

Swami Chalah watched Paul in silence, finishing his glass of chai and wiping the remnants from his lips with his finger. "Meditate on it, my friend. The answer will come."

Paul remained on the ashram steps as the swami draped the end of his robe over his arm and stood. He looked out into the night once again before going inside.

SADHANA

The Sadhana candle withered and sputtered before ripening into a plump flame. Paul had become lost in it, staring deep into the mellow glow until everything else in the room was adrift in an inky sea. Breathing was clemency—each inhalation imitating the one before it, surrendering deeper to peace. Each discharged breath was liberation.

Submerging into a mindless cloud, Paul felt detached from his extremities. Images floated through his mind like raindrops, dribbling out and taking with them fixation and interpretation. Impressions of Gwyn, of Tatleen, and of his own mother came and went. His mother's image was one he'd fabricated as a child, and though years had passed the picture of her in his mind had not.

Emerging from his daze back to consciousness, Paul felt the Sadhana book in his hands. It was his mother's book. As he had in the past, Paul flipped it open at random. Beneath the undulant light of his candle was a story told by Buddha.

A young widower, who loved his five-year-old son very much, was away on business when bandits burned down his whole village and kidnapped the widower's son. When the man returned, he saw the ruins and believed his child had been killed in the fire. After grieving uncontrollably for several days, the man collected the ashes, placed them into a beautiful velvet bag and held a ceremony. Whether working, sleeping or eating, he always carried the bag of ashes with him.

One day his son escaped from the bandits and found his way home. He arrived at his father's new cottage in the middle of the night and knocked on the door. The father asked, "Who is there?" and the child answered, "It's me, Papa. Open the door, it's your son."

In his agitated state of mind the father thought that some mischievous boy was making fun of him, and he shouted for the child to go away. The boy continued knocking, but the father refused to let him in. Some time passed, and finally the child left. From that time on, the father and the child never saw one another again.

After telling this story the Buddha said, "We all seek truth and honesty. But sometimes you take something to be the truth that is not. If you cling to it so much, when the truth finally comes in person and knocks on your door, you will not open it."

Twenty-three

Just when we had nearly given up all hope, Curtis Tam called with new information. Airport security in Helsinki had found a possible hit on one of their surveillance camera tapes. A man matching Paul's description had been seen shouldering his way through a jostling crowd at the Aeroflot ticket counter on the morning following his cancelled flight. But by now, the lead was weeks old.

The Terminal 2 cameras had captured the grainy image just before a flight to New Delhi, via Moscow. It was a hopeful turn; the best we'd had since Tam took the case on. And if true, it suggested a high probability that Paul did make it to India. What happened to him after that however, was still something of a mystery.

In any case, Tam had conveyed his optimism, and Mr. Griffiths seemed at least a little more positive in the few days that followed.

* * *

Even before daylight crept into the halls of the ashram, Paul was up helping Sree prepare breakfast. Together they served the widow women who had lined the alley behind the kitchen, but Tatleen was not one of them.

After serving the ashram residents, clearing the tables and washing the dishes, Paul spent the bulk of the day bathing some of the elderly men, shaving them and clipping their nails. He had asked Swami if he could leave for a while in the afternoon, so he could spend time in the temple that he had seen while having dinner with Gwyn.

The Krishna-Balaram Mandir complex was as busy as it had been the last time Paul was there. But now he actually went inside the temple and spent time there as if he were one of the Hindu worshipers. The black and white tiles felt cool beneath his bare feet as he made his way toward the back of the sanctuary.

SADHANA

It was a huge, odd-shaped space with several fingers pointing out from the main room. Each accommodated a small shrine with one of 330 million Hindu deities—all subordinate to a massive altar in the main hall. This held golden likenesses of Lord Krishna and his elder brother, Balarama, both accentuated by over 1,000 flickering candles.

It surprised Paul that nobody seemed to take notice of him. Happily, he was able to spend a couple of hours, sitting against a marble pillar, meditating and listening to devotional chants.

Paul stretched his legs on the temple steps after having been coiled cross-legged on the floor for so long. He hesitated while passing the restaurant where he and Gwyn had eaten the previous evening. The sun had just dropped below the rooftops and the snappy balm of roasting spices floated in the air, producing in him a guilty yearning for his credit card-filled wallet.

He thought of the dismal ending to last evening, lamenting to some degree his uncharacteristic secession from a state of desire. It made him wonder if his decision had been a mistake, if he had lost further opportunities to connect with Gwyn, and if his refrain from her invitation had caused an ally to become an enemy. Mostly though, Paul second-guessed his machismo, which in turn served as ample proof that his male ego was still in need of restraint.

Paul's detour past the Asha Heath Care Centre was intentionally unintentional. He hoped to run into either Gwyn or Tatleen, but definitely not both.

Gwyn was sitting on her late afternoon bench behind the clinic gate. In her hand was a plastic jar, from which she spooned a tan paste into her mouth as if it were scoops of ice cream.

Paul had come upon her with a suddenness that accounted for the charitable-looking wave he offered her. He immediately felt like a clod, and motioned to the guard as if he had intentionally come to see her—which in partial truth, he had.

He stood before Gwyn, trying to read the label off the jar from which she busily excavated.

"Prutina," she said, holding up the container for Paul to see. "It's India's attempt at peanut butter."

"Oh." Paul realized his responses were getting worse instead of better. "Hey, I wanted to apologize about last night. I wasn't really myself."

Gwyn gazed up at Paul, a visual assay of his merits. Even in his loose-fitting tunic, the contour of his toned chest and broad shoulders were apparent. "You know what Charlie Brown says?"

The boyhood cartoon flashed in Paul's head, but he was afraid Gwyn was talking about a different Charlie Brown, and anything he answered would no-doubt make him sound even more ridiculous.

Gwyn set the spoon in the jar. "*Nothing takes the taste out of peanut butter quite like unrequited love.*"

Confusion washed over him, but she was quick to backstep. "It's just a joke, Griffiths." Gwyn stood and dusted off her kaki shorts. "You know? Just lightening up the conversation?"

"Well, I'm sorry, nevertheless."

They walked out past the guard, turning right at the roadway.

"I've got a few minutes before my staff meeting," she said. "But I wanted to talk. I've been doing some thinking, and after last night I think I need to get a couple of things off my chest."

Tatleen hurried across the street, conscious of the setting sun and all too aware of the prevailing sentiment about unescorted women—especially at night. It wouldn't be the first time someone mistook her for a street whore.

She ran up to the guard at the clinic gates and in Hindi she asked, "Have you seen the American man?"

"Walked in that direction with Ms. Gwyn," he answered, motioning up the road.

"Do you know where they were going?"

The guard shrugged then sat back down on his plastic chair, ignoring the *untouchable* widow woman.

Tatleen bowed her appreciation.

As she headed off in the direction the guard had indicated, Tatleen felt a peculiar emotion—at once both shameful and excited. She had something important to tell Mr. Paul Griffiths, and it could not wait. She hoped he would find happiness in her news, and that made Tatleen feel alive. It was something to look forward to. And it was her desire to please Paul that both gratified her and besieged her with guilt. She was a widow. Her husband had died. She had been cursed, and was condemned to a life of prayer to atone for her misfortunes.

Tatleen knew that the last time she was truly happy was as a child in the caring arms of her father.

"Tatleen!"

She turned to see Paul and Gwyn emerging from a cluster of stalls on the fringe of Sadar Bazaar.

"Mr. Paul Griffiths!" She bowed her head to acknowledge both he and Gwyn before continuing. "There is important news I must tell you."

Gwyn's eyes rotated in arching disfavor as her lips pressed painfully against one another.

"What is it?" Paul's slackened arm slipped free of Gwyn's grasp.

"It's Mr. Gopal."

"The man on the third floor?" Paul's shoulders dropped. "Tatleen, I'll be glad to help him when I get back."

Gwyn's castigating smile was even more severe. "Yes, Tatleen. Paul can deal with that when--"

"Forgive me, Ms. Gwyn." She turned her attention to Paul. "I was serving a meal to Mr. Gopal tonight when he mentioned that he was once a security guard."

Gwyn rolled her eyes again, but Paul was not so quick to dismiss her.

"Go on, Tatleen."

"He told me that many years ago he worked at the Bind-Chem facility near Aligarh."

Paul was listening intently now.

Tatleen continued. "His job was night watchman at the plant. He told me that he was employed there for two years, until it was shut down in 1983."

"Did he know my uncle?" Paul took a teetering step into the ambiguous bog separating the two women.

"No," Tatleen said. "Mr. Gopal never met your uncle."

Gwyn stepped forward and reclaimed Paul's arm in hers. Her sympathetic tug casting an image of she and Paul on the same team— of similar mindset: *Poor Tatleen, she's such a simple woman.*

Tatleen took a bold step closer, so close that she was staring directly into Paul's eagerly awaiting eyes—blocking out everything and everyone else.

"Mr. Gopal was working at the job site the night of the chemical spill. He was inside the office near the front gate, and he saw . . . he saw what happened."

* * *

"I was a young man of only 22-years when it happened. Three children already and a fourth on the way."

Tatleen translated while Mr. Gopal sucked air, as if just speaking the words deflated him.

"Nearly a child, myself." He coughed into his cupped hand and wiped the blood-tinged phlegm on the bed sheet. "It was my first real job. I had studied for five years in school, and was hired by CISF. The day they assigned me to the Bind-Chem plant was the happiest day of my life."

Paul turned to Tatleen. "CISF? What is it?"

Tatleen looked at Mr. Gopal with an expression he must have understood, because he spoke to her without further prompting.

"Central Industrial Security Force," Tatleen repeated back. "Indian parliament approved it that year, and I was in the first training regiment. I had worked my way up and was only months from being appointed Assistant Commandant." His head dropped. "And then, Aligarh."

"I'm still not clear," Paul said. "Did you work for my uncle or not?"

Tatleen's chopping Hindi discourse poured out, refashioning the question. Paul surmised that she was trying to put into context at least some aspect of the Griffiths family picture, and the reason why it was an important point.

Paul's eyes watched Tatleen closely, savoring her emotion like a first sip of coffee. The woman was intense, yet respectful and tender at the same time. She was also beautiful in a way he had never noticed beauty.

Mr. Gopal was silent for a long while after she finished. He glanced at Paul before continuing.

"It was a good government job," he spoke in Hindi and Tatleen translated. "I worked for the Ministry of Home Affairs in New Delhi. CISF sent its employees to guard industrial instillations throughout India, over 300 of them. Atomic power plants, oil fields and refineries, shipping ports, and so on. It was a great blessing that I was assigned to the Aligarh Bind-Chem facility. Nothing ever happened there."

The old man paused, nearly out of breath. And Tatleen, her cheeks burning with excitement and her eyes sparkling like a flare in the night sky, translated every word back to Paul.

He stared into the heat of Tatleen's gaze, forcing himself to focus on her words.

"That night," Paul said. "You were there."

"Yes," Tatleen said. "He was there." Then, turning back to the sobbing Mr. Gopal, she began translating again as he spoke. "I shamed myself by falling asleep in the plant foreman's office. His name was--"

"Bhupinder Magar." Tatleen finished the sentence for him, gasping the words like a dying prayer.

The room fell silent.

Paul stepped closer to her, for the moment abandoning his own line of questioning. He placed a hand on the back of Tatleen's trembling saree. The cultural *taboo* went unnoticed by Mr. Gopal, but the stirring tonic of Paul's touch served to further stoke the blazing pyre inside Tatleen.

Mr. Gopal nodded solemnly. "Magar. Yes, Bhupinder was an honorable man. He did not deserve the fate that befell him."

"What happened that night?" Paul asked. "What did you see?"

The old man took in a deep breath. "It was the drinking man—the American that Bhupinder Magar replaced as the boss. His name was O'Bryan. He must have come to the plant very early in the morning. I heard something outside, and when I looked out the window I saw him. He was running away from the tanks, toward the gate."

Paul and Tatleen glanced at one another and then back to Mr. Gopal. Tatleen offered him a sip of water, which he took.

"There was steam. Steam pouring from the chemical tanks. The smell, it was terrible. It strangled me, and I didn't know what to do." Gopal began to sob again. "I didn't know what to do."

Tatleen sat down next to him, nodding. She understood his dilemma, connecting with it in some way. It was as if she had accepted his pain and guilt as her own. She looked up at Paul, almost apologetically. It was the flaw in her country. More than a shortcoming, it was their cultural disgrace—placing the value of steady work above all else.

"The American ran out through the front gates, and I never saw him again." The old man took another sip of water, wiping his eyes with the bed sheet. "I couldn't believe he had done such a thing. There is no experience in Indian society that prepared me for this. We hold our jobs at the highest level, only the deities are above them."

Gopal had placed his employment upon the highest pedestal—a pedestal to which he was handcuffed. And somehow Tatleen knew and understood that. His decision had been prejudiced by the dangling promise of promotion. Money. So instead of reporting what he had seen, and risking his family's livelihood, he had lied. *I saw nothing.*

"I told the investigators that I found the tanks spilling chemicals into the ground while I was making my rounds. I told them that I had tried to shut them off, but was overcome by fumes."

When Tatleen finished interpreting, Paul slumped in the seat next to the bed. His hand dropped from Tatleen's back, and now it was she who wanted to caress him.

"You never told anyone the truth," Paul said.

"I lied. I lied to all of them." Mr. Gopal coughed and then stared at Tatleen with red-rimmed eyes. "I'm so sorry."

The words were Hindi, but their meanings vibrated through Paul. It was clear that the old man had carried the burden of deceit for over thirty years. Gopal had allowed Tatleen's father and his family to lose respect and fall into dishonor. Bhupinder Magar had been blamed in the media and by the government, and even worse, by the community, for the terrible tragedy. Mr. Gopal had not only let an innocent man go to jail, but ultimately to his death. And all of it to keep a steady job.

The blood inside Paul pumped into his head like an oil well. He wanted to reach down and slap the man who had caused Tatleen's family so much pain.

Paul studied Tatleen. Her graceful face was full of compassion. In her eyes he saw no hint of resentment or hatred, only humility. It was as if she had somehow detached herself from the personal insult of the old man's actions, or inactions, and surrendered her outrage to forgiveness. And she had done it in the blink of an eye.

It was a kind of grace and a beauty Paul had never experienced. Never.

Who am I to harbor such outrage and anger, when someone who had suffered far greater has rendered such forgiveness?

Mr. Gopal gradually turned to face Paul, his smoky black eyes swimming in remorse. He spoke softly, hesitatingly, in his native tongue. When he finished, Tatleen turned to Paul with the same look in her eyes.

"I think I must tell you something unpleasant, she said to Paul. "This man, Mr. Gopal, he says to me that your uncle was killed."

Paul stared blankly at her.

"This, he says, happened in the United States after the chemicals were spilled from the tanks."

"When?" Paul was crushed, his face drained of color. "Does he know who killed him?"

Gopal spoke again, and Tatleen listened.

"He says that it was talked about during the trial."

"What trial?"

Tatleen's chiseled features were unyielding. "My father's trial." She took a breath and rubbed the side of her neck. "This was the reason that no other action was taken by the Indian government. Bind-Chem's assets were seized and my father went to jail as the responsible party."

Paul glared back and forth between the two. "But that's not fair. That's not what happened. Your father didn't do anything wrong."

Tatleen took a step back, as if separating herself from the entire affair. She had shouldered enough. "This is India," she said quietly. "In the eyes of the State, the damage caused had come into alignment with the penance paid. The owner was dead, the foreman sentenced to prison and the company's entire fortune taken by the government. There was harmony . . . karma."

Paul stood silently. Finally asking, "So, my uncle is dead?"

Mr. Gopal's raw eyes watched the two of them, not understanding, but sensing their despair.

Tatleen spoke to Gopal and he responded with only one word.

"Accident," she said.

Paul stared into her eyes. Neither of them said it, but again, the word *karma* was there, suspended in the air between them.

He shook his head. For this man to show up now, at this place and at this time, was yet another extraordinary coincidence which nobody could have ever predicted—another swipe of fate's indelicate hand.

Later, after comforting Mr. Gopal and easing him into a peaceful sleep, Tatleen spoke again to Paul. "Something else I must say to you." They had left the dormitory and paused in the hallway overlooking the garden. She gazed out over the rooftops, dark and silent under a tangle of wires, as she searched for her words. "I have behaved as an ordinary woman. In doing this, I have dishonored myself."

Paul thought of the things Gwyn had told him about Tatleen. It was a trigger that quickened his heartbeat, yet he said nothing.

"I am *not* an ordinary woman," she said. "In truth, I am far less than that. In some respects, I am not even a woman."

His eyebrows wrinkled. "Of course you are. What are you saying?"

"From perspective of Indian society, I am nothing. I was once a married woman with a child. Now I am a widow—a burden to my relatives. I have nothing to contribute, not as a mother, not as a family member, and not as a citizen of my country."

"I know all about Naagesh," Paul said. "And I know that you are one of the singing widow women."

Tatleen nodded slowly. The realization that Gwyn had told him her secret was firmly fixed in Tatleen's mind, but her expression showed nothing. It didn't matter.

"I have wanted you to know these things about me," she said. "It was wrong of me to conceal them. I have dishonored my faith and the memory of my husband."

"Nonsense." Paul reached a hand toward hers and she stepped back. "Tatleen, you didn't do anything wrong. Being a widow doesn't make you any less of a person. No less of a woman."

"That is not the way *we* view things." Tatleen tucked a swatch of fabric across her face below her nose and eyes. "I must now only give praise through prayer and song and by showing compassion. That is how I must live my days."

"But you're still young," Paul said. "Young enough to start over, meet someone else and build a life."

From behind her saree, Tatleen smiled at the American's lack of understanding. "It's a rare thing when a widow remarries. Who would have her?"

Paul's palms turned upwards and his mouth sprung open, as if an entire sea full of other fish were swimming around them.

"And Naagesh? You must still care about him." Paul now had a sense as to why Tatleen had felt responsible to return the gift he had given the boy—she was his mother, and she still wanted to instill a sense of value and responsibility. "You love Naagesh, don't you?"

"Of course I do." Tatleen's eyes flashed with emotion. "That is why I could not leave him alone with my husband's family. I had to take Naagesh with me."

"I don't understand. Why did you have to leave in the first place?" Paul tilted his head in confusion. "Didn't your husband's family feel badly for you? I mean, wouldn't they want to help you and Naagesh?"

"Let's walk." Tatleen turned toward the staircase. Descending the steps in front of him, her breathing turned to wild gulps of air—unsteady and rushed. Her trembling hand gripped the handrail. When they emerged onto the cool grassy courtyard, Tatleen slowed but kept her back to him. "I'm sorry," she said, wiping her eyes.

"That's alright, Tatleen." Paul stepped closer, up to her back. "There's so much about Indian culture that I'm ignorant about. We don't have to talk about any of this if you don't want to."

"No," she said. "I want to tell you this. I have wanted to let you know who I really am, ever since you first showed such kindness to me. Even then, I wanted to stop you. I should have stopped you. I should have said, don't be so kind to me. I am nothing. Even less than nothing. I don't even exist in my own country."

Again, Paul put his hand on her back. This time she pulled away.

"My husband was older than me. He had worked with my father, and had come from a working family. He was able to provide well, so the marriage was arranged. I was twelve years."

Paul's head became heavy, as if filled with giant waves of water—sloshing and pounding inside it. He steadied himself against her, and she turned to face him.

"When my father went to jail and the plant closed, my husband had no work. And then my husband became sick, probably from the toxic water in the wells. His care was expensive and we were not able to pay for medications and treatment. I found out that I was pregnant just before Tavish—that was my husband's name, Tavish—just before he died. Naagesh was born with deformities, which we think was also a result of the water, as many children in the village were born with health problems. His condition meant that he would never be able to work or contribute to the family. And I, as a widow lacking skills and standing in the community, would never be able to contribute either."

"But that wasn't your fault," Paul said.

Tatleen smiled. "Indians have a different concept of fault," she said. "When a woman is attacked, raped, the crime is often blamed on her. The woman is said to have been dressed inappropriately, or had behaved in a seductive way, or shouldn't have gone into an unsafe area. In this way, again, there is cause and then there is the result. Damage caused and penance paid. They are in harmony."

"So what happened?" Paul said as they walked through the gate and slowly down the alley. "Did Tavish's family force you to leave?"

"Yes." She turned her head away, just short of the truth.

Paul sensed it. "There's more."

Tatleen took another few steps. "Yes, there's more." She stopped in front of a large archway—its heavy timber door cracked and peeling from disrepair. "My husband's family beat me, and they refused to feed Naagesh. They forced me to cook and clean for them. And when that wasn't enough they made me beg for money on the streets. And when that wasn't enough, they wanted me to . . . they wanted me to sell myself."

Paul stood with his mouth open, but his words were shackled somewhere inside. Words he could not even form in his mind.

"When I refused, they threatened to beat Naagesh. They said they would kill him if I didn't pay them money each day." Tatleen took a breath, tucking a stray lock of hair under her saree. "That is when I took Naagesh and left."

She faced away from Paul toward the building. He stepped closer, resting his hands on her shoulders. It was then that he was able to actually sense, for the first time, her state of emaciation. He gently caressed what felt like little more than a coat hanger with a garment draped over it. She pulled away again, but less vigorously than before. Then she stopped altogether.

"Tatleen," Paul whispered. "You're so thin."

She turned to face him. Tatleen's coffee eyes were heavy with moisture. It snaked down her cheeks in glistening streaks.

"Do you eat?" he asked.

Tatleen slowly shook her head. "Most of what I earn, I take to Naagesh. The orphanage where he stays is run by a Hindu charity, and there is little to eat there."

"Can't he stay with you?" Paul kept hold of her.

Tatleen shook her head again as she reached for the handle on the heavy wooden door. Paul heard the groan of rusted hinges as she pulled it open, then he stepped back to view inside the building. It was ghastly—a muggy cell, devoid of natural light and fresh air. The room was littered with women—mostly old—lying by the dozens in gaunt heaps on the dank concrete floor. One woman squatted over a plastic bucket in the far corner of the room. A few candles positioned intermittently throughout the hollow chamber, casted undulating ghoulish shadows around its dark periphery. The smell was horrific.

Paul stumbled backwards, and then looked at Tatleen with eyes that could not hide their revulsion.

"You ask me why Naagesh can't stay with me, why I gave him up?" Tatleen glanced back into the room as several of the women stirred and rustled at the intrusion. "Because this is where I live."

Twenty-four

I hadn't heard anything more and was beginning to wonder if the Russian airline was just another dead end. But just a few days later, Mr. Tam called with an update. He had learned that Paul Griffiths had been listed on the passenger manifest of Aeroflot flight #3661, transferring in Moscow to New Delhi, India. He had actually been confirmed on the flight, and by all accounts had arrived at Indira Gandhi International Airport the following evening.

A collective sigh was released as word passed from one employee to another. We barely had time to cheer the good news when the next blow stuck: Paul's suitcase had been found unattended at the curbside in New Delhi. His clothes, wallet and all his money—abandoned there.

* * *

Tatleen had bared her soul to the American, and though it had been an undertaking of great importance to her, she still didn't know exactly why she'd done it. Other than seeing that Paul was a kind and compassionate man, there was little about him Tatleen understood.

The story Gwyn had told her about Paul was disturbing, of that she had no doubt. Tatleen placed truthfulness above most things. But she no longer cared to know what was fact and what was not. She did not feel she had a right to it. Paul's transgressions were between he and his god, and Tatleen wanted it to stay that way. By showing him the widows' shelter, she had intentionally pushed him away. Again, she didn't understand exactly why she had done that, either.

The meaning of this man in her life had become as mysterious as the uncomfortable stirrings she felt with each touch of his hand. Tracing these threads to their emotional source was like searching for the cotton plant responsible for a single fiber floating in the breeze. So she sang and she prayed for forgiveness.

"I want to go home." Paul's childlike plea in front of his flickering candle was heartfelt. "I honestly don't think I can take anymore of this place." He closed his eyes, but couldn't blink away the image of the squalid room that Tatleen called home. The place wasn't fit for animals, he thought. The idea of her living there was utterly revolting.

He suddenly began to cry. As if he had run too fast down a hill, Paul was now tumbling uncontrollably. He struggled to gulp in air, but his hard, spasmodic sobbing came from somewhere too deep to restrain.

When the tears finally stopped, Paul leaned back onto the bed. His breathing had slowed and he was no longer shaking. He stared up at the chipped paint on the ceiling, trying to gain some understanding of what it was he was feeling. Disgust, shame, guilt . . . and he wanted nothing more to do with Tatleen. Nothing.

Paul quickly slammed the door to his mind, locking and bolting it securely. *Done!*

The thumping rotation of the fan reminded Paul of his first night in the country—never so afraid, never so alone. He glanced over at the chair to inventory his belongings, just as he had that morning in New Delhi. He didn't own much, but Paul realized he still had the expensive watch his father had given him. It was the security blanket he had clung to since arriving in India, knowing he could hawk it anytime for a ticket home. Paul considered it now, more seriously than at any other time during the trip.

Then he noticed the stupid painted elephant. He had given the trinket to Naagesh and Tatleen had returned it. Paul shook his head in frustration. "This country is too damn strange for me."

I think it's time to cash in the watch.

He laid his head back on the wafer pillow. Gwyn's image popped into this head, and he was drawn down that river of thought. She was, after all, a seductive little thing—clean and American. They could have fun together. Carefree fun. Meaningless and mindless. Best of all, Gwyn didn't sleep on the floor or use a bucket for a toilet.

The next day Paul walked over to the clinic to see her. He had decided to stoke the embers that had ignited with such ferocity only a few nights before. He would use the information from Mr. Gopal as a pretext for his visit.

"Well, look what the monkey dragged in." Gwyn pushed back from the papers on her desk. "Yet another visit from my fickle friend."

This may be tougher than I thought. Thankfully, the words were spoken only in Paul's mind.

"Mind if I sit?"

Gwyn motioned toward the chair.

"You okay?"

"Great." Gwyn's mouth barely moved.

"I thought I'd come by to tell you about this guy I spoke with. An elderly man at the ashram."

Gwyn put no effort into an appearance of interest. "Gopal. Yeah, I heard Tatleen tell you about him."

"Anyway, this guy knows the whole story. He--"

Gwyn cut him off. "Hey, before we get too far into this . . . are you expecting Tatleen any time soon? I mean, I'd hate to have you run off again in the middle of another conversation."

"I'm sorry, Gwyn. I know I deserved that." Paul took a breath. "No, that won't happen again, I promise."

Gwyn nodded, as the trace of a curve exposed itself at the corners of her lips. "Okay."

"Okay." Paul made use of his blue eyes to plea lenience. "So it turns out that some drunk who worked for my uncle sabotaged the place. Gopal saw him do it!"

"And he didn't tell the police?"

Paul shook his head. "Was in line for some kind of promotion, and too afraid he'd lose his job. I'm sure the guy feels like shit now, but, whatever."

Gwyn rolled her eyes. "These Indians and their jobs."

"But the other thing he said was that he heard my uncle died in some kind of accident."

Gwyn eyed Paul to gauge his grief, but strangely there seemed to be none. "So, your uncle is dead?"

"According to Mr. Gopal." Paul stared out the window, thinking. "If it's true, and depending on where and when it happened, it might prove that he's not my father."

"So how do we find that out?" she asked.

"I thought we might be able to--"

"Do an Internet search." Gwyn pursed her lips. "So that's really the reason for the visit. You just want to use my computer."

"No, not at all." Paul slid his seat closer to the desk. "In fact, I woke up thinking about you this morning, and I wanted to see you. Either way, I wanted to apologize."

Paul's explanation seemed to sweeten the mood. Gwyn logged into the computer and slid the monitor around so they both could view it.

"What was your uncle's name again?"

"Paul."

"Oh yeah, same as you." Gwyn tapped the keyboard.

"Paul James Griffiths," he said. "And this time leave out the word *India* and type in *accident*. Gopal said it happened somewhere back in the states."

One hit looked promising, though it led them to another link. Gwyn followed it to Mayville Sentinel Newspaper archives. She scrolled down to a December 15, 1983 issue in which a multi-vehicle accident dominated the headline.

An aerial photo of a snowy crash site made Gwyn turn away.

Paul angled the monitor toward him and studied the picture briefly before reading the article: "Six vehicles including an ambulance piled up in a chain-reaction crash in a snowstorm on Interstate 90 early Thursday morning, killing two motorists and shutting down the highway for nearly 10 hours."

Gwyn reached over to put her hand on Paul's arm, but his eyes didn't leave the screen. "Police closed a mile-long section of I-90 in both directions near Dunkirk after the 1:20 a.m. accident. Killed were Paul James Griffiths of New York and his sister-in-law, Leigh Abigail Townsend of Chicago."

Paul didn't even feel Gwyn's grip tighten as he reread the last line of the article to himself. Scanning to the end of the page, he came back to *that* line and stared at it again. He peered into the monitor, as if the names might miraculously change. They didn't.

"Paul?" Gwyn's voice crept into his periphery. "Are you alright?"

Paul swallowed a knot in his throat. "I think so," his words dry and croaky. "So that's what happened to my mother." He slumped back against the chair. "And my long lost uncle actually *was* my father."

"We don't know that." Gwyn turned the monitor back and shut it off. "You don't know the whole story."

"You mean why my mom and her husband's brother were in a car together, 500 miles away from Chicago? Yeah, I'd like to hear that story. C'mon, Gwyn. What else could it be?"

Gwyn's eyes dropped and she said nothing.

"I need to face facts, Gwyn. My mother was a two-timing cheat who probably never loved my dad in the first place." Paul sat there, eyes focused on a scenario he had no doubt about. "No wonder Loring always hated his brother. Who could blame him? The guy was a backstabbing rat."

"Can't you talk to your father about it?"

Paul shook his head.

"He's not even my father," he said after a pause. "Loring must have hated *her*, too. Anyway, no, I can't talk to *him* about it. Like I already told you, if I go home I'll be thrown in jail. And even if I try to phone the estate, the cops will trace the call."

Gwyn put her hand over her face and shook her head. She hadn't gotten any particulars from her call to the program director. But Gwyn definitely had the impression that Paul's legal problems were not as daunting as he made them out to be. She considered admitting to Paul that she had called the director to ask about him, but she knew he wouldn't be pleased. Paul had received enough of a shock for one day."

Paul's mind was elsewhere now. He actually considered the pros and cons of heading back to Long Island. If his dad got the attorney to work on the judge, and Paul was able to explain his stolen bags and the mix-up with the CRF group, he might be able to avoid a prison sentence.

Paul stood, yawned and stretched.

Gwyn saw it as forced; meant to make him appear relaxed and unfazed, ready to discus the weather.

She stood, too. "I suppose you'll find your way to Tatleen after leaving here." Gwyn's words held none of the sarcasm they had in the past. Before Paul could answer, Gwyn continued. "I just want to say that she's not really as bad as I made her out to be. Tatleen is actually a very nice woman, and I feel badly for ever speaking ill of her."

Paul studied Gwyn, wondering why the sudden change of heart. "Doesn't matter," he said. "Her life is proving to be more reality than I can handle. Not really sure what I was thinking, but I'm definitely done with all that."

Now it was Gwyn who studied him. Something in the vehemence of his words settled harshly on her—too harshly to be spoken by one who truly doesn't care. Gwyn was suddenly aware that the opposite of love is not hate. It's indifference.

And Paul's sentiments when it came to Tatleen were anything but indifferent.

Gwyn's eyes searched his for more clarity. "Can I just ask one question?"

Paul took in a breath and let it out.

She said, "How did you end up with that trinket?"

"The little elephant thing?" Paul's tone was one of confusion. "The swami at my ashram gave it to me. Said someone found it outside, I think. Why?"

"I saw Tatleen hand it to you the other day, just outside the clinic."

"Oh that." Paul tilted his head back with a dismissive laugh. "I had given it to Naagesh, and I guess Tatleen didn't want him to have it. So she was just returning it to me."

"Naagesh? Is that the boy?"

Paul nodded.

"You even know her son?"

"Sure," he said. "I've run into them a few times. But I never knew he actually belonged to Tatleen until--"

"Until I told you." Gwyn's eyes gazed off in thought. She hadn't really recognized the depth of Paul's relationship with Tatleen until that moment. Not just his knowledge of Tatleen's son, but his apparent acceptance of the boy had added a nebulous layer to the dynamics of his relationship with Tatleen. It confused and disarmed Gwyn.

"Like I said, I'm done with all that." Paul looked off into space.

The silence that followed confined them. Paul rubbed the bridge of his nose, hoping to think of a transition for a smooth exit.

"Well, as you can see I have work to do." Gwyn motioned at the desk, saving Paul the search for an excuse. "And sorry about your mom and uncle, whatever he turns out to be."

The words she had chosen, more a closing than an opening, told Paul that she was of the same mind. Neither of them saw any value in pushing an empty cart any further up the hill.

Paul thanked Gwyn for her help and headed back to the ashram. Their minds each lingered in restless thought, both feeling frustrated and unfulfilled—as if they had worked on a jigsaw puzzle, only to find the last piece missing. But for Paul, it forced a decision. It was the final straw.

The walk back to the ashram would have taken him past the temple of the singing widow women, which he wanted to avoid at all costs. Instead, he turned down an alleyway that led him past the shanty orphanage where Naagesh lived. Paul was at a loss as to whether or not he wanted to see the boy—he did and he didn't.

"Hallo, Paul!" Naagesh's scrawny voice called from the curtained doorway. "Hallo, Paul." Propping himself onto his side, the boy leaned over the wooden threshold and managed an excited hand gesture. "Hallo, Paul."

Naagesh's sweet smile and practiced greeting gripped his heart. Paul knelt on the ground, just outside the opening, and clasped hands with the little guy.

"Hello, Naagesh." Paul cupped his hand around the side of the boy's dirty face. Naagesh wore a faded soccer shirt and pajama pants that had been cut off at his stub knees. The boy's nose was runny and his hair was a nest of twigs, but it was clear from his immense grin that none of that mattered. He was truly elated to receive a visit from his American friend and Paul was equally as excited to see him.

Again, as with Paul's previous appearance at the orphanage, a handful of the other children bounded out to gawk at the tall foreigner. The novelty quickly faded and the orphans ran off, kicking an empty plastic bottle back and forth in a makeshift game of soccer.

Paul used his tunic to wipe Naagesh's face, and the unlikely pair continued playing like schoolyard friends. Paul hammed and Naagesh mimicked, and both of them laughed recklessly. Their surroundings paled around them as their worlds melded into one. They were consumed with one another.

Unseen at that moment was Tatleen. She had made her way down the alley toward the orphanage, stopping suddenly when she saw Paul. She slowly backstepped until she was a sound distance from them. With her white saree and willowy body tucked into the shadows of a doorway, Tatleen watched her son. Her heavy heart, now made buoyant by the boy's palpable love for the American man, began to beat with pleasure again. What she saw inflated her like the warm breath of love. It had been so long that Tatleen had forgotten what joy was actually like. She had only experienced such a feeling with Naagesh . . . and from her father.

Later, when Paul's visit bordered on disruptive and the orphanage housewoman had poked her peevish face out from the next room, he headed back down the alley toward the ashram. Tatleen compressed herself into the darkest recess of the building, a plastic bag, a discarded piece of fabric, or another nameless street person. Paul passed her without a glance, but suddenly stopped and turned. He ran back to the orphanage, as if he'd left something of importance.

Naagesh was still wriggling in the crook of the doorway when Paul got there. He swooped the boy up in his arms and embraced him tightly. Naagesh nuzzled against Paul, head-to-head, both wearing the same broad smile. Setting the boy down again, he and Naagesh exchanged a *high-five*.

"Goodbye, Naagesh."

The child's dark eyes stared back at Paul, trying to understand the meaning of the man's teary gaze. He put his tiny brown hand on Paul's cheek and gently stroked it.

Paul set the boy down and turned away to cloak his emotion. He walked back toward the ashram, unable to look back.

Awake and with his mind swirling in thought, Paul laid in his room awaiting daylight. When it finally came, Paul had made his decision.

Swami was praying in the courtyard when Paul stepped out to greet him. The warm dew, floating upward and disappearing into the sunlight, heralded the cruel heat of a new day.

Paul extended his hands toward the swami, and in the cup of his palms was the wristwatch his father had given him. "Can you help find someone who will give me money for this?"

The swami regarded the watch, but did not reach for it. "It is a fine piece of jewelry. Does it have special meaning to you?"

Paul frowned into his hands. "This is a Patek Philippe, Aquanaut. It's worth thousands of dollars."

Swami smiled warmly. "But what is its value to you?"

Paul shook his head. Clearly, the swami wasn't understanding what he wanted. Paul looked at the watch again. "My dad gave it to me," he said. "But I need to sell it so I can buy a ticket home."

"A gift from your father," Swami said. "To sell such a precious thing for a jet airplane ticket . . . You must have extreme longing to go home and see him."

Paul shook off the swami's faulty assumption. "So, do you think you can help me?"

"Yes," answered Swami Chalah. "I will help you."

Paul wasn't sure what he was supposed to make of Swami's answer, or what he should do next. The swami never moved to take the wristwatch and never made any further inquiries, so Paul simply nodded his gratitude and headed up to his room.

Paul looked around his tiny sleeping quarters, the place he had called home since his arrival in Vrindavan, and the place in which he had searched so much of his soul in an effort to find enlightenment. The entirety of his worldly possessions was laid out on the bed, and all of it could fit in Paul's black leather satchel. He sat there beside his things, thinking.

SADHANA

A tap on his door raised Paul from the depths of dark reflection. Having lost track of time, he ascended up through fathoms of awareness until he was fully present. He could not tell how long he had been in that state. In the hallway was Swami Chalah, hands together in prayer, bowing a pardon for interrupting Paul.

"Come in, Swami."

"I will not disturb you any further." The holy man's grin bobbled slightly. "As you asked, a jet airplane ticket has been purchased for your flight back to New York City."

Paul tried to blink his mind into comprehension. "Already?"

"Your reservation is on British Airways number 256, leaving Delhi airport in the morning hours of tomorrow." Swami handed Paul an envelope, tattered and stained from repeated use. "Some rupees for food, and also enough for a train ticket to New Delhi."

Paul didn't know what to say. He grabbed his wristwatch from his pile of belongings, but Swami quickly offered a palm into the air between them. "Please keep your father's gift. It has much greater value than the contents of the envelope."

Emotion filled Paul's throat instead of words. It showed in his eyes, making any further attempts at conversation pointless. Paul leaned into the holy man and wrapped his arms around him. They embraced one another for several seconds. When Paul eased away again, the two men locked eyes.

Swami's smile was warm and knowing. "I pray you find what you are seeking."

The two men stood facing each other as Paul thought about Swami's statement. He wondered: *What am I seeking?*

"The truth." Paul heard his voice say the words before he had even completed the thought.

Swami nodded and looked fondly at Paul. "The moon is true, is it not?"

Paul shrugged. "Yes, it's the moon."

"Yet, its light and image are reflected in a tiny dewdrop of water. Is not that small image also true?"

"Well, yes and no. It doesn't represent the actual size of the moon."

Swami smiled in sympathy and kindness. "You seek the truth but you have been injured by deceit. Would you believe the truth if you found it?"

An answer did not come to Paul. He had become immersed in distrust, even of himself. He no longer knew who he was.

287

"Real truth is enlightenment," Swami said. "And at the root of enlightenment is compassion. Travel well, my friend."

Paul stood alone in his tiny room, unmoving. He tried to gather the seeds of knowledge Swami had given to him, but they slipped from his hands. Paul's mind was a scramble of contrasting emotion and thought, none of which he was able to fully grasp.

He looked around the tiny space, taking in the smell, taste, look, and feel of it, regarding it as the loving companion he would never see again. Paul put his meager belongings into the satchel; his passport, the Sadhana book, the elephant trinket and the envelope Swami Chalah had given him. Then Paul noticed the small stub of his Sadhana candle sitting on the windowsill. He tossed it in with the rest of his things, before slinging the bag over his shoulder and leaving the room.

Standing in the road in front of the ashram, Paul felt the feverish heat of the new day. It entombed him in a muggy cell that he was now eager to escape—even if it meant exchanging one prison for another.

He walked out to Gandhi Marg and got into a tuk-tuk. Paul did not speak to the driver, other than to direct him to the Mathura Junction train station. He paid the driver and bought a New Delhi train ticket with rupees from the envelope. There were more bills inside it, which Paul knew were meant for meals. He did not feel hunger, only nervous anticipation.

At 6:48 p.m., #1237—Punjab Mail pulled up to the platform, and Paul squeezed into Sleeper class with a thousand hurried travelers. The sweltering car and the oppressive tang of its passengers was dizzying. Paul could only close his eyes and hope for a wisp of air as the train began moving again. He had wanted to relax in meditative thought during the ride, but he found himself unable to focus on anything but the unbearable heat and utter discomfort of the train car.

The gradual absence of farmland and the thickening structures whizzing past the barred window alerted Paul to his pending arrival. More decrepit shacks, stacked one on top of the other like toy blocks, and dirty faces with sad eyes—burnt match heads lining shoulder to shoulder at the side of the tracks. The twisted maze of electrical cables overhead and tuk-tuks by the hundreds in jagged rows, meant the 2½-hour journey was finally over. *Welcome back to New Delhi.*

Though the air upon stepping off the train was no less stale than inside it, Paul had room at least to move. Unlike the last time he was in Delhi, nobody approached him and nobody begged for money from the *American*. He fit in with his surroundings—he was one of them.

SADHANA

In the rattling quiver of the tuk-tuk, Paul regretted not taking a real taxi from the station to the airport. After all, he now had the money. Vibrating through Gol Dak Khana roundabout onto Baba Kharak Singh Marg, Paul's thoughts turned inward.

Something about India had liberated him. Paul felt capable and real. The frantic country had been trying and uncomfortable, but at the same time it was a challenge he had faced. Alone.

The buggy convulsed off of Delhi-Gurgaon Expressway toward the airport and memories of his arrival percolated through him. It seemed like so long ago. So much had happened since then, and there were so many things Paul had learned about himself and about life. He asked himself what the point was to it. Was there a lesson somewhere in all of this?

The tuk-tuk motor quaked and spit to a stop at Terminal 3. Paul paid the driver and stepped out into the snarled clamor of Indira Gandhi International Airport.

A legless beggar sat propped against a pillar. In his hand was a candle, extended out to all the passersby. Paul chuckled to himself, realizing he was the same guy who had sold him the Sadhana candle when he first arrived. "You're still here," Paul said with a smile as he passed the man.

A look of recognition flashed in the beggar's eyes, but Paul was certain there was no way he could remember him. A stout Caucasian man passed Paul, hastily exiting the terminal. He was older than Paul and dressed in a suit, as if he had an important meeting to make.

The legless man held a candle up, offering his goods to the visitor.

"I don't need a candle, Pal." The man tossed a few rupees onto the ground next to him. "Here, get yourself some chow."

Paul's gut twisted into a knot.

The candle salesman turned his head slightly, then picked up the notes and handed them back to the well-dressed American. It was clear he did not want the man's charity, and only intended to transact a legitimate sale.

"Crazy fool," said the American, snatching the rupees back and stuffing them into his pocket. "That was more than you'll make all week."

Paul's stomach wrenched tighter as the man strode away and hailed a cab at the curb.

That was me, Paul thought. He watched the man ride away in the cab, oblivious to his surroundings. Oblivious to life.

Paul was unable to move. The actions of his foul-mannered countryman had booted Paul, forcing him to come face-to-face with himself. He imagined the other man's arrogant wealth was equal to his own, and like Paul, he had only come to India because he had to. The man repulsed him, but Paul knew deep inside that it was that same part of himself that he found most repulsive.

Paul wanted to resurrect his appetite for the flight back to New York, but his gut burned like an incinerator, scorching his self-worth until there was nothing left but a black soul.

"Who the hell am I?" Paul said aloud. "What have I done?"

As Paul watched people pass the legless man, an image of Naagesh blotted out the scene. Tatleen's little boy was like a salamander, not fully at home in the water or on land. There was no place for a legless boy like Naagesh in India. Paul's eyes misted over and he felt weak. He turned abruptly and entered the terminal, determined to leave all this hurt and suffering behind—after all, he was only one man in a country of over 1.2 billion. What could he possibly do about it?

The chaotic scene changed markedly once Paul was inside the gigantic concourse. A modern space of glass and steel, cooler and slower moving than outside, Paul felt as if he had stepped back into civilization. But even with the improved landscape, he could not shake the constricting anxiety tightening around his chest.

Paul stepped into the British Airways queue and made his way up to the ticket counter. His hands slowly began to tremble as Naagesh's innocent and loving face filled his mind. Paul took in deep, steady breaths, but was unable to block out the vortex of images. He closed his eyes and stood there at the counter, clenching his teeth and urging himself to do it.

Suddenly, Swami's words reverberated in his ears, as if roaring through a hollow canyon.

"The root of enlightenment is compassion."

Twenty-five

On the off chance that Paul had somehow managed to get in touch with the CRF group, Mr. Tam thought it worthwhile to follow-up with them. He had apprised Mr. Geerts of his attempts to phone Gwyneth Eichler at her office in Vrindavan, but thus far she had not returned his calls.

It seemed that Indian law enforcement contacts were less reliable than in Finland, and the flow of information across the vast network of states and union territories was a mess. According to Tam, politicians comprising India's 39 political parties heavily influence local police jurisdictions, making each an independent entity. As an added snag, one-third of India's parliament currently faced criminal charges—making Tam's inquiries susceptible to extortion and subterfuge.

A silver lining to the India cloud, and it wasn't much, was the fact that Paul had a contact person through CRF. Whether or not he could get in touch with her remained to be seen.

In any case, Mr. Griffiths saw only a *worst-case scenario* for Paul. And I believe those days and nights of worrying were the source of Mr. Griffiths' eventual health problems.

* * *

Hazrat Nizamuddin was not the same Delhi railway station Paul had originally arrived at, nor was it where he had requested the tuk-tuk driver to take him. Paul was on the other side of New Delhi from where he wanted to be. But it was a train station, nevertheless.

The ticket counter was a broiling madhouse, and like other single file lines Paul had waited in, there was no semblance of either single file or a line. Sandwiched in the center of at least two-dozen surging and heaving men, Paul could barely see the ticket window. After being flattened like a piece of naan bread, he finally gnashed his way to the front of the line by making use of his size and fitness.

Thankfully, Paul's unspent food money was enough to purchase a Sleeper car ticket back to Mathura Junction. He had a scant 14 rupees left over. But the *Nizamuddin-Kota Superfast Special* wasn't to depart until 5:15 a.m. the following morning, which meant another bone-bruising night on a concrete station platform.

Hundreds of other travelers seemed to have little problem slumbering through the bedlam, but Paul was miserable. The irritating squawk of the woman's recorded voice over the loudspeaker, the odor of urine emanating from the man next to Paul, the rats scurrying about with complete impunity, all worked in concert to fleece Paul of his much needed sleep.

He was hungry and sore. Several times during the night, Paul wondered if he had made the right decision to stay. He hadn't been allowed to exchange his return ticket, and the airline would not extend Paul a credit. With only a handful of rupees left, Paul had no idea how he would manage his way from the Mathura Junction station to Vrindavan, 15 kilometers away.

As the first searing rays of light glazed the platform, two large, rusted wheels trundled within inches of Paul's head. Wooden carts, pushed by tiny men with chai-colored skin and bloodshot eyes, began their monotonous trek up and down the station's seven platforms. Paul sat up and gazed longingly at a cart piled high with bananas. They were discolored and scrawny by civilized standards, but Paul still found himself unable to resist one. He fished around for a couple of rupees, but the seller did not have sufficient change this early in the morning. So instead of one banana, he simply handed Paul three.

A rustling sound came from behind a garbage can near where Paul sat, as if someone were sweeping the floor. He glanced over his shoulder to see a woman, apparently unable to walk, sliding herself and her folded legs along the ground on a soiled piece of cardboard. Riding upon it with her was an infant. Paul watched the woman use her calloused black hands to tip the trashcan and rummage through its contents for something to eat.

Paul separated two bananas and handed both to the woman. She accepted them with hands pressed together and fingertips to her bowed forehead. She then broke bits of it off, pinching it with her fingers into a paste that her toothless mouth could swallow. She fed the open-mouthed infant the same way, as if it were a chirping baby bird.

SADHANA

Feeling a moderate amount of guilt for not offering her and the child all three bananas, Paul only partially enjoyed dining on the remaining piece of fruit. He watched the woman struggle across the platform, wondering what tragedy had sacked her mobility. Again he thought of Naagesh, and then of Tatleen. Paul's cramped joints and grieving bones brought with them a wave of sadness. Tatleen slept on a bed of cement every single night. Her comfort bar couldn't get any lower.

As it turned out, the *Superfast Special* wasn't as super or as fast as its name. The train was delayed due to some kind of accident on the track, and ended up taking longer than the mail train that brought Paul to Delhi the day before. No matter, he was relieved to arrive in Mathura before noon. With no money for a tuk-tuk ride, Paul knew his only option was to walk back to Vrindavan.

An image of an old woman Paul had seen, walking shoeless along the road on her pilgrimage, limped into his mind. If she can do it, he thought, I ought to be able to do it, too.

It took Paul the entire day of walking. He moved carefully through the dark, staying well off of the roadway. Pagal Baba Temple, its top floor reaching 11-stories high, was visible from more than a mile away. Paul finally spotted the glimmer of its spotlighted marble arches as he trudged along Mathura-Vrindavan Marg, and knew he was getting close to the town. It was late however, nearly midnight, and Paul wondered whether he would be able to find her at the late hour.

He passed by the orphanage where Naagesh lived. The hut was dark and there was no sign of movement inside. As Paul continued down the alley, a lone dog barked from somewhere inside the labyrinth of walled yards. Then came the voices of the widows, warbling in the night. Paul turned down a side road and followed the grooved pathway to the widows' temple. There he found a covey of women shrouded in white—skittering Bush Quails, flushed from their thicket. As if on cue, they each covered their faces, and then, one-by-one, they ducked inside the temple.

Paul strained to see if Tatleen was in the group, but there were too many of them. At least two dozen. And it was dark, and they all looked the same. He waited there for a few minutes, watching for Tatleen. Then he rounded the corner to the large wooden door. He paused there, knowing that behind it sat the putrid dungeon that hundreds of women called home.

It was a private thing—an aberrant sanctuary for widows in an otherwise cruel and inhumane culture. No matter how repugnant the conditions were, modest meals, a dry floor and a roof overhead were the only luxuries life afforded these women. He wanted to open the door, but he couldn't do it. This place offered the only dignity these women had left. He would wait outside for Tatleen to either return from the temple or come out of the sleeping quarters.

He dreamt a bird was on his shoulder, pecking his head. Paul awoke without opening his eyes, recognizing at once that the incessant pecks were actually raindrops. He scrunched his body closer to the rock wall behind him, but any effort to shield himself from the muggy downpour proved unproductive. Paul wished he had never left the ashram; for a moment he entertained the notion of going back to beseech the swami for a place to sleep. But for all the help Swami had provided, Paul's thanks had been to go to New Delhi, only to return again. And in doing so, wasting the airline tickets. Paul had, for all intents and purposes, *permanently* checked out of the ashram.

It was a disjointed, fidgety sleep, crippled by soggy discomfort. The rain ceased sometime before sunup, but the craggy cradle of the alley made certain the throbbing in Paul's hips remained. He was aware of voices and the light of a new day, and he felt the damp earth beneath him. Several minutes passed while Paul wallowed out of his quicksand lethargy.

"Hallo, Paul!"

He opened his eyes and Naagesh was an inch away, a huge almond eye staring back at him. Paul's face immediately spread into a smile. "Naagesh! What's my little man doing here?"

Naagesh pulled at Paul's arm, smiling and chattering to his mother in Hindi. Paul looked past the boy to Tatleen, who stood in the mud-puddled alley behind him. He couldn't quite read her face, but it appeared neither warm nor cold. Her expression was like a woman waiting in a subway line: serious, polite, but detached. *Neither warm nor cold.*

Paul peered up at her through his mottled beard. "What are you doing here, Tatleen?"

She motioned toward the door, and with just a hint of sarcasm she answered, "This is where I live." She let the silence that followed ask the more obvious question.

"Oh, you're probably wondering what I'm doing in the alleyway," Paul said. "I fell asleep out here last night."

Tatleen nodded. Again, her silence turned the light back to Paul.

"You're probably used to this kind of thing," he said. "Sleeping in the rain and everything." Paul immediately regretted the insensitive remark. "I didn't mean. What I meant to say was, I'm not at the ashram any longer, so I had to sleep--"

"Yes, the swami told me that you had left." Tatleen glanced up the alley toward the ashram. "I was under the impression that you had returned to the United States."

Paul struggled to a hunched vertical position, balancing tediously as if standing on ice. He abruptly reached over and tousled Naagesh's hair. "Hallo, Naagesh! Hallo, Naagesh. Hallo Naa . . . gesh."

Paul's nervous attempt at deflection came off as if he were mocking the boy. His lame parody crashed to the ground with a thud. Thankfully, Naagesh was none the wiser. But Tatleen just eyed him.

There was a collision of words, as Tatleen and Paul tried to speak at the same time. Then an awkward silence as they each acquiesced to the other.

Finally, after another uncomfortable lull, Tatleen spoke. "Why are you here, Paul?"

Her tone was more direct than Paul had ever heard, and it was the first time she had used only his first name. "Fair enough," he mumbled to himself.

Tatleen lifted Naagesh to her hip and stepped back, leaving Paul room as he straightened himself and brushed the ground's crusty remnants off his stained clothes.

"I came back to talk to you," Paul said. "Actually, I wanted to talk to you about Naagesh." Paul made an impish reach toward the boy's hair again, but Tatleen stepped further back.

Several women filed out of the doorway behind her—all of them with probing black eyes, and all of them moving forward as if they hadn't noticed their fellow, *untouchable* widow, talking with the man. An American man.

When the women had gone, Paul continued. "I don't want Naagesh to grow up a burden. I mean, I want him to have self-respect and be able to do things . . . you know, like play ball and run around."

"Thank you," Tatleen said. "Your blessing for Naagesh is very comforting." She bowed and started to back away.

"No, no." Paul sprung forward, hands outstretched. "That's not all. I have money, Tatleen." He paused, as if those words could part the sea. Paul's disclosure didn't have the intended effect. "A lot of money," he added.

"Forgive my shallowness," Tatleen said. "But what has any of this to do with Naagesh's self-respect?"

Paul tossed his head back and let out a puff of air. "I want Naagesh to see a doctor. A real doctor, and I want to pay for it. I'm going to see that he gets a good pair of crutches—even better, a wheelchair! And not one of those kinds he'll have to wheel himself. An expensive one, electric, with a rechargeable plug-in battery."

Tatleen stared back as if Paul had offered to send the boy to the moon. She had never heard of such a chair, and couldn't imagine how Naagesh would maneuver it in the scrawny orphanage. "What would he plug it in to?"

"Come with me, Tatleen." Paul extended his hand again to guide her, but less abruptly this time. "Please. Just come with me for a few minutes, so I can explain what I mean."

She nodded, but held Naagesh tightly in her arms. The three of them walked to the end of the alley and Tatleen guardedly followed him onto the main street. Paul took her elbow to lead her and Naagesh safely across the road to the Asha Health Care Clinic.

"Mr. Paul Griffiths," Tatleen said. "Why are you wanting us to come here?"

"Just follow me," he said. "And Tatleen, I really liked it better when you just called me *Paul*."

They passed the security man, who recognized them both and didn't bother to get up. Paul led her down the driveway to the side of the main complex, stopping at the CRF office where Gwyn worked. Tatleen tendered a confused expression, and her dubious eyes never left him as they continued into the building.

Gwyn set down her tea with a thump, and stared up at the three intruders without a word.

Paul motioned for Tatleen to sit, but she chose to remain standing. He turned back toward the desk and said, "We need your help, Gwyn." His open hand flailed in the direction of the boy. "I want to get Naagesh in to see a good doctor. As soon as possible, and money is no object. We need to get his life back on track."

Both women looked at Paul as if he had lost his mind.

SADHANA

After a few seconds, Gwyn pushed her chair back from the desk. "It's too early for this." She tossed her pen on the stack of papers she'd been working on. "What the hell has gotten into to you, Paul? I thought you flew home, anyway."

"Changed my mind." He put a hand on top of the grinning boy. "So, do you think there's any way you can help us?"

Gwyn looked back and forth at the three of them, taking it all in. Finally she let out a sigh. "Paul, that's not what we do here. CRF is all about vaccinations, and medications and education. That isn't even what the Health Care Centre is about. Their doctors can't fix this boy's legs. Nobody can. There are no legs to fix."

Paul stood there, poised like a swimmer on a starting block. "But what about . . . I mean, can't somebody try to . . ."

It took a minute for his fervor to melt into dejection, and when it did, Paul flopped into a chair across from Gwyn. "I'm not going to just sit here and do nothing." His eyes began to fill with tears. "I can't stand the thought of Naagesh living his life like this."

"Paul?" Tatleen set the boy onto the chair next to him. "What is this really all about? Can you tell me, please?"

Paul blinked and rubbed his eyes before answering. "This whole thing, this entire situation is really getting to me. I've already lived my childhood like this. I know what it's like growing up alone, without a mother."

Tatleen and Gwyn connected glances for a second, as they both began to make sense of Paul's fluctuating emotions. It seemed as much about *him* as about Naagesh.

"Only he *has* a mother." Paul turned to face Tatleen. "But he can't even live with you. He'll never be able to live with you. Or work and earn money, not without some help, some intervention." He palmed his eyes roughly. "And that place you sleep, Tatleen . . . It's just a terrible, terrible situation. The thought of it just makes me . . . ." Paul paused a few beats. "I have an idea. You and Naagesh can come back to the U.S."

Squinting frowns froze on the brows of both women. Their eyes were fixed on this man who appeared to be having some kind of breakdown.

"There's work there," Paul continued. "Naagesh can go to school, a private school. And you, you can get a job—cleaning—at the estate! You can work there and get paid good money for it. You can even stay there—we have the employees' quarters. You won't have to live in squalor any longer." Paul gulped in a quick breath before continuing.

"And we can get horses again, and I can teach Naagesh to ride. We'll have to figure out a way to strap him onto the saddle though, but I'm sure we . . . yeah, this is going to work. What do you say, Tatleen?"

Gwyn slowly touched a finger to her pursed and grinning lips—now fascinated by the drama playing out in front of her, but also a little saddened by it.

Tatleen's face was a mixture of shock and outrage. True to form however, when she finally spoke it was with respect and humility. "I'm very sorry, Paul. I think I must have somehow given you a mistaken impression."

Paul's face twisted in confusion.

Tatleen shook her head. "What would make you believe that I would ever leave India?" She reached over to stroke Naagesh's cheek. "I love my country. This is my home."

Gwyn swiveled her head back toward Paul. "Your turn."

Paul ignored the quip. "But Tatleen, what about the things you told me? About the beatings and about Naagesh—his deformity and his inability to contribute to society? What about how everyone treats you here?"

"These are unfortunate things," she said. "But these are the lives we have been born into. I accept my life as it is, my past, my present and my destiny. Both the good and the bad."

Paul hung his head, and Naagesh reached over and ruffled his hair.

Paul sat up with a strained smile. "What about him? What about Naagesh? Can't we at least try to make his life something better?"

They all sat in silence. Nobody was really certain what Paul meant by *something better*. Not even Paul.

"Jaipur." Gwyn's perky voice suddenly said. "What about going to Jaipur?"

Paul and Tatleen stared across the desk in puzzlement.

"There's a foundation there," Gwyn said. "It's near our CRF headquarters there. We've actually referred patients to them in the past. I'm not sure exactly what they do, but I know people with deformities and missing limbs travel from all over India to get there."

"Yes!" Paul slapped a hand on his leg. "Yes, I remember seeing crippled people driving around on yellow carts."

"*Disabled*," Gwyn said.

"Yeah, that's what I meant." Paul jumped to his feet. "Anyway, these guys pedaled the contraptions with their hands, all over the streets of Jaipur."

Gwyn nodded as she wrote down the name of the place. "This foundation has a long name, but everyone knows its acronym: BMVSS." She handed the slip to Paul.

"Forget about an electric wheelchair, we're going to buy Naagesh a pedal cart!" Paul's clasped hands implored Tatleen. "C'mon, Tatleen. What do you say?"

"What do I say?" Tatleen thought she must have missed the question.

"Let's go to Jaipur." He read from the slip of paper, "We'll find some way to get there, and one way or the other we'll locate this BDSM whatever place. Once we get one of those carts for Naagesh, we're golden."

Tatleen stiffened. "I'm sorry, no. I can't leave Vrindavan. I'm a widow. My life is devoted to prayer and service to others."

"You're also a mother," said Paul. "What about service to your son?"

Gwyn tilted her head again, this time to look at Tatleen. There was no response from her.

Several seconds of silence passed. "How would we even travel to Jaipur," Tatleen asked.

Gwyn's head cocked toward Paul.

He unslung his satchel and dug through its contents, trying to find his watch.

"Forget it, Griffiths." Gwyn shook her head mockingly. "I'll chip in my part toward this heartwarming charity. Our CRF bus is going back to pick up a new group of volunteers. They leave here tomorrow, so if you can be ready by then, we'll give you a lift as far as our headquarters in Jaipur."

Paul came around the desk and hugged Gwyn. She winced at the fumes from his soiled clothing. Then Paul hugged Naagesh, who grinned at the odd game. But as Paul turned toward Tatleen, she held up a firm hand. Then she slowly brought both hands together in prayer and touched them to her head.

"Thank you, Mr. Paul Griffiths," she said. "Naagesh and I will go with you to this place in Jaipur."

"One more little issue," Gwyn said. Looking as if she had just bitten into a lime, she held up a slip of paper. "I've gotten a few calls from this investigator. Haven't called him back yet, but from the messages he's left it sounds like he's very interested in finding you."

"What?" Paul's face went slack. "You don't know me! Tell him you never saw me! As a matter of fact, don't tell him anything. Don't even call him back!"

Gwyn rolled her eyes. "Don't be ridiculous, Paul. I can't just ignore him and not return his call. I could lose my job."

"Gwyn, please." Paul flashed a glance toward Tatleen and Naagesh. "I need some time, at least enough to get out of Vrindavan. Please, can you give me until tomorrow?"

Gwyn nodded.

Twenty-six

It was November 11th – Veteran's Day. We had all found something to keep us busy, knowing Mr. Griffiths preferred to honor the memory of his father privately. I saw the first rays of sun glancing off the top of the flagpole, yet still no flag had been hoisted. He had been out there for over an hour, and nobody had thought to check on him.

When I found Mr. Griffiths, he was crumpled on the lawn behind the koi pond, confused, pale and only semi-conscious. Emergency services were summoned, and he was transported to Southampton Hospital's emergency department.

After conducting an examination and taking a chest x-ray, Mr. Griffiths' personal physician, Dr. Moretti, came out to the where Rupert and Nathan Geerts were waiting. He told them that Mr. Griffiths had suffered from an infection of the alveoli, the sacks inside his lungs—basically a bacterial pneumonia. He prescribed antibiotics and decided to keep Mr. Griffiths under observation for a few days.

The doctor appeared to be non-committal about the risks of the illness, but did ask whether Mr. Griffiths had been under stress. He was given a brief summary of the events involving Paul's trip to India, and how the recent turn of events had affected the senior Griffiths.

Dr. Moretti advised that lung infections are generally not too dangerous if they are detected early, but unfortunately, that wasn't the case with Mr. Griffiths. Both of his lungs were filled with fluid and the lab was running gram strain cultures to identify the bacterium type. The doctor strongly encouraged Rupert and Mr. Geerts to locate Paul and let him know what was going on.

I believe it was the attorney, who telephoned the director of CRF International. He brought Mrs. Beckham up to speed on recent developments relative to Mr. Griffiths' health, and of the urgency to locate Paul. Geerts also mentioned that a private investigator had been hired, and that the man was trying to get in touch with Gwyneth Eichler.

Beckham must have promised to do everything in her power to locate Paul, because there was certainly an air of relief around the grounds. All of the staff now wanted Paul to be home—less for any stability he would provide, as virtually no one expected that, but more for the boost in spirits we all thought his return would have on Mr. Griffiths.

* * *

"Is your father a kind man, like you?"

Tatleen's question had stumped Paul. He didn't see his father as kind, and certainly didn't view himself that way, either. "My father, or more accurately, the man who raised me, is the type of guy who takes up an entire room."

"A heavy man?"

Paul shook his head. "No, not in that way. It's like, Loring casts a big shadow wherever he goes. That's like saying that he's the man in charge—always in control."

She nodded. "But he is kind to people?"

Paul shrugged. "He's got friends. I mean, a lot of people seem to like him." There was a long pause as Paul thought about it. "It probably wasn't that easy for him, raising me alone."

"A man wouldn't do that in India." Tatleen's voice sounded soft and sleepy next to him. "He would give the child away, sell him to a farmer, or leave the boy for relatives to raise. If the man was wealthy, he might send his son away to school."

"He didn't do that." Paul's eyes stared off into the rolling fields of dry grasses. "Loring was certainly wealthy enough, but no, he never sent me away. I lived my whole life on the estate, with him."

"And you have no sisters or brothers?"

Paul shook his head again.

"Like me," she said.

They rode in silence, both thinking about their lives and how different they were from one another.

Tatleen's eyes were bleary, dimmed from exhaustion. "What does your father do to earn so much wealth?"

"Semiconductors," Paul answered. "He owns a company in the City."

"Ah, computers." Tatleen smiled drowsily. "Many Indian people attend school to become programmers."

302

"Yeah, but his company has more to do with the glue they use to hold the stuff in place." Paul leaned toward Tatleen, making the most of the quiet, one-on-one time. "I guess Loring came up with a better way to attach the components together.

"A significant contribution," she said.

"I guess." Paul slumped down in the seat and gazed up at the inside of the bus. "I think it was more about timing and luck. Coming up with an adhesive that improved conductivity, sure improved his financial portfolio."

"Still, a very ingenious thing." Tatleen stared upwards at the same place on the ceiling of the bus. "A definite family talent, this glue-making."

Paul turned to look at Tatleen. "How do you mean?"

"Bind-Chem." She tilted her head slightly toward Paul. "Your uncle's company in Aligarh. They made glues and adhesives used for the binding of books."

The rhythm of the road rumbling beneath the bus had serenaded Naagesh to sleep some time ago. Now, as they stared off in thought, its soothing melody tranquilized Tatleen into quiet dreams.

Paul sat there, staring up and thinking about what Tatleen had just told him. He had never considered the name of the company or what they manufactured. Other than the use of toxic chemicals, their purpose had never occurred to Paul. Thinking about it now however, seemed an incongruity of logic. The odds of such a coincidence between Loring and his twin brother had to be astronomical—both of them involved in the same type of invention. *How likely was that?*

More deception, Paul thought. Every time he pulled an answer from the muck of family lies, another mystery bubbled to the surface. For the first time, he was beginning not to care—at least not as much as he had in the past. Paul glanced over at the window seat where Naagesh slept soundly, and then he watched Tatleen resting between them. Finally something mattered more.

Tatleen's head bobbed with the contour of the road, finally settling into the cushion of Paul's shoulder.

Though he was wide-awake, Paul closed his eyes and immersed himself in the thicket of Tatleen's unwitting tenderness. He knew he was defrauding the widow of a touch she would have recoiled from had she been awake. But she wasn't awake and he felt no shame in it.

The Mahwa bypass looked like a wide bite taken out of the Agra to Bikaner road—a heavily used route to the Taj Mahal. Within the past year, two major accidents had dominated Indian news—one in which an overloaded bus skidded off the road, landing upside down in a ravine, and the other, a tour bus whose driver was drunk and fell asleep. The latter had struck an overpass abutment and burst into flames. Both collisions resulted in dozens of fatalities, as well as a great deal of pressure on the Rajasthan state government.

A line of buses and trucks sat in a smoky, unmoving clot in front of the safety checkpoint on NH-11, just south of Mahwa. Although taxis weren't part of the Road Safety Council's mandate, they too were stopped—but only for the purpose of collecting a police-imposed tariff from the unsuspecting sightseers.

The CRF bus slowed as traffic congealed into an oozing jam ahead of them. A comatose policeman stood near an open lane next to the line of busses, half-heartedly waving other traffic around them. Other vehicles—rickshaws, tuk-tuks, animal-drawn carts, motorcycles and bicycles—were all being allowed through without inspection.

There appeared to be some confusion as to which of the two lanes the CRF bus should be directed into—its Indian driver sitting patiently behind the wheel while the officers debated the issue.

"Is there something wrong?" Paul asked Tatleen.

She sat forward and looked at the goings on, then spoke to the driver. He glowered at Tatleen in the tiny rearview mirror and responded with a one-word answer. His disgust for the widow was more than apparent in the man's expression.

"An inspection," Tatleen said.

Paul returned the driver's dirty look in the mirror. Tatleen, unbothered by the interaction, adjusted in her seat so that the sleeping Naagesh could rest his head on her lap. Because he had no lower legs, Naagesh was easily able to lay coiled on a single seat.

The police officer approached the driver's window and there was a lengthy exchange between he and the driver. From the glove box, some papers were passed to the officer, haphazardly perused, and handed back. The officer stuck his entire head through the window, surveying the three passengers.

A mild look of distaste crossed his face as he regarded Tatleen, then his eyes settled on Paul. *"Aap ke rashtreeyatha kya hai?"*

"American," answered Tatleen.

SADHANA

"Passport!" the officer said—his unambiguous demand needing no translation.

Paul unzipped his satchel and handed the passport over the driver's shoulder, to the officer. The man examined it with more scrutiny than he had the vehicle registration, and then consulted with another uniformed officer before returning the passport to Paul.

After several minutes more of a bantering delay that involved the two officers and the driver, the CRF bus was allowed to go around the other buses and continue on its way. Tatleen's mesmerizing eyes reflected the late afternoon sun, deep and rich and warm. They studied Paul closely for a few seconds that seemed longer to Paul. And then she turned toward the window, tucked her saree across her face and lowered herself gently across Naagesh.

Paul replayed her glance several times, trying to read into its substance. He found these cultural nuances difficult to interpret, especially when it came to Tatleen.

Settling back into his seat, his head was full—too full to sleep or relax. Weighing heavily was the fact that Paul's mom was killed in a car wreck—not with her husband, but with her husband's brother. And the most recent in the series of troubles, the Indian police now had his passport information. And all of it cogitated under the shroud of Tatleen, and whatever *feelings* he had for her.

The bus stopped at a Parakram Petrol pump station, and Paul stepped out to stretch his legs. They had been on the road for over three hours, and by his estimation less than thirty minutes of driving remained.

Paul gazed out at the chalky landscape, a hodgepodge of listless wheat fields, brick-makers and tile kilns. He stared up the dusty road in the direction from which they had come, half-expecting to see Indian police cars in pursuit of the CRF bus. Only a lone man pushing a broken bicycle was in sight, with a soulless Mimari cow plodding behind him.

The bus driver motioned Paul back aboard and they continued the journey toward Jaipur. The bus bounded over a dried rut as they merged back onto the highway, and Paul felt Tatleen's watchful eyes looking up at him. He let her continue observing, as if he didn't notice. It felt nice to have the interest of a woman of such depth and goodness.

After a while she spoke. "I have been told that you are not a good man, Paul. But your manner has shown me only kindness and caring."

It wasn't so much a question, and Paul wasn't sure what his response would be if it was. *What had she heard?*

"I'm not worthy even to ask." Tatleen hesitated. "But if you ever wish to share what is inside of you, I promise to listen with ears of compassion and a heart without judgment."

Paul studied the woman next to him. Her warm eyes held only a primitive sincerity that was both naïve and true. So unlike the cagey urban cynicism he'd known throughout his life, it only made Paul want to unburden his hurt, his distrust, and pour himself and his screwed up life onto her. Tatleen's overture had been as difficult for her to offer, as it would be for Paul to answer.

She nodded, her eyes never leaving his.

"This person who told you, Gwyn I suspect, was right," he said. "I'm not a good man. I only came to India in order to stay out of jail." Paul shook his head and lowered his chin to his chest. "I wish I could tell you that I'm someone else . . . someone like you see, kind and caring. But that's not who I am. I've spent my whole life thinking only of myself. And without my father's money, I'm nothing. Worse than that, I'm less than nothing."

Tatleen stared into his marbled eyes, but her expression was that of someone taking in a Michelangelo painting for the first time. "I've not known you as a wealthy man," she said. "And until yesterday I had neither seen nor heard anything of your father's prosperity. Yet I have only experienced unselfishness and compassion from you. In your presence I have felt respected, and I know you have been very kind to Naagesh. He cares for you very much. I'm sorry Paul, but those things are not the mark of a bad person."

"Thank you, Tatleen." Paul saw that Naagesh had woken up, and he took the boy onto his lap. "But you didn't know me back home. I've done some terrible things, hurt other people, that's why I'm here."

"I know about the car crash, but I'm sure it was only an accident." Tatleen timidly put her hand on Paul's. "One who thinks he is free is free, one who thinks he is bound is bound. As we think, so we become."

"I only wish that were true, Tatleen." Paul's grimy hand coursed back through his hair. "This isn't a *mind over matter* kind of thing. You don't know how many times I've wished I could wake up and find that all of my legal troubles are gone. But I'm afraid that my past is catching up with me. The police back there on the highway, they saw my passport."

Tatleen nodded. "A routine inspection."

"Or maybe not. Those guys looked real closely at it, and they had a lot of questions about me. They know my name now. If they run a check they'll find out that I'm a wanted man back in the states." Paul paused, thinking back over what she had said. "Wait a minute, Tatleen. How did you know about the car accident? I never told Gwyn that."

Tatleen's eyes were downcast, as if she felt she was to blame for something. "I'm not sure how it is that Miss Gwyn knew--"

"But it was Gwyn who told you, right?"

"Yes, Paul." She looked back up. "That night when you were going to meet me. Ms. Gwyn told me what you had done. It was later that night that I saw you together with her, in the clinic courtyard."

"Kissing each other?"

Tatleen nodded.

"That was a big mistake. I should never have trusted her." Paul straightened in his seat and glanced out the windows in all directions. "Somehow Gwyn must have found out what happened. By now there's gotta be some kind of reward, and I wouldn't put it past her to tip off the cops in order to cash in."

"I'm not understanding all of these things," she said, "but I don't think Ms. Gwyn would do anything to hurt you. I believe she also cares for you."

The driver said something over his shoulder and Tatleen repeated it to Naagesh.

"What did he say?" Paul's question was a tad loud, bordering on accusatory.

Tatleen took her hand off of Paul's. "He said, 'We're almost there.'"

Paul steadied himself on the seat cushion in front of him, still glancing out the windows, front and back. When the CRF headquarters building came into sight, he let out a long breath. The bus pulled to a stop in the narrow driveway and the driver got out. He stretched his back and lit a cigarette.

Someone called down from a second floor window and the driver answered in prattling Hindi.

"They're asking for you," Tatleen said to Paul. "That man in the upstairs window, he asked the driver if you were with us."

"I knew I couldn't trust Gwyn!" Paul took Tatleen by the arm and quickly ushered her around the back of the bus. "Take Naagesh, quickly. Give me a 30-second head start, and then tell those men that I had to use the bathroom and I'll be right back. Then slip away, as fast as you can, and meet me in an hour."

"Where? Where do I go?"

Paul looked around frantically. "That way," he said, pointing in a northerly direction. "We passed a park on the way here, with some kind of castle or something."

Tatleen squinted desperately back at the road.

"It was right after we turned off the main highway."

"Yes, I remember," said Tatleen. "A museum."

"Okay, good. Just meet me out in front of the museum in an hour, but make sure you're not followed."

Tatleen's wide eyes strained to remember all of Paul's instructions. "Thirty seconds?"

The man in the upstairs window suddenly emerged from the front of the building. Paul dove onto the ground and slithered toward the bushes like a serpent. Naagesh saw the familiarity in his funny impersonation and began laughing loudly.

A CRF security guard came out of the building behind the man and they both strolled toward the bus. Not with any haste or urgency, but as if they had nothing better to do than join the driver in a smoke.

"Mr. Griffiths?" the security guard called out in English. "Are you there?"

A rustle emanated from the bushes as Paul tried to conceal himself. And then, from the depths of the thick foliage came his hoarse whisper, "Now, Tatleen. Now!"

She twisted Naagesh's face away from the bushes and stepped around the bus. "Mr. Paul Griffiths will be back in a moment."

The other man asked her in Hindi where Paul had gone, but before she could answer, Naagesh twisted back toward the bushes, pointing and laughing.

"He's relieving himself," she quickly said, feigning a look of embarrassment.

He shrugged and both men casually leaned back against the bus.

"I must go now," she said. Then turning toward the driver, she thanked him in Hindi, for the ride.

The driver grunted his response, and the other two men barely looked up. Carrying Naagesh on her hip, and without shoes, Tatleen made a hasty exit down the road and around the corner.

Certain that the authorities were closing in on him, Paul tried to scrounge his way through the brush toward the road. It was a noisy effort, akin to a hippo rolling on dried leaves, and both men turned to look. In a panic, Paul jumped to his feet and started running.

"Mr. Griffiths," the guard called after him. "Please come back. I have a message for you from Gwyneth Eichler."

Paul heard only his name being hollered out. The rest of it was drowned out by his tromping footfalls through the shrubbery, and the manic thwacking of his size 11 sandals. The tan security uniform the man wore was enough to convince Paul that it was now official: He was not only a fugitive in his own country, but in India, too.

He sprinted across the road and through a bank parking lot. The guard, an employee of Marwar, a private security company contracted by CRF, made a half-hearted attempt to chase after Paul. After a few meters he stopped and rejoined the other man and the bus driver.

"I wonder why he ran away," said the guard in his native tongue.

The other man snickered, "Maybe a bee stung his pecker."

The driver laughed a stream of gray smoke through his nose, and then he passed a cigarette to the winded guard. The man who had made the wisecrack turned back toward the headquarters building.

"I have to call Ms. Eichler now," he said. "I'll need to let her know that I couldn't deliver her message to the American."

Paul ran down a series of narrow roads and through a bazaar full of jewelry and clothing. Some of the people browsing stopped to chew on the image of the tall man dashing through the teeming marketplace. Literally nobody ran in India, unless they were either pulling a rickshaw or dodging one.

Once certain he had eluded his pursuers, Paul slowed and tried to blend into the crowd. He looked around at the sellers hawking their goods and eyeing the latest salvo of potential customers. Paul was sure they were all watching him. A wooden stall stacked with pajama pants and matching tunics caught Paul's eye, and he considered getting a new outfit, maybe shaving his beard—anything to disguise himself.

With no money, he saw that the only way to do it would be to steal a razor and some new clothes. Paul quickly came to his senses, then made his way through the bazaar and out to the main road. He had gotten turned around, and it took him several more twists and wrong way alleys before getting back to *Jawaharla Nehru Marg*, the main road the bus had taken when they arrived.

With daylight draining rapidly from the orange sky, Paul hustled toward the museum to meet with Tatleen and Naagesh. He maintained a conscious monitoring of passing traffic as he advanced in furtive, checkerboard moves along the side of the road.

It had been much longer than an hour by the time Paul spotted the huge, park-like roundabout that encompassed the Albert Hall Museum. Across the road was a sign pointing to the Ravindra Manch cultural center, a cricket ground, and the Jaipur Zoo. All Paul could think of, besides steering clear of the police, was how much he would love to take Naagesh to see those things.

A black, wrought iron fence surrounded the massive museum building and two guards stood on either side of the entry gate. Paul spotted Tatleen's faded white saree in the shadows of a tree in a secluded corner of the park. A pleasing tingle crept up from his stomach as he saw her eyes looking back at him.

She was seated on a low curb with Naagesh in her arms, trying to get the attention of a bird hopping along the fence. The boy's face turned into a moon-shaped grin when he saw Paul skirting the edge of the flower garden.

"Hallo Paul, Hallo Paul!" Naagesh bellowed out, his arms waving wildly.

Paul took the boy from Tatleen's arms and held him up over his head. To Naagesh's delight, Paul swung him around so he was positioned like a frog on Paul's back. With his thin arms clamped tightly over Paul's shoulders, the little jockey rode the jouncing stallion up and back across the grass. Again, Paul could see that the boy craved attention from a male role model. Tatleen had recognized it much earlier, and delighted in it.

Afterward, they all sat side-by-side on the planter stones—Paul and Tatleen, with Naagesh propped between them.

"Where do we go now?" Tatleen asked.

Paul looked around the park. A few lights had come on nearer the street, and the rest of the museum grounds had faded to dark. The last of the public patrons were leaving through the front gate as the security guards began locking the grounds for the night. Naagesh gazed up at Paul. Though there was only love in the boy's eyes, Paul knew they belied his exhausted little body and the emptiness in his stomach.

"I'm sorry, Tatleen." Paul put an arm around her son. "I didn't plan this very well. It's probably too late to find the place Gwyn told us about, and now we're stuck with nowhere to sleep." He rested his chin on the top of the boy's head. "I only have a few rupees left, but maybe we can at least find something for Naagesh to eat."

Tatleen held out a handful of odd-sized coins. "Perhaps these will help."

"Tatleen?" Paul cupped his hand beneath hers and examined them. "How? Where did you come up with this?"

"Before you arrived here," she said. "I sat with Naagesh near the museum gate. Some of the people, they gave--"

"You were begging for money?" Even if Paul had been able to disguise his appalled expression, it resonated in the tone of his voice. He heard it himself and immediately gripped her hand. He closed his eyes. "I'm sorry, Tatleen. I'm so sorry I said it that way. It's just . . ." Paul took in a breath and let it out. "In my culture, there's this whole stigma around homelessness and begging."

Tatleen nodded genially, her soft eyes bearing no animosity. "I don't know that word, *stigma*, but I do understand humiliation and shame. These *stigmas* in our cultures may not be so different from one another. Perhaps in India we just have more people and less to share."

She had made a humbling point.

"You're right," said Paul. "It's probably a terrible thing to have to do, no matter where you live. A last resort, I suppose."

Tatleen dropped the coins into his hand. "Nobody begs for food when they're not hungry."

Paul stared at the coins in his palm, still thinking about what she had just said. He'd seen panhandlers in Manhattan that hadn't missed a meal in their entire lives. Others wore nice clothing or jewelry, or talked on their cell phone while asking for handouts.

Unintentionally, Tatleen had made another good point—one that illustrated a major difference in the two cultures: their definitions of needy.

Dark clouds crossed the sky as if someone had pulled a blanket over the three travelers. Whether or not rain was on the way, the night promised to be one better spent under shelter.

Tatleen pulled her tattered saree around her shoulders as best she could, and wrapped her arms around Naagesh like a life vest. Identical sets of almond eyes sought an answer in Paul's.

"Do you think you can walk any further tonight?"

"Yes." Tatleen unfolded onto her feet.

"Good, okay." Paul lifted her son onto his back. "I'll carry Naagesh, but I'll need you to ask somebody for directions."

"Directions to where?"

"The Sunder Palace. It's a small hotel here in Jaipur."

Tatleen's enthusiasm faded into regret. "I'm sorry, Paul. Those coins I gave you, even when combined with your rupees, they're not enough to pay the price of a hotel."

"That's true," he said. "But I know someone there who may be able to help us."

"You have a friend here in Jaipur?"

Paul hesitated. "I'm not sure he'd actually consider himself my friend, but, I don't know. Maybe he would."

"Who is this person?" Tatleen asked.

"He is a tuk-tuk driver who gave me a ride the last time I was here. His name is Juber Kazi."

Faith drained from Tatleen's eyes. "A tuk-tuk driver?"

Twenty-seven

I wasn't really with it then, none of us were. With Mr. Griffiths lying in a hospital bed over in Southampton, most of his staff was mired in worry—some unfortunately, about their job security rather than their boss' health. And, as always, the employee rumormongers buzzed the estate like hummingbirds, spreading a cross-fertilized version of Mr. Griffiths' latest prognosis. Their consensus was that the boss wasn't doing well; in fact he had become more ill since being admitted.

In the meantime, word had come back rather quickly from Mr. Tam. The glum whisperings batted the staff like dominoes: *Loring Griffiths' son had vanished . . . again.*

No real explanation followed the tragic communiqué, but it seemed that Paul had been swallowed up by the Third World sinkhole of India. And this woman, Gwyneth Eichler, who worked for Mrs. Beckham, had supposedly been in contact with Paul, but now had no way to find him.

It made no sense to us. Nevertheless, the staff wasted no time in speculating about the types of ghastly curses dwelling in a place such as India. Paul was already dead as far as some were concerned, and that would undoubtedly signal the beginning of the end for Loring Griffiths—and by way of employment, their jobs here on the estate. One landscape supervisor actually up and resigned on the spot, opting instead for the secure work at a golf course over in Sag Harbor.

Meanwhile, Loring Griffiths' particular strain of bacterium seemed to be resistant to the first-line antibiotics normally used to treat his condition, and he was transferred to the intensive care unit. His doctors continued working vigorously, battling each downturn with more aggressive countermeasures.

And still, there was no word from Paul.

* * *

Jayanti market was just one warehouse in a series of hundreds that comprise Indira Bazaar. The sprawling marketplace sat just off of M.I. Road, the highway bisecting the north and south sides of Jaipur.

Paul and Tatleen had walked nearly two kilometers. Naagesh, though he never complained, could barely keep his grip on Paul, and Tatleen's tiny feet looked like alligator hide. Paul knew that he had to find a safe spot to stop for the night.

"Watch out for the glass." Paul sidestepped a pile of umber shards.

Tatleen followed him around it. "It is *kulhar*," she said. "The cups for serving *lassi*."

Paul stopped to marvel at the mounds of broken stoneware. "And they just throw them on the ground after they drink from them?"

She gazed down at the mess, then back at Paul. "What else?"

Just then another terracotta cup struck the dirt, its fractured chaff flying in all directions.

"What is this stuff they drink?"

A tall man wearing slacks and a dress shirt stood on a landing just above street level, summoning Paul inside. "Come in good sir. Try our *lassi*, the best in all of Jaipur."

Paul caught the glint of excitement in Naagesh's tired eyes. Taking Tatleen by the arm, he ushered her up the few steps to the *Lassi Wala*.

The owner started to extend his palm to block the widow and her deformed son, but Paul's steel scowl backed him down. Lifting one dubious eyebrow, the man stepped back to allow them entry.

"Naagesh and I don't belong in here," Tatleen said. "It's an indignity that upsets customers. And that man, the owner of the place, he wants us to leave."

"Too bad. He'll just have to get over it." Paul's volume punctuated his words. "Our money is as good as anyone else's. And we're going to sit right here and drink our *kulhar*!"

"The drink is called *Lassi*." Tatleen's hand covered her nervous smile. "*Kulhar* is the cup."

"Whatever." Paul turned in his chair, his hand whipping the air. "Three *lassis*, please. And we'll take them in a *kulhar*."

Tatleen bowed her head as if in prayer, but it was all she could do to suppress her grin.

The owner collected the cost of the drinks, as if he couldn't believe they had so much as a 5-paise coin between them, and then sent an underling over to serve the trio. The waiter set the cups down on the small table, without a word.

Tatleen was a child the last time she had *lassi*, and Naagesh had never even tasted it. Neither had Paul. But for all the aggravation, at that moment all their senses savored the creamy drink. Naagesh's twinkling eyes flashed between the *lassi* and Paul, as if trying to decide which of them he loved more. It was the best thing he had ever tasted.

The owner dipped his head almost imperceptibly as they exited, then quickly scanned the scene outside in the hopes that none of his contemporaries saw the widow and legless boy leaving *his* shop.

Down the road a bit, Tatleen asked a midget if he knew where they could find the Sunder Palace. He glanced around, scratching his hairless brown head. The little man was no taller than Naagesh, which the boy found amusing, yet he was the friendliest stranger they had encountered thus far. As they conversed in Hindi, Paul reasoned that the man must have understood the pain of being an outcast. He pointed west on M.I. Road, then gestured a series of twists and turns, which thankfully Tatleen seemed to follow.

By the time the threesome turned onto Sanjay Marg it was well into the night and a mist of warm air formed tiny droplets on their heads. Naagesh had fallen asleep on Paul's back, but Tatleen padded along behind them, her body motionless except for her churning feet. The hotel was dark when they arrived, and the front gate had been closed and locked for the night.

"Do you want Naagesh and I to wait here while you go in and find your friend?"

Paul's face contorted. "Yeah, well, if I remember correctly, the guy doesn't actually work here. But I think he said his father and brother do."

"In American culture," Tatleen turned with a puzzled expression, "someone with such a vague connection, such as perhaps the father and brother of a taxi cab driver you once met . . . they would help you in the middle of the night?"

Paul saw the innocence of her question, and at the same time recognized the logic in it. How absurd his behavior was. This kid who had given Paul a ride over a month ago might not even remember him, much less want to help him. And the guy's brother and father? Paul wanted to kick some sense into himself.

"No, probably not." Paul eyed the empty street, struggling to come up with some pretense of an idea. Then he spotted a faded tuk-tuk parked on the sloping dirt, directly in front of the hotel gate. "C'mon, let's get in."

Tatleen frowned. "You would take another person's tuk-tuk?"

Paul laughed. "Of course not. The three of us will have to sleep in here for the night. It'll keep us dry."

Tatleen regarded the arrangement, appearing to have some reservations. Paul imagined she had slept in much worse conditions, and that her concerns had more to do with propriety. The mist maturing into steady drops of rain apparently tipped the scale in Paul's favor. She climbed into the front seat, leaving the larger passenger seat in the back for Paul and Naagesh.

Moments later the black clouds opened. It sounded like handfuls of coins dropping onto their aluminum shelter. But Paul felt content lying across the seat, Naagesh's tiny body wheezing gently beside him. A feather-duster soft hand brushed across Paul's forehead and he looked up. Tatleen's placid face gazed at him over the top of the seat.

"Thank you, Paul."

Quenched by her touch, he smiled back. Paul reached up and placed his palm flat against her much tinier hand. After a second or two Tatleen crimpled back onto her seat while the rain continued to lick at Paul's feet. He reclined as best he could, unable to compress his rangy limbs fully inside the tuk-tuk.

It was an uncomfortable, broken sleep for Paul, but one with the unexpected element of contentment. Curled around Naagesh, and knowing that he had Tatleen's trust, Paul felt affirmation. Something about the situation tasted of adulthood, masculinity, maturity. It was the first time Paul had ever led, and the first time anyone had followed.

Rattled to attention, Paul stared into a crooked mustache perched over a disorderly collection of teeth. The man in front of him yelled and screamed, spewing a sooty vapor of cigarette smoke into Paul's face. Paul struggled to right himself as the man nattered on, shaking a bent finger at him. And though Paul couldn't understand a single word, the man's point was clear enough: *Get out of my tuk-tuk.*

Tatleen was already out, a good 10-meters away, bowing her apologies. Paul scooped Naagesh in his arms and slid off the seat. The tuk-tuk owner backed off a bit as Paul stood up—a whole head taller than the man.

Paul followed Tatleen's lead, dipping his head in supplication, but the man only shooed him out of the way. The owner then climbed in, started the motor and drove off.

Tatleen watched Paul's expression carefully. "That man. I think he was not the friend you spoke of?"

Paul's laugh cascaded out, causing his entire body to cough and shudder. Imagining how it must have appeared to Tatleen only made him howl harder. Tatleen guessed from his reaction that the man was not Paul's friend, and she too began to chuckle. Naagesh grinned happily as if included in the joke, but the true source of his joy was in seeing his mother smile.

"C'mon," said Paul. "Let's go inside and see if we can find my friend."

Paul carried Naagesh, and Tatleen shadowed them up to the front gate. It was locked, so Paul rang the buzzer.

"Yes, what do you want?" came a man's voice from somewhere among flowering Magnolias. He had apparently heard the ruckus involving the tuk-tuk owner, and had come out to have a look. He was a profuse man who appeared to be suspended behind the white blossoms. Bobbing down the path, Paul saw he wore a purple tent of a shirt, tucked into maroon slacks that were several shades away from a decent match.

"Hi, I'm looking for an old friend by the name of Juber," Paul said, passing Naagesh to Tatleen.

The man's eyes never left Tatleen and the boy, even while speaking to Paul. "You are staying here? A guest at Sunder Palace?" he asked, removing his eyeglasses.

"Not yet, but I'm thinking about it," Paul said.

"We have no vacancies," the man snapped. "And I don't know the person you look for."

"Perhaps you could ask someone inside," Paul said. "I'm sure he told me that he has family working here."

"The only person named Juber is a young man, not old." He turned and waddled back up the path.

"No, no." Paul tried to wave him back to the gate. "That's the guy I'm looking for! I didn't mean *old friend* as in, old age."

But by then the man had reached the door. "Go on," he brushed the air with his hand. "You rascals get away from this place, before I call the authorities."

"I only want to find . . ." Paul gripped the gate with both hands, but the man had already gone inside.

"Paul." Tatleen backpedaled into the street. "We should go before a policeman comes. That would not be good for either of us."

He knew she was right. Paul glanced back up the incline once more in the hope that another employee might appear, but no one else came out. He called out a couple of times to nobody in particular, not wanting to return to Tatleen with no friend, and worse, no plan. Realizing an even more dismal scene would be getting captured and hauled off to jail, Paul finally decided to leave.

He hurried to catch up with Tatleen who was already half a block away—Naagesh percolating wildly against her flank. The faster Paul walked, it seemed Tatleen hastened her pace that much more. Soon she was running, or as close to it as one can do with no shoes and a legless child as cargo.

When Paul saw Tatleen had broken into a sprint, he followed suit. "Tatleen! Stop!" Suddenly, he felt like the fat kid in the schoolyard . . . *Hey guys, wait up!*

She turned her head slightly without breaking stride, and on her face was a look of terror. Paul couldn't understand. Had he screwed things up one too many times? Had she had enough?

Naagesh's head bobbed over Tatleen's shoulder with the same frightened look, and then Paul realized he was not the source of their panic. A blotchy gray shark of a dog shot out from a driveway, its back legs sliding sideways for purchase in the gravel and its jaws snapping at the air. Two other dogs of similar looks appeared like torpedoes on the same trajectory, galloping a few meters behind the first. Paul had seen these three mutts before, but this time they tasted the flavor of fear.

A guttural roar rattled from deep in Paul's lungs, as he exploded into an all-out footrace. He scanned the dirt sidewalk for a stick, a pipe, or a brick, anything he could use to equalize the fight. He waved his arms in the air, hollering again as loud as he could. The two hindmost desperados turned at the noise, slowing now, confused by the threat behind them.

Paul scooped up a broken chunk of brick and heaved it at them, missing by only a few inches but peppering both dogs with shrapnel. The two cowards split course, each veering to opposite sides of the street, diminishing their confidence and causing them to abandon their initial target.

Unfortunately, the ringleader was now close to lunging range of Tatleen's fast-moving legs. Paul was still too far away to reach them in time to help.

318

SADHANA

A green and yellow wreck of a tuk-tuk abruptly appeared, weaving lopsidedly around the corner ahead of Tatleen. Its driver, apparently sensing the urgency in Tatleen's frantic manner, swerved around her and cut across the predator's path.

The unexpected turn of events served to befuddle the dog temporarily, as he first had to avoid running into the vehicle and then reevaluate his attack, now considering another player. And even before the dog could do that, Paul surprised him from behind with a solid kick in the ribs.

What might have been a career-ending blow yielded little more than a high-pitched yelp. Paul figured he owed the disappointing kick to his haggard state and the floppy leather sandals he wore. In any case, the dogs fled and Paul felt that he'd somewhat redeemed himself.

"Are you alright?" he asked Tatleen.

"Yes, thank you, Paul." She struggled for breath. "Dogs. They are a deathly fear of Naagesh's, ever since he was bitten by one with rabies."

Naagesh's fright had been trumped by Paul's soccer kick, the boy's smile evidence of Paul's ascension to hero status.

Paul patted Naagesh on his back. "How old was he?"

"He was an old dog." Tatleen seemed puzzled by the question.

"I mean, Naagesh. How long ago did this happen?"

Tatleen nodded a clearer understanding. "Naagesh was bitten only two months ago. That is why you saw us at the Asha Health Centre each week, so Naagesh could receive his inoculation treatments."

"Did he actually have rabies?"

"Naagesh was treated right away, so they were able to prevent it."

"No, the dog. Was it rabid?"

Tatleen squinted through one eye, wondering if she would ever be able to fully understand the English language. "The dog was never captured. But rabies is a big problem in India, especially in the rural areas. I was told by Naagesh's doctor that over a third of the rabies fatalities in the world occur here."

Tatleen rattled off something to the driver who had helped her, then clasped her hands in prayer and bowed to him.

Paul turned back toward the tuk-tuk, idling in the middle of the street. "Yeah, thanks a lot for the help."

"Hello again, my friend." The driver sat there with his hands on the cocked wheel, watching Paul with a sly smile. "The dogs, he nearly eating you for breakfast," he laughed.

"Juber?" Paul moved around the front of him to get a better look. "It's you!"

"To your service, sir."

"I was looking for you," said Paul. "You remember me, right?"

"Yes, I take you to English school in Malviya Nagar."

"Yeah, sort of." Paul turned to make introductions. "This is my friend, Tatleen, and her son is Naagesh."

Juber made quick work of them, eyeing Naagesh's deformed legs and noting Tatleen's widow saree. In Hindi, Juber asked her if she spoke English.

"Yes."

Juber's eyes and cheeks grinned as one. "This is good thing. I will practice my English speaking with both. And little Naagesh," he said, motioning to the boy. "He is next one to learn."

"Juber, we need your help." Paul stepped closer to the tuk-tuk. "Naagesh has no legs."

The young man leaned over the steering wheel to glance at the boy, then at Tatleen, and back to Paul—his expression trying to make sense of Paul's statement of the obvious. He turned off the engine and suddenly there was quiet. "Only God can give Naagesh legs."

Both Paul and Tatleen smiled, but for different reasons. Paul thought it amusing how Juber had misunderstood his point, but Tatleen smiled out of agreement with Juber.

"I know that." Paul fished through his satchel. "But there's this place we heard about; we need to take Naagesh there." Paul found the slip of paper bearing the foundation's name. "BMVSS," Paul read out loud. "We haven't got much rupees, but if you could possibly take us there . . ."

Tatleen saw Juber's expression and understood it. She spoke a few Hindi words to him and he spoke back. They both focused back to Paul.

"Today is a national holiday," Tatleen said. "Nothing is open."

Paul slapped his forehead. "You've got to be kidding me."

"No, this is true." Juber stepped from the tuk-tuk, leaving it in the middle of the street. "Two holiday today. *Guru Nanak Gurpurab* for Hindu, and *Ashura,* very important day to Muslims. Many peoples, they do fasting, and not eating the foods today."

Paul rolled his eyes, exaggerating his frustration. "So what now, we have to wait until tomorrow?" Though he didn't say it, Paul's manner held them and their *ridiculous* Indian religions responsible for the setback.

SADHANA

Nobody said anything. The dogs had returned to their hovel, no longer interested in harassing out-of-towners; Naagesh had calmed himself into a curious assessment of his caretakers, and the adults all struggled to untangle the cultural milieu that had taken over the middle of Ajmer Road.

"I must go now," Juber said. "Some passenger, they come to train station at Jaipur Junction. "I return in three hours more to give ride for you."

"To where?" Paul's frustration was evident in his voice.

Juber got into the tuk-tuk. "To my home. I show to my family, you."

He drove off, and that was that.

"A holiday," Paul said, turning to Tatleen. "Now what? We have to wait until tomorrow?"

"Perhaps. But I think waiting one more day will not make any difference." She glanced in the direction of the departing tuk-tuk. "Your friend, Juber, invited us to visit his family's home. That is very significant in India."

"Yeah, I'm sure it is. I totally get that. But we didn't come all the way here to socialize; we're here to get Naagesh onto one of those yellow sleds. Not to mention, the longer I'm out here in the open, the higher the risk of getting caught."

"The local police," Tatleen said. "They are not so sophisticated, and they don't have technologies you are accustomed to in the West. I came to realize this during my father's trial."

"Maybe." Paul took Tatleen's elbow and led her and Naagesh out of the street. "But I have to assume that by now, my photo has been sent out to every beat cop from Bombay to Calcutta."

Both cities had long since changed their names, but Tatleen only sighed a dutiful affirmation.

"So, he invited us for dinner." Paul was warming to the notion. "Maybe it isn't such a bad idea that we lay low with Juber's family til things settle down. Besides, we can all use a good meal."

Paul's thoughts migrated to his paltry finances. After their big *lassi* splurge, only a few coins remained in his possession. "I've read up a little on this sort of occasion. C'mon, let's find a market. One thing you don't want to do is show up to someone's home empty-handed."

Tatleen hadn't been a penniless widow her whole life, in fact she had been raised with a fair knowledge of cultural etiquette. Yet rather than intrude on Paul's civics lesson, Tatleen listened to him with her heart.

A kilometer away from the train station they spotted a two-wheeled cart propped level against a tree. Upon it was a random assortment of goods: cigarettes, necklaces, ink pens, a miniature checkerboard game, a spongy replica soccer ball, and a variety of boxed candies.

Paul held the collection of odd-shaped coins in his palm, fingering through them as if calculating their value. Tatleen carried Naagesh further down the road and waited in a shady spot.

"I'll take this and this," Paul said to the vendor.

The man wagged an index finger—its overgrown nail thick and yellow. He groaned his displeasure with the offer. Paul nodded, trying to play the ignorant American card for all it was worth. Taking the man's hand in his, Paul emptied the coins onto his palm.

"Thank you," Paul said, with a bow and prayerful hands. He took the items and bowed again before the reluctant merchant changed his mind. Paul squeezed the spongy ball into his satchel and held up a box of sweets victoriously.

As Paul got closer and Tatleen saw what he had actually bought, the corners of her eyes wrinkled into a grin. "Zoordar Bomb," she said.

Paul tilted his head to read the writing on the box. "It's good, right? A small present to give Juber's parents?"

"Sour candies in the shape of a bomb, yes." Tatleen held back a chuckle. "Many children are fond of them, also."

When Juber returned to their agreed upon meeting place later that afternoon, Paul and Naagesh were asleep in the shade beneath a stand of Sorghum. Tatleen prayed at the side of the road nearby. With her saree pulled over her head, she was an understated lotus flower—its milky petals barely noticeable against the tan dirt.

Paul heard the rattling motor approach and was already standing when Juber pulled up. He lifted Naagesh into the tuk-tuk's seat and then offered a hand to help Tatleen to her feet. It was a perplexing gesture, as it was both uncommon and unnecessary. She stood in one, solitary scissoring motion from the exact location where she had sat. When Tatleen realized what Paul had tried to do, she thanked him.

Inside however, Tatleen continued to be drawn to this man, away from her simple and predictable life. His intense blue eyes could stop her heart, and a simple touch from him caused it to beat wildly.

"You are widow woman?" Juber asked Tatleen, as she took a seat next to Naagesh.

"Tatleen's husband died and his family refused to take care of her." Paul's hostility was hardly concealed. "Let's just say they weren't very nice to Naagesh, either."

Paul felt Tatleen's hand slide over and squeeze his knee, while Juber's dark eyes peered back in the mirror. Tatleen's tightening grip made clear the silent reprimand for Paul's unfiltered and unsanctioned biography of her life.

Juber simply nodded his lament. "Some peoples, this happening to here in India."

They rattled along the main highway, barely exceeding the speed of a camel-led cart full of wooden sticks. Juber turned left near the bazaar where they had bought the *lassi*, into a slightly less populated and more rundown section called Berava Basti. He finally stopped the tuk-tuk at a dirt roundabout clogged with a huddle of empty tour busses. They were quiet and unmoving, like logs stranded at the bottom of a dry lakebed.

"These peoples, they all coming to see Nahargarh Fort." Juber pointed to the top of a bluff where a stone structure seemed to collapse under the weight of a choking brown sky.

He left the tuk-tuk at the side of the road, unbothered by having to walk the rest of the way to his home. The daily gridlock was apparently an acceptable tradeoff for tourist revenues. Juber's proud grin conveyed that it was a way of life—barely an inconvenience.

Paul heard bleating sheep or goats—some boisterous animal thumping around inside a nearby pen. His mouth suddenly watered at the image of a hot meal of mutton, potato pakora and vegetable curry. Then, stepping over a muddy froth dribbling from an open pipe, Paul reached back to take Naagesh from Tatleen and help her navigate around the muck.

Three homes were stitched together, seemingly pushed into the side of a doughy hillside. The clay bricks from which they had been constructed were uneven and of different colors, as if laid by several different people over a period of years.

"My brother, he is owner of this," Juber said, motioning proudly toward a black Bajaj motorcycle leaning against the wall.

A collection of sandals sat at the door, reminding Paul of yet another courtesy he had read about in his travel guide. He turned to Tatleen as he kicked off his sandals. "Make sure you and Naagesh remove your shoes."

She glanced down at her own bare feet and then at Naagesh's forsaken knees. With giggling eyes, Tatleen looked back at Paul. Recognizing his asinine lapse, he shook his head then squeezed a silent apology into her nervous hand. It was enough to comfort Tatleen's fluttering apprehension.

The home was dark and wafted its own unique scent—the place's history, its residents, its foods, its summers and its winters, its births and its deaths. They clung to the walls like old coats of paint.

Juber's parents were quiet and serious, younger than Paul expected. He imagined their families had forced the couple together when they were young, believing them to be a suitable match.

The man stepped forward to welcome the visitors. Paul bowed and handed him the box of Zoordar Bombs.

The man spoke to Juber who translated to Paul. "We are Muslim," said Juber. "My father, he say to me, we do fasting for Muslim holiday. He wishing to offer you something, but no food is prepared for eating until tomorrow."

Paul tried to speak up over the growl of his protesting stomach. "Not necessary at all. Please tell him we're just very honored to have been invited into his lovely home."

Tatleen also bowed, and then Juber translated Paul's words back to them. At the conclusion of his rendition, smiles were passed around the room from person-to-person, more bows were taken, and then more smiles. Someone had to be the first to stop, and it was Juber.

"Come, sit. We will have chai, yes?" Juber motioned to the group of adults, then left the room to heat the milk.

Juber's father asked Paul a series of questions, which were translated by Tatleen: *Do you have family? Is it difficult to be away from them? What is your education level? What is your profession? How much money do you earn?*

Paul's eyebrow inched upward as the questioning progressed. "Wow, they kind of put it right in your grill."

Tatleen, guessing at Paul's meaning, said, "Indians regard family and education and career very highly; that is why they are interested in these things—especially when its someone from America."

Paul did his best to respond, skating around the family issue. He told them that he had attended New York University—which sounded good, though he omitted the fact that he had never graduated. And thankfully, Juber returned with tea before Paul tried to tackle the question about earning money.

SADHANA

A coy smile idled in Tatleen's eyes as she and Paul exchanged a discreet glance. Her understanding of him felt as foreign to Paul as this country, but both offered a quenching serenity he had not experienced in any relationship.

Apparently Juber's father wasn't quite finished with his inquiry. He spoke and Tatleen translated. "Your father and you are very close?"

Paul weighed his response. "We live very near one another, and see each other every day."

Mr. Kazi nodded, the fingertips of both his hands lightly touching. "Family is more than simply a word. They are the roots that secure us, the water that nourishes us, and the sun that provides us growth." He poured the silky mix from a steaming pot, offering the glass to Paul. "In family relationships the most important things are trust and loyalty."

Paul clasped hands and bowed his thanks. The man's words were an offering of unification—an endorsement of their common beliefs. Paul saw it on his host's face, in the harmony of his consenting grin. The smile Paul sacrificed in return felt forced and deceitful.

"I have had some issues with my family," Paul said. He set his glass down and waited for Tatleen to reconstruct his words. She watched Paul cautiously for a moment before repeating what he said.

Mr. Kazi sipped from his glass, his eyes appealing for Paul to continue.

"I've had a rough relationship with my father . . . the man who raised me. There has never been real communication between us." Paul tilted his head back and let out a deflating breath. "It has always been one-sided and on his terms. The truth, whatever that is, has always been under his control. Trust and loyalty? Not sure I've ever experienced them."

Tatleen translated, her face flushed with trepidation and her words, even in Hindi, sounding hesitant. Despite Paul's emotion-filled disclosure, it delighted him that Tatleen was so affected by it. He wanted to reach over and take her hand, but resisted for both religious and cultural reasons. Women had their place, but it didn't seem to be as a contributor in this type of setting. Mrs. Kazi sat quietly on her cushion away from the table, and though Tatleen's status as a widow didn't seem to bother them, her role as a translator was tolerated, though nothing more than that.

Instead of demonstrating his sentiment for Tatleen, Paul lifted a beaming Naagesh onto his lap.

"This man who raised you," Juber's father said, recognizing the wording Paul had used. "He has been untruthful in his dealings with you?"

Tatleen's interpretation was followed by a nod of her head.

"Yes," Paul agreed.

Their host bowed his head. "Prophet Muhammad taught us to always speak the truth, even if there is anxiety or fear in doing so. There is always freedom in speaking the truth."

"I wish my father believed that," Paul said. "I feel like I've wasted my whole life waiting for him to give me a little honesty."

"This can also be seen as a blessing," Mr. Kazi said. "Without such people in our lives, we would not be able to practice patience." He adjusted himself deeper into the pillow. "Then too, we are often misled about a person by seeing only a tiny part, and confusing it with the whole."

This reminded Paul of the story of the three blind men and the elephant. It was becoming a common theme, though he wondered what more he could possibly know of Loring Griffiths that would excuse his deception.

Their host asked, "Have you a place to sleep tonight?"

"No, we don't," said Paul.

Mr. Kazi spoke again and Tatleen waited patiently with downcast eyes before translating. When she looked up, her face bore a look of terror.

"We have little space here, but my brother-in-law lives in a larger house next door." Tatleen swallowed, and was about to speak again when Paul interrupted.

"That would be fantastic. As long as it's no trouble, we'd love to stay the night with him."

Tatleen's eyes widened as she completed the entirety of the translation. "My brother-in-law is the head constable for the state police."

Paul's throat tightened as he looked across at his grinning host.

Twenty-eight

Tam had put out feelers to contacts within the U.S. Department of State, Transportation Security Administration, and for whatever it was worth, law enforcement agencies within India. So far he had come up with nothing concrete.

There was discussion between Nathan Geerts and Mr. Tam about Tam going to India, but at that point it hadn't been resolved. Tam's position was that until they were able to zero in on a specific location, traveling there would be unproductive. The place was simply too big and too difficult to navigate. Tam believed he could be more effective with his computer and phone, working out of his Hong Kong office.

Meanwhile, the bacterial source of Loring Griffiths' pneumonia had spread into his bloodstream. According to his treating physician, significant swelling was found in the lining around Mr. Griffiths' heart, and the doctors were losing the battle against the disease's progress.

* * *

Mr. Kazi's offer to stay with his brother-in-law stalled over the table then danced among them like a sassy child. Yet nobody said another word. Eyes flashed back and forth between Paul and Tatleen. The idea of a place to stay the night had been an attractive one, that was, until Paul learned they'd be staying with a policeman. But in his haste to secure a decent night's rest—his first in several days—Paul had prematurely bellowed his acceptance. An acceptance that was so obvious that it needed no translation.

Tatleen was now stuck. She lacked the standing to speak about such issues, much less overrule Paul and refuse to stay the night. She kept her eyes lowered, hoping that Paul would come up with a decent excuse as quickly as he had come up with his acceptance of their offer.

Paul was in a state of panic, as wild thoughts flashed in his head. He wondered if this whole thing had been some kind of elaborate sting operation, a setup. He envisioned himself tossing hot tea at his host and making a run for the door.

Without so much as a sound, Naagesh squirmed off of Paul's lap and wriggled over to his mother. He tugged on her garment and spoke to her in Hindi—just loud enough so that everyone in the room could hear.

Tatleen nodded to him, tucking the boy under her arm. "I'm so sorry," she said to Paul. "Naagesh doesn't feel well. I'm afraid we should go." She then repeated the apology to Mr. and Mrs. Kazi.

Paul looked at Naagesh, watching his face as he lolled against his mother, holding his stomach and moaning. What Paul saw reminded him of a younger version of himself—feigning an illness to avoid going to school. As the adults stood and bowed their appreciation, apologies and sympathies, Paul caught a quick look from the boy. His cunning expression and satisfied grin confirmed what Paul had suspected.

"I drive you," said Juber, jumping to his feet. "Walking not so good for sick boy."

Paul hustled Naagesh out of the house and down a dirt path, the entire time listening to Tatleen's nattering chastisement of Naagesh from behind. Not knowing which neighboring home belonged to the policeman, Paul held Naagesh high in front of him, using the boy to shield his face. Juber sprinted just ahead of them, motioning onward through the lattice of narrow lanes, toward where they had left the tuk-tuk.

They were all nearly out of breath by the time they found it. The clustered tour buses were all gone and the green and yellow tuk-tuk sat resting in the shade, waiting.

"Fast," said Juber. "We go now."

The urgency in Juber's voice took Paul by surprise, a cold splash of sobering guilt. "Juber," Paul said as the group came to a gasping stop. "I'm really sorry to have done that to your parents."

Juber stood in the dusty road, trying to comprehend the words and their context.

"I have to confess something to you," Paul continued. "I don't think Naagesh is really sick, in fact I pretty much know it. For reasons I can't explain right now, we just couldn't stay the night. We had to leave right away."

Juber calmly reached under the seat of the tuk-tuk and took out his powder blue, short sleeved driving shirt. "I know you not want for to sleeping at police constable house. I see a scared in the eyes of you when my father say it."

"How could you tell that?"

He smiled at Paul. "And also I see Naagesh," he said, slipping the shirt on and buttoning up the front. "In eyes of him, I see happy boy. Not sick boy."

Tatleen bowed as she passed, and stepped into the backseat. Paul followed her, sandwiching Naagesh between them.

"Speaking of which," Paul said to her. "What was that all about? Did you get mad at Naagesh for faking it?"

Tatleen gave the boy a shameful glance. "When Naagesh saw you hide from the security guard at the CRF building, he must have realized you are a fugitive from justice. His understanding of adult matters is that of a child. But he's a smart boy, sometimes too smart for his own good. I told him that God will punish him for pretending to be sick when he is not."

Paul gave Naagesh a wink behind Tatleen's back. "I don't know about that, but he sure saved my hide."

Juber's inquisitive eyes seemed perfectly framed in the rearview mirror, observing quietly.

"I'm sorry to drag you into this," Paul said. "I don't want to get you into any trouble. You can drop us anywhere around here."

"Police constables," Juber said, ignoring Paul. "They making some checkpoints at highways. I help you going safely passing."

"Why would you do this for us, Juber?"

"Mr. Paul is my friend." Juber turned in his seat, temporarily abandoning any attention to his driving. "Not important for Juber to know all things. Only duty to help my good friend." Juber turned his focus back to the road. "So, where you want we are going?"

Paul took out the piece of paper Gwyn had given him. "BMVSS."

Juber stared blankly into the mirror. "Not know this address."

Tatleen spoke to Juber in Hindi, and his face ignited in recognition. "*Bhagwan Mahaveer Viklang Sahayata Samiti*," he said. "Making Jaipur famous is this place. Many peoples, they hear about the Jaipur Foot."

"Then you know how to find it?" Paul leaned forward, placing a hand on Juber's shoulder.

Juber nodded. "Also in Malviya Nagar. Close to where I taking you last time you come here to Jaipur."

The ride into the Malviya Nagar district took 45-minutes, partly because of the muddy condition of the roadways and partly due to the low speed of the sweaty, overworked tuk-tuk. In addition, Juber was concerned about a police checkpoint at the roundabout near Rajasthan University and decided to detour through Ganesh Colony, catching the NH 8 bypass road south.

Businesses were closed due to the holidays, and by late afternoon the mostly industrial streets were bereft of their normal congestion. The group arrived as the final steamy rays of sunlight reflected on the glass and concrete hospital. Juber's coughing tuk-tuk pulled to a stop beneath a drab, morbid-looking statue of a one-legged man on crutches. The 14-foot likeness, clearly that of an ethnic Indian, was clad in only a simple *dhoti* around his waist. His body lacked any evidence of muscle or fat, seemingly representing the common man.

Parked under a weeping tree was a decrepit white van with a large red cross hand painted on its side—a rough attempt to identify it as an ambulance.

A half-dozen men and women sat scattered about the driveway—all of them with the same vacant look of hope and despair, and each of them missing at least a limb, some more. One young man about the same age as Paul used his only arm to pull his body onto a low concrete curb. He sat upon a folded blanket, which had been bound with tape and string to what remained of his amputated thighs.

"What is this place?" Paul stepped slowly off the tuk-tuk, his face slack and his mouth barely moving. He gazed around, taking in each of the mangled souls.

Juber asked a question in his native tongue, though not directed to any one of the wrecked patients in particular. One man responded, and another next to him added a few words. Juber nodded gratefully and turned back to Paul.

"This place, it closed because holiday." Juber motioned toward the men he had spoken with. "This peoples, they waiting for to opening in the morning."

Paul glanced around again, trying to imagine a comfortable way to pass the night. Other then the copious blanket of wide palms overhead, there was little to protect them should it rain again. Aside from that, the driveway was no more than hard-packed dirt. There were no benches, and not even a patch of grass upon which to lie. A couple of the waiting patients had staked out the low brick planters, affording them something to lean back against.

"Thank you, Juber." Paul turned and hugged his friend. "I can't even tell you how much I appreciate what you've done for us."

Juber stiffened slightly against the embrace, for no other reason than a true perception of deference to the American twelve years his senior. "My honor," he said.

He got back into the tuk-tuk and drove off.

Paul took Naagesh from Tatleen and settled him into a dirt depression beneath a thick palm. Paul and Tatleen sat on either side of him like bookends, and all three reclined back against the tree. The ground was unforgiving and relentless beneath them, but only Paul regarded it as an unnatural condition.

The trio huddled quietly as another steamy downpour passed over them like an inhuman enemy. Suddenly startled awake, Paul flinched and stiffened to the sounds of loud breathing and feral movements around the dark courtyard. At one point the rain finally stopped.

"You are guarded." Tatleen's voice whispered to him in the dark. "You find it difficult to trust others."

Paul knew it was true, but had never seen it as a problem. "Yes, sometimes very difficult. I guess I'm just a little cautious with people I don't know."

"And what of those you do know?"

"Hmm." Paul looked out as shards of moonlight fell through the clouds. "As long as they don't lie to me. I've had more than enough of that in my lifetime. No one wants to be a chump."

Tatleen listened quietly, not fully understanding. "We are alike in that way," she said. "But also not alike."

"I'm not following you."

"My mother used to tell me a story about how she and my father came to call me Tatleen."

Paul could barely make out her gentle features in the dim light.

"She told me that I was like a little bird when I was born—unable to see, speak or fly. Not yet able to sustain myself with food or water, and completely dependent on my mother for nourishment and warmth. She said that my world was simple then, and my only truth was her nurturing love. They worried that once my eyes opened and my wings sprouted, I would fly from their nest. I would hear and see and experience wonderful new things—bright and pleasurable things that would draw me away from that which is real. They feared that the truth would become unclear and would lose its color, so they named me Tatleen. The meaning is, *one who is absorbed in the ultimate truth.*"

Paul pondered the name's meaning. Ultimate truth was a worthy goal, he thought. One he had hoped his sadhana practices would bring. "That is a good thing," he said. "It sounds a lot like me, I guess. I'm pretty much absorbed in finding the truth. But then how is it that we are *not* alike?"

"I was taught that outside things are not real—they can be made to appear a certain way, either pleasing me or hurting me. But the *real* truth comes from within me. It is that which I own, and it is only through that truth that I can truly live a life in peace and harmony."

The half-moon had disappeared behind the building and Paul felt Tatleen adjust herself as Naagesh slid onto her lap. She leaned back and a bit closer to Paul. His heartbeat quickened and he suddenly felt no discomfort from the ground. He moved his hand slowly through the blackness until his open palm found Tatleen's face. He cradled it there, touching her cheekbones with his thumb and gently caressing her forehead. Then he ran his fingers along her hairline to her temples. Paul sensed Tatleen's breathing deepen as he tentatively traced the outline of her lips with his fingertips.

Though Paul expected her to, Tatleen did not pull away. Whether it was because of exhaustion or the cover of night, he didn't know. Nor did he care. She was awake and they were sharing something that needed nothing else, no words or sound. It felt innocent and at the same time, intimate. It was in that darkest part of the night that they both found to be the most illuminating.

A scalding glare reflected off the ambulance windshield, bullying Paul from his only sleep of the night. He shielded his eyes and dislodged himself from the tree. Tatleen and Naagesh were gone.

His body hurled insults as Paul struggled to a brittle stoop. Over a dozen more people had come during the night, mangled and maimed, cripples and amputees, some with prosthetic limbs, strewn about the front of the hospital like dismantled toys.

Turning in circles, Paul called out for Tatleen. The other resting campers stirred and some squinted up at him, but none of them showed much concern. Just then Tatleen rounded the side of the building with Naagesh.

"He had to use the bathroom," she said.

"There's a bathroom?" Paul perked up, unconsciously adjusting himself.

SADHANA

Tatleen's unmoving eyes told him that it was just an expression. There was no bathroom and they had made use of the privacy afforded by the dense vegetation around the hospital property. Paul felt foolish, as he trotted off to do the same.

Paul returned from around the far side of the building to find the hospital's front door now open. He hurried to catch up with Tatleen and Naagesh, who had joined the others. They all moved like leaves in a muddy ditch, flowing slowly toward a drain.

Nobody was inside to greet them, just a large, round high-ceilinged room with rows of folding chairs. A bank of windows on one side looked onto an interior courtyard where dozens of yellow pedal carts sat stacked, one on top of the other.

"Look," said Paul, nudging Tatleen's elbow. "That's what we're going to get for Naagesh. They've got a bunch of them!"

But she wasn't looking at the yellow carts; her attention was on the broad, paneled wall across from her. "A message of welcome and acceptance to all who come here," she said.

Paul gazed at the wall and the dozen or so pictures that hung there. Doesn't seem like much of a welcome, he thought, just a bunch of cheap prints. "I don't get it."

Tatleen motioned toward the row of framed images. "That one is a picture of the Prophet Muhammad, the highest of Islam. The next one is Jesus, symbol of all Christians. And there, to the right, are many of the Hindu deities; Shiva, Vishnu, Krishna, Ganesha."

"What's that one?" Paul asked, pointing to a colorful painting of a meditating Asian.

"A symbol of Buddhism." Tatleen stroked Naagesh's hair as he sat quietly on her lap.

"What do they all mean?"

"The images are a welcoming to all people, regardless of religious belief. Their culture, their language, their status in society, these do not make a difference. Even those who cannot read will understand this message."

Paul wondered how he had missed it. Then, as he glanced around at the others waiting there, he realized why. He had never been poor or disabled. He had been welcomed wherever he went—the recognition of his family name and his wealth had made certain of it. And then he came here to India, and he had nothing. No name, no money and no friends. But he had been welcomed anyway.

A woman doctor came out carrying a clipboard and spoke for a moment with Tatleen. She then bowed a prayer-hands greeting to Naagesh and nodded to Paul.

"Naagesh is next," Tatleen said.

The doctor sat down next to Naagesh and asked him questions, then made notations onto her paper as he quietly answered her.

"What did she want to know?" Paul asked.

But the doctor stood and directed them into the next room before Tatleen could answer.

They passed another woman in the hall, huddled against the wall with her weight on one leg and a wooden crutch. Her white saree resembled the one worn by Tatleen, and Paul noticed that beneath her cloth scarf, the woman's head was shaved. Tatleen greeted her with a subdued blessing, which the woman returned.

"Is she also a widow?" whispered Paul.

"Yes, from the south. Tamil Nadu, I think."

"This way." The doctor took them into a long narrow side room.

At one end of the room was lighting equipment mounted on a metal pole. It sat directly opposite a raised platform with handrails attached at either side. In the center of the platform was an adjustable leg rest that could swing to either side for support.

"Can he balance here?" the doctor asked, moving the leg rest to one side and lowering the handrails to Naagesh's height.

Naagesh said something in Hindi, and Tatleen smiled.

"He assured the doctor that he could do it." Tatleen said to Paul, as she set the boy carefully onto the contraption.

Paul watched as Naagesh held tightly to the rails, his right stump perched on the leg rest and his left one hanging free. The doctor activated a small black box aimed at him from across the room, and suddenly a vertical red laser projected onto Naagesh's tiny body. It ran down the center of his left breast, following the line of his torso, over his left hip to the nub of his knee. The doctor adjusted Naagesh, and then repeated the process on the other leg.

Paul whispered to Tatleen, "Why are they doing all this?"

"I don't understand it either," she said. "Perhaps to make certain he will fit safely into the pedal cart.

Paul nodded. "Makes sense, I suppose."

The doctor recorded some measurements onto her clipboard and then motioned them along.

Paul lifted Naagesh and followed Tatleen and the doctor into the next room. There a man stood over a large plastic vat, pouring chalky powder into it from a brown sack. Dust filled the air, drifting slowly to a tile floor already caked with it.

The man hefted Naagesh onto a table and began wrapping each leg with soggy gauze. The doctor stood beside them.

Paul dipped a finger into the milky slag "I haven't been in one of these casting rooms since I crashed Lou DiNunzio's motorcycle."

Tatleen wrinkled her brow, trying to determine if this DiNunzio person was germane to Naagesh's treatment. Paul saw her look and swatted the comment away.

"They sure go to a lot of work," he said. "What's it all for?"

"Paul, I am worried about the cost of this. I will not be able to pay for these kinds of tests." Tatleen moved closer and whispered. "Should we decline this evaluation and just tell them what we need?"

"I still have my watch," he said. "Whatever the cost, I'm pretty sure that can cover it. If not, we'll find a way to pay."

Tatleen shook her head. "I cannot accept your generosity. Naagesh cannot accept it either. I'm very sorry, Paul, but I am afraid this is just too much. I won't allow it."

Tatleen stepped toward the doctor and Paul reached for her arm. "No, Tatleen."

"Yes, Paul."

Both the doctor and the man plastering Naagesh's legs stopped and turned their heads. "Is there something wrong?" asked the doctor.

"You must not do this," Tatleen said. "It's the money . . . the price of all these measurements. We came to this place to get my son one of those yellow carts stacked there in the courtyard. Nothing more."

The doctor smiled, seemingly amused by Tatleen's emotional plea. "Those?" she glanced toward the courtyard. "The carts are provided for people with deformed legs."

Paul rolled his eyes. "What do you call those?" he motioned toward Naagesh.

She smiled again. "Naagesh has no legs. We save the carts for people who have legs that don't work. The most common is a syndrome called caudal regression. People born with short legs, missing leg bones, severely deformed limbs. You've seen them, they look like small flippers attached at the upper thigh—nothing else upon which to walk or bear weight. Caused by vitamin deficiencies or untreated diabetes. Very common here in India."

Paul took his watch out of the satchel. "Couldn't you please make an exception for Naagesh? He's such a good kid, really smart, and he's got his whole life ahead of him. I'll pay whatever you want for a yellow cart."

"Are you the boy's father?" asked the doctor.

Tatleen looked humiliated as Paul floundered for an answer. Finally he said, "No, I'm not. His father died and Naagesh never had a chance to know him. I'm . . . sort of like an uncle to him, I guess. And I'm also a good friend of his mother's."

Tatleen's look softened at Paul's depiction.

"They're lucky to have such a concerned friend," the doctor said. "But I think we can do better than a cart for Naagesh. We are going to build legs for him."

Paul's eyes grew wide. He could hear Tatleen gasp next to him. Her hands sprung to cover her mouth, but the tiny trill of weeping escaped through her fingers.

Paul knew he couldn't pay for that, at least not without the help of his father. "How?" was the only word Paul's mouth was able to form.

"We're just about finished here," the doctor said. "You go have a seat in the waiting area in the next room and I'll be right out to explain everything to you."

The plaster man eased the molds off each of Naagesh's legs, and gave him a wet rag to wipe off the remnants. Paul was still in a state of shock as he hoisted the boy onto his hip and followed Tatleen into the next room. A string of metal seats were fused together in one long row against the wall. Several amputees sat waiting, all with bits of plaster still evident on the fabric of their rolled up pants and shirtsleeves.

Two seats were left, which Paul ushered Tatleen and Naagesh into. He stood beside them, still trying to grasp what the doctor had said.

Tatleen thought she had misunderstood the woman. She was afraid to tell Naagesh, for fear she had somehow gotten it wrong. And then there was still the money issue. Even if her understanding was accurate, there was no possible way Tatleen could pay for such a thing.

Just then the doctor came out and squatted in front of Naagesh. "I'll speak English since you'll both understand me, and I'll translate for Naagesh."

"No, please don't." Tatleen's eyes were full of skepticism. "Please explain it to us first, and then I can tell Naagesh. If for some reason this doesn't work, I don't want him to be disappointed."

SADHANA

"I understand." The woman set her clipboard on her bent knees. "I am Harnam Chandra, lead physician here at the institute. I apologize for not explaining the process sooner, but most patients come here with an understanding of what services we offer, and what, if anything we can do to mitigate their particular affliction."

Tatleen nodded and held Naagesh's hand.

"The foundation operates through donations and from some grant funding, but not by charging those we help. Many are among the most needy in our society, and among the least able to pay."

"Are you saying there is no cost for this?" Tatleen gripped her son's hand tighter.

"No cost." The doctor shook her head emphatically. "It is our mission to provide artificial limbs, calipers, wheelchairs, crutches and hand-paddled tricycles to those who need them, wherever they come from, free of cost.

"And you can help Naagesh?"

Doctor Chandra nodded. "What we have done is taken a cast of Naagesh's legs, where they terminate at the knee. We fill that with a resin, which we will use as a reverse mold to attain an exact replica of his limb. It will ensure a precise fit for the prosthetic legs."

Paul felt his own legs weaken. Nothing had prepared him for this. His greatest hope had been a wheelchair for Naagesh, and then for a pedal cart. But the thought of prosthetic legs had never even crossed his mind.

"How long do they take to build?" asked Paul. "I mean, this whole procedure must take days, weeks, even months."

"In most cases, only a few hours."

Paul made no effort to conceal his doubting expression.

"This process is patient-centric, not doctor-centric or hospital-centric," she said. "There is no Medicare, no HMOs are involved, no insurance forms to fill out. We have the materials to construct the entire replacement limb right here, so the waiting period and the red tape has been eliminated."

"Still," Paul wasn't convinced. "All the technology that goes into one of these things."

"Not as much as you might think." The doctor motioned toward a man seated next to Naagesh. "No computer chips, no circuitry."

Paul frowned at the man's pasty rubber leg. It looked too small for the guy, and the foot was flat with streaks of black showing through, as if it were a shredded whitewall tire.

"The technology we use is simple, and well suited for conditions in this part of the world," said the doctor.

Paul leaned down to take a closer look at the man's leg. "Is that what it will look like?"

"Not like that one," she said. "He's been walking around on that leg for twelve years. Patients are supposed to come in for a replacement whenever they've outgrown it—four years at the longest."

"You've been building these for twelve years?"

"Longer than that," the doctor laughed. "We constructed our first limbs in 1975, for a total of 59 patents. Last year we made over 24,000 of them—all custom fitted, and for patients from all over the world.

The doctor excused herself and disappeared into another part of the building.

"Are you getting all of this?" Paul turned to Tatleen.

Her face was pale and her eyes stared back in disbelief. "Should I explain to Naagesh?"

Paul shrugged. "It's starting to sound like a legitimate thing."

Tatleen resisted telling Naagesh about it, fearing that the whole scheme was too good to be true. And Naagesh never asked; he was used to sitting around watching other kids play, and being ignored. He had no expectations whatsoever.

A few hours passed and Doctor Chandra returned. She told them she would take Naagesh with her for about an hour, so she could check his fittings and engage him in physical therapy. Tatleen and Paul sat stunned, as the doctor lifted the smiling Naagesh from the seat and rounded the corner with him in her arms.

Tatleen kept her head down and her hands clasped in prayer. As the end of the hour neared, Paul became more conscious of his jittery breathing. He realized that the outcome of this single day could change both Tatleen's and Naagesh's lives forever.

His body tensed as time writhed slowly into the second hour. Paul closed his eyes and leaned his head back, trying to relax himself. He wondered if he, too, should try prayer. Just then he felt a silky warmth cover his open palm. Paul looked down to see that Tatleen had slid her hand over his. He turned to her, to look into her warm brown eyes, but she was not looking back. Her gaze was fixed on the doorway across the room. Tatleen's grip tightened as her mouth slowly dropped open, yet not a sound escaped it.

Paul followed her line of sight across the room. There in the doorway, stood Naagesh—his smile as proud as the moon.

Twenty-nine

It seems that Mr. Tam had been able to conduct a fair amount of his investigation from his Hong Kong office.

Of particular interest were the results of a more in-depth telephone interview with Gwyneth Eichler, CRF's deputy director of volunteer and community partnerships. Though most of this had not been shared with the general house staff, I found one piece of information quite unexpected: Paul was traveling in the company of an Indian widow and her son. According to the information provided by Eichler, Paul had sought a ride for the trio, from the town of Vrindavan to the CRF headquarters in Jaipur.

That information, apparently reliable, buoyed those of us who were privy to it. The fact that Paul was alive was the best news any of us had heard since the episode began. His association with the woman and her son however, didn't seem to fit anything even remotely recognizable in Paul's pattern of relationships.

In any case, Mr. Tam seemed to have a good lead as to Paul's destination in Jaipur—apparently he was headed to some kind of a specialized hospital. That news, on the other hand, was somewhat concerning, as one could only imagine what manner of malady would befall someone traveling through India. And the speculation that Paul might actually be ill or injured and in need of hospitalization only served to worry us anew.

The investigator had booked the first direct flight from Hong Kong into New Delhi. The six-hour trip would put him "boots on the ground," in investigator parlance, by the following morning. Tam's game plan, as I understood it, was to hire a driver/interpreter and attempt to intercept Paul at the hospital in Jaipur.

Nathan Geerts informed Mr. Griffiths about Tam's progress, trying his best to put an optimistic spin on it. But Mr. Griffiths said little in response to the news. He was tired from all the medications he was taking, and his body was worn down from fighting the infection. My boss also seemed saddened by the whole series of events as they related to Paul's traveling to India in the first place. It was apparent that the longer this went on, the more he blamed himself.

Our hope was that Mr. Tam would locate Paul quickly and return him to New York without delay. I don't think it an exaggeration to say that at that point, Mr. Griffiths' life depended on it.

* * *

All at once Naagesh's body seemed to accommodate his face and head, almost making them appear small in comparison. He had grown 17-inches in the past two hours, and suddenly looked five years older.

He wobbled a bit as he clamped a pair of wooden crutches under each arm for balance. He had never walked in his life, and the pitch and yaw of it was an unfamiliar sensation. He felt like a bird, soaring high in the air, having only been that far from the ground when carried in someone's arms. It was frightening and thrilling all at once.

He looked at his mother across the room, wobbled again, but maintained the focus on whichever leg he was moving. "One step at a time," he said in Hindi, as he transferred his weight onto one foot and then aligned the other one next to it.

Tatleen was a tearful mess, encouraging her son in between gasping prayers of thanks. She ran to him and stopped a few feet away, her hands wide apart. Naagesh took several tentative steps until he submerged himself into her open arms and the furrows of her saree.

Paul was right behind her, clapping and hooting wildly, and wiping tears from his own eyes. He felt like a father, bigger than life and engorged with pride. Wishing he had a camera to capture the moment, he looked frantically around the room.

"Doctor Chandra, can I borrow your cell phone?"

The woman paused a second before taking it from her lab coat and handing it to Paul.

Paul motioned for Naagesh to take more steps, and then he backed across the room, peering through the phone's viewfinder as he recorded it. Other patients were forced to stumble out of Paul's way, and a metal leg brace was knocked over, but everybody in the room was equally cheered by the scene. And Naagesh was definitely gaining speed and competence with his new legs.

"Where should I forward this?" Dr. Chandra asked as Paul handed the phone back to her.

Paul thought for a minute, considering the liability of what he was about to do, then took a long breath. "Go ahead and send it to my email." He enunciated his email address to the doctor while she typed it into her phone. Paul's cautious vigilance had served him well, and he realized that by doing this, he was leaving a trail for the police. But the significance of the occasion was worth the risk, he thought. And besides, he would be long gone from Jaipur by the time the police traced the email back to the doctor's phone.

Naagesh had spent a full hour with the doctor, sizing, adjusting and walking on his new prosthetic limbs. He was as eager as any patient they had ever worked with. "Everything you know," they told him, "Everything you are used to will have to be relearned. You will have to climb down to sleep instead of climb up; you will have to bend down to wash and bathe instead of sliding yourself beneath a faucet, and you will have to learn to pee standing instead of lying on your side."

The boy was elated. All of these had been only dreams of a young man who was certain he would never experience them. In a very literal sense, it was as if a whole new life had been given to Naagesh.

"You must be thankful," Tatleen kept reminding him. "This blessing would not have been bestowed upon you unless you were deserving of it. But don't presume you will enjoy a life beyond that which you were born into. You are still a boy with no legs, born to a father who is now dead. Your mother is still a widow, Naagesh. We have nothing."

Naagesh answered in his native tongue. *"Yes, Mother."* Then he gave her a crafty smile. *"But I do have legs, Mother. And I can walk just like other boys."*

Tatleen couldn't argue that point. "This man who has been so kind and who has helped you, he is not the same as us. He does not understand our faith, our culture, our country, and we could not understand his. He is an honorable person, but he will never be part of us. We are too different, and his life in America offers things we shouldn't dare to imagine. Remind yourself of that."

Her words of warning and guidance had been offered in Tatleen's own language. Paul suspected he was the topic of discussion, though he walked next to the boy with no understanding of the conversation Naagesh was having with his mother. Paul glanced at the boy, noting his slumped shoulders and disheartened expression.

The heat had baked the ground outside, and the long driveway provided a solid and level practice pad. Paul worked with Naagesh on his balance, and also at helping him acclimate to the hinged knee joint. There was some timing involved in allowing the lower leg to swing fully into position, before placing weight on it and moving the other leg. As Naagesh started to get the hang of it, it became clear he would not need the crutches for long.

The satchel Paul carried also held the small, spongy soccer ball he had negotiated from the roadside merchant when he bought the candies for Juber's parents. He had planned to give it to Naagesh at some point, never suspecting in a million years that the boy might actually be able to kick it.

Naagesh bellowed with excitement as the ball bounded across the dirt toward him. A frenzied sally of Hindi words sprung forth as he closed on the ball. He stabilized himself with one crutch before kicking it back in Paul's general direction.

The sense that someone was watching him made Paul turn toward Tatleen. Her moist eyes looked deep into him, and he could see there was more than just gratitude.

She stepped close to Paul. "It would take a lifetime for you to fully understand what you have given to Naagesh. From his first memories, he has sat alone while other children have played. This thing you have done for him and for us . . . this wonderful thing. It is real and true and honest. What you have done defines you. It is who you really are, and it replaces all that you find shameful in your past."

Paul wanted to speak, but emotion snagged his words in his throat. Tatleen took another tentative step forward, her deep eyes sure unflinching. She reached toward Paul and with a willowy embrace, hugged him tightly. Her gaunt arms chafed at his sides like windblown branches against a window. He held her against him, indulging himself in the tenancy and dominion he felt—a proprietary sureness that, as nearly as Paul could figure, came with the responsibility of caring for others. Whatever it was, it felt true and it made him feel like a man. At that moment he felt as if he would never let go.

"Paul Griffiths?" The calm but sure voice cut across the yard from the mouth of the driveway. It sounded neither English nor Indian, but it carried with it an air of authority. "Quite a few people have been looking for you."

Paul's body tensed, and Tatleen felt his chest rise and fall against hers. He didn't turn around, in fact he didn't move at all. Except for his eyes, which scanned over Tatleen's head, away from the sound of the voice toward the rear of the property. Paul saw the thick shrubbery and the vine-covered fence beyond it. His body flinched in Tatleen's trembling arms, and she tightened herself to him. She stretched upwards onto her tiptoes, until her lithe brown lips touched his neck.

He felt her warm breath pressing into his skin as she whispered into his ear. "Please, Paul. Don't run away. Trust in yourself—the honorable man you are and the good you've done for others. No matter what, nobody can take those things from you." Tatleen pulled back to look into Paul's eyes. "Have faith that karma will right all wrongs and light the path to the truth."

"Mr. Griffiths," the voice called out again.

Paul released his hold on Tatleen, slowly raising his arms in the air. In case these cops had a gun trained on him, Paul didn't want to give them a reason to shoot. He saw Naagesh teetering on the dirt drive behind Tatleen, his inquisitive brown eyes taking it all in.

Turning around to face his accuser, Paul saw the nicely dressed Chinese man in dark slacks and a white collared dress shirt. He wore round glasses and sported a trim, athletic build. Standing next to him was an older Indian man in a well-worn tunic, brown slacks and sandals. Not at all the Special Forces team that Paul expected to be hunting him.

"Tracked my email account, huh?" Paul cast a knowing smirk. "Wondered how long it would take you guys."

The man ignored the question. "My name is Tam," he said. "Curtis Tam. I'm an investigator from Hong Kong, hired to locate you and facilitate your immediate return to the states."

"Hong Kong." Paul dropped his raised arms. "What, you're like some kind of mercenary or something?"

"Not exactly." A dry chuckle escaped Tam's lips, though his staid expression did not change. "I'd like you to accompany me back to New York, however. Apparently there's an issue of some urgency." Tam motioned toward the man next to him. "My associate, Mr. Singh will drive us back to New Delhi where I have already booked our return flight."

Paul stepped toward the man, then turned and placed his hands behind his back. Tam eyed him curiously.

"That won't be necessary, sir," Tam said.

Paul was surprised the lawman was playing it so casually. Tam wore no weapon, as far as Paul could see, and apparently he had no intention of placing Paul in handcuffs. Deducing that the investigator must be well-trained in the martial arts, Paul considered himself, for all intents and purposes, Tam's prisoner.

"What about them?" Paul asked, motioning toward Tatleen and Naagesh. "They need to get back to Vrindavan.

Tam glanced at his driver. The Indian's eyes narrowed as he assessed the widow before he finally shrugged and then nodded his approval.

"Mr. Singh will drive them back to Vrindavan after dropping us at the airport." Tam then motioned to Singh, who went to bring the car around. "Have you any bags, Mr. Griffiths?"

"No, no bags."

Tam gave Paul a look—something that could have been taken as haughty and disdainful, until Paul looked into his eyes. Then he saw a second thought, and maybe a slight nod, like someone reconsidering a first impression.

"What?" Paul cocked his head.

"Your luggage went missing at the airport when you arrived, yes?"

"How would you know that?"

"It came up during my investigation," said Tam. "Since your last credit card usage was during your layover in Helsinki, I contacted authorities at the airport in New Delhi to find out whether you ever actually made it to your intended destination. They advised me that your luggage had been recovered and was being held for you."

"Interesting."

"They dispose of unclaimed items after a certain time period. I took the liberty of submitting a claim so they would hold your things."

Paul nodded a trite thanks. He let Tatleen and Naagesh into the back seat, then followed them in. "Well, where I'm headed I won't need anything more than a toothbrush anyway."

Tam imagined the lavish surroundings Paul had undoubtedly become accustomed to at his father's estate in the Hamptons. "Yes, a back breaking life awaits you, I'm sure."

Paul envisioned himself pounding out license plates in the penitentiary, but mentioned nothing more of it.

After a few minutes of silence Paul asked, "Can I ask how long you guys have been tailing me?"

Tam had switched to sunglasses now, and Paul couldn't see his eyes. "Not long," said Tam. "Maybe a week. Apparently your father's attorney, Nathan Geerts, has an urgent message for you."

Paul tried to twist the tension out of his neck. "I'll bet he has." Paul imagined that Geerts was fuming after having negotiated the soft sentencing on Paul's behalf. Although it didn't seem so at the time, Paul suspected that his forced voluntary trip to India was getting off easy for a felony hit & run. "You know, it wasn't my fault that I missed the CRF bus when I first arrived here. I hadn't any intention of going on the lam."

Curtis Tam didn't have a clue to what Paul was talking about. He hadn't even been told about Mr. Griffiths' illness; only that Paul had gone missing and needed to return to the United States immediately.

As they pulled into the circular driveway in front of the terminal, Paul slipped a hand discreetly into his satchel. The car came to a stop and Paul sat motionless, tears welling in his eyes. He turned and took Naagesh in his arms, infusing him with all the praise, adoration and love he could not express in words. Paul leaned away and raised a hand, inducing a lackluster *high-five* from the boy.

Naagesh's eyes widened with joy when Paul pressed the small circus elephant trinket into the palm of his hand.

Tatleen leaned forward and began to protest, but Paul held up a resolute palm. "The elephant is my gift to Naagesh. Accepting it is your gift to me."

Paul looked past the boy into Tatleen's stoic face; there he saw both her beauty and her strength. Her circumspect expression was like someone on death row, hoping in vain for an appeal. She was used to bad news and disappointment in her life; had lost love, family, and self-respect. This feeling was not a new one.

Paul recognized in her eyes, that whatever he meant to Tatleen, whatever feelings she had embraced, she could just as easily release. In this way she was the exact opposite of him—Tatleen had absolutely no sense of entitlement.

Everything he felt, everything he wanted to say had become twisted into an intricate knot inside him—one that would take time and clarity to fully unravel. Both Paul's affection and his confusion were communicated through his grasp of Tatleen's delicate hand.

The investigator got out of the car and Paul followed him into the terminal. He could not look back.

As Mr. Singh drove away, Tatleen's attention was drawn to a shiny object lying on the seat between she and Naagesh. There sat Paul's expensive wristwatch.

Tam made his way through the crowded Terminal-1 rotunda with Paul closely following.

Paul squinted up at the overhead sign. "Domestic Terminal?"

Tam continued walking. "It's where recovered property is kept." He pulled a small bound notebook from his pocket and glanced at the page. "Old Udaan Bhawan. This is the place."

Paul followed Tam into the glass office, where Tam spoke as if he was the owner of the missing luggage. Paul took his passport from his small satchel and showed the man, who handed over the duffel bag without further question.

Inspecting the nametag to make certain it was his, Paul turned back to the man behind the counter. "Can I ask, how is it that you ended up with my bag?"

The man typed the claim number into a keyboard in front of him. "It was turned in to us," he said, glancing at the screen again. "A legless beggar selling candles outside found it on the curb several weeks ago. Poor guy drug it into the terminal by himself and handed it over to a security officer."

Paul unzipped the bag and browsed quickly through its contents. Nothing was missing. His wallet, credit cards, money, none of it had been touched.

Tam slept easily during the long flight back, but Paul did not. He was sorting through the past three months. It felt as if his entire life had been put into a shredder, turned into confetti, and now Paul was trying to piece them all back together.

They arrived at JFK to find Terrence waiting at the baggage claim level, just outside the doors. The attorney, Geerts, sat talking on his cell phone in the back seat of the sedan.

"Yeah, he's here now." Geerts glanced up, his finger holding his earpiece in place as he eyed Paul up and down. "What in God's name are you wearing?" Without waiting for an answer, Geerts slid over and continued talking into the dangling mouthpiece. "We'll be on our way to meet you at Southampton Hospital."

Tam leaned around Paul to hand Geerts a card. "I'll be staying in town for a couple of days if you need anything else."

"Thanks, Curtis. We'll be in touch."

Paul's head swung back and forth following the exchange. He watched Tam hail a cab and ride off. "Wait a minute," Paul held the car door with a stiff arm. "Where is he going? Or better yet, where am I going?"

"You need to see your father." The attorney said.

"What about the whole jail thing? I thought I was--"

"Just get in, Paul." Geerts motioned to Terrence, who started the car. "We'll talk on the way to the hospital."

"The hospital?!"

"Yes, your father's very ill."

Paul got in and as soon as the door was closed, Terrence sped off. "Will someone please tell me what's going on?"

Geerts removed his earpiece and turned off his cell phone ringer. "It's your father, he's taken ill."

"Yes Nathan, you already said that." Paul pushed his duffle off of his lap. "What's wrong with him?"

"He's been fighting a bacterial pneumonia, and somehow it's gone into his bloodstream."

Paul turned away, an unfocused gaze out the window. "How bad?"

"It's pretty bad." Geerts cleared his throat, a suspense-building pause that Paul was certain he had practiced to perfection in the courtroom. "I'm not sure he's going to be able to beat this thing, Paul."

He couldn't tell if the attorney was just being dramatic, or if the situation was as grave as it sounded. "What does the doctor say?"

"He said to find you and get you home."

Paul turned back from the window, toward Geerts. "What are you telling me, Nathan? That's why I was brought back here?"

Geerts nodded. "Yes, of course. Why? What did Tam tell you?"

"Not much, really, just that you had something important to talk to me about. But he also made it pretty clear that I was under arrest."

A demeaning scoff fizzled out of the attorney, as if his lips had slipped off a balloon he was blowing into.

Paul squinted back into the past few months. "You know, I didn't hook up with the CRF group in New Delhi, Nathan. What about the judge? What about the deal you brokered to keep me out of prison?"

Geerts palmed the few remaining hairs on the top of his head. "You're not going to prison, Paul. As for this whole CRF thing, you'll have to talk with your father about that. All I can say is that I hired a private investigator on your father's behalf, to find you in India and bring you back here. As far as I know, nobody else is looking for you."

"And the hits just keep on coming." Paul turned away again, not even seeing the passing landscape.

"There's something else we may need to talk about, Paul."

He didn't respond to the attorney. After several seconds Paul slowly turned back toward him. "And what's that?"

"I know it's a distasteful subject, and perhaps a bit premature, but there is the issue of your father's estate. I think we need to discuss it."

"You're right."

The attorney slid his briefcase onto his lap and unclasped it. As he began to reach for a packet of paperwork, Paul interrupted him.

"I mean, you're right, Nathan. The subject *is* distasteful and it *is* premature . . . not to mention, disrespectful and totally uncool. We're talking about my dad here."

Nathan Geerts had never heard Paul refer to LJ as "Dad." He also sensed other changes, much deeper than the odd outfit he wore.

"Tell me something, Nathan." Paul leveled a no-nonsense look at Geerts. "What do you know about his twin brother?"

Geerts' eyes bulged over the top of his wire-framed glasses. He smoothed his hairs again, and then cobbled together an artless frown. "I'm sorry, Paul, I'm not sure what it is you're asking me."

"Oh, I think you know exactly what I'm asking." Paul's glare was locked on his face. "It's a simple question. Did you know him?"

Geerts snapped his briefcase shut. "Whatever it is you're getting at should be addressed with your father, not me."

Thirty

My understanding was that Mr. Griffiths had been under sedation, but he had perked up a bit when told that his son had been found and was on his way home.

Paul returned from India in the hands of Curtis Tam, and despite the bizarre clothing and scraggly beard, he was by all accounts in good physical health. The investigator had escorted him all the way to JFK where Nathan was waiting. They took Paul straight to Southampton Hospital, so he could see his father.

* * *

It was clear to Paul that whatever Nathan Geerts knew about Loring's twin would remain locked up tight inside him. His misguided loyalties notwithstanding, Geerts might have just as easily claimed it was an attorney-client privilege.

Paul turned his gaze back to the window again, thinking how odd it seemed now, to be surrounded by taxis, cars and Christmas shoppers instead of carts and rickshaws and farm animals. The cool air even felt unfamiliar as Paul watched the Sunrise Turnpike course by, mile after mile past leafless trees. It was difficult to imagine that only 15-hours earlier he was in India with Tatleen and Naagesh.

He missed them. But it was already starting to feel like a dream, slowly fading in the light of a new day.

The Town Car pulled into the hospital lot where Rupert stood waiting. Paul got out before the driver had a chance to open his door.

"Thank you, Terrence." Paul said over his shoulder, as he hustled past Rupert, toward the hospital entrance.

Rupert followed him with his eyes, then stayed at the car to have a word with the attorney.

"How is Paul?" Rupert asked.

Geerts shook his head. "I'm not sure . . . different. He's asking what I know about his uncle."

Rupert stared back without responding. "Strange," he finally said. Then after another pause, "I hope he has the good sense not to confront Loring with those kinds of questions, especially now in his weakened condition."

Monitors pulsed and beeped in the corner of the room, as oxygen hissed from a tube taped under his father's nose. Paul didn't broach any subject with his father, other than to tell him that he was there. He whispered it into his ear, but LJ's eyes remained closed.

He wasn't sure his father was even aware enough to feel his presence, but it didn't matter to Paul. His dad was obviously very ill, and Paul was used to being around sickness. He sat next to the bed and held his father's hand. "I'm here, Dad."

Paul returned to the hospital every day. Over the next three weeks, he sat with his father, watching him, listening to him breathe, reading his Sadhana book and thinking.

Loring's heavy sedation kept him nearly comatose during Paul's visits. According to Dr. Moretti, the measure was necessary to prevent any stimulus to his father's body and brain. It was supposed to help him heal, but nothing seemed to be working.

Every now and then Loring stirred. Paul felt his father squeeze his hand a few times, and once he opened his eyes and tried to speak. The only thing Paul could make out of his words was that his father was sorry for something.

LJ repeated it again, squeezing Paul's hand and trying to sit up. "I'm sorry. I wish I had never—"

"Don't worry, Dad. Just take it easy." Paul eased him back down. "You need your rest."

Paul had a pretty good idea what was bothering his dad—he could list them all, from Paul's mother to his uncle, and everything in his life in between. Even his forced volunteer mission in India, which Nathan had finally broken-down and admitted. All lies and manipulation.

Looking down at his dad again, Paul saw someone different. Loring appeared weak and feeble. He wasn't the formidable adversary or the controlling villain that Paul had remembered. He was only a man. A man who was close to death and who regretted what he had done in this life.

SADHANA

It had rained all day—an icy December shower that wanted to be the first snowfall of the season. Paul got back late from the hospital and a pink VW Bug was parked in front of the main house. Paul didn't know why, but something about the car gave him an odd feeling—probably because it fit in out there in the Hamptons about as well as a horse and buggy.

Paul started for the pool house, but stopped halfway down the path as a thought waltzed through his mind. He looked back at the car. Gwyn.

Slipping inside the main house, he quietly eased the front door closed behind him. As Paul stood in the vestibule, he heard Rupert and Gwyn talking in the library, to his right. He paused there, savoring Gwyn's light laugh, barely audible above the crackling fireplace.

"I'm amazed," Rupert said. "You don't read much about that."

"That's because the Indian government doesn't want the rest of the world to know. They have more TB cases than any other country, 2.2 million, to be exact. And India has the second highest rate of drug resistant and multi-drug resistant strains of tuberculosis."

Rupert asked Gwyn if she would like more tea. Paul listened to the movement, maybe the teapot, a spoon being stirred, and then Rupert settling back onto the couch. "I wonder why they would try to keep something like that covered up."

"Because their health care system sucks." Gwyn took a tempering sip of her tea. "The government has neither the drugs necessary to treat their patients nor the resources to get the drugs to them."

Paul stepped around the corner. "Well, on that happy note . . ."

Gwyn stood and they hugged. She kissed Paul lightly on the side of the face, but he couldn't tell if there would have been more to it had Rupert not been sitting right there.

With his legs crossed and a cup and saucer in his hand, Rupert observed the interaction as one would watch a horserace they had not bet on. "Gwyneth's insight about India's health problems has been scintillating. She's quite brilliant."

Paul pulled back to take in the whole of her. "Yeah, she's definitely something. How long have you been back, Gwyn?"

"Nine days." She set her cup down and tucked her hair back behind her ears.

Rupert took the opportunity to gather the tea service. "It has been a pleasure to finally meet you, Ms. Eichler."

"Thank you, Rupert. You, as well."

As Rupert left the room, he pulled the doors closed behind him.

"I have to say, I'm surprised to see you." Paul eased her onto the couch. They sat together next to the fire.

"I know." Gwyn fought through her apprehension. "Well, you never did give me your phone number . . . and, so, I got your address from Sheryl. Remember? She knows your dad. How is he, by the way? Sheryl told me he was in the hospital."

"Not great." Paul said, leaning back and resting an arm behind her. "It's kind of a day-to-day thing. Sometimes he looks like he might be doing better, and then, wham—next day he's nearly down for the count."

Gwyn wasn't sure what to say next. From all accounts, Mr. Griffiths was very critical. She wondered about the questions Paul had about his mother and his uncle, and whether he had gotten a chance to talk to his dad. Instead of asking, Gwyn just reached over and hugged him.

She smelled good. Something like vanilla or flowers, Paul thought. He watched her from the side as she stared into the amber flames, then he leaned his head back and rubbed his eyes. Why had she come, and where did he want this to lead?

Gwyn smiled and then playfully bumped him with her elbow. "Lighten up, Griffiths. I just dropped by to say hi."

She leaned forward to stand up, but Paul took her arm before she made it to her feet. "I like you, Gwyn. I like you a lot."

Cupping his face in her hand, Gwyn stared into his eyes. "We're alike, you and me. We would fit together pretty well."

Paul nodded. He knew what she meant—they were the same. The same look, same age, status, social circles. Gwyn was right, a perfect fit.

She stood suddenly and he followed. They hugged and she pressed a slip of paper into his hand. "My cell number is on the back of my card."

As Paul moved to kiss her on the lips, she slid a hand up between them. With her index finger pressed on his lips, she leaned into him until they were face-to-face.

"Give yourself time to adjust," she said. "India is a powerful place, and it will take you awhile to absorb all that you've been through. When your life quiets down a little, and you have some time to sort everything out, then give me a call . . . or not. Whatever you decide."

Paul watched Gwyn as she picked up her purse and sweater and headed for the doors.

"I'll let myself out."

He sat back down in front of the fire and stared into it.

Vaguely aware of a phone ringing somewhere else in the house, Paul eased his mind back to the present. A minute later there was a tap on the doorframe outside the library.

Rupert eased between the double doors. "Paul, the call was about your father."

By the time they got outside, Terrence had already brought the Town Car around and had it idling there. Paul got in and Rupert sat up front.

"Nathan will meet us there," said Rupert.

The hospital was only five minutes away, and Terrence was trying to make it in four. The narrow streets were wet and probably slippery, but thankfully nobody else was out at that time of night.

Paul stared out the window as they passed the Old Southampton Cemetery. He realized he needed to get used to the idea that his dad may not be around much longer. Paul wondered if Loring would be buried there, along with the heavyweight hall-of-famer, Jack Dempsey.

Probably somewhere else, he thought. With his twin brother, Paul, or even next to his wife—wherever it is that they were laid to rest.

Dr. Moretti met them in the small waiting area outside the critical care unit. "Loring seems to have taken a turn for the worst," he said. "We've taken him off of the sedatives and he's coming around a bit. This might be the only chance you'll have to—"

Paul held a hand in the air and dipped his head. "I get it, doctor. Thank you."

The automatic doors slid open behind them and Nathan Geerts walked in. Rupert stepped over to meet him, and turned him around. They both walked away, huddled in conversation. Paul figured they were giving him time alone with his dad.

The lights were low in the room, and the air inside had a distinct chill. LJ stirred and then opened his eyes when Paul walked in. When he was able to focus on Paul, he reached out to him with a hand tethered by wires and tubes. Paul sat on the edge of the bed.

"I'm not going to beat this thing." LJ's voice was raspy and weak. "This is one time Loring doesn't get to have it his way."

"Don't think like that, Dad." Paul gripped his hand. "You're—"

"I'm not . . . your dad." LJ let out a sigh, as if the words had dislodged a plug that had been stuck in place for decades. "I've wanted to say those words for so long. And I want to apologize for never telling you about--."

Paul gripped his hand tighter and gazed into LJ's glassy eyes. "None of it matters to me anymore. You may not be my father, but you've been my dad since I can remember. You raised me."

He placed his other hand on LJ's chest as a tear trickled from the corner of his dad's eye.

"You knew." LJ coughed then steadied himself.

Paul shook his head. "I found out while I was over there."

LJ nodded, his expression conceding defeat.

"I learned my mom's real name." Paul weighed whether or not to tell him more. "And I read about the crash that killed her and your brother, Paul."

The spillway opened and LJ's eyes were awash. "No," he gasped, waving a pale hand in the air. "That wasn't him . . . I am Paul Griffiths."

Paul stood. LJ kept a grip on Paul's hand so he wasn't able to back away. The two men stared at each other without saying a word.

"How?" Paul finally asked.

"I had traded passports with him, so I could travel back and forth without the government knowing. Lore didn't even know. And when the accident happened the police found the passports—mine and your mom's."

"So, they were my parents, my real mom and dad—Loring and Leigh."

The withered man nodded. "Abby. She hated the name Leigh."

"Whatever. And you just let everyone think it was you who died, because?"

LJ wiped his face with his faded cotton smock. "Because—"

Paul cut him off. "Never mind. I forgot about the big chemical spill. I get it now. You didn't want to lose everything and go to prison."

LJ shook his head. "I had already lost everything. And I would have gladly gone to prison. I couldn't live with what had happened to all those people in India; and my brother was gone, and I knew I would never get the chance to do right by him. I wanted to die."

Paul wasn't sure if he believed him or not. But it didn't matter. He was no longer bitter.

"There was nobody left in our family, Paul." LJ motioned for a sip of water, which Paul gave him. Then he eased back into the pillow. "You would have gone to an orphanage or been put up for adoption. Even if I had been able to beat the criminal case against me, do you think any judge in the world would have granted me custody of a little baby?"

Paul leaned back, raking his fingers through his hair.

"Believe it or not, I loved Lore. He was more than a brother."

"And you also loved his wife," Paul said, now with a different view. "It was your handwriting. You wrote the letter."

"Yes, I wrote the letter, and yes, I did love Abby." LJ coughed again. "But I hated myself. And when I had a chance to live the rest of my life as Loring, and raise their child, I did it the best way I knew how. It was the only way I had left to try to make up for what I had done to them. I wanted to give you everything I possibly could, and I wanted to honor your parents—the two people I loved most in the world. That is, until you." LJ coughed again, struggling to catch his breath.

"We really don't have to talk about this anymore tonight, Dad." Paul adjusted the oxygen tube under his dad's nose and rang for the nurse. "You need to take it easy and get some rest."

The nurse came in and began checking the electrodes taped to LJ's chest. She glanced at Paul with a look that answered any question he may have had about his father's prognosis.

"Dad, I meant what I said." Paul leaned around the nurse to make sure LJ could see the truth in his eyes. "You have been a good father to me, and even though I haven't always shown it well, I truly appreciate everything you've given me."

Paul stopped to talk with Nathan and Rupert in the waiting room. He told them that his dad was worn down and had experienced intermittent breathing problems while he was in the room with him. Paul waited outside while the two men paid a brief visit to their boss.

Nathan decided to spend the night at the estate, rather than drive back out to the City. It was still raining, and a somber mood had settled over the group. Nobody spoke on the way back to the house.

It was a rough night; Paul was unable to fall asleep. He stared up at the ceiling of the pool house, his mind spinning in circles—about the man who raised him from infancy, the real parents whom he had never known, Gwyn. And there was Tatleen. She and Naagesh had cleaved so deeply into his heart, been so meaningful in his life. They were so real, painfully real, and yet Paul had blossomed in their company.

But now was a different story. The sparkle of his New York life fogged the memories and dimmed the feelings. Paul felt like a phony— a chameleon, altering his exterior, conforming to the prevailing environment. He got out of bed and dug through his bags. At the back of his closet he found his small satchel containing the Sadhana candle.

Paul lit what remained of the 2-inch waxy stub, and placed it in an empty glass on the nightstand. As he watched the flame, just as he had during his trip, Paul knelt on the floor in front of it.

"I practice this Sadhana with the intention of living an honest, ethical life, and to reach enlightenment through offering myself as a servant to others."

It had meant something special in India. But now Paul saw only his distorted reflection in the glass, wavering in the refracted light of the candle. Was this just a meaningless exercise he had done every night? Is there really a purpose to seeking enlightenment? He asked himself aloud, "What is the truth?

Noises outside the pool house shook Paul from his thoughts. Distressed conversation at the door and then a knock. "Paul!" It was Rupert's voice calling to him from the landing outside.

Paul took time to dress before answering the door; he did not rush. He felt it in his heart, they had come to tell him that the man he had known as his father was gone.

The memorial service for Mr. Griffiths' was held in Southampton, so the estate's staff and employees of LJ's Manhattan-based company could attend. Having conducted some research on his own, Paul planned to take his father's cremated remains back to Chicago for a much smaller service. Rosehill Cemetery was where Paul's biological parents, who had also both been cremated, were interred.

Paul had purchased an adjoining niche on the same memorial wall in the lower mausoleum, where the two brothers would be placed side-by-side. Patricia Ruth Griffiths and James Victor Griffiths, Paul's grandparents, also had burial plots at the same cemetery.

A snag in the plan came to light when Paul started looking into transportation regulations. Airline policies regarding the shipment of human remains, even cremated, were a cluster of red tape. He would need to submit the death certificate, a cremation authorization form, a cremated remains receipt and an authority of the authorizing agent form—whatever that was.

Another problem was the weather. Chicago was an arctic mess, and it was doubtful that either O'Hare or Midway would remain open very long. And since both Rupert and Nathan had also planned to attend the interment, Terrence prepared the family limousine for the 14-hour drive.

Little conversation had taken place between Paul and the two men since the night of his father's death, and this was a drive that Paul was dreading.

They left the estate with the pinch of a 4:30 a.m. wind. The large sedan rocked back and forth, buffeted by sudden gusts. The two men talked quietly on the opposite seat, while Paul plugged the headset into his ears and closed his eyes. They arrived at the Majestic Hotel near Lincoln Park at dinnertime. All four men got separate rooms—Paul, Rupert, Nathan, and the driver, Terrence.

Paul presumed the other three would be heading out to get dinner and drinks somewhere, though he had no interest in joining them. Instead, he ordered a large sausage and mushroom from Pie Hole Pizza Joint, and had them deliver it to his room. It was Monday, and with only two weeks left in the regular season, he hoped Chicago would get a wild card playoff spot. But even their Monday night game barely held his interest.

Paul couldn't rid himself of the vacant feeling that pelted him like the rain outside—it was a hollowness that he chalked up to the loss of his father. Strangely, he felt more homeless now than even the night he'd spent in the rainy alley outside the widows' temple.

The interment itself was held early the following morning—a quiet affair, save for the squeak of wet rubber soles echoing off of the marble mausoleum floor.

It was through a filter of mixed emotion that Paul viewed the service, maybe even more so to see the niches holding the remains of a mother and father he never knew. He wondered how different his life might have been.

The emptiness didn't leave him. He gazed out the window during the ride back, mile after mile of farmland. He thought back to the life he had before India—fun and carefree, but also shallow and selfish. Then Paul looked at his future, wondered about his newly acquired wealth, and imagined how Gwyn might fit into his world. What would that life offer him?

Finally, somewhere near Toledo, Nathan Geerts spoke. "Paul, we need to talk."

Paul looked back from the window. "About what?"

"First off, you can't continue to ignore the elephant in the room; the deception about who your father was."

There was a quiet pause while Paul thought. "Funny thing about an elephant, Nathan; if you were to experience only a single feature of one, you'd never have a complete understanding of what it is."

Nathan and Rupert glanced at one another, then back at Paul. "What are you talking about?" Nathan asked.

"I'm saying, I can see the whole picture now. More clearly, I'd have to say, than I ever did before. I understand everything about my life that I need to understand. I'm saying that for me, there is no *elephant in the room.*"

The attorney brushed away the metaphor. "Well, as long as you understand. Nobody ever intended to hurt you with this; it was just better in the long run for you not to know."

Paul nodded and turned back to the window.

"Other than that one lie, we've all been straight with you—your dad, me and Rupert." Nathan slipped on his glasses and opened his briefcase. "Now, about the—"

"There is never just one lie," Paul interrupted. "There are always two; there's the lie you tell someone, and then there's the lie you tell yourself to justify it."

Paul saw Terrence glance up at him in the rearview mirror, and for a second their eyes locked.

"I've been your father's counsel for a long time, since before you were even born." Nathan removed his reading glasses and continued talking. "He was a good man and a good friend."

It felt as if Geerts was giving Paul a lesson, but rather than argue, Paul simply nodded. Rupert must have sensed it, too, because he seemed reluctant to join in.

"He used to screw with his brother about that woman . . ." Nathan let the statement die when he realized he was talking about Paul's real mother and father. "What I meant to say was—"

"Forget it, Nathan, I know all about that, too. Believe it or not, he actually loved my mother."

Geerts wanted to debate the point, but Rupert nudged him into subjection. Paul detected a slight nod of Rupert's head.

"At any rate," said Geerts. "Once he learned of the pregnancy, everything changed."

"Changed, how?"

"Well, I think he realized how your father—your real father—truly felt about Abigail. And how she really felt about him, I guess. He was ready to give everything to them, as kind of a wedding gift."

Paul eyed the attorney. "What do you mean, *everything*?"

"His fortune. Everything the company was worth." Geerts shrugged as if he had never understood the sentiment—which he hadn't. "He took your real dad's passport with him to Germany, so he could close the deal and then have all the funds transferred into your parents' accounts."

"He was using the passport to dodge the government," said Paul. "He told me that, himself."

Rupert finally spoke. "That's true to some extent, Paul. But he was selling off the plant in India—he wanted out. And he hoped to make it right with them—your mom and dad—make up for all the troubles he'd caused in their relationship."

Paul squinted his skepticism.

"It's true," Rupert continued. "Except two terrible things happened on that day: the spill at the Aligarh plant, and the car accident in Pennsylvania. Bind-Chem was worthless after that, but *Paul*, the real Paul, didn't care. He was inconsolable about the death of his twin brother, and the fact that he had never gotten things straight with him. He became acutely depressed, and if it hadn't been for you, I think your father would have taken his own life."

"You know," said Nathan. "I was with him right after the India thing. He embraced fatherhood as if it were his lifeline. But he grieved about those people in India. That's why he eventually set up the fund under your mother's name. He's given hundreds of thousands to that organization."

"Set up the fund with what?" Paul asked. "I thought you said he had lost everything."

There were a few tough years after he took you in. The two of you lived in a studio apartment in Hoboken, but I'm sure you were too young to remember. Rupert had to leave his employment for a bit, and I continued to help out on a pro bono basis. Meanwhile, your dad continued to work on new glue compounds, but without using banned chemicals. Eventually he saved up enough to start a small company."

"You were only a toddler," Rupert said.

Paul shook his head, having never heard any of it before. "So what happened?"

"Lenovo happened." Rupert glanced toward Nathan, who raised his eyebrows and shrugged.

Paul caught the exchange and shook his head. "What is Lenovo, more secrets?"

"No. No secrets," Rupert continued. "I'm just not sure how much you want to know."

Paul turned up his palms. "Uh, how about the truth?"

"IBM found that your dad's epoxies were a perfect bonding medium for semiconductor applications." Rupert looked as if he were gazing back through years of dust. "It was a tenfold improvement over what they had been using—thermal conductivity, low out-gassing and moisture absorption, better electrical insulation, all of it. IBM paid to use his adhesives in their very first personal computer—that was way back in '84. They wanted to buy up your dad's patents, but at a bargain basement price."

"Anyway," interrupted Nathan. "A Chinese startup company called Lenovo Group approached him with a better offer. Even though he didn't want to get involved in a foreign venture again, the price was too good not to."

Paul rubbed his bleary eyes. "I hope you're not going to tell me he accidentally poisoned a bunch of villagers over in China."

Nathan shook his head. "Not at all. This was low risk, high profit. In fact, years later the Lenovo Group ended up acquiring IBM's personal computer business, anyway. And Griffiths Semiconductor, Inc. still gets a percentage of each sale. Terrence came on the staff around that time, and then little-by-little your dad hired back many of his original employees, including Rupert and myself."

Paul sat back in his seat, tired and emotionally drained. He rubbed a hand down his face, trying to make sense of all that he'd learned. It was almost too much to absorb, but at the same time it was like wiping the steam off the lens through which he had always viewed his world.

"Speaking of money," said Nathan. "We'll have to schedule time to go over your father's investment portfolio. As you already know, you are the sole heir to his estate—Griffiths Manor, the company, all of it."

The notion was still an awkward one, even though anticipated. Paul sat quietly, letting the reality of it sink in. The entire concept felt unfriendly, as if he were accepting something that didn't belong to him. Tatleen's theory about karma played in his head: *God is very fair and gives us exactly what we deserve in this life.*

The attorney continued, "Now that you'll have everything you could ever want—"

"How could you possibly know what I want?" A hint of irritation punctuated Paul's words. *He* didn't even know what he wanted.

Nathan chuffed out a laugh, then looked over at Rupert for backing. "Give me a break, Paul. I've known you since you were a kid. A zebra doesn't change his stripes. All I'm saying is that you'll have enough money now, that you can live whatever kind of life you want."

"The world according to Nathan Geerts." Paul turned back toward the window and stared out into the night. Nobody spoke, allowing the tension to settle like dust on a sunlit windowsill.

Rupert tried to change the subject. "That young woman, Gwyneth, from CRF. She seems quite friendly." His intent was not nearly subtle enough to help. Instead, it seemed to add weight to the heavy mood.

"Yep, she's nice." But the comment got Paul thinking about Gwyn, and of the question he had asked himself earlier: *What would that life offer me?* He had thought about his past during the last few months, and was now trying to envision his future. But Paul hadn't considered the present. He wondered what it was he truly wanted in life?

The limousine pulled into the roundabout outside the Griffiths estate just after midnight. Rupert and Nathan got out and went into the main house.

Terrence's eyes stared back at Paul.

Thirty-one

I looked in my mirror that night and saw the same crystal blue eyes that had stared back at me twenty years prior. He asked me if I had known the truth all along. And since I had made up my mind long ago never to lie to him again, I admitted to him that I knew.

Paul moved across to the seat behind me and placed his hand on my shoulder. He realized then that I had heard everything from where I sat. Years of information—good and bad—that gave me a clearer picture of Paul's life than he ever had. It had been more of a picture than I ever wanted to have, and I hated knowing that he had been deceived. Worse still, that I had been part of it. So I told Paul that, too.

He asked if I had anything to do with the book, Sadhana. My eyes welled with tears as I turned to face him. I told Paul that I knew that the book, and probably the letter, too, must have meant a great deal to his mother; that Mr. Griffiths had me look for it in her things after she passed. He was so broken during those days that he just couldn't do it himself. From that day on, Mr. Griffiths kept the Sadhana book hidden on a top shelf in his private library; only Rupert and I knew about it.

Paul was surprised that Rupert was aware of it as well, but if it weren't for him I would never have had access to it. Rupert would never have gone against Mr. Griffiths, none of us would. But I think he felt as badly about the deception as I did. I imagine he also wanted Paul to know the truth. That's why he brought the book to me the morning we drove Paul to the airport. And when I carried the luggage to the trunk of the car, I slipped Sadhana into his duffel bag. Whether or not anything would come of it in India, giving the book to Paul felt like years of shame had been unburdened.

The back seat was quiet for a long while, and I imagined that Paul was working through the bitter loss of trust that comes from betrayal. He finally got out then stood next to my open window. He made no reference about what he had just learned, but asked me if I would mind waiting for him. And of course I didn't mind, it was my job.

SADHANA

Ten minutes later, I saw Paul jogging back up the path from the pool house. With an unflinching look of resolve in his eyes and a small duffel bag under his arm, he opened the passenger side door and slid into the front seat next to me. He said he needed me to drive him to one more place that night, which, of course, I agreed to.

He told me that while in India, as well as at his father's bedside, he had thought a lot about the meaning of *truth*. Trying to uncover it for years, Paul said, he'd been waiting for someone to hand it to him, as if it were the main ingredient in a recipe—the recipe for a happy life. He had finally come to realize that if you have to look elsewhere for it, you will never find it.

We sat there in the warmth of the idling car, speaking for the first time as true friends—no guile or deception to separate us. Paul had learned a great deal about himself in India. He told me that his truth was not in the past or the future, as those are either memories or hopes—neither being tangible or real. Instead he had found his truth in the moment; in the things we can hear, smell, taste, touch and feel.

"Right now is what truly matters, the *only* thing that matters," he said. "The real truth is what's inside *me*—what gives *my* life meaning."

I nodded, but I could not hide my smile. Paul had grown into the man I had always hoped he would become. The person I knew he was capable of being. He had not only found out who he was, but he knew who he wanted to be.

The limousine pulled away from the house, down the long, tree-lined driveway toward the Bluff Road. With the lights of Griffiths Manor fading behind us, I asked where he wanted me to drive him that night.

Paul tilted his head back against the seat, as if a wave of abundant satisfaction had washed over his body.

"Take me back to the airport."

* * *

Me and my friend, Juber, taking a break during a visit to Amber Fort –
Jaipur, India (September, 2012)

Other books by this author are available in print and on Kindle can be found at Amazon.com:

COMING SOON

It's Only a Badge   Barkers & Bones   Malfeasance

www.ingramcontent.com/pod-product-compliance
Lightning Source LLC
Chambersburg PA
CBHW070908260626
47162CB00007B/2593